Mary E Jackson

The Spy of Osawatomie

Or, the mysterious companions of old John Brown

Mary E Jackson

The Spy of Osawatomie
Or, the mysterious companions of old John Brown

ISBN/EAN: 9783744790192

Printed in Europe, USA, Canada, Australia, Japan

Cover: Foto ©Andreas Hilbeck / pixelio.de

More available books at **www.hansebooks.com**

The Mysterious Companions

OF

OLD JOHN BROWN.

By

MARY E. JACKSON,
STAUNTON, KANSAS.

ST. LOUIS, MO.:
W. S. BRYAN, Publisher.
1881.

DEDICATION.

———◆———

TO MY FRIEND,

MISS ANNIE CHILDRESS,

Of PAOLA, KANSAS,

I humbly and affectionately dedicate this story.

THE AUTHORESS.

HANNAH MOORE said, "All for the best," and thus we find it through life, if we can bring our minds to dwell upon the bright and reject the dark sides of life's pictures.

In perusing this book there will be found dark pictures, yet bright ones predominate. Thus it is in the history of any people.

Now while our glorious Republic flourishes and history lives there will ever exist a picture in the gallery of Time, depicting the passing scenes in Kansas during her struggle for Freedom.

"*Ad astra per aspera*," the motto of our State, is well chosen. If any State, through tribulations, trials and asperities became one of the stars constituting our glorious Union, Kansas is the one.

It is twenty-four years ago, when the boom of the invader's cannon and the rattle of his musketry, replied to by the detonating crack of Sharpes' rifles in the hands of Captains Brown's and Cline's men, was heard at Osawatomie.

The writer, then a little child, living near, heard the fearful sounds of that memorable battle. Even the shouts of the Missouri leaders urging their men to charge upon the block-house were heard.

Thus growing up amidst these scenes, a true narrative of those early days has been penned.

To-day as she sits by her window listening to the rattle of the wheels and the whistle of the locomotive at Osawatomie, her thoughts revert to the destruction of that town twenty-four years ago to-day by the torch of the invader, and with Hannah Moore she exclaims, " All for the best."

STAUNTON, August 30, 1880.

CONTENTS.

THE SPY OF OSAWATOMIE.

CHAPTER·I.

"DICKEY DEANE'S" HOME.

A FINE mansion, built in the old Scotch style. The surrounding grounds artistically arranged. In front of the door, to the right of the path, stood an evergeen: a cedar, which had been brought from the far West, and bore no resemblance to its fellows. At the door of the mansion two persons were standing.

Such was the beautiful scene we gazed upon as we journeyed through the old Granite State on a frosty morning in November, 18—.

The mansion was the home of Roderick Leland, a Scotch nobleman who had fled to America, years before, for the preservation of his life. Among the freedom-loving Americans he had found friends, and soon won the love and esteem of all with whom he associated.

By his industrous habits he had amassed a fortune, and after leaving the city where he had labored, he found himself among the White Mountains, beneath whose tallest peak he built his mansion home, and brought thither the belle of Boston as his happy bride.

Yes, Leona Deane, the gayest of the gay, had left the fashionable world, where she had reigned queen of all the gay circles, and, with her chosen husband, had settled among this wild scenery, declaring that until now she had never realized the full meaning of "true happiness."

Ten years had scarcely passed, when death crossed that threshold and carried away the beautiful young wife and mother. A sweet-faced girl of eight summers stood by the bedside of the dying mother, while the fond father held a laughing, blue-eyed baby-boy in his arms, which he presented to the dying woman for a parting kiss, as his own tears rolled as drew-drops from his face upon the hot and fevered brow of her whom death had claimed. Thus home was robbed of its choicest jewel, and sorrow reigned for years.

Six years have passed, and we see those two persons standing at the door of Cedar Hall, watching the first snow-fall of the season: a gentleman of some forty-five years, and near him a young miss of fourteen. They were Roderick Leland and his daughter Ona. He had lived with his children and servants since the death of his wife, and had given his exclusive attention to teaching them, never missing an opportunity to avail himself of anything that would prove advantageous to them. Ona had grown to be not only surpassingly beautiful, but also very intelligent.

"What a beautiful tree!" exclaimed she, as she watched the snow-flakes falling upon the boughs of the cedar tree. "I never before observed it was so

different from those on the lawn.   Where did it first
grow, papa?   Did you plant it here?"

"No," said Mr. Leland, stepping out in the falling
snow.   "This tree came from the West, years ago;
it has a romance of its own: it also has a secret to
keep."

"What is it, papa? I should like to know."

"I will tell you, for in so doing, I only obey the
injunction laid down in the written pledge, but I
must exact the promise from you that you will keep
the secret and obey the instructions contained in the
pledge.   The present, to my mind, is a fitting opportunity to convey this sacred trust to you.   Yes,
in the first snow-fall of the season, and on the anni-
versary of your fourteenth birth-day."

Ona was somewhat surprised, yet said, "I will
keep the secret, papa, and endeavor to live up to the
precepts of anything that teaches to be great and
good."

Mr. Leland took a silver locket from his pocket,
saying, "Here is a silver case; within its lids you will
find the lesson you are to learn.   This was given to
me by two masked men.   They also brought the
tree which you so much admire.   We planted it here
by the light of the moon; it now belongs to you, and
if all works well, you will, sometime, visit the spot
where it grew.   You will find that there is a great
work before us.   You have reached that age when
you should lay some plan of life.   Learn to depend
upon yourself.   Be neither a drudge for some man,
nor a slave of fashion.   Men labor for fame and happiness, why should not women do the same? Let

not your favors be bestowed upon any on account of wealth or position; treat all deserving ones with the same kindly, genial courtesy. Be true to yourself and you will always be prosperous and happy. I shall be absent a few days in Boston, which will give you ample time to reflect upon what I have said."

"Yonder comes a carriage, containing, no doubt, some of your abolition friends," said Ona. "Goodbye, papa," she exclaimed, as she hastened to her room, while he sought his library to arrange some papers, preparatory to starting for Boston, to attend a meeting of the Anti-Slavery Party, of which he was an enthusiastic leader, and the carriage, as Ona had suggested, contained some of his co-laborers in that work, Cedar Hall, his home, being a favorite resort of the adherants of that party. Such was the home, the surroundings and the instruction of Ona Leland, better known to the world as "Dickey Deane, The Spy of Osawatomie."

As Mr. Leland stood arranging his papers, his thoughts reverted to the scenes of his early life among the Highlands of Scotland, and the Kirk of Glenarreu. His meditations were interrupted by the entrance of a stranger, whom the servant had announced. In those brief moments he had thought, almost expressed, his thoughts audibly. "What is to happen! I am so nervous this morning, some evil seems to be approaching. It cannot be that in Scotland they have learned of my home, ferreted out my seclusion, after so many years have elapsed. To be sure, I can not always hope to be thus secluded. The time must come when all will be known to the world. I will be bold." Thus his thoughts flew to the past, present and future, until, thinking of the stranger awaiting him in the parlor, he cleared his face of the sad expression which had gathered there and repaired to the parlor, to entertain his guest.

The stranger was a young man, scarcely twenty years old. He was very handsome, his costume indicating that he belonged to the aristocracy of England. When Mr. Leland entered, he was perusing a paper which he had taken from a neatly-arranged table, and observing the entrance of his host, he laid it aside. Mr. Leland beheld him with amazement, at last stammering, "Who are you?" as he fell, unconscious, to the floor, much to the surprise of his visitor, who thought, "What can have so unmanned this proud being before me?" as he called his servant to assist his prostrate master.

CHAPTER II.

THE SILVER CASE.

ONA tripped through the hall and up to her room, closing the door behind her. She stood before a large mirror, which reflected back a beautiful image. She viewed herself as she slowly shook the melting snow-flakes from her blue velvet dress and heavy black cloak. They clung with more tenacity to her golden curls which, her father had frequently told her, resembled her aunt Theodocia's, who was a pet sister whom cruel circumstances forced him to leave, yet whose image time could not erase from his thoughts.

Ona thought, at this time, of the remarks her father had frequently made regarding that sister. The presence of the silver case in her pocket, led her to investigate it more thoroughly. On one side was engraved a negro, bound in chains, while a white man stood near, ready to break the chains with a heavy axe. Under this was engraved, "If our nation prosper, the slave must be free." "We cannot be prosperous while the clanking of chains is heard in the land." On the other side was engraved a woman reaping a field of grain, while the sheaves stood thickly around her. Beneath were the words: "Women sow and reap. Why not own and represent?"

"A lesson taught on each cover," said Ona. Opening the case, she discovered a thin sheet of paper, closely folded, which she removed and read carefully. After which she exclaimed, "What a pledge! What a lesson taught by it! Can I ever live up to all that is there prescribed? There is so much work to do! Can I be of any use in that work? I shall put forth every effort for the benefit of the oppressed? I may never hope to become a Madam Roland or a Joan of Arc, yet I am determined to follow out the obligation imposed upon me by and through this pledge. This must be kept a secret. I must not disclose its contents." Thus soliloquizing, she read and re-read, until she became entirely familiar with its contents, after which she replaced the paper in the case, and locked it safely in a secret receptacle, where she knew it would be safe.

"What can I do in such affairs, with none to counsel? none from whom I can ask instruction? I dare not ask regarding what I most desire to learn. I must know. I shall go immediately and ask papa." Saying which, she hastened to the hall on the way to the library, just as the servant announced the stranger. Gliding noiselessly to the banister, she looked down upon the stranger as he passed through the hall below. She started back in surprise. Never before had she beheld so handsome a person as this richly-attired Englishman. "I surely have seen him! No. It is his resemblance to the picture of Lord Byron that causes his appearance to be so familiar," said she, as she gazed in silence and admiration.

At last, recovering from her surprise, she turned to search for Aunt Nancy, who had been a member of the Leland family since Mr. Leland's marriage with Leona Deane, whose childhood days had been watched and guarded by the same Aunt Nancy. She had remained with the family and cared for the children with a solicitude that would well become many mothers. She was bound to the family by no other tie than that of friendship, cultured by long association. She was poor, but possessed a strong and well-balanced mind, well stored with a knowl-

edge of the world and its ways. She had taken the
place of mother to Mrs. Leland, when she was left
an orphan, at an early age, dependent entirely upon
the charity of relatives. Her sufferings of mind,
during that time, had been related frequently to Mr.
Leland, during their married life, and the impression
made upon his mind had, no doubt, influenced him,
in giving instructions to Ona, and advising her to
develop some plan of life, which, should circumstances prove adverse, would place her in a position
where she would not be dependent upon the charity
of friends.

Ona found Aunt Nancy in the nursery, endeavoring to put Robie to sleep. She entered, and seating herself quietly at the window, awaited Aunt
Nancy's leisure. She soon became lost in contemplating the beautiful scenery by which the mansion
was surrounded, made more beautiful and entranc-
ing by the weird circlets of snow, which festooned
every bough, and hung in immense wreaths over
every projecting rock. She was, at last, aroused
from her reverie by Aunt Nancy, who exclaimed,
suddenly, "Where have you been, Ona? or where
are you going?"

"I have been out upon the lawn watching the
snow."

"Why are you so sad? Is it the snow, dear?"

"No, I love to watch the snow-flakes fall. I feel
well, but I am sad because I have nothing to do, I
have no other troubles. I am fourteen years old,
to-day, and have, as yet, developed no object in
life."

"Nothing to do, child! when this great world is full of the poor and ignorant, who need your assistance, and yet you have nothing to do! You, with all the luxuries of the world, yes, all that wealth can procure, and yet you are unhappy!"

"Yes, Aunt, I am unhappy, because I have nothing to do. What is your advice? shall I get married?"

"No! no, child, never get married, that is, not until after I am dead."

"Why so, Aunt?"

"Because, you can be something more than a mere drudge or showy flower in this life. You have a bright, active and intelligent mind that should be devoted, in youth, to something that will give you fame, wealth and happiness."

"Were you ever married, Aunt Nancy?"

"Yes, I was, and to my sorrow," and she bent down over the crib where Robie lay sleeping, to hide the tears which came to her eyes, in spite of all she could do.

"Is your husband dead?"

"No, he is living."

"What is his name?"

"Guy Wren."

"Guy Wren!" said Ona to herself.

"Yes, Ona, I have been married, and am sorry to say it. If I had known of one-half of the trouble I was compelled to endure, I should have remained single, but I did not dream of trouble when I was young, and was only a child when I married Guy Wren, that is, a child in the experiences of the ways

1

of the world," and she bent over the sleeping child
again.

" Tell me the history of your life, Aunt, it may,
perhaps, be a lesson to me."

CHAPTER III.

MR. LELAND AND THE STRANGER.

BEFORE assistance could arrive, at the call of
the stranger, who had imperfectly called, on
account of his own excitement, Mr. Leland
had recovered and occupied a chair, looking ghastly
pale. The stranger rose from his seat, not fully recovered from the excitement, and approaching Mr.
Leland, said: "My name, Sir, is Hayden Douglas,
I am sent here by the Anti-Slavery Society of Boston, on important business."

"I understand," answered Mr. Leland, motioning
him to a seat, at the same time closing the door,
while Hayden drew from his pocket a large roll of
papers which Mr. Leland, who seated himself on the
opposite side of the table, received, and appended
his name to each paper. But very few words were
exchanged during the operation; Hayden did not
wish to ask questions, and Mr. Leland, although anxious to know, dared not ask the young man who he
was, or where he came from.

After Hayden withdrew, Mr. Leland ordered his

carriage, and was soon on his way to Boston, following closely his recent visitor.

Mr. Leland was unhappy. The stranger had left him with a heart-sickness which he had never before experienced. When contemplating the recent episode, he trembled as men seldom tremble. As he sat in his carriage watching the falling snow, he lived over his past life. He, in imagination, revisited the scenes of his childhood—the highlands where he roamed, a happy, good-natured lad; his mother, father, two brothers and his only sister, the pet of all. Then came his days at school; his early days at Rugby; his happy days and genial companions at Oxford; the vacation days when he visited his home, accompanied by a gay young English classmate; the rambles and sports among the heather. Then came sad thoughts, brought about by the presence of Hayden Douglas. Where was that companion of his youth? Moldering in the grave—laid there by the hand that had been grasped in friendship. The thoughts of that companion sent a chill to his heart. It was now twenty-five years since that time. Yet it now rose up with striking distinctness; he, with gun in hand, returning from hunting in the mountains, saw his friend, sitting beneath a large tree, pencil in hand, sketching a view of the landscape. The next moment he stood beside that friend, in the agonies of death. It was only a moment he tarried to staunch the life-blood that was flowing from his breast, made by a ball from the gun in Roderick Leland's hand.

Roderick, seeing that his friend was dying, picked

up his gun, and under cover of the approaching darkness, made his way out of the country where he would be recognized. Ere many days he found himself on a vessel bound for the city of New York. Thus he severed his connection with the land of his birth, for fear of unjust censure for a careless act.

He had never communicated with his friends; and had not heard even indirectly from any of them; while they, believing him to have been murdered by highwaymen, had ceased to search for him. He loved his life, and feeling that he had disgraced himself and his family by the murder of his friend, resolved to spend the remainder of his days in seclusion in America. He was troubled when thinking of his visitor of the morning. "I know he has Gordon blood in his veins, and looks the picture of Cyril the day I killed him, but it cannot be he is of that family. No, he is from another branch of the Gordons. Hayden Douglas!" he said slowly. "I know the Douglases, but he is not of that family." Thus Roderick Leland mused to himself as he journeyed toward Boston. At dark he stopped at a wayside inn, but his morning visitor had passed on to the next one. Mr. Leland was disappointed when he learned that the young Englishman had passed an hour before his arrival. His slumbers were disturbed by seeing his old-time friends pass before him, yet he could not address them. When morning came, he was haggard and worn, as though he had not closed his eyes during the night. Being weary, he did not look over the names on the register at the hotel. Merely signing his name at the

"Oakland House," he withdrew to the room assigned him, ordering his refreshments sent up. The tread of footsteps on the hall did not molest him, neither did the merry voices in an adjoining room disturb him. Could he have raised the curtain which conceals from view those who are near, he would have discovered those whom he thought far away; he would have been surprised, had he known who occupied the adjoining room, but he was still, in imagination, far away in Scotland, when kind repose came to his weary eyelids. When he descended to breakfast, there were none at the table whom he knew. Having finished his meal, he withdrew to the bar-room just as two Englishmen entered the dining-room. They were of the upper class, and showed by their dress and manners that they had spent but a brief time in America.

CHAPTER IV.

AUNT NANCY'S STORY.

"YES, the story of my life would be a lesson for any girl, Ona, but it may be of no use to you, if you have made up your mind to marry."

"I do not expect to marry for a long time, and then I want a good man, so please tell me the story of your life, and I will glean from it the lesson it contains, and heed your advice."

"Well, it is a long story, but sad and true, too sad for a young mind, like yours, to comprehend. I may not tell you all, but sufficient for you to know what I have suffered, both in mind and body. My father and mother were poor, they had a small farm and stock enough to keep them in comfortable circumstances, and at sixteen I commenced teaching school for my support. I had been educated at home, and I felt as proud as any young girl could feel, when I came home with the earnings of my first school. I saved nearly every dollar, and during vacation, worked for my clothes. I went on in this way, without change, for several years. When I was about twenty-four years old I met Mr. Wren, a singing teacher. He was educated in all the English branches, but expressed a preference for music, and while attending one of his schools, I became acquainted with him. He seemed so earnest in his attentions to, and in expressing his regard for me, that I felt assured, in my own mind, that he really loved me. I knew nothing of his people, and had been taught to look upon the bright side of life, to judge the faults of others lightly. Generally speaking, if a man has not stolen a horse or murdered a fellow-being, he is a good man. But I am wandering from my story. I do not know as I loved him, as women sometimes do, but I know, I never loved any one else. In course of time we were married. My parents were well pleased and thought I had done remarkably well in being so happily settled.

" Two weeks afterward we went to the farm he had bought, bought with money saved from my teaching. I had not seen the place until I went to stay. I was really sick at heart, when I saw the desolate and neglected place. The house, a log one, and small at the best, was open between every log, so that a cat could have jumped through anywhere. No work had been done towards making it comfortable. I went to work arranging the furniture, which I had purchased with my own money, before we were married. He sat reading the paper while I worked. As the days passed, he did nothing, except go to see his folks, who lived about a mile from us, and occasionally go to the post-office. Cold weather came, and the house had not been repaired. My early teaching had been, that men should rule and women must obey, and not speak on any business, unless consulted. But, one day, I ventured to speak, in a hesitating way, about the house needing repairs, and suggested that, if he would procure the lime, I would point and fix it up for winter. Then came a volley of abuse. He was reading, as usual he threw down his paper and began cursing me. I shrank back in fear and crept out that night and cried until I was sick. I ought to have died for being so foolish as to stay longer with him, but I did. His mother scolded me from day to day. She said, I spent too much time keeping house, I had better be doing something to make my way, and not wait for Guy to have me to support. Two years passed, and if I had not had an abundance of bed clothing, we would have suffered from the cold. I had gone

to work, as his mother had told me to.   I served,
wove and spun for the neighbors, taking in pay all
kinds of provisions and produce, while he sauntered
about, playing cards, and not earning a cent.   That
will give you an idea of my married life, child.   I
had married a man simply because he was stylish
and had plenty of book-learning."

"Were his people good, Aunt Nancy?"

"They were not.   He was just like his father.
The way you bring up a boy, is the way he will
always be; it is the truth.   Mind what I tell you.
That family expected the women to be slaves, just
as any other uncivilized family expects, the same as
the Indians do.   You know, Ona, that all the primitive tribes make slaves of their women.   Years
passed on and we still lived in the miserable hut.   I
had two children, a boy and a girl.   The boy was
two years older than the girl.   I had to work to keep
them from starving.   When the boy was fourteen,
we sold our land, and bought a house near the village.   I was better contented.   I was further from his
folks.   I could take in washing, and my boy could
run of errands and earn for himself a few dollars.
I had still heavier burdens to bear.   Wren was of a
jealous nature.   I never dared sit down at the table
with men.   If I did, he would surely curse me.   He
abused me constantly about different men who
brought and came for their washing.   Abuse had
become part of my life.   When sickness came, and
death took my two children within three weeks, you
may be assured I was then sad and miserable.   They
had been a great support to my aching heart.   But

they were gone. I soon left home, and went to work by the week. We had been married twenty years, and my household goods were all worn out. Not a single article of any kind had been bought for the house. I did not weep at the thought of leaving home. I went to the house where your mother lived, and there I found a good home, and when she married Mr. Leland I came to live with them."

"What became of Mr. Wren?" asked Ona.

"I do not know. When I first left him, I left a note telling him I had left and was never coming back, because, during the previous night, he had so abused me that I was afraid to sleep, lest he should murder me during the night. The next morning, after he had gone to town, I left and kept hid, telling your mother and her aunt regarding his cruel treatment. Soon after they moved to Boston, and I went with them. I often saw him passing on the street, but he never found me. I have told you my story. What do you think of it?"

"I think, aunt, you had more patience and a better temper than I have. I would have left him the first time he abused me."

"That would be the proper course to have pursued, but it is all past, and I care not to recall one moment of that life."

"What can I do, Aunt Nancy?" said she, at the same time thinking of the conversation between her father and herself that morning, and comparing it with the sayings of Aunt Nancy. "I mean, what can I do that will make me useful and of benefit to others?"

"I do not know, Ona, what you can do. You must think of this for yourself and see what you can do, and if you can devise no plan, I will then assist you. There is one thing I would suggest. Every woman should learn to cook and attend to ordinary housework at least."

Ona went to her room. "I am free to do as I wish. I will begin at once. I must see all the girls in the neighborhood this afternoon." Seating herself at the desk, she soon had written a note of invitation to each one of them, and going to the kitchen, she sent Walter Strawn to deliver them immediately.

Ona's home was an elegant mansion, while her village companions lived in log houses or pine cottages, yet that made no difference with Ona Leland. She had not been taught to value people by their surroundings, and she had fully determined, since she had listened to her father's instructions, and heard Aunt Nancy's story, to assist in the elevation of her sex.

Walter had gone to deliver her messages, and repairing to the kitchen, she said, "Mary, I wish you would prepare tea for my company, this afternoon, and allow me to assist you."

Mary looked up surprised, exclaiming: "You help me? What do you expect to do?"

"I wish to learn to cook and become familiar with the manner of doing housework."

Mary knew Ona Leland sufficiently well to understand that she was determined to do as she proposed.

"Do you want to begin now?" asked Mary.

"Yes, if you please," and putting on a neat apron, she went to work in earnest, assisting in the preparation of dinner. She remained in the kitchen until the arrival of her young friends; then, repairing to her room, she arranged herself neatly, to entertain her company, eight or ten happy, laughing girls, who were ever anxious to visit Ona, and always happy in her presence. She was so situated as to be able to contribute to the happiness of her associates; her neatly arranged and commodious home being, to them, a pleasure as well as a wonder; their fathers being mechanics and occupying humbler, yet none the less happy, homes. After tea they adjourned to Ona's private room, where they were surprised by her carefully closing and locking the door, retaining the key.

CHAPTER V.

THE MYSTERIOUS STRANGERS.

HAYDEN DOUGLAS left Cedar Hall a little perplexed at the strange actions of Roderick Leland, but he was so bewildered by the recollection of the soft, blue eyes peeping over the banister, that more serious matter would rest only temporarily in his mind. "I believe I am in love with her," he said to himself. "She is his daughter. I have certainly met him some place, or, at least, have heard his name." Thus soliloquized the young nobleman as he was hurriedly driven toward Boston.

He was some two hours in advance of Mr. Leland. Alighting at a hotel, he entered the reception room, where he found a middle-aged man awaiting him. Their meeting was cordial, Hayden being the first to speak, asking :

" Did you find the library ?"

" Yes, and will have them ready to send off to-night."

After supper they repaired to the room which they occupied together. Hayden was soon absorbed in a new story in a late London paper he had just received, while the older gentleman proceeded to arrange a number of dusty books which lay upon the carpet. One by one he opened them and noting the name upon the fly-leaf, placed them carefully in boxes, preparatory to shipping them to England. They were a portion of a library belonging to Lord Gershom, and were left to his relatives, the greater part belonging to the gentlemen in whose possession they now were.

Lord Gershom was an exile and had spent his last days in Boston, and was laid away in a quiet grave-yard without pompous display, as would have been the case had he died in England.

Hayden read some two hours, and then commenced some of his wild pranks, such as whirling tables and chairs upon one leg, without disturbing their contents, such as books, lamps and brushes, at the same time singing some pathetic love song, accenting each syllable clearly and distinctly, while his

companion worked away, seemingly unconscious of
his presence. The sole cause of his unrest being
he had nothing else to do. Ten o'clock found Hayden in bed, his companion still poring over his musty
volumes, examining each one, as though he expected
to find something that had been lost for ages. Picking up a rusty-looking book, entitled "Scottish
Chiefs," he opened it, and starting in glad surprise,
he beheld beneath the name of Lord Gershom another name. Could his eyes deceive him? No! there
it was, the name of Roderick Leland, written in a
truly Scotch hand. The stranger turned each leaf
carefully, but that was all he could find, and turning
to it again read that name, Roderick Leland. "He
has written that name with his own hand; but when
was it written?" No clue was to be found as to that.
"Roderick surely lives, for this book was published
since he disappeared. Can it be that he is living!"
said the Englishman, as he again turned to the name.
"No, he is not alive, or he would have returned ere
this time. But this name! Who put it here to tor-
ment me?" When Hayden awoke the next morning he did not observe that his companion had not
retired during the night, or was, even now, looking
pale and careworn.

Had he but spoken one word regarding his meeting with Mr. Leland, years of anxious care and expectation would have been avoided to two persons,
who had sought each other for years. But he did
not mention the scene at the Leland mansion to his
companion, yet it was frequently in his thoughts.
When they sat down to breakfast, neither was aware

that the object of his solicitude had just disappeared.
After breakfast, Hayden entered the bar-room, but
meeting with no familiar face, he started out, without a definite idea as to where he was going. Suddenly he came face to face with the small, smooth-
faced man who had persuaded him to join the Anti-
Slavery party. This was their first meeting in
America.

"Captain Brown! I am glad to meet you," said
Hayden, as they cordially grasped hands. "May we
be ever seeking the right for our fellow-beings, and
to ever instruct each other as we meet from day to
day. Let me say, further, Captain Brown, I am
ready for any work you have in hand."

"Be ready, Douglas, I will call upon you some
day, ere many years go by."

"Some one is watching us," said Hayden, and
they separated, Hayden going on down the street,
where he saw Mr. Leland, standing in a group,
consisting of members of the Anti-Slavery Society.
He could not catch Mr. Leland's eye, for he was too
deeply engaged in conversation to observe a passing stranger. Hayden continued his walk down the
street, returning in half an hour. As he passed the
group of men the second time, he observed that his
friend Brown had become a member of the group.
He paused sufficiently long to note the topic of conversation, and sauntering leisurely along until he
reached the hall where the society were to assemble.
Although the hour was early, many members had
already arrived. He looked for his companion, but
he had not yet arrived, neither did he arrive with the

crowd at the opening of the meeting. Mr. Leland
and Capt. Brown entered together.

Boston was the birth-place of Abolitionism, and
the home of the most earnest workers in the cause.
As the members came in, Hayden recognized but
few that he had met at previous meetings in New
York. A number of ladies were present at this
meeting, a peculiarity he had not observed elsewhere.

At the close of the meeting Mr. Leland addressed
the audience, complimenting them upon the presence of ladies, and gave a few broad hints favorable
to women taking part in their work and doing what
they could in assisting to overthrow the institution
of slavery, which he regarded as the greatest crime
the American people had tolerated. Not slavery of
Africans alone, but the slavery of women also.

Hayden looked in astonishment at the speaker.
A new train of thought, which had never before
been presented, took possession of his mind.
Women as slaves! He had traveled through the
Old World and saw the women bearing heavy burdens, but he never once thought that they were
compelled to work, while the husbands, fathers and
brothers were spending their time in the grog-shops.
He had seen the German and English women carrying the hod, and hitched, like brutes, to water-sleds.
They were women, and if Americans could complain
of the treatment *their* women received, what should
England say regarding such treatment among her
poorer classes? "It is time some one should wake
up to this matter," he said to himself. "We must do

as Mr. Leland had said, 'Educate both sexes, and make them equal in all positions. In that lies all the hope I have of making them free.'"

The meeting adjourned for dinner. Hayden found his companion still busily engaged in packing his books.

Mr. Leland descended the steps of the rostrum to converse with some of the ladies of the society. Little did he think of the new torch he had lighted by speaking in favor of the freedom of women. Such words were sown on good ground, and took deep root in the minds of many thinking, reasoning men. Yet there were some, both men and women, whose minds were narrow and warped by the contamination of previous customs, who scoffed at the remarks. Such persons were neither capable of doing nor being anything more than common help or laborers, because they had neither energy nor enterprise to make an effort tending toward their individual elevation.

Mr. Leland was aware that he had touched tender chords in many minds. Some beat responsive and in unison with his ideas; others the opposite, but he did not waver. Some one had to begin the battle, and he was ready at any time to champion the cause of liberty. Energy was never lacking in any of his undertakings.

At dinner he saw Hayden and another English gentleman by his side. He recognized Hayden as the same person who had visited him. A shade of gloom passed over his brow as he noticed Hayden's gaze settle upon himself. He took no particular notice of Hayden's companion. He was thinking of the youthful form he had left lying on the green sward twenty-five years ago, as he continued his dinner in silence.

CHAPTER VI.

PAT DEVILIN.

WHILE Mr. Leland and his fair daughter stood watching the falling snow-flakes at Cedar Hall, another scene was being enacted far away across the broad Atlantic, in the city of Dublin. Two boys sat in the doorway of a bread shop; the elder deeply engaged in repairing an old-fashioned carpet-sack, while the younger sat, for some time, a silent spectator, finally exclaiming, "Are you going to leave us, Pat?"

"Yes, I am, but who told you I was going?"

"I heard you tell those Americans that you were going to leave for the United States some time this week."

"Yes, Mike, I am going, but don't say anything about it until I am well out of reach."

Pat Devilin, the elder of these two Irish boys, was about seventeen, while the younger was not more than ten years old. They sat in the doorway of their father's shop while he had gone to dinner. Pat was stitching the carpet-sack in which he had stored

2

his few articles of clothing, and a supply of bread
and cheese for his lunch until he had secured quarters on the vessel that was to take him to America.

"I am going now, Mike, before father comes back,
and remember, don't you tell him where I am until
I have had time to cross the channel to Liverpool,
and grasping his sack, he held out his hand to his
brother saying, "I will send for you before long, so
don't fret or tell any one about my going," and joyfully started away.

The boys' father had died when they were young.
Their mother had married again, but fortunately,
they had a kind and indulgent step-father, who furnished Pat with a liberal allowance of spending-
money, which he had saved until he had sufficient to
pay his passage to the New World.

Mike shed a few tears as he watched the receding
form of his brother. When his father came he left
the door without saying a word. Pat found a light
craft almost ready to leave for England, and he engaged passage. The Captain had known Pat for
years and did not suspect that the lad contemplated
leaving Ireland forever, neither did Pat tell him.
When ready to leave Liverpool, the Captain searched
for Pat, but he was not to be found.

Pat had wandered down to the dock as soon as he
could leave the Captain unnoticed. There he found
an American ship ready to sail for the New World.

"The Lone Star," said he to himself, after he had
taken passage and was on board. As he gazed in
admiration upon the stars and stripes floating aloft,
he questioned that flag in his mind as it majestically

floated in the light breeze. "Silken flag! I wish you could talk, and then you would tell me all I desire to know. Did you wave over the people in their strife for freedom? Are you a comrade of the one in which the brave Count Pulaski's form was wrapped after he had given his life for the liberty and freedom you proclaim? I have read of your floating over a lone grave on an island in some inland sea. I cannot tell why I love you more than I do the flags of other nations, but I do, my heart beats with rapture and joy on beholding thy bright colors. I, too, may acquire honor and fame in the land, whose freedom thou dost represent." He gazed until his eyes were moist with fast gathering tears, and turning away, he gazed out upon the broad expanse of waters. The ship was plowing through the mighty waste of waters with her weight of human beings from all parts of the world, each seeking the land where freedom reigns and oppression will soon be unknown. As Pat's thoughts reverted to the scenes of his home life, his heart grew sad. The thoughts of leaving all that was near and dear to him, neither were they dispelled when sweet sleep came to his tired eyes, he thought of his mother weeping as she knelt by the side of the cradle containing his baby sister, grieving over the conduct of her lost boy, although alive and well, she could think of him only as lost.

The next morning Pat felt more cheerful. The sun shone out bright and clear, and Pat thought nothing of last night's troubles as he stepped on deck. There was a charm for Pat about that American ship; everybody was busy; no idlers were seen

among the crew, and he wished within that he was a
member of that crew.   As he turned his attention to
the passengers, he observed a gentleman of about
sixty years, who occupied an easy-chair.   He saw
that the old gentleman eyed him closely.   Pat was
anxious to know what caused the proud Englishman
to devote so much attention to him, a poor Irish lad.
He felt uneasy, lest he should prove to be some gentleman from Dublin, who would embrace the first
opportunity of sending him back to Ireland.   So he
shied around and kept away from the old gentleman.

The next day, as Pat was perusing an old American newspaper, he was surprised, on looking up, to
behold the same gentleman near and watching him
as closely as he had done on the preceding day.

"Can you read, my lad?" asked he, in a kind and
friendly tone, drawing near.

"Yes, sir; I am reading an American paper which
a passenger loaned me."

"Where are you from, my lad?"

"I am from Dublin, sir."

"Are you going to remain in America?"

"Yes, sir."

"Going there to make a great name for yourself?"

"I hope so, sir," said Pat.   But little did he think
that there was a work to be accomplished in that
New World in which he would take an active part,
and in so doing, enscribe his name high upon the
Temple of Fame.

"How long shall you remain in America?" continued the old gentleman.

"Always, sir; I am never going back to Ireland."

"Are your parents living?"

"My mother is, sir. My father was drowned at sea."

"What is your name?"

"Devilin, sir: Pat Devilin."

"Devilin! What was your mother's name?"

"My mother's name, sir, was Lena Burns."

"Lena Burns!" gasped the old man. "Is she living in Dublin?"

"Yes, sir, I left her on Monday last."

"I knew you, Pat, when I first saw you. You have found a friend, Pat Devilin," said the man, coming near to Pat. "Your mother, Pat, is my daughter."

CHAPTER VII.

THE INDEPENDENT BAND.

WHEN the girls found themselves locked in Ona's room, they looked at Ona in surprise, then looked at each other. What, thought they, is to be done? Some trick of Ona's, some sleight of hand performance, was the object of their playmate's fastening them in. She being the acknowledged leader in all their sports, Ona was the first to speak. "Girls, be seated, please. I have a new game, a play we have never yet learned." Each miss seated herself with surprise and expectation depicted upon her countenance.

Ona felt embarrassed, but she remained standing and addressed her hearers in a low, sweet, serious voice, saying: "Girls, I am fourteen years old to-day, many of you are about the same age. I want to tell you, that this morning I formed new resolutions and partly developed new plans by which my after life is to be governed, and I earnestly desire your co-operation. I have called it a 'new play' for the purpose of enlisting your attention more thoroughly, yet it will have its bearing upon our whole lives. First, I am determined to acquaint myself with several useful trades, and in so doing, endeavor to elevate myself above the station generally allotted to woman. Will you join me in the undertaking?"

"My gracious! What can we do?" exclaimed Lillie Brooks.

"You can accomplish anything you earnestly undertake, as for me, I shall learn to cook, make watches, clocks, and such articles," said Ona.

"You work? indeed, Ona Leland?" laughed Lillie Brooks.

"Yes, I don't expect that my father will live always, and if he should lose his property, what should I do in my present circumstances regarding a knowledge of work. It is true, I could teach school, but why not do something I like better and make more money?"

"You must be going crazy, Ona?" said Sallie Strawn, and all joined in a hearty laugh at the absurdity of the idea of her being crazy. Ona smiled at their sport.

"I will do what I can," said Lillie Brooks, "but I do not know what to do first."

"What does your father do?" asked Ona.

"He makes brooms."

"Then that would be a good place for you for a while."

"Me make brooms? Who ever heard of a woman making brooms?"

"What do you do at home?"

"I milk the cows, churn, help do the washing and cooking, and ever so much."

"Did you ever assist your father in the shop?"

"Yes, indeed, several times."

"Is it hard work?"

"No, not very."

"As hard as churning and washing?"

"No, no, not half so hard."

"Why then could women not work at such work."

"O! It would look so odd, that's all."

"But don't you suppose the first lady teacher seemed odd, as she took her place? I think she did. Then is there any reason we should wait for some-one to begin this work?"

"You are right, Ona," answered a number of the girls at the same time.

"How many of you will be ready to join me in this work? Are there any?"

"Yes," said some half-dozen, "I will, if my mother will let me."

"I will attend to that part, if you will only set your hearts entirely upon trying to be something more than drones and drudges," continued Ona.

"Now I will take your names and the calling or occupation you prefer, if you wish me to assist you,"
said she, producing pen and paper. "I shall sign
first, then you who wish to sign, can do so, I will fill
out the preamble to-night, as it is growing late," and
so saying, she signed her name with "Baking, Watch-
making and Repairing" appended as her chosen
trades. Soon each one in the room had chosen a
calling, and their names added to Ona Leland's on
the little page.

"Now, what can we do, Ona, about finding situa-
tions, so we can learn the trades we have chosen?"
asked some.

"I will attend to that if you desire me to do so, I
will secure a place for you to serve your apprentice-
ship in, myself with the rest. Now let me say, you
must be as still as 'mice in the meat-chest.' Do not
whisper one word, even to your own folks, keep all
your business to yourselves, and you will prosper
better in all your undertakings. I can talk to your
parents with better prospects of success than you
can, and if any one opposes, I can, I think, easily
overcome their opposition." Thus ended the first
meeting of the "Independent Band."

CHAPTER VIII.

THE MYSTERIOUS STRANGERS AGAIN.

HAYDEN and his companion sat side by side, but the old gentleman did not observe the one at the opposite end of the table, but sat with his head bowed down. A shadow was upon his countenance. He had spent a sleepless night over the book which contained Leland's name.

Mr. Leland was the first to leave the table, as he left the room the mail was carried in. A letter was handed to the old gentleman; breaking the seal he read it carefully two or three times.

" Is it from Theo. ?" asked Hayden.

" Yes, it is from Theodocia, I must go soon. I shall leave this afternoon."

" Why so soon ? Can you not defer your journey and attend the meeting this afternoon ?"

" No, Hayden, I cannot break my promise to Theodocia."

" I do not ask you to break your promise, Sir Charles, but I would like for you to attend this meeting, if you can possibly do so. I know how deeply you are interested in Theo.'s welfare, and realize fully the comfort your presence would convey to her mind. Could I feel that my presence would contribute to her welfare, however small the degree, I should forego any other engagement in order to accompany you to her bed-side. Be the bearer to her of my most kindly regards and sympathy. Good-bye."

Thus the two friends parted, one to wend his way back to England, where a weak, worn and weary woman waited to bask once more in the sunshine of his smile, and again listen to his cheerful, kindly voice which had often, in times past, dictated words of advice and wisdom.

The other watched the coach conveying his friend until it was lost to view, and mechanically wended his way to the hall where the society assembled, but it had lost, for the time, its interest. His thoughts were away in Merrie England, or following his departed friend.

Hayden remained in Boston two days, when he proceeded to Washington, where he intended to pass the Winter.

In that year occurred one of the most important events that had ever been recorded in the history of the world. The introduction of the electric telegraph, the construction of which created an excitement which called together people of all nations and climes, who assembled at Baltimore and Washington, making those cities all aglow with life, vivacity and intelligence.

Hayden had traveled over the greater portion of the Eastern and Southern States, gathering up the political views and observing the general customs of the people. From these observations he had drawn his own conclusions. The striking contrast presented to his mind by the customs and habits of the different sections, were indelibly impressed upon his mind. In the one, each man followed earnestly some avocation in life; the population was active, energetic, industrious and intelligent. In the other section, where idleness prevailed, there was little energy manifested, and intelligence was the exception instead of the rule. The people were indolent, slow in movements, languid in the expression of their countenances; both mind and body in a dormant condition. Being of a joyous, happy temperament, Hayden's ideas assimilated more readily with those of the people of the East than with those of the South. Yet he admitted with the candor becoming a gentleman, that the natural acquirements of many of the Southern people were of a superior quality, and when the energies were called into play to develop the mind, success crowned the effort, producing many bright lights in the world of literature, science and politics.

The three political organizations had caused considerable excitement this year in Washington City. The Anti-Slavery had for the first time appeared as a distinct party, and put a candidate for President in nomination. With this party Hayden Douglas became identified. He liked their precepts and their energy. Although an alien, he loved the Americans and their ways far better than he did his own early companions and their principles. He saw intelligence in every household in the New England States, and women were not slaves. They sat at the head of the table, and conversed freely on topics religious, scientific, political, and, in fact, any subject of conversation was readily handled by them as well

as by men, and with the fluency and ease of the nobility of his own country. Free speech is allowed, and
why should not woman be free to express her opinion upon current questions commensurate with her
intelligence?

One day, as he and an English friend were walking down the avenue, he remarked to that friend after this manner: "We English will learn from the
Americans, in fact, we can not help it. If we associate with them, their principles of liberty and freedom will fasten upon us. We may not immediately
recognize the change; possibly not until we again
mingle with our own countrymen at home. Then
our minds will revert to scenes and incidents in
America, and the habits and manners of American
people will rise up before the eyes of our minds, and
in comparing them with those at home, we will be
compelled to decide in favor of American principles,
as tending to harmony, arrangement and general
beauty. Notice, for instance, the deference shown
here to women; no matter what the habiliments
may be, whether plain calico or royal purple and er-
mine, and observe further, the effect of such universal equality upon the women themselves. All classes
are courteous, kind and seemingly happy, a cheerful
smile ever plays upon their countenances; not to the
detriment of regality. No! No! the same independent expression is behind that smile, and through it
gleams with more beauty. I tell you, that right here
in America is where the grand thought was conceived and will be fully developed, declaring woman
to be the equal of man in everything."

Hayden Douglas was of an impulsive nature, an enthusiast in everything in which he became interested. Endowed with finer feelings than the majority of men, he grasped readily the finer points of every thought; the heavy and more burdensome was left for those of a more argumentative turn of mind. While others were laying the solid foundation stones, he was reveling among the frescoes of the superstructure. Leisure hours were spent in cultivating the muse, and frequently fine sentiments would flow from his pen. Gifted and schooled in social etiquette, he enjoyed the society of the Americans, and still further resembling them in his restlessness of disposition, he felt at ease in their midst. When the entertaining season opened, none entered upon its pleasures and enjoyments more readily than did Hayden Douglas.

One day, at dinner, he received a letter; he broke the seal and read the few lines which it contained. It was written in a feminine hand. After reading it a number of times, the pallor heightening in his face at each reading, he withdrew to his room where he threw himself upon the bed and gave way to sobs and tears, as he contemplated the sad news. He was thus thinking and grieving over his sadness, when some one approached his door and rapped gently. Hurriedly arranging his collar and brushing his hair, he prepared to answer the summons.

CHAPTER IX.

ONA'S SUCCESS.

WE next find Ona Leland sitting near the large oven in a baker's shop. She remained silent for some moments, her mind reviewing the past, not of her own life, but of that of her ancestors, of which she felt more than an ordinary degree of pride. Yes, she was proud that the crimson blood which coursed through her veins was tinged with the pure Scottish blue blood of the Clanronald family who fought under Charles Edward on the fatal field of Culloden. Ona Leland was a Macdonald in her bold determined manner. Her father's mother was a sister of the brave Marshal Macdonald of Bonapart's army, who, when he had merited the displeasure of the Great Soldier, through his defense of Moreau, the "Hero of Hohenlinden," was relieved of his command, but through the necessities of war was reinstated and retrieved the smiles of his chief, and at the same time won his Marshal's baton for invincibility and stubborn fighting at Wagram, where he broke the enemy's center and carried the tri-color of France triumphant to the opposing camp. Ona had imbibed his spirit and determination. She was bold, daring and firm, fully determined to overcome every obstacle that tended to hinder her progress. Flattery was a poison drop in her cup; open, candid and outspoken, she praised wherever praise was due, she censured where blame belonged; ever endeavoring to inculcate into the minds of her young friends the same power to distinguish right from wrong and as readily choose between them.

Her thoughts had wondered to her illustrious ancestors; she had reviewed their actions with pleasure to herself when her reverie was disturbed and the object of her mission brought to her mind by the entrance of Mrs. Jones, the proprietor of the shop, to whom she spoke, saying: "Mrs. Jones would you like an apprentice for two or three months?"

"I don't know, we have tried two boys and they were worthless, and I told Mr. Jones we would never try any more."

"Would you take two good, industrious girls?"

"I don't know. How old are they?"

"Fourteen years old."

"Who are they? Do they live near?"

"Yes, they live near the village. I am one and Ida Brown is the other?"

"Well, I do declare! You learn to cook, Miss Ona? You cooking with those little white hands? What can you be thinking about?"

"I desire to learn to cook and do general housework, I may be compelled to do so some time, and if I learn now, I shall be prepared when circumstances require it."

"Well! Well! Will wonders never cease? The idea! You compelled to cook, as rich as your father is. Why, I am surprised! Roderick Leland's daughter learning to cook?"

"Mrs. Jones, I am no better by nature than you are, and perhaps not as good by practice. I know I am not in cooking, for I know nothing about it."

"Well, if you are determined to learn, come on when you get ready and I will teach you and Ida Brown all I can."

"We will come next Monday morning," and Ona turned her steps toward the broom-factory of Mr. Brooks, to intercede for his daughter Lillie. After talking an hour in a persuasive manner, she convinced Mr. Brooks that she was taking the proper course.

"Three out of eleven provided for," said she, thinking herself fortunate.

The tailor, watch-maker and dry-goods merchants were each visited, and the proprietors seemed greatly surprised to find young girls applying for such positions. Had they made application in person, they would not have been so fortunate, perhaps. But Ona, being rich and independent, had considerable to do with the favorable view taken of her applications in behalf of her young friends.

She had to find places for but two more. She accordingly called on Mr. Black, a dry-goods merchant, who welcomed her obsequiously, by saying: "How do you do, Miss Leland? I am happy to see you this morning. I am always pleased to have the ladies call, and more especially you. I could not keep store if the ladies were as hard to please as the men are. I was saying to Mrs. Black last night that this would not be a hard world if men were as good-natured as women. What do you think about the women and negroes voting, Miss Ona?" at the same time patting her familiarly on the shoulder, "Do you think they will some time?"

"I do not know," she replied, stiffly.

"Well, I would like to see you at the polls voting. Really I would, Miss Ona."

At length Ona found opportunity to state her errand. Mr. Black turned pale and red by turns, and finally found courage to express his opinion.

"Really, I do not need any one at present, except on Saturdays, and then Mr. Briggs, the teacher, assists me. He is a young man and very anxious to accumulate money with hard labor; he is a good clerk. I pay him one dollar and a half a day."

"But, Mr. Black, those two girls could do a great amount of work in one day without costing you anything, except a little trouble in instructing them."

"It does seem to me that women are growing bolder and more presumptuous every day. I do not think it becoming for women to seek or occupy positions outside of their calling. Such actions, on their part, unless prevented, will bring our country into disgrace."

"Mr. Black, is it any more debasing for women to clerk in business houses than it is for the wives of some merchants to chop wood?" asked Ona, the Macdonald fire of her nature rising to its full height, as she administered this gentle reminder to Mr. Black of his home affairs, and hastily bidding the old flatterer adieu, she called at Mr. Crowell's store. He was of a different character—slow to speak, and reserved in manner toward strangers. He met and addressed her in a kindly tone as she entered.

3

Her interview with Mr. Black had excited her somewhat, but Mr. Crowell's kind tone and gentle manner reassured her, and she soon made known her errand.

Said he, in reply: "Yes, I will take two apprentices, and be glad to get them, besides I will agree to do a good part by them."

Pleased with her success, she hurried home to make known her plans and partial success to Aunt Nancy, not forgetting to report her interview with Mr. Black.

"I am not surprised to hear of Mr. Black's talking as he did. He is just like his sister, Mrs. Dr. Harris, who, it is generally admitted, is the meanest woman in the neighborhood. I have known the Black family a long time, and have yet to learn that they possess any redeeming quality."

"Why, I thought they were good people," said Ona.

"No, they are not, and it is well for your friends that he refused to take them, and let me say more, you and your young friends will be vilified and slandered unmercifully by Mrs. Harris for this step you have taken. It matters not what any person does that brings them before the public, even in the remotest way, Mrs. Harris is sure to find something to condemn in their action, and if she can find no good open ground, she is sure to manufacture something especially for the occasion. If you do not hear from her, I am wonderfully mistaken."

Ona, in deep meditation, withdrew to her room. As she was laying aside her wraps, she thought of her promise to assist Mary, the cook, in preparing supper.

While thus engaged, she was called to the hall, where she met Walter Strawn, a young man who was in her father's employ.

"What do you wish, Walter?"

"I have a present for you, Miss Ona. Please step to the door."

Following him to the door, she beheld on the lawn a beautiful sleigh.

"This sleigh is for you, Miss Ona. I made it during leisure hours, and secured the trimmings of Mr. Smith, by assisting him gather corn, on pleasant nights, last fall."

"I thank you kindly, Walter, for the beautiful present, and I assure you I shall prize it highly as an evidence of your industry. I see I shall need an outfit of cushions for my sleigh, and I authorize you to procure them. Here is twenty dollars; whatever sum is left, you can devote to your own use. I feel confident that you will use it properly."

Walter accepted the money with many thanks, and in a brief time procured the necessary upholstering for the sleigh. During the afternoon, Ona had the horse hitched to the sleigh, and accompanied by Aunt Nancy and Robie, with Walter for driver, called on the parents of the girls who had chosen to become clerks in the various shops. She found some of the parents opposed to the scheme, and in order to accomplish her purpose, she was obliged to pay them certain sums per week out of her personal funds. Aunt Nancy and Robie remained in the sleigh until they came to the last house. It was the home of Walter Strawn, where Sallie, his only sister, lived with his feeble mother and three small boys. Sallie was a favorite of Ona's, and they were frequently together. The dwelling was of logs, standing on some unimproved land belonging to Mr. Leland. No carpet covered the slab-floor, and only a rude fireplace gave them warmth. On the bed, in one corner, lay Mrs. Strawn, pale and emaciated. Ona soon made the object of her visit known.

"No, Ona, Sallie cannot go. I am not able to do the work, besides she has no suitable clothes."

Ona glanced toward Sallie, who was standing at the window, weeping silently. Then turning to Walter, asked in a low tone, "What can we do?"

"I do not know. I would like to have Sallie go, but you can see from our surroundings that we are not able to hire any one to assist mother if she goes away, and it is too far for her to go and return each day."

"Can we not rent a house in the village so Sallie can board at home and attend to her duties in the store?"

"Yes, if we had the means to spare," said Mrs. Strawn.

"Walter has sufficient to pay the rent a month or two. After that we can make some arrangement that will prove satisfactory. So cheer up, Sallie; all is for the best."

The next morning Ona and Walter drove to the village. Walter was sent on a tour of inspection and inquiry, from which he soon returned, saying: "I find but one vacant house. It is a large one with five rooms."

"That is not very large. Let us drive around and see it."

After an examination, Ona said: "This is the very house. How much rent do they ask?"

"Three dollars a month, cash down."

"Here is the money; go and secure it while I see if I can find some one to clean it."

Walter went out, and Ona passed down the steps leading to the alley where Mrs. Fox, the washer-woman lived, who received her with the exclamation: "Goodness sakes! where under the sun did you come from? Are you lost, Miss Ona?"

"No, Mrs. Fox, I came to see if I can employ you to clean this house near yours, so Mrs. Strawn can occupy it."

"Of course I will clean it, and not charge a cent for the work. I am so glad Mrs. Strawn is coming back to her old home, for this once belonged to Mr. Strawn, as did the whole village, but he got sick, and soon he had to sell all he owned."

"Did he own and lay out this village," asked Ona.

"Yes, my child, he did, and it makes me mad to see some folks living in style, while Mrs. Strawn is so poor."

Ona felt a greater anxiety than ever about the family since she had learned that they had once known better days.

"I will send Walter over this afternoon with a cooking stove and he can assist you, so that you can finish the work to-day."

As she was about to leave, she saw a woman hurrying towards where she and Mrs. Fox were standing.

"That," said Mrs. Fox in an under tone, "is Mrs. Harris, she is out on some slandering expedition, I know, for she is unusually excited over something."

As Ona departed, the Doctor's wife entered saying, "Good morning, Mrs. Fox, you had an early visitor this morning, was it that Leland huzzy?"

Ona's cheeks burned with vexation as she heard the remark of the Doctor's wife, and she felt inclined to return and defend herself against the unjust aspersion which she felt would follow the introductory remark of the Doctor's wife.

CHAPTER X.

HAYDEN IN TROUBLE.

HAYDEN DOUGLAS opened the door and was surprised at beholding an acquaintance in the person of Arthur Holmes.

"I have found you at last, Mr. Douglas, but why are you so pale? Are you sick?"

"No, I am not really sick, yet I am suffering somewhat from indisposition, induced beyond doubt by a severe headache."

Arthur Holmes was of English parentage, born in America, and as regards his habits, manners and sympathy, he was wholly American. Hayden had been prepossessed in his favor at their first meeting, and as the acquaintance grew, he had learned to depend upon him for favors, which he would otherwise have been compelled to forego.

"No doubt you have a headache, I should, were I compelled to stay in this place, and my object in calling upon you at this time is to cordially invite you to make your home with me. I need not tell you that my father's house is commodious, and I am earnestly seconded by him in extending this invitation to you."

"I am at a loss for words to express my appreciation of your kind invitation. I have more than once felt a repugnance when contemplating my surroundings at the hotels. I long for the comforts of home life. I hope you will not deem me inconsiderate in thus readily accepting your kind offer."

"Thank you, you are doing our house an honor, and I hope, under our home administration, to see the rose's bloom soon again upon your cheeks."

Even with bright anticipations of congenial surroundings and associates, the gloom cast upon Hayden's brow by the reading of that letter would not be dispelled. Arthur watched him closely, to ascertain, if possible, the cause of his melancholy. During their conversation one day, Hayden voluntarily communicated to Arthur the cause of his sorrow, his history from childhood to the present time, concluding with this remark: "To you alone have I communicated all that I know regarding my own history, and you can readily imagine, when contemplating it,

that my gloomy spells are not mere delusions, but
are based upon grounds sufficiently strong to cause
me to appear sad and dejected at times."

When we have sad thoughts and brood over them,
we are apt to be depressed in appearance, but when
we meet one whom we can trust, and converse freely
regarding our troubles, our minds are sensibly relieved of their burdens.   Thus it was with Hayden,
from the day he recited his troubles and grievances
to Arthur, he appeared more cheerful than he had
been for months.   He mingled with cheerful company and became a regular attendant of all the fashionable parties and entertainments with which Washington is replete.   None became so popular with
both sexes as Mr. Douglas.

From among the many fair ones that graced
Washington with their presence, none were fairer
and more attractive than Lillie Calhoun.   By an affinity unexplicable, these two young persons had
sought each other's society.   The devoted attention
of Hayden was kindly appreciated by Miss Calhoun,
and his ardent words, as he expressed his heart-
utterances, met with a reciprocity of feeling on her
part.   We pass over the various entertainments during that unusually gay winter, until the last, which
was designed with an elaborateness that far surpassed
anything that had preceded it.

The invitations were out, and the stately mansion
of the Arnolds was resplendent with light, and rare
flowers decorated the rooms.   Caterers from New
York and Philadelphia vied with each other in the
costly and symmetrical table ornaments.   Special mes-

sengers were in attendance from the tropics, bearing
the richest fruits and choicest viands. The grand,
the elite, the bon-ton of Washington were to meet
for the last time during the season. Many who had
actually surfeited of amusements,. felt the early fer-
vor coursing through their veins and were preparing
to grace the stately halls with their presence.

Guests began to arrive at an early hour. Among
the first were General Haynes and his family, of Atlanta, Georgia. Their entrance created a sensation
among the guests already assembled, as they took
their places in the elegantly furnished parlors. Ava
Haynes, the oldest daughter, was a warm friend of
Lillie Calhoun, whom she soon sought out and led
quickly into the conservatory.

Ava was very beautiful and had, until Lillie came,
reigned as the belle of the city, but she manifested
no displeasure toward the sweet Southern beauty who
had superseded her, but rather more earnestly sought
her friendship. She was not of the true, pure, con-
fiding nature of Lillie. She had, in the early season,
become acquainted and flirted with Hayden, and was
charmed with the young Englishman. She felt
vexed when she saw that his most earnest attentions
were bestowed upon Lillie. Her deportment toward
either manifested no pique, and she chose Arthur
Holmes as her most intimate friend. While she, to
all appearance, was infatuated with the attentions of
Arthur, she harbored away down, deep in her heart
the determination that she would not surrender the
effort to win the attentions of Mr. Douglas.

As she and Lillie passed through the hall, she

glanced quickly into each apartment to discover if either Hayden or Arthur were present. Not seeing them, she felt relieved, and began the conversation by saying:

"Lillie, you are looking better by far to-night than I ever saw you. You are grand; you are superb, and I am really sorry to be compelled, by a sense of duty, to speak upon a subject that, no doubt, will cause you to feel sad."

"Ava, do not keep me in suspense. I cannot imagine what your remarks may be, but if they are 'prompted by a sense of duty,' I humbly bow to the shrine of that duty."

"I hope you will not censure me. My object in calling you aside, is to convey to your mind the fact that certain reports derogatory to the social standing of Mr. Douglas are current, and as a friend I thought it best to advise you, that you may no longer compromise yourself by associating with him."

"I can not be other than surprised at the assertion you have just made, Ava. I have known Mr. Douglas and have associated with him, to a greater or less extent, more than others, and have yet to experience the fact that his deportment has been other than that of a gentleman. You must be more explicit in your accusations, otherwise I can not give them credence."

"My information, dear Lillie, does not affect his deportment. It refers more directly to his social standing. It is his parentage."

"O, indeed! Were his parents poor?"

"No, not that. It is rumored that his genealogical record is not legally traceable. In fact that he is a son of the erratic Lord Byron, whom he wonderfully resembles, and I believe it is true."

A wild light gleamed from the eyes of Lillie Calhoun. A pallor overspread her face as she reeled, and would have fallen to the floor, had not a strong arm been thrown around her. Hayden was approaching, and heard the last words, "it is true," when he noticed the reeling girl, and sprang forward in time to receive her in his arms ere she fell. He held her a moment, himself almost unconscious.

As suspended animation resumed its office, and she fully realized her surroundings, the quickly-returning blood mantling her cheeks, she stepped back, rejecting his kindly-offered assistance, exclaiming:

"Can such be true! Am I to be thus cruelly robbed of all budding joy and anticipated happiness!"

Although Hayden felt that he was in some manner connected with the statement of Ava which had affected Lillie so strangely, yet he desired to learn from her own lips the cause of her perturbation. Therefore he followed Lillie, she not being cognizant of his presence until he addressed her as she stood in the brilliantly-lighted hall, asking:

"Why, Miss Lillie, are we to be thus suddenly deprived of your company?"

She turned quickly, and recognizing him, said:

"I wish you would order my carriage, Mr. Douglas. I desire to return home. My indisposition is so great that I cannot longer remain."

Hayden offered her his arm and leading her to one of the many beautiful parlors, saw her comfortably seated and departed on his mission.

Soon Lillie passed from the house escorted by Hayden. By the sparkling gas jets Ava Haynes saw him assist her to enter her carriage, himself following. Ava felt annoyed at the prospect of losing Mr. Douglas, as she had planned to dispose of Lillie only, hoping then to secure Mr. Douglas for herself. But being disappointed, she endeavored to forget Douglas, and to all appearance was quite happy when she found Arthur Holmes by her side. As they sauntered leisurely from the crowd, Arthur said quietly, "What has become of Miss Calhoun and Mr. Douglas? Have they spirited themselves away, hoping to bask in scenes more celestial?"

"Lillie was suddenly attacked with a sick headache, from which she suffers so much annoyance, dear girl, and Mr. Douglas, feeling troubled on her account and for her safety, has accompanied her to her father's residence."

Ava knew that she was telling an untruth, she knew that Lillie Calhoun was heartsick, made so by the cruelly false insinuations conceived in her own malicious brain and uttered by her own perfidious lips. She knew that her own despicable mind had evolved the poisonous words which went like viper tongues to the heart of the gentle and loving girl.

Hayden on the journey home spoke but few words to Lillie, which she answered in sad, dejected tones. As he assisted her to alight from the carriage, he said, "Now, Miss Lillie, before we part, please tell me what has so wounded your feelings and placed such a seeming barrier between us?"

"I cannot, Mr. Douglas, it would be useless for me to repeat what I have heard. It is enough for me to bear it, without inflicting pain upon you by reiterating. Allow me to bid you good-night."

She was gone. Hayden wended his way to the residence of Mr. Holmes, entering his own room, he threw himself into a chair, his mind tormented with conflicting thoughts, his heart beating rapidly in uncertainty. He attempted to review the past, but his excited and bewildered mind could fix itself on nothing definitely, further than his anxiety to fathom the reason of the sudden withdrawal of consideration for him on the part of Miss Lillie. Said he "she has learned, from some source, my past history, no doubt and with additions *ad furitum.*" Thus cogitating he fell asleep, and was aroused only by the entrance of Arthur, who jokingly said:

"You, too, are sick, old boy, I suppose because Miss Lillie experienced so sudden an attack of headache?"

"No, I am not sick," said Hayden, "but I am in receipt of bad news, is what causes my apparent depression."

"I will not, to-night, inquire the particulars of your sad news, for I am too sleepy. I will hear it in the morning, at which time I can sympathize with you as fully as now, when I am tired."

Thus speaking, the light-hearted youth withdrew and was soon asleep in an adjoining room.

CHAPTER XI.

THE SLANDERER.

"MRS. HARRIS! Why should you speak so harshly of one who never did any harm to any one and is trying to do all the good she can?" said Mrs. Fox.

" I don't think she is doing any good, just think of what she was adoing yesterday morning, agoing all over town begging of men to take those green country girls and teach them to be ladies. Why, Mrs. Fox, I cried last night until I was almost sick, just athinking of these innocent girls being ruined."

" Mrs. Harris, I think they will do very well. They go into the shops and stores by twos, and what harm can come of their learning some trade?"

" They will make harm of it, and one thing I want to know, who will there be to do our work in the kitchen, if those low-down girls try to come up with us? I don't intend they shall ever associate with my girls."

" Mrs. Harris! I have to work hard, yet I am well pleased to hear of these girls having easy lives planned out for them, and I am glad that Strawn, if it is a small village, has one brave, intelligent girl in the person of Ona Leland."

" You may think she is something above the average, but I don't, and I told brother if he had taken in those girls, I should have disowned him."

Mrs. Fox did not indulge in gossiping, neither did she uphold those who did so, but when Mrs. Harris introduced her brother, Mr. Black, and inferentially held him up as a paragon of perfection, she could not repress her indignation, and addressing Mrs. Harris, said :

" If your brother never does a greater wrong than assisting those girls, he will be sure of a seat in Heaven, and if he would cut more wood and feed. the hogs at home, perhaps his own wife would be a happier woman."

"Mrs. Fox, you know that my brother's wife is nothing more than a crazy old woman, and she is fit only for a drudge."

" She may be crazy now, Mrs. Harris, but she was not when she was a girl at school. I knew her well, and have often spoken of the smart girl Mr. Black got for a wife when he married Ella Carmean."

" You may think so, but I don't," said she, as she hastened away, to the great pleasure of Mrs. Fox, who well knew that Mrs. Harris was anxious to have some one join with her in abusing her neighbors, especially the women.

When she left Mrs. Fox, her temper was at its extreme height. She could not bear to be crossed in the least thing she undertook in defaming any one, and the only wonder is, that she did not include Mrs. Fox in her category of those deserving abuse for the bold stand she had taken in defense of the girls. She knew of one person who would sympathize with her, it was her brother. She accordingly wended her way to his place of business, there to give full vent to her vituperations.

CHAPTER XII.

PAT DEVILIN'S NEW HOME.

P AT'S new found friend and grandfather was an
Englishman, known as Sir Richard Burns.
His daughter, Lena, had married against his
wishes and he had disinherited and disowned her.
She had gone with her husband to Ireland, and her
relatives ceased to hear from her; they supposed she
was dead. Her father's heart softened toward her.
when she had gone, and he inwardly and silently
grieved and blamed himself for his hasty and inconsiderate action, yet he would not publicly put forth
an effort to find her, being governed in such matters
by a false family pride.

Feeling assured that Pat was really a son of his
long-lost Lena, he felt proud of him, and often found
himself gazing unconsciously into the face of the
noble-looking lad. In his features he could trace
the lineaments of the lad's mother, his own proud
daughter. From the boy's eye flashed the same
determined look that he beheld in the expression of
his mother, when she chose between wealth and station and the man whom she worshiped with a wealth
of love gold could not buy, although he was pecu-
niarily poor.

Pat, on the other hand, did not feel elated at the
prospect of being tied to his wealthy relative. He
had started out to make a stir upon the busy stage
of life alone. His plans were not matured, but he

felt since he learned that he was to be the especial charge of his grandfather, that he had not in reality gained the freedom for which he had so ardently longed.

As days rolled on, Sir Richard became more ardently attached to his grand-son. Pat found his feelings changing toward the kind old gentleman. Sir Richard spared no effort to make Pat happy and comfortable, and soon after they landed in New York, Pat was wonderfully surprised on being conducted to one of the largest and finest dwellings in the street where his grandfather resided.

"Pat," said Sir Richard, "this is my home, and I want it to be yours."

"Thank you, grandpa, I will stay with you until I find employment. I promised Mike I would send him some money as soon as I could earn it, so he, too, could come to America when he is a little older."

"I will furnish you all the money you may need for yourself, besides allowing you to send some to Mike all in good time."

Pat expressed himself as well pleased at the kindly offer of his grandfather, as well as with his luxurious surroundings. Yet, with all its grandeur, it was not his own quiet, happy home in Dublin, where his sad-faced mother was thinking of her boy who had wandered far to distant lands; where his brother Mike, as he found himself alone, would drop a tear as he thought of Pat, so far away; where little Mary was looking anxiously from the window for his return, expecting some new toy each day. When Pat would think of those at home, the tears would voluntarily

· 5

chase each other down his cheeks, until he would arouse himself by saying: "Never mind, boy, the time will come when you can send for them to come to happy, free America, and then all will be well."

One day, after his grandfather had called him to his library, he said: "My good lad, here is some money to send to Mike. Tell him I sent it with my kindest regards."

Pat stood a moment in silence, and then, in a faltering voice, said: "May I send some of it to sister Mary? She will be disappointed if I do not send her something as well as Mike."

"Pat, girls should not expect to get money as a present. They have no use for it, and it is not customary to consider them the equal of boys, or to treat them as well."

"I know it is not customary to treat them so, grandfather, but custom does not make it right. I shall never treat my mother or sister in any such way. They are as good as Mike or myself, and deserve equally good, if not better treatment. And more, I will leave any country whose customs are like those of England, in that respect. That is why I am in America to-day. I admire their laws, and love the freedom which their customs give."

"What do you know of America?"

"What I have read and heard from Americans who visited Ireland."

"Do you think you shall like it on account of the respect shown to women? Are you in sympathy with the idea that women should enjoy the same rights that men have in public affairs and in inheriting property?"

" Ye ;, sir, I would like to see a general law pass d
which would make my mother and sister my equal."

" Pat, what has turned your head on that subject?"

" It is not turned, sir, I have always believed that
was the right way.   I know of one circumstance that
I can never forget."

" What was it?"

" Well, sir, a gentleman, an Englishman, had two
children, a son and daughter.   He sent the son to
school, and being confined to the house for a number
of years, he compelled the daughter to remain at
home and care for him, which she did until he died.
When his will was read, it gave all his possessions to
the son with the understanding that he was to care
for his sister until she married.   The son began traveling and when he returned he was penniless, having
lost his money in gambling and thrown it away in
dissipation.   The daughter was by force of circumstances compelled to make her own living.   To-day
she is working herself almost to death to earn a
miserable small sum in a dress-maker's shop."

" Well, Pat, should not women work as well as
men ?"

" Yes, sir, and they should have opportunities to
become educated as well as men.   With an education and a share of her father's property, that girl
could have done well in life and been well cared for."

" Pat, I think you only see one side of this question ! "

" I hope not, sir, I remember a remark frequently
made by my mother, who said, " She would rather
bury her children when small, than to be so unrea-
sonable in the division of her property."

Sir Richard made no answer to this remark. He began to think there were two sides to the subject. He thought of his own roving son, who sent to him frequently for hundreds of dollars, which he never denied him; but his daughter, who had married Pat's father, had never received a cent from him, and she had nursed him and managed in every possible way to make him comfortable, when she was at home, yet he had never before so considered the matter. Pat's conversation had struck a tender chord. Turning to Pat, he said, "Come to my library again to-morrow morning, I will then make arrangements to send you to school and at the same time send some money regularly to your mother for her to distribute among the children or use as her judgment may dictate."

Pat left the room highly elated in spirits, to anxiously await the coming of the morrow.

CHAPTER XIII.

ONA AT WORK.

ONA LELAND stepped into her sleigh with an angry frown upon her brow, which was soon dispelled as she thought of the Strawn family. "I wish we had a stove for mother," said Walter, as they drove toward home. "I must endeavor to find one this afternoon."

"I was thinking that that stove in the wood-shed would answer for a while. It is comparatively good, and was rejected by papa only on account of its being too small for our use. I can polish it myself. There is also a good heating-stove in the cellar. It requires some trifling repairs on the door. You can leave it at the shop when you take the cook-stove."

Walter and Ona set to work immediately on their arrival home. They brought the cook-stove from the wood-shed. Ona soon found the furniture belonging to it, while two of the men assisted in loading it, together with the heating-stove, on the heavy wood-sled. One of the men accompanied Walter to assist in placing the stove in the house. The smith soon repaired the broken door, and. ere long the stoves were in position. The man brought a load of wood, which he cut in proper lengths. The fires were started, and the house soon became comfortable.

After the sled had gone, bearing the stoves, Ona asked Aunt Nancy and Mary to assist her in fitting up a carpet from the many rejected ones at the Leland mansion.

"I have instructed Dick to procure the dimensions of each room. I want to surprise Walter as well as the balance of the family," said Ona, and they began to unload old chests and search the closets, bringing from the various receptacles pieces of both new and old carpet, besides three sets of green damask curtains, which were too short for use at home All hands went to work sewing and piecing the strips of carpet, and when Dick returned they were ready to fit it for the three rooms of which he had the measurements.

"There is a piece of oil-carpet in the garret, which will do for the kitchen. It has some holes in it, but they will come on the edge of the room as it is small."

The next morning Ona asked Walter to have the large sled filled with straw and driven to the gate, as she had some articles which she wished to take to town. Walter was surprised, after various bundles were loaded, to see Miss Ona, wrapped in her rich warm cloak, climb into the sled. But greater was his surprise when he found those bundles consisted of carpets for making his mother's new home more comfortable. Walter was delegated to purchase some tacks and ask Mrs. Fox to assist them. By the united efforts of the three, the carpets were down and the stoves polished by noon-time. After dinner the windows were cleaned and the curtains hung.

"That is really a cosy house now," said Mrs. Fox, as Ona went with her to dinner. Walter having gone for a further supply of wood.

The next morning Walter took Ona's sleigh, and Dick the wood-sled, and carried his mother and her family with their scanty furniture to their new home. Great was the surprise of Mrs. Strawn and Sallie when they were invited by Ona to occupy the comfortable house as their home. Mrs. Strawn's feelings could not be controlled, she sank down overcome, when her mind reverted to the past; to the time when she had in affluent circumstances occupied this house; to the time when her husband was living and comfort and plenty surrounded her, then she lived over again the trials, tribulations and hardships she had endured since his death. Now, that comfortable surroundings were again hers, she lifted her heart in silent, yet fervent prayer, to the Great Ruler, asking that from the abundance of His good gifts He would bestow liberally on one who had thought kindly of the widow and orphans.

Ona had brought some favorite house plants to ornament the sitting-room, and all felt joyous and happy. What a change had taken place in a brief time! From the dark, dingy, desolate log-house to the large, warm rooms, well-lighted, comfortably furnished, and pleasantly located. While the family were joyous and happy when contemplating their changed surroundings, their happiness did not exceed the happiness of Ona, who felt that she had found a work to do that brought its recompense in smiles and happy heart-beats. She soliloquized, "If I could only visit the cities where are many poor families, I would do more than is being done for them. I would enlist the sympathy of the wealthy, and have them appropriate articles cast aside by them, toward the amelioration of the needs of the poor. Why should we keep stored away as rubbish that which would make many families comfortable. I know it is a sin to be so thoughtless and penurious."

She was right. We should think of those who are more needy than ourselves and contribute to their comfort, according to our means. Many an article of clothing and furniture we could, without feeling the loss, donate to such purpose.

On Saturday evening Mr. Leland returned. Ona was overjoyed at seeing him. She told him what she had done during his absence.

"You have done well, my child, for one week. May you continue in well-doing as you grow older."

"I wish I had sufficient money to purchase that house for Mrs. Strawn," said Ona.

"How much will it require, my dear?"

"Three hundred dollars."

"That certainly is cheap. I will give you that amount, and you can buy it and present it to her."

"I would much prefer that you purchase it, papa. I am inexperienced in the matter of deeds and property transfers."

"I will hold the matter under advisement," continued Mr. Leland.

On Monday morning the apprentices made their appearance. They were industrious girls, happy and cheerful as could be. Ona seemed to be the only sad one among them. Her father had been summoned to go as a messenger to Mexico, and his business would detain him some months. Ona had been deprived of his society but a few days at any time previous, and she could not feel other than sad at the prospect of being separated for so long a time as the immediate future promised.

He accompanied her to the village and purchased the house for Mrs. Strawn, giving the deed into Ona's possession, to be delivered that night. He called upon his friend, Mr. Crowell, to whom he entrusted his business transactions, with the care of his family, until his return. Bidding Ona good-bye, he started for Washington City, to receive instructions preparatory to continuing his journey to Mexico.

The girls were soon busy at their respective labors, not dreaming of the terrible storm of scandal that was gathering around them.

CHAPTER XIV.

HAYDEN GOES WEST.

"WHAT in the deuce was the matter last night that you did not return to the party, Hayden?"

"I can assign no definite reason, but I suppose some one has been interesting him or herself in a manner prejudicial to my affairs."

"It can not be. You certainly are mistaken."

"I feel confident I am not mistaken."

"What do you know to confirm your suspicions?"

"I accidentally overheard part of a conversation between two persons. Of course my surmises do not form sufficient grounds for an open accusation, yet the impression left upon my mind by occurrences which immediately followed, and the futility of an attempted investigation afterward, leads me to imagine that my surmise, as stated to you, is correct."

"What did you learn from Miss Lillie?"

"Not a solitary, direct expression, pro or con. Her evasive answers only add inferentially to the strength of my surmises."

"Well, let them all go, is my advice. Do not suffer your mind to be worried over 'trifles light as air.' These little peculiarities and differences often arise in a life-time, and I believe that 'indifference' is the best application we can make to overcome such friction. Let's away to breakfast, I am hungry."

Hayden mechanically followed Arthur into the dining-room, piqued because he could receive no sympathy from him. Arthur was too light-hearted and frivolous to grieve over the loss of a friend, when he could convince himself that he, individually was not to blame. Hayden was different, honorable, honest, candid and affectionate, he could not battle with circumstances, especially, such as were adverse to the promptings of his heart's sympathy and affection.

After breakfast they strolled upon the street, each with a different motive. Arthur to enjoy the exhilarating effect of the pure atmosphere and bright sunlight, both of which Hayden was unconscious, as he peered anxiously into the various carriages carrying visitors to the trains, on their way home. He hoped to get but a glimpse of one fair face, but it came not and his despondency hung like a cloud over him as he returned home.

Entering their room, Arthur said, "Now that the season is over, Washington will be virtually dead until next winter. Your introduction has been an exciting one, and up to the present seems to have produced a gayety in your feelings which you did not possess when I first met you. Now that you are sad, which I hope may not be your lot eternally, I suggest that we search for more inviting fields, for I, light-hearted as I am, cannot endure the ennui of Washington 'out of season.' What say you to a trip to the West?"

"Start to-day, if you choose, I am ready at any time. Anywhere to forget the past. Away to the mountains of the West where I can look from some lofty peak upon the rising sun which lights a civilization that has been to me a cheat and a delusion."

"We cannot start to-day. We shall have to go to St. Louis and from there I know not where, before starting for the West."

The morning papers of the next day contained news of the departure from the Capital of several prominent families, among which were the names of the Calhouns and Haynes.

"Good-bye to Southern friends," said Arthur, laughingly ; but Hayden felt a pain pierce his heart, and inwardly expressed a strong desire to hail the first cab and follow them. Where the treasure is there will the heart be also.

In a few weeks the young men were in St. Louis, preparing for the trip overland to the West.

"How are you going, Arthur? In a buggy?"

"No, indeed, we shall be fortunate in obtaining passage in a large farm-wagon, and I assure you, we will be more fortunate if we retain it and our scalps to return with."

As they were searching for an appropriate outfit, they were accosted by a lad of about seventeen, who said :

"Hello, is this you, Arthur?"

" Yes, Pat, how did you ever get to America ?"

" I did not walk all the way, I assure you. How have you been since I saw you in Ireland?"

" I have been well, Pat. When did you arrive ?"

" Last fall "—and Pat related incidents of his voyage to America; the finding of his grandfather, and facts of his regard for and influence over the old gentleman.

Arthur had traveled in Ireland and become acquainted with Pat and Mike Devilin, and recognized Pat readily on meeting him in St. Louis.

" What are you doing here, Pat ? "

" We are preparing to go West."

" Going West ! Who is going with you ? "

" Grandpa and two men. One they call Brown."

" Where are they now, Pat ? "

" Back on the corner where I met you."

" I want to see them. Let's go now."

They retraced their steps, Hayden bringing up the rear. Pat halted before a small group of men, and introduced Arthur and Hayden to his grandfather and Captain Brown. Pat watched Hayden closely. He had seen many handsome men, but he thought Hayden far exceeded any he had ever seen in personal beauty. He dared not question Hayden as to who he was. When the friends separated for the night, Arthur induced Pat to accompany himself and Hayden. When they were safely ensconced in their room, Pad plied Arthur with questions concerning Hayden. To an interrogation of Pat's, Arthur answered :

" Yes, I know his history, Pat, but it should not

concern us. Why are you so anxious regarding him ? "

"Because I think he is a relative of Lord Byron."

"Did you ever see Lord Byron ? "

"No, I never did, but I have seen his picture frequently."

"He does resemble Lord Byron in appearance, besides he writes well, but we should not judge people by their appearances."

"Why not, Mr. Holmes ? "

"Because here in America there are so many nationalities represented that we can not judge one by the other. Persons from one country may resemble those from another, when we know that no relationship can exist between them."

When Arthur had finished the last remark, he found Pat safely enclosed in the arms of Morpheus, oblivious of passing events.

CHAPTER XV.

THE SLANDERER FOILED.

Foolish woman ! what can you gain
By flounting out those words of shame ?
A just reward on earth you'll meet,
Ere you approach the Judgment seat.

MRS. HARRIS walked rapidly to her brother's store, where some half-dozen idlers sat around the stove. A glance around the room conveyed to her mind that none were there who would fail to agree with her. Seeing her brother approaching she said hastily:

"Good morning, brother!"

"Good morning!" returned he in a gruff tone. "What has brought you here so early?"

"I came in to see if you were as crazy as the rest of the men in this village."

"I am not crazy. I do not comprehend you! What do you mean?"

"I mean what I said. The men have all gone crazy about accepting the services of them hateful, no account girls, who have come to town to learn trades."

"I do not know. It seems they have and—"

"It *seems* to you. Don't you see, when your eyes are open?"

"Yes, I see what is coming. Those girls will all be ruined, and—"

"I say they are ruined now," put in Mrs. Harris, "when a girl takes one step in the wrong direction, she is lost right there, and lost forever. Those girls are lost to the world now, and I feel sorry for them and their families."

"I know they are lost, sister, I would have given Ona Leland some good advice, but she has so much of the old man Leland's fire in her eyes, that I was afraid to undertake it."

"What has been done?" asked one of the loungers.

Mrs. Harris soon informed him as to what the girls had done, and added, "That everybody is talking about them already, and the young ladies in town are not going to associate with them, and they need not come out to church, for we have fully decided to 'turn the cold shoulder' on them. Just to think of their impudence, coming to town to learn a trade. I think they will be gadding on the streets all the time or buggy-riding with their employers."

" Yes," said Black, "that will be the talk."

"It is already, and that is why I came to see you. I thought, perhaps, I would find one or two of them here, clerking for you."

" No, I was too sharp for them."

" I am glad there is one sensible man in this town. Just think of them, they look like being city ladies, don't they? I hope they will sink down to perdition. They had better stay in their own sphere. Who is there to do *our* work when *they* get too nice to work. I am not going in the kitchen to make a slave of myself when those country girls are sailing 'round so fine, I am bound on that. The idea! They setting type and measuring goods with all the dignity of a man. I won't stand that," blurted out the woman, as she, almost out of breath, brought her hand down heavily upon the counter.

" I don't see what we can do about it, sister Sarah?"

" Why, get them out of this, is the only way, of course, and I will commence this very day," said she as she flounced out of the room.

The next day she made several calls and told at each place what she had heard. How that the people were not going to put up with those girls staying in those shops, and that there was talk about them already in the stores. "I don't blame the men for talking," she would invariably say, and edge it off with "I know I would, if I was in their places."

By Monday noon she was raving. She had seen the girls, after dinner, returning to their work, and turning to the Doctor, her husband, said she was going out that afternoon to see what was going to be done.

"I think you had better remain at home, as I have to go out in the country to visit a patient, and shall not be able to reach home before night."

She sank down and cried as though her heart was broken, until the Doctor had gone, when she hastily donned her wrappings and sallied forth upon her mission. She called first upon Mrs. Fox, whom she found washing.

"Didn't you wash this forenoon?" enquired she.

"Yes, I did my own washing, but I am now washing for Mrs. Strawn."

"What! Mrs. Strawn! This poor woman over the alley! What has she to hire with?"

"Walter pays me fifty cents a week to do their washing for them."

"He had better keep his money and let that lazy Sallie get to work."

"Sallie is not lazy, Mrs. Harris. She is far from it."

"Well, *you* may think so, but *I* cannot see it in any other light. The whole family are worthless, except to eat."

"Yes, they have what some term the worst disgrace of all, hanging over them—they are poor. I

knew them when they first came here; when Mr.
Strawn was alive and had plenty of money. Then
they were fine folks, but, it is true, now they are
poor. Their property was sold before they could
make arrangements to pay their doctor's bill and
such other things as they were compelled to have.
I am glad Mr. Leland has bought that property for
Mrs. Strawn."

"Done what!" gasped Mrs. Harris.

"Mr. Leland bought that nice residence this morning, and gave it to Mrs. Strawn."

"Well, I declare! that shows what the Strawn
family is. What right had Roderick Leland to be
giving them a house?"

"I think they need friends from somewhere."

"Do you think they are better than the rest of
us?"

"By nature they are good people, and have been
unfortunate. Why should they not be assisted?"

"You are blind, Mrs. Fox! Don't you know it is
a disgrace for any one to do as Mrs. Strawn has done
and her family are doing? I know it, if you don't."

"I can't agree with you, Mrs. Harris. So you
need not complain of them to me."

Mrs. Harris was offended and hastily departed.
She had intended calling on her brother, but she retraced her steps, stopping in to see how each neighbor was getting on and relating what she had heard,
adding that the widow Strawn and Roderick Leland
were going to be married.

By the time she reached home it was all over town
that Mr. Leland's trip to Mexico was a humbug;

5

"that, in fact, he was soon to return and marry the widow Strawn" and that they were to live at Cedar Hall, and Aunt Nancy was to go to the village and take care of the children of the Strawn family. ·

Such were the various reports that Mr. Crowell heard on his return home at night—Mrs. Harris had called on his wife and told her the news. Mr. Crowell merely said: "Three Black Crows."

The following morning Mrs. Harris started out to consult her brother. She found the store full of idlers, as usual. She was bold, although she feigned modesty. In a moment she "opened her batteries" of abuse upon the Strawn family, and the girls who were serving apprenticeships in town. She reiterated her statements of the previous day with the "purchase of the house by Mr. Leland" added.

Black stood with his back toward the door, engrossed with the narration of his sister, and did not observe the entrance of Mr. Crowell, who stood an unobserved auditor of all that was being said, until at the mention of Mr. Leland's name. Then concluding he was right in his suspicions as to the source of the "talk" of the community, he walked up close to her, saying:

"Now, Mrs. Harris, if you are through, I will say a word. I have heard your scandalous remarks personally this morning, as well as heard of your vile talk at previous times throughout the village. I shall be glad if you desist from further gossiping on this subject, especially about these innocent girls whom I have promised to protect, which I propose doing. All other means failing, I shall appeal to the majesty of the law for their protection."

Mrs. Harris quailed before the positive words of the stern-countenanced man, and drew back in silence. Black stood speechless, while the crowd of loafers gathered close about the stove, fearing an onslaught from the bold, upright man who had thus summarily silenced Mr. Black and his more vituperative sister.

With his last remark, Mr. Crowell withdrew from the store. Mrs. Harris soon followed, without a word in defense of her own dear self or brother. Black became absorbed with his books, and the crowd of loafers left one by one, until none remained.

CHAPTER XVI.

HAYDEN AND PAT ON THE PLAINS.

ALMOST a week was spent in St. Louis before the travelers could pursue their journey. Wagons were to load, and everything made secure before starting on "the trail," as the road was called, which they followed in crossing the country. Not one of the party from the East, except Captain Brown, had ever experienced the rudeness of "camp life." The only hardships they had undergone was in crossing the Atlantic. They gazed in astonishment as the long line of wagons, each drawn by six mules, passed by, while the drivers rode one of the wheelers. At last came the empty wagons which were to carry the travelers and their baggage. The constant cracking of the whips and swearing of the drivers were annoying to men who had been accustomed to refined society.

"My first meal in the open air," said Sir Richard, as he sat down to the long rude board which took the place of table. Tin cups, pie pans, coarse iron spoons and heavy steel knives and forks took the place of china and silver ware. Bacon, beans, black coffee, rancid butter and miserably prepared bread, constituted the one course for dinner. The meal was not relished by the sight-seers, but the bracing atmosphere of the country, with abstinence from dinner, gave them a relish for supper that would have made any meal, however crude, palatable. As time passed on, they began to admire the primitiveness of camp life, although at night they were often weary of the trouble and vexation of the slow journey. The days were passed in watching for wild game, which they killed to take the place of old bacon and dried beef, which on account of its toughness, Pat had named China meat.

Said Pat, in a letter to his mother, "We have, indeed, jolly times, your father is too old to fully appreciate the fun there is in 'camping out.' After a long day's travel and many interesting sights, it is excellent sport to gather around the camp fire and listen to the thrilling stories told by the teamsters, who have frequently conducted strangers across this country. Stories of adventures on the plains are the predominant features of the evenings' conversation."

During the journey, after they had advanced well

into the wild country, Pat caused a sensation which will be remembered by many of the old teamsters on the trail to Santa Fe.

The day was dark, a heavy mist falling, which promised that an unusually dark night would follow. As they came near their camp-ground the wagon-master called out lustily, "Corral to-night!"

"What does he mean by that?" asked Pat of the teamster.

"He's afraid of wolves; watch and see how it is done," answered the teamster.

Pat stood by to see the "corraling" done. The wagons were placed in a circle, the mules were placed on the inside, while the camp-fires were built on the outside. Pat soon learned that the country abounded in wolves and that such a night as this was generally favorable for their depredations, and the precautions taken by the wagon-master were really necessary.

As they sat around their fire, wolf stories were told by the score, until Pat's nerves were so unstrung that in imagination he could see wolves in all directions, with their green eyes glaring upon him from the Egyptian darkness which surrounded the camp. When the time came for retiring, Pat was anxious to sleep upon the high bed, made by placing plank across the sideboards, thus converting each wagon into two beds, but Arthur would not agree with him. They had scarcely crept in bed, when the yelp of a wolf near by, almost took Pat's breath. He covered his head with the blankets and nestled close to Arthur. When he fell asleep, he dreamed that wolves had attacked the train on all sides and seemed determined to destroy his life especially. He began to defend himself by kicking and scratching. Above were sleeping Brown, Hayden and Sir Richard. Pat gave them a lift at his first kick that aroused them. They called to him to lie still, but Pat, still asleep, and in his dream closely beset by wolves, began kicking harder and faster. At length the planks were displaced and down came the three men on Pat and Arthur. The fall aroused Pat who was really frightened, until he heard the voice of his grandfather reprimanding him by threatening to disinherit him, if he continued to prove so cowardly. During his kicking, Pat had injured one of his toes, which gave him great pain and afforded a theme for jesting and amusement among the teamsters, who took delight in teasing him about his wolf scare.

Hayden and Pat became fast friends and passed a great deal of their time together. Hayden knew how fearful the Irish are of wild beasts and reptiles and his killing of many snakes that Pat had found, caused the boy to think him very brave, and thus for protection, he remained with Hayden. Pat had not seen all of the peculiarities of the Western country. Thus far the days and nights had been balmy and pleasant, except an occasional threatening storm which blew over. They were now some three hundred miles west from St. Joseph, it was near the last of May. As they wended their way westward, a dark cloud loomed up directly in front of them. The zig-zag lightning played across its face at intervals. It was too far away to hear the accompanying thunder. It approached. Pat was watching it closely. Some seconds after an unusually vivid flash of lightning a low rumbling sound was heard, Pat clung closer to Hayden. The wagon-master dashed past each wagon on his fleet pony, shouting, "Corral, boys!" The train was drawn in a close circle, the mules unhitched and secured, and all were awaiting the result.

The storm came booming on, first a strong wind, which carried an immense cloud of black dust and charred weeds, the debris of the last fire, followed by a deluging torrent of rain, which seemed to pour its whole force upon the wagons and mules of the train. Vivid lightning flashed upon all sides, sharp peals of thunder echoed everywhere, and the coarse voices of the teamsters, endeavoring to quiet the affrighted mules, all created a scene Pat did not care to behold, at least so we suppose, as he sought out a wagon and was soon hidden under the blankets and bedding.

After the storm had subsided, Hayden searched for his new friend, Pat. At last finding finding him ensconced among the blankets, addressed him by asking:

"What is the matter, Pat?"

"Nothing, Mr. Douglas, only I don't admire the war that has been going on."

"Why, my boy, there has been no war."

"I tell you I call such a racket as that, war. I don't like this part of the country."

"You have not seen all that is to be seen here, my lad. We will soon see the Indians and their wigwams, and the towns of the little prairie dogs, and a thousand other things."

"Well, I'm tired of this place, and don't think I care to see more of it."

The storm had passed. The thunder rumbled in the east, while the sun shone out as she shines only in the West.

Hayden gazed rapturously on the scene before him—the beautiful landscape, clothed in green; the larger rain-drops glistening in the sunlight like so many diamonds; the refreshing breeze following the storm; all awoke the finer feelings in Hayden's nature. And Pat even regretted having hidden during the tumult.

We will not follow our travelers during the summer months as they saunter about the streets of Santa Fe. Suffice it to say that they spent the time pleasantly with Spanish guides, riding up and down the valleys; climbing the foot-hill ranges; chasing deer and antelope, and deporting themselves generally as men who are determined to extract pleasure from every draught in life.

In September they determined to return to New York. Pat had begun to love out-door life, and urged Arthur and Hayden to remain, but as they had nothing in common with the West, Pat's entreaties were in vain. In answering one of Pat's questions one day, Hayden said:

"Man is happier in his primitive life, that is why the camp-fire has its charms for us; it is the wild nature lurking within us, and yet we can trace our civilization back through our progenitors for centuries. The white child soon becomes wild, but it is almost impossible to civilize a wild man. Even in childhood they are wild, and it seems impossible to eradicate the wild principle."

"Are all wild people mean?" asked Pat.

"No, they are of different dispositions, similar in that respect to the white race. Yet it is generally understood that all uncivilized and barbarous races are cruel to their females, they being made the slaves and drudges of the men."

"I think there is a sprinkling of the wild in ourselves," said Pat.

"What do you mean, Pat?"

"Just what I say. Women are not treated as they should be. What is your opinion, Mr. Douglas?"

"I have studied that matter carefully. I have cause. My whole life has been clouded, because of that great bugbear that woman must be silent; have nothing to say or do, except to do as she is told by the proud 'lord of creation.' I am determined to see what I can do in their behalf."

"And I'll do the same, Mr. Douglas."

"Very well, Pat, here is my hand. We shall meet in after years. Don't forget what you have promised me. Now farewell."

In a moment Sir Richard and Pat were gone.

The above conversation took place in a Boston omnibus. Pat had bidden his friend Hayden farewell, to visit his grandfather's home in New York.

Hayden sat thinking of the change a few hours could bring about. Friends separated, perhaps to meet no more. When comfortably seated in his room at the hotel, he felt sorry that the autumn winds had warned them of the approaching winter, which drove them from the plains, as it does the buffalo and deer. Thought he, " I must find something to busy my brain about. Inactivity kills a man far more surely than disease."

While thus musing, a message appeared, apprising him that he was needed in the village of Strawn, in New Hampshire, immediately.'

CHAPTER XVII.

SIR CHARLES IN EUROPE.

HAYDEN DOUGLAS and Sir Charles bade each other farewell as the latter departed for Europe at the summons contained in the letter received when he was wondering over the name of Roderick Leland, which he had found in the dusty book. The letter Sir Charles read that morning caused a deep feeling of sorrow to fill his mind, which was plainly depicted upon his countenance.

As the ship bounded on its way through the blue, laughing waves, none was as anxious as he to set foot on English soil. The day came at last, when the passengers landed at Liverpool and were soon hurried across to London. Immediately upon his arrival, he hastened to a small white cottage in the suburbs. The blinds were closed, and a death-like stillness reigned over all. With a trembling hand he rapped upon the door. It was gently opened by a handsome, well-dressed girl.

"And you have come at last, Sir Charles," said she, in an undertone.

"Yes, Viva, I have come home. How is Theodocia ?"

"She is very poorly to-day," replied the girl as she conducted Sir Charles into an adjoining room, where, upon a snow-white bed, lay a beautiful woman. Her black, glossy hair and lustrous eyes adorned the most regular features ever met with. One glance at that face invariably compelled another. It was a French face. It was surpassing beautiful, made more attractive by the flush which always accompanies that fell destroyer, consumption, which had laid its grasp upon this beautiful being at the bidding of the grim monster, Death, whose insatiety is ever grasping for the choice flowers of the land. The sufferer opened her eyes as the newcomer approached her bed. Recognizing him, she said, calmly :

"You have come, brother ?"

"Yes, Theodocia, I have come," said he, bending over the frail being, "I came as soon as I received your letter, written by Viva."

"I was sorry to be compelled to write to you asking you to come, and would not have done so had it not been your earnest and last request when you bade me adieu."

"My purpose was to come soon, and only hastened at your request, which did not interfere the least with my business."

"Where is Hayden ? Did he come also ?"

"No, he did not come, but would have done so,

had Viva's letter intimated that he would be looked for along with myself."

"I do not desire him to spend his time while young, in earnest solicitude regarding me. I am pleased that he is away. I would prefer to have him away, where his thoughts will be free and untrammeled. His life has been one of sorrow and gloom, may it be brighter in days to come."

Sir Charles' thoughts dwelt upon the book which he had in his pocket containing the name of Roderick Leland, which he desired to show to her, but fearful of exciting her he refrained, and finally deferred doing so until to-morrow, when she would be better. But many "to-morrows" came and went and they still watched by the bedside of the woman who daily grew weaker, at last becoming unconscious of those around her. In her delirium she talked of childhood days in Scotland, of Hayden on the plains, for whom she seemed to be searching, yet she could not find him. She at length opened her eyes and gazed about her.

"Has Hayden come?" asked she.

"No, Theo., he has not come."

"Tell him I am sorry to have him gone at this time, but I cannot wait longer, I feel that my last hour is at hand. How gladly do I welcome death that frees me from a life of grief and misery. Bury me in some quiet cemetery, place a plain marble slab at my grave, mark the dates of my birth and death, and then my name Theodocia, 'she of the broken heart.'" As she uttered the last word, she quietly crossed over the dark "River of Death."

The next afternoon a few friends followed the hearse from the cottage, while the only mourners were Sir Charles and the simply attired young lady who leaned on his arm. As they wended their way slowly toward the cemetery, they passed near a large mansion, whose shadow fell across their path. " My God! must even her funeral procession be shaded by that gilded home of sin," said Sir Charles as he observed the place and its shadow. As he noticed the form of a gaily attired lady pass one of the windows, he thought, "You may smile and strive to gather happiness at the expense of home, joy and comfort to others, but a just retribution will follow you, and your punishment shall surely come. She, whom you by vile machinations robbed of home, husband and name, is now passed from earth away, and as her angelic form joins the band of redeemed saints, and her sweet voice adds to the melody of the heavenly choir; just so surely will the avenging angel record your name upon his book, for a just rendering of justice in the great hereafter."

He and Miss Viva returned by another street to the now desolated white cottage, where he secured everything, and settling with the servants, locked the doors and drove to his own home, a fine residence in the fashionable part of London, saying to his grieving companion, "Viva this shall be your home when not at school."

"Thank you, Sir Charles, I can never properly acquit myself of the obligations I am under to you, who has proved indeed my friend."

The housekeeper conducted her to an elegantly

furnished suite of rooms, informing her that they were designed especially for her individual use. The young lady, a mere child almost, surveyed the apartments briefly. Upon the wall hung two pictures, as she approached she found them to be portraits. One was a lovely girl, apparently in her teens, the other a handsome youth, whom she thought at first glance to be Hayden. "No," said she, "it is the picture of some one I never met, or I should be able to recognize the beautiful face." A gloom was cast upon her brow when she ventured to ask Sir Charles concerning the portraits. "Those belong to the family, Viva, and not until Theodócia is avenged, will they be placed in the family gallery, so do not ask more concerning them."

Viva remained but a brief time at the mansion of Sir Charles, that gentleman early made arrangements for her to enter school, which she soon did, thus leaving him alone with his servants.

He did not write to Hayden until some weeks after the funeral. The letter did not reach him until his return from the West. Almost a year had passed when it came to hand, just as he was preparing to leave for the village of Strawn.

CHAPTER XVIII.

THE KIDNAPPERS.

MR. LELAND returned from Mexico late in October. He found all the girls yet at their work where he had left them, except Ona, she had left the bakery and was now at work in the jewelry store. The others were now receiving compensation for their services, and their employers were remarkably well pleased with them. Mrs. Harris, had, after being warned by Mr. Crowell, desisted from further persecution of the members of the "Independent Band," as the girls' organization was styled.

Ona gained permission of her employer to spend a week at home on the return of her father. Mr. Crowell had informed her of the slander inaugurated by Mrs. Harris, after it had been suppressed. She accordingly related her information of the affair to Mr. Leland with the account of her progress in the calling she had pursued.

"You have accomplished much for one of your age, but the work, my child, is just beginning," said Mr. Leland.

The next day being the Sabbath, Ona attended the village church as was her custom. Although the weather was unpleasant, by reason of the snow which had fallen the previous night, quite a number were present. Among the attendants Ona observed

two strangers. The mere glance she gave them revealed the fact that they were rough and desperate
men. They occupied a seat just behind where she
sat with some children who were members of her
Sunday school class during the Summer season.
During the service the men were constantly whispering, but Ona could not learn the subject of conversation, nor could she distinguish their words, until as
the doxology was being announced, she heard one
of them say, "I learned that they have gone to
Northfield and will return on Wednesday night sure."

"At home Wednesday night," said she to herself,
after services were dismissed, and taking another
look at the men, she found them of sallow complexion and a peculiarly mean expression of countenance.
Watching them as they entered the village hotel, she
accompanied Mrs. Strawn home, and sending one of
the boys to Cedar Hall to advise her father of her
purpose of remaining in the village until the next
morning, quietly entered the hotel and secured a
room opposite the one assigned to the strangers.

She withdrew to her room early on the plea of indisposition. Carefully closing her door, she sat down
to wait. Some two hours passed before they came
to their apartment, she extinguished her light and
slightly opened her door. She heard them securely
fasten their door. In her stocking feet she silently
moved across the hall and took up her position near
their door. At first she could hear only the murmur
of their voices, not being able to distinguish their
words. She stooped and applied her ear to the key-
hole. They were speaking in a low tone. Soon

they spoke louder and she was enabled to note their conversation. She was amply repaid for her daring. She had heard all she desired to know. She withdrew to her room, where securing her shoes and wrappings, and taking the lamp, crept quietly down stairs to the kitchen where she left it burning on the table, as she hurried out of the back door.

The weather was growing colder. The snow was nearly a foot deep and still falling, but she thought not of wind or snow as she hastened toward Cedar Hall. Wearied with her walk through the deep snow and against the cold, piercing, driving wind, she reached her home. For some time she thought she should be unable to arouse the inmates, as her summons remained so long unanswered. She had already repeated her summons. Presently the door was opened by a servant who was surprised at finding Miss Ona there at such an unusual hour.

"I have some strange news for papa, please notify him of my arrival and say that I shall wait for him in the parlor," said she to the servant.

On receiving the instruction of the servant, Mr. Leland hastily attired himself and repaired to the parlor where Ona was awaiting him, she having replenished the fire and was drying her shoes, when he entered.

He soon learned the nature of her errand, and after considering a few moments, he repaired to his library, where he wrote a brief note, which he instructed a servant to deliver to the party addressed, in Concord, as soon as possible. "Take the fastest horse, and do not spare him," said he, in giving further instructions to the wondering servant.   6

The servant hastened away, and Ona expressed her intention to return to the hotel. Her father objected, but after hearing her reasons, he withdrew his objections, and taking her up behind him on his horse, she was soon left near the hotel. She glided into the kitchen, where she found the lamp as she had left it. Going, noiselessly, to her room, she was soon asleep.

Mr. Leland continued on to Mr. Crowell's, whom he aroused and informed of the facts that Ona had learned, which surprised that gentleman very much.

Mr. Leland rode rapidly home, to await further developments.

When Strawn was first located, a family of blacks by the name of Curry, had settled near the village. They had belonged to a Baptist preacher in Virginia, who had given them their freedom. They came to this quiet mountain village and had here found a home among the whites. Every one had a good word to say of the Curry family. They were industrious and thrifty. Their little home was paid for, and they had improved it wonderfully. A neat white cottage and a beautiful lawn in front, were the pride of Mrs. Curry. She labored hard to keep the place in order, while Mr. Curry was busy on the farm. They had four children, the oldest a boy, about twelve years old.

When Ona Leland heard those two men talking in church concerning some one being in Northfield who were expected home on Wednesday night, she well knew to whom the parties referred. She knew that the Curry family had gone to that place to visit their former master, who now resided there. She also knew of their expected return on the night mentioned by the strangers. As soon as she heard the remark made by them in the church, she felt that any concern such men would express for any colored family, boded no good to that family. Her only object in attempting to learn more, which she did at the hotel, was merely to confirm her suspicions, and as we before remarked, she was amptly repaid for her daring effort by hearing their entire plan canvàssed between them.

The next morning she arose early. When breakfast was announced, the strangers came in and seated themselves beside the girl, who now, that she knew their plots, could see "rascal" plainly depicted in each of their countenances, although they talked loudly of their appreciation of the neighborhood and their purpose of buying property and settling there. They left during the afternoon, informing the landlord they would return on Wednesday.

Mr. Leland, Mr. Crowell and Ona were the only persons of the entire village who knew the object of the strangers. They thought it advisable to notify only members of the Anti-Slavery Society, which Mr. Leland had already done by dispatching the messenger to Concord.

On Wednesday, about noon, the two persons returned, as they had said they would. Late in the afternoon, a large covered wagon approached the tavern, from which three men alighted.

"They have come," said Mr. Crowell to Ona, as he met her on the street.

"Yes, I observe they have, are you prepared for them?"

"I do not know, no one has come yet, but I feel assured that our friends will be here all in good time."

Ona entered the sitting-room of the hotel as if she was a regular boarder, manifesting the utmost indifference for those around her. The two strangers occupied different parts of the room. She watched them closely, as the new arrivals entered. As each one entered, merely a glance of recognition was given, not one word spoken. They had their horses cared for and partook of their supper with great glee, perfectly unconscious that their vile plot was known to the child who sat at the same table.

Ona went up stairs, leaving all in the sitting-room. In a few minutes she passed down another way and hastened home.

"Walter, are there any strangers here?" she asked innocently.

"Yes," said he, "there are about a dozen men in the parlor with Mr. Leland."

She clapped her hands joyfully, much to Walter's surprise, and hastened to her room. Taking a seat near the east window, she could note the arrival of the Curry family, when the light which they would necessarily make, should show from their room windows. She sat there a few minutes and observing the light, and at the same time seeing the strangers pass, exclaimed "they have come, we must be off!" She rushed down and calling her father, told him that the Curry family had reached their home, and also that the strangers were passing that way.

As she passed the door, she observed among the guests one man, who on account of his remarkably beautiful appearance, both in feature and dress, attracted her especial attention. " That is the stranger I saw here one year ago, he closely resembles portraits I have seen of Lord Byron, even if he is masked," thought she as she ascended the stairs to her look-out at the window.

Out in the cold the men glided from Cedar Hall with Mr. Leland as guide. When they had approached sufficiently near to observe any demonstration that should be made against the house, they secreted themselves behind some fallen trees in the snow. A half hour passed when a small form, enveloped in a long cloak, approached and giving the signal of the party, joined them. Not a word was whispered by any one as they watched the house near them.

" Listen ! " whispered one, "they are coming."

Soon two figures cautiously approached the rear of the cottage, just as the light was extinguished by the unsuspecting inmates as the last one retired. In a moment the two in the garden were joined by three more, who came from the timber in the rear. All was quiet for a half hour, and the watchers began to grow uneasy, lest they had fled. But they soon came hurrying around to the front door, the foremost carrying an uplifted axe, with which to break down the door.

CHAPTER XIX.

"BILL QUANTRELL"—HIS EARLY LIFE.

"WHAT is the matter, Chatty Granger?" asked Mattie Starr, the village school-mistress in a quiet little village in Ohio, as one of her pet pupils came in crying.

"Oh, Miss Starr! I saw some boys killing some kittens out yonder. They were pulling them to pieces alive, and they were such pretty kittens."

Miss Starr hastened out with pointer in hand, to prevent the boys acting so cruelly. They saw her approaching, and fled, leaving a little white kitten, the last of four, dying.

She returned to the school-room, heart-sick, exclaiming: "Never was there so much cruelty practiced in any place as there is here, and I am sorry that one of my otherwise best pupils is the ringleader."

"It is Bill Quantrell," said two or three of the children at once.

"Yes, I know who it is. He will be guilty of something worse than killing innocent kittens, unless he changes his nature by careful cultivation of right doing," continued Miss Starr.

"I hope somebody will kill him before long," sobbed Chatty.

"Oh, no, Chatty! that would be wrong."

Late that afternoon every eye was turned upon

the mean, sneaking-looking boy of some twelve or thirteen years, who walked into the room and took his seat.

He was tall and slim. His complexion was of a sallow tinge; his eyes pale-blue, and his hair a dirty white. His head was small and round, yet heavy above the ears. Such is the picture of the meanest boy in the village of Osage.

The children looked at him, and then at their teacher. She glanced at the cruel boy, but he was, seemingly, engaged with preparing his lesson for the next day. Not until the last bell tapped did he lay aside his books.

"Stay here, William Quantrell, after school is dismissed. I wish to talk with you," said Miss Starr.

He hung his head and resumed his seat.

After the children had departed, Miss Starr seated herself at the desk, dreading to begin the reprimand she felt it her duty to give the boy. Finally she said: "What will become of you, William, if you continue to act cruelly toward animals?"

He made no answer, and she continued:

"Such cruelty will lead to something worse as you grow older, if not checked while young. You *must* inaugurate a reform. I have heard so much regarding your cruelty since I came here. The wanton killing of those innocent kittens this morning being the first that has come directly to my notice, I could not let it pass without saying something. You cannot restore the life of those kittens, and I do not propose to punish you. I only want to impress upon your mind the cruelty of such acts. How unmanlike they are! I hope you will not be guilty of such acts in the future. You have heard of men who slaughtered their fellow-men, have you not? Well, no doubt, they began their career of crime when young, by being cruel to birds and beasts, and made no endeavor to cultivate a different nature, until they sought for higher objects to destroy, and finally ended their days in the penitentiary, or suffered themselves a felon's death. Let me say again, You must do better, otherwise you will soon be practicing your cruel acts on your companions, instead of brutes. Now go home. I have said all I ever intend to say to you."

He gave her a scornful, vicious look, as he turned to leave the house. What influence could a kind-hearted girl have over such a demon mind as he possessed? Every person in the village feared him, lest he would do them some mischief. One time, the sexton's daughter entered the church to ring the bell, he followed near, and when she had entered, he closed the door and locking it, threw the key in the creek near by. One boy witnessed the trick, but dared not speak of it.

Such was the early life of one who has done the world much harm and whom we will meet during the turbulent times in the West.

CHAPTER XX.

FOILED.

"WAIT until they break down the door, before we start," said one of the watchers as they arose from their hiding-place.

The axe came down on the door, splintering it considerably and arousing the inmates, who called out, "Who's there?"

No answer came from the outlaws as the axe again fell and another panel was broken.

The family were thoroughly aroused by this time and were out of their beds.

"John, bring me the teakettle from the fire-place," exclaimed Mrs. Curry. "I will scald the villains."

John appeared with a kettle of hot water and a dipper; before the door could be broken down Mrs. Curry had thrown the hot water through the broken panels.

In vain did they attempt to force open the windows, and upon the house they went, tearing off the roof.

"I will watch here and you mind the chimney, John," said Mrs. Curry.

One attempted to pass down the chimney, Mr. Curry seized a bed and threw it on the fire to smoke him out.

Mrs. Curry had to abandon her place at the door to guard a window which was giving way. Two of the villains were anticipating this opportunity, and kicking down the already shattered door, rushed in before the frightened inmates could offer further resistance.

"Come on boys," shouted the two who had entered the room.

Down they came from the roof and rushing in, exclaimed, "let us gag first and tie afterward," and seizing the two nearest, proceeded to gag them.

The family were so frightened they knew not what course to pursue, it being nearly a mile to the nearest house.

The silent watchers with revolvers in hand were soon on the spot. Rushing through the door, they soon surrounded the kidnappers, who were taken entirely by surprise. Now *they* were bound instead of the colored family.

"Some one has betrayed us," said one, and each looked wildly at the others.

The kidnappers were tied and the Curry family set free. They could not tell who their deliverers were, for they all wore masks except one little, blue-eyed one, who wore a long cloak and jaunty cap with a blue tassel on one side.

After the confusion had subsided, a messenger was dispatched to the village to procure a wagon to convey the prisoners, and also to notify the proper authorities of their arrest. As they sat awaiting the arrival of the wagon, Mr. Leland, still under mask, endeavored to learn from the prisoners their intentions toward the members of the Curry family in thus assaulting their home.

Douglas Hayden's thoughts were in another direction. He knew that he had entered the same house he had visited one year previously. His thoughts were not so much of the excitement his presence had caused Mr. Leland, as they were of the handsome blue eyes he had observed watching him from upstairs. Now that the kidnappers had been secured, he took a cursory view of those whom he had assisted in the work. Soon he saw a pair of blue eyes watching him from under a jaunty cap. Could it be they were the same he saw a year ago at the Leland mansion! They were very much like the same!

He sauntered near to the wearer of the jaunty cap and impressive eyes, and after a few common-place remarks, politely inquired her name.

The eyes were cast down; a flush suffused the face and neck, as, in a trembling, low voice came the words: "Dickey Deane."

Hayden was more perplexed than ever. "Dickey Deane!" said he, thoughtfully, as he turned away to meet the new arrivals with the wagon. When he would have resumed the conversation, "Dickey Deane" was gone!

The next morning Hayden took the stage to Concord, none the wiser as to whom he had met, yet all the while cogitating over the name of "Dickey Deane."

When the prisoners were taken charge of by the civil authorities, the masked men dispersed, and friends gather in to congratulate and comfort the Curry family.

The news of the capture of the kidnappers spread

far and wide, and long before noon an immense throng of people had gathered on the streets of Strawn, many of the indignant populace shouting, "Hang them! hang them!"

At the preliminary trial they pleaded "guilty," and were held over for the next court.

They said they intended carrying the Curry family South, to sell into slavery.

The whole village was in a state of excitement as to who had betrayed these men. Many offered any sum to know. Ona was at her customary work, and none suspected her, she being but a woman, and in those days women never did a good deed—in the estimation of men—unless to look in various ways after the especial comfort of the "lords of creation."

The prisoners were kept in town that night. Mr. Leland was one of the guards appointed to watch over them, he having returned from Cedar Hall, where he had gone to rest.

None knew who the prisoners were. When asked that, of course had given names, yet Mr. Leland and Mr. Crowell knew, by the expression of their countenances, they were giving assumed names, and they communicated their suspicions to Ona.

The villains were anxious to converse with each other, but no opportunity for so doing was given by the vigilant guard.

With one exception, their appearance would not be called attractive, and that one attracted especial attention on account of its repulsiveness. None could look upon him without being convinced that he was a man of vice and crime. Women gazed upon him with a shudder. As his villainous eyes gleamed upon them from under heavy brows, they conveyed to the mind of the observer, the true prototype of a murderer.

After the excitement had died away, Ona called on Mr. Crowell, who was seated at his private desk, writing.

"I came in," said Ona, "to ask if you have any idea as to who sent for these villains. Some one must certainly have informed them regarding the presence of the Curry family, as well as of their isolated situation."

"I had never thought of that," said he, "but I think you are right. These men would never have found their way to this secluded place without information from some one acquainted with the surroundings. I wish we could procure satisfactory information as to who the person is."

"I have a plan by which, I think, I can ascertain, but before saying anything regarding it, I must see papa and have his advice."

Ona returned to her work. Mr. Crowell sent for Mr. Leland and communicated to him Ona's suspicions and said, "I feel that she is right."

"Yes," said Mr. Leland, "why did not we think of this in the first place. We must ascertain, if possible, who this serpent is, that is dwelling in our midst."

"Ona says she has a plan that seems feasible to her, she wishes to consult with you regarding it. I have every confidence in her ability, although I know nothing of her plans."

"If she has given the matter proper consideration, I shall have no hesitancy in allowing her to undertake it. Ona has already been our greatest help in intercepting these villains."

Mr. Leland sent for her and the three consulted for some time. When they separated she went to the house where the prisoners were held. She told the lady she desired to remain there all night, as her father was one of the guards, and she would feel much safer near him. The lady consented and Ona made herself at home. She went to first one room and then another, examining each door and its fastenings. At last she found one that suited her, and informed her father which it was.

When the prisoners were ready to retire, Mr. Leland selected two of the most loquacious and locked them in that room, being careful to noiselessly unlock the door.

In one corner of the room was a large closet containing cast-off clothing, in fact it was a general receptacle for old rags. Ona had secreted herself in this closet before the prisoners were brought in, and had made herself a snug little bed of the old clothing. The bed in the room was located conveniently near the closet. She lay there with the door slightly open. After the men had retired she found that the pocket of the old coat she had chosen for a pillow contained some snuff and she was fearful the inhaling of it would cause her to sneeze and thus betray her presence.

She gently pushed the coat out of her way and settled down to await developments. In about an hour one of the men said :

"I wonder if we are alone?"

"I don't know," said the other.

"I will light a paper and see," continued the first speaker.

"No! no!" said the other, "they would think we were at some plan to escape, and would place a guard in the room."

Ona trembled, lest they should inaugurate a search and find her. She was confident they had heard her as she shoved the seat along the wall.

A few minutes passed, when one said, in a loud whisper: "What is your name? and where did you meet the other boys?"

"My name is Jackson. I met them at Concord. What is your name?"

"Guy Wren. I have been in this business fifteen years. I have an old woman here I would as soon kidnap as any nigger, if I could only get the chance. She lives with that fair, curly-headed fellow with blue eyes, one of the leaders of the party that captured us."

"Why did you leave her?"

"She was not worth a cent to work when she began to get old, and I did not want to keep her. It is enough for an old man like me to take care of himself; so I did everything I could to make her leave. She has considerable money by this time, and I am bound to have it, if I have to kill the whole Leland family to get it. I have a friend here who keeps me posted on her affairs—the same one who let us know about this nigger family who have escaped this time, besides getting us into a heap of trouble."

"Who is your friend?"

"His name is Black. He runs a store in this village, but makes more money in other ways. He would have got three hundred cool, if we had got these niggers South."

Ona had heard the entire conversation, and from it had learned, not only that her surmises were correct, but also who the person was that had given the information. They continued to talk about other matters until near two o'clock the next morning. When she was convinced that they were asleep, she crept from the closet. Closing the door carefully, stole softly out, and seeking her own room, retired.

In the morning she went to Mr. Crowell's store, where her father met her. She told what she had learned. Mr. Leland had not before manifested the least degree of excitement, but now he became thoroughly aroused. The threat that his family were to be murdered, was more than his nature could endure.

Their first action was to write a note to Mr. Black, informing him of the knowledge of his complicity with the kidnappers, and advising him to leave the country immediately, which was signed "Citizens."

Mr. Leland accompanied the prisoners to the county town, where they were to be tried. They were found guilty of "disturbing the peace," and fined, except Guy Wren. Mr. Leland had him sent to jail to await another court.

Ona said to her father, "We will not tell Aunt Nancy that Wren was among the prisoners."

"For the present, while he is in jail, we will say nothing about it to her, but we must, in time, give her sufficient information to place her on her guard, for he might, if he is cleared, do her some harm, possibly murder her. Oh! such a thought is horrible. Is there not some process of law by which such men can be kept in imprisonment?"

"Not under our present system, my daughter. Evil-minded and wicked, as such men are, they have their friends, parties who can use them for dirty-work, who upon the grounds of 'sympathy' will help them when they are in trouble."

After paying their fines, the outlaws left for Boston, leaving Wren behind.

Ona, when considering the past, was more thoroughly convinced of the truth of Hannah Moore's saying, "All for the best." Had I not secreted myself in the closet, Wren would have been at liberty, and in all probability, would have killed all of us, to secure Aunt Nancy's property and all he could carry of ours, but now he is safe.

Upon further consideration they concluded to inform Aunt Nancy, which Ona did on the following Sunday.

"That is what I have expected since I left him," said she. "Yet I have endeavored to say as little harm of him as I could, in fact, none publicly, I am sorry he is in jail, but while he is there I am safe."

Ona was weary on retiring, and did not awake until the family had eaten breakfast and Mr. Leland gone to the village. "It is now one year since papa gave me that locket," thought she, as she glanced from the window, the snow reminding her of the time.

7

CHAPTER XXI.

THE MEETING.

By the window I am sitting
Watching feathery snow-flakes flitting,
And my mind is slowly sifting
Thoughts that have so long been drifting
Toward this one, for whom is breaking
The heart that has long been aching.

THESE were the lines Lillie· Calhoun wrote in her diary as she sat by the window in the upper parlor of the "Grand Central," a hotel in Washington, on the same morning that Ona Leland was thinking of what she had accomplished during the past year.

Lillie having finished the lines placed beneath them the date, Nov. ——, 1845. Closing the book, by some mishap it fell from her hand and rattled down to the pavement below. She leaned from the window to note its location and became absorbed in watching the falling snow, when she again turned her attention to the book, it was to see a young gentleman lift it from the snow and glance upward to see. where it came from, but no one being visible, he put the book in his pocket.

Lillie sat thinking of the loss of her book until her mind drifted into another channel. She thus soliloquized : "A year ago to-day, I came here happy, happy in the bloom and freshness of youth, happy in bright recollections of the past, and cheerful anticipations of the future. But now how is all the brightness of the past dimmed? How is all the prospective lustre of the future tarnished? Why is fate so unjust, to raise our hopes and then ruthlessly dash them to the ground? Why is society so cruel, that we must ostracise an affinity that is given only by heaven, in obedience to its arbitrary rules? Why did I come here again? Why did I not remain in the seclusion of my own, heretofore happy, Southern home? I thought to live down in the whirl of excitement the heart lonliness that makes even Washington a solitude. I thought to meet him for whom my heart yearns. I thought to meet him and learn from his own lips that 'report' was a falsifier. I may never see him. Could I but tell him my sorrow and troubles, I know I should no longer brood over them, even if his ear was not turned in sympathy toward me. Even if his heart is turned to adamant, my mind would be relieved of an oppressive burthen and my heart of a crushing weight. I will wait and see."

She was very pale, a shadow had gathered upon her brow, an anxious, expectant look flashed from her eyes, to be followed by an expression through which one could seemingly look into the depths of her heart and there read its sorrow and feel its pain.

She had visited many of the watering-places during the summer and had spent the autumn in Canada. Many were the admirers that begged for the sunshine of her smile, but she turned from them all. She was indeed a true woman; she loved but one, and that one alone could restore the roses to her cheeks.

Among the gay and beautiful that graced the magnificent parlors of Washington society, the inquiry was often made regarding Miss Calhoun, the belle of the previous winter.

She could not be persuaded by her friends to appear in company, and yet she remained at the hotel. She returned but few calls and those were of her most intimate friends. The winter had almost flitted by and she had neither seen nor heard of Hayden, yet she felt sure he was in the city. Ava Haynes called, but never mentioned the name of Hayden. Her purpose was severing the friendship between Lillie and Hayden, and further than that she had no anxiety.

Often Lillie drove out alone, hoping for even an accidental meeting with him. One bright day, in the latter part of February, she was driving very slowly, feeling sad and dejected, as she met carriage after carriage, often recognizing some familiar face. At length she noticed one bearing the coat of arms of an English nobleman, attended by servants in livery. As the carriage approached, she took particular notice of its inmates. She started in surprise and anguish of mind, for there sat Hayden Douglas and by his side sat Ava Haynes. One glance told her how she had been betrayed by the heartless Ava. She saw her triumphant glance as they passed, but Hayden did not lift his eyes, he seemed in deep meditation and did not observe the sweet pale face of Lillie.

Mortified and dejected, she returned to her room, where she gave vent to her sorrow and grief, through the volume of tears, that no power of will could restrain. Then, for the first time, she realized the entire selfishness of the world. She thought of how Ava had poured into her ears vituperative evidence of the social standing of Hayden, and after prejudicing the mind of her auditor against him, quietly and hypocritically appropriated him as her friend, and gloating over her success in poisoning the mind of a fair and virtuous woman against a true and just man.

Amidst her sorrows, the triumphant glance of Ava would appear before her mind's eye, and arousing her pride, she determined to not tamely submit.

She soliloquized: "Next Wednesday evening is that set apart for the last entertainment of the season. Shall I attend? Yes. I shall advise none of my purpose. I shall address Madam DeLand immediately to forward my new dress. I shall have my pearls reset."

She acted accordingly, sending her maid to post the letter and leave her jewelry at Barnes' for repairs.

She seemed a different woman. That one scene had changed her nature. Expectation of the future infused new life in her system, and vivacity gleamed from her eyes and glowed upon her cheeks. She felt a determination to vindicate herself, and if need be, assume the aggressive against one who, in the person of Ava Haynes, had acted so falsely.

The day before the party, much to Lillie's surprise, Ava made a passing call. She was coolly received, and treated reservedly. She soon became aware of the coolness of her reception and the haughtiness of her entertainment, and made her adieu, fully realizing, at last, that she had acted unbecomingly, and feeling that her duplicity had been detected, but feeling that she had secured the friendship of Hayden, her misdeeds gave her little anxiety.

On Wednesday Lillie's new wardrobe arrived, and was carried to her room so secretly that not even the inquisitive servants imagined the contents of the box. Late in the afternoon she opened the box and shook out the beautiful and costly blue satin dress, which was elaborately trimmed with laces and flowers. Accompanying the dress were shoes and stockings to match. Calling her maid, she began her toilet. Her hair was tastefully arranged; a cluster diamond held some of the longer curls in place, while from among the loose ones peeped a small bouquet of forget-me-nots.

She stood before the mirror, arrayed in her handsome dress. She was startled at the reflection. On her neck glittered the beautiful pearls; a diamond brooch held a bunch of forget-me-nots at her throat; curls floated around a brow denoting intellect and refinement, while her low dress displayed the shapeliest form ever beheld. For the first time, she felt a degree of pride never before experienced.

"You are so pretty, Miss Lillie," said her maid, "I am glad you are going out to-night, for Miss Ava's maid told me that you would not appear any more, because there was a young man you wanted, and that Miss Ava took him away from you, and you were staying at home, dying of a broken heart."

" Does Miss Haynes tell her love affairs to her servants?" asked Lillie.

" Yes, marm, I think she does, for they always tell me who Miss Ava loves, and I suppose she always tells them."

" Whom does she love now?"

" I forget his name, he is the son of some English lord, and is very rich. He has the finest carriage that has ever been in this country."

Lillie felt grieved at herself for allowing her curiosity to lead her to seek information from her servants. She had fully determined that those who had vituperated Hayden to her, should yet feel her influence. She made no reply to the volubility of words used by her maid.

The last entertainment of the season was to be held at the unassuming residence of Senator Taylor. The parlors were already crowded when Lillie, leaning upon the arm of her escort, entered. Her companion was a stately and handsome young naval officer, her cousin. Many were the handsome faces already there, but none compared in beauty of feature, harmony of attire, and happy expression with the beautiful blonde who had just entered. Her eyes sparkled as brightly as her diamonds. The general murmur of admiration which greeted her entrance, attracted the attention of Hayden, who was enjoying himself, seemingly, by conversing with Ava in an adjoining parlor. As she passed the apartment their glances met momentarily. Passing from the room into the conservatory, she seated herself near a table laden with choice flowers.

As she sat admiring the elaborate arrangement of the flowers, the hum of admiring voices proclaimed the entrance of some attractive or important personage.   As she arose from her chair to observe the new arrivals that were calling forth such an expression of admiration, her eyes fell upon a face fairer than her own, a face that had never known cosmetics, a face which shone with the pure whiteness of nature's own coloring, while her cheeks glowed with the bright tints of the rays of the setting sun.   Her lips were cherry red, half parted in a pleasant, winsome smile. Lillie gazed upon the stranger with delight.   "I love that child, for she is only a child in appearance ; how gracefully she moves from room to room.   What a halo of youthful, exuberant joy and happiness seems to surround her.   How tastefully she is dressed, how everything harmonizes with her complexion.   Her dark blue silk and white-rose trimmings, those silver snow-flake resting on her golden curls are true to nature.   She is pretty.   She has no knowledge of her attractiveness and that fact lends grace to her movements and adds more beauty to her appearance."

As Lillie toyed with her fan, thinking of the beautiful girl, she heard a step by her side, turning quickly, she beheld an extended hand and heard a well-known voice exclaim : "I have found you at last, Lillie ! "

It was Hayden ; he had sought for her as soon as he could, without abruptness, relieve himself of the care of Miss Ava.

They conversed a few minutes, when Hayden proposed a promenade. Taking his arm they moved leisurely from parlor to parlor, so wrapt in their own thoughts and expressions, as to be entirely unconscious of the murmur of delight expressed by others at their appearance. They passed near Ava, but Lillie seemed not to regard her presence.

"Look, Hayden, can you give me any information regarding that beautiful child-lady standing near the piano?"

"I can not positively say who she is. I did not hear the announcement of her name, after she had created such a sensation by her entrance," said Hayden. "But I am quite positive I saw her one year ago last autumn in New Hampshire. I had but an imperfect view of her face, but her eyes attracted my especial attention by their brilliancy."

"I became entirely enraptured at her entree this evening, and even now am compelled to admit that I am deeply in love with that fair young being."

"I am surprised. I was not aware that ladies ever became enamored of other ladies."

"I hope, by the assurance I have given you regarding my feelings for that lady, that such a statement will not surprise you in the future. I have lady friends whom I love ardently, aye! devotedly."

"Perhaps, Miss Lillie, it was of one of those lady friends you were thinking when you let your book fall from the window."

"I have not the faintest idea as to what you refer."

As he produced a handsomely bound, gilt-edged day-book, she exclaimed: "That is certainly my book. How did it come in your possession, Hayden?"

"I picked it up on the day of my arrival here, as I was passing the 'Grand Central.' On opening it, I saw it was yours. Let me assure you, Lillie, the sight of your name, in your familiar hand, brought again into active life the feeling which had not died —only become dormant in my breast. My heart throbbed with a new and stronger pulsation than had been its wont since I parted with you last winter. I felt a delicacy in approaching you to-night, but my observation of the occasional sad expression that would intrude itself upon your countenance, led me to feel that I was connected with your thoughts, as you have been with mine, since we last met. I have repeatedly asked Miss Ava concerning you. She invariably told me that you had returned home soon after the season opened, and not seeing you, I was led to believe such was the fact. Perhaps it may have been, and that you have only returned to be present at this grand 'break-up.' "

"No, Hayden, I have been in the city all winter. 'Tis true I have been out but little. Miss Ava has called upon me at my hotel frequently. I am surprised that she should endeavor to impress you with the idea that I was not in Washington."

"Since we have again met, and understand each other 'as of yore,' I will not repeat other remarks regarding yourself made by Miss Ava, which I now know to be false. We will let it all pass, and hope that the great firmament of the undeveloped future may contain brighter constellations than has fallen to our lot in the past."

When Ava saw Lillie and Hayden together, she

at once realized that her plots were discovered, yet she felt no admonitions of an accusing conscience for her perfidious acts.

Ava Haynes was not the woman to love or ardently cherish a love extended to her. Her only desire seemed to be to excel others in attracting the attention and winning the admiration of men. She was not beautiful, even if she was attractive. She was a perfect dissembler. She desired to so impress each new acquaintance, that he would bow humbly to her slightest wish and acknowledge her as the reigning queen of his heart. Such an influence she never could wield over Hayden; although he seemed charmed with her presence, and happy in her society, yet she never could induce him to speak of love or adoration. She felt piqued at the failure of her plans, but not a line of her countenance indicated the inward feeling.

"When may I look for a return of my book?" said Lillie to Hayden.

"Miss Lillie, since this little book has fallen into my possession I have cherished the hope that I would be permitted to retain it, and now since I have met you, let me earnestly entreat that I may not be denied the pleasure so fondly hoped for. I am about to sail for England and in my previous contemplations of that voyage and its following travels, I assure you this little book has played a prominent part. It has and shall be a reminder of happy days in the past, and I now hope it may prove a talisman which will vouchsafe still more happy ones in the future. I am loth to part with it."

"You may retain it, Hayden, but let me ask, how long shall you remain in England?"

"I *had* thought I should never return to America, but I have very recently changed my mind. The time will come when I shall feel·that I must return. In fact it is a duty I owe you Miss Lillie, to not allow the future to be overcast with shadows, as the past has been, when such can be so easily dispelled by the sunshine of love. So you may anticipate my return as soon as I can possibly arrange the business which calls me away."

"Be assured Hayden, I shall look anxiously for your coming."

"What rapturous music," both exclaimed in a breath.

"Who is the performer?" querried Lillie.

They entered the next room and beheld seated at the piano, the same sweet-faced girl. She was singing an old Scotch song, her voice so sweet and earnest in its appeal, so life-like in the rendition of the sentiment, so affecting in its execution that tears dimmed the eyes of her auditors.

Hayden stood by Lillie after the song was ended, conversing on various topics, especially the dangers attending an ocean voyage. As the time of parting drew near, he detached a beautiful ring from his watch-chain, placing it on her finger, said, "Let this be a momento of my love for you; wear it while life lasts and may the hand that it decorates cool my fevered brow and press my burning cheek, as I pass happily away to prepare an arbor for your coming in a world where love reigns supreme."

With light happy hearts, joyous thoughts, and bright anticipations, they parted. He to wonder why people, aspiring to be considered refined and intellectual, could debase themselves as Ava had done, and only for a selfish motive. She, woman-like, to forget the past with its sorrows and grievances, and to live in the sunshine of the immediate present, and contemplate the lustrous brightness of the future opening before her. Even her dreams partook of the same nature, she dwelt in realms of bliss, perpetual joy flowed as a stream to make glad her heart.

CHAPTER XXII.

THE WIDOWED AND WIDOWER.

AFTER Mr. Black received the note conveying the knowledge of his complicity in the Curry family abduction, he made hasty preparation to leave the village. He was wondering who had betrayed him. He was enraged beyond all question, on account of the turn affairs had taken. His naturally vicious temper demanded some one on whom to reak his vengeance. None other appearing, he vented his spleen upon his innocent wife, by furiously beating her. She was so badly bruised that she was unable to leave her bed for days, and for attention she was compelled to depend upon the charity of the neighboring women.

Black sold his store to his wife's cousin and departed for the West, failing to induce his wife to accompany him, she, in fact, not being able. News eventually reached Strawn that he had joined the Mormons. Mrs. Black made a comfortable living by boarding her cousin and his wife. She frequently assisted him in the store and became an excellent saleswoman, and now that she was no longer under the domineering influence of her brutal husband, her refinement and intelligence became noticeable and truly appreciated. Thus she experienced greater enjoyment than at any time since her marriage.

While Black was making preparations to leave, Mrs. Harris was expressing much sympathy for Guy Wren, who was in jail. She attributed all his misfortune to the previous bad conduct of his wife. She knew Wren was a good man, but he had suffered in mind on account of family troubles, and any crime or misdemeanor he committed was traceable to his wife, and she should be the one to suffer. Mrs. Harris made it a rule to blame women for all the wrongs committed, and invariably found some woman at the bottom of all the mischief done under her observation. Such weak-minded creatures are a curse to their sex.

She attempted to administer a reprimand to Mrs. Black for refusing to accompany her husband, but the attendants caused her to refrain as soon as she began her bemeaning lecture. She left the house in high dudgeon, and hastening home, spent her fury upon her husband, the doctor, who was one of the mildest-tempered men in the country. He was wearied in watching with one of their children, night after night, besides waiting upon other patients during the day. After she had finished her tirade of abuse, he calmly informed her if she was not pleased with her home and husband it would be better to find a more congenial place. She hastened to her room, and when called the next morning, it was discovered that she had gone.

She had taken all the money she could find, together with her clothing, and departed during the night. The stage picked her up on the road the next morning, but her final destination none could ascertain.

The doctor found a newly-married couple, who rented his land and occupied his house, taking care of his children and providing meals for himself.

The neighbors were pleased when she left—she had been a town scourge; a genuine, untamed shrew.

The doctor received no word from her. He never mentioned her name, unless it was first mentioned in his presence.

Ten years passed by and he removed to the city of New York where he found practice more remunerative and he had more time to superintend the instruction of his children, or at least, have a watchful care over their instruction.

His daughters had grown to be lovely girls, and by his careful supervision all the contaminating influence, set by the example of their mother, had been eradicated from their minds. They recognized the protector in their father, and his kindness, mildness and general suavity of manner, gave him the place in their minds, of mother, a name they had scarcely understood when applied to her, whose foibles and peculiarities they could never entirely harmonize · with such an endearing appellation.

Mr. Harris' professional duties called upon him to traverse the allies and by-ways of the city. During one of these trips on a cold afternoon, he noticed a woman whose peculiarity of movement attracted, momentarily, his attention. " Certainly it cannot be Mrs. Harris," he mused, " she had more than a thousand dollars in money, sufficient to keep her above want for years." · He soon dismissed such thoughts from his mind, and in his rounds thereafter took no notice of the miserable hut, except an occasional mental comment on its unusually squalidness. But as he had no warning of the severe winter storm that was soon to visit the city, so he had no knowledge or idea of the storm so soon to agitate his motives. To him "a shadow was on the wall," yet he divined it not, although he had noted its presence.

CHAPTER XXIII.

ONA IN WASHINGTON.

MR. LELAND was called to Washington City after the affair concerning the Curry family, and he proposed to Ona that she accompany him, to which she consented.

Mr. Leland had an intimate friend in Washington,

Mr. Henry Wise, a prominent abolitionist, in fact the leader of the Anti-Slavery party in the city. Immediately upon their arrival, Mrs. Wise became so infatuated with Ona that she at once began to prevail upon Mr. Leland to allow her to spend the winter in Washington. But until Ona herself expressed a desire to remain, he did not consent. Mrs. Wise was pleased with her pretty face and sweet voice, her shapely head graced beautifully formed shoulders, but most of all the firmness of her character as expressed by her demeanor, attracted Mr. as well as Mrs. Wise. Ona's mind was properly developed and abundantly stored with useful knowledge and she conversed fluently on general topics of interest. All these, added to her musical knowledge, made her really an attractive personage.

Mrs. Wise had endeavored to introduce her into society during the early season, but Ona would not acquiesce in the proposition. She preferred roaming at will, unnoticed, through the different departments of Government buildings, becoming familiar with the routine of work in each, and finally, when urgently pressed, she consented to attend the last entertainment, where Hayden and Lillie, with others, so much admired the stranger who discoursed such sweet music, and otherwise won their admiration.

That attractive stranger was Ona Leland. Mrs. Wise had taken great pains to make her guest the most attractive and accomplished lady present, and had most admirably succeeded.

Such fashionable life did not meet the approbation, neither did it win the approval of Ona. She said to

8

Mrs. Wise one day: "I had rather be at work in the kitchen than be compelled to entertain these giddy-minded callers. I must have something to do here in this busy world. I cannot imagine what satisfaction there can be in a life spent in idleness when there are so many opportunities to do good and but little effort required, and even if we do work to accomplish good, assuredly it is time and labor well expended."

Many long letters found their way to members of the "Independent Band" from Ona, portraying her loneliness, even when surrounded by the gay and fashionable of the world. She told them how precious time was wasted in catering to the dictates of "Dame Fashion" by many whose abilities, both natural and acquired, if properly trained and applied, could be productive of so great good; those who instead of informing themselves upon the current questions of the day and expressing their opinions freely upon them, as is their God-given privilege, thus paving the way or laying the foundation stones for a structure which should elicit the admiration of the world when contemplating the privilege granted to women in America, that of being as God had created them, equal in all respect and under all considerations to the so-called "Proud Lords of Creation." Instead of thus seizing upon the opportunities presented, their whole time was being consumed in preparing for and attending the numerous fetes given in this gay and profligate city. Thus she would write to them of things of interest she had learned; of the abounding skill displayed by American minds, as exemplified by the thousands of models in the Patent Office; of her visit to the Department of Agriculture, where she had penned condensed reports from all the States and Territories, treating of the productiveness of the soil, its adaptation to various cereals, its property in producing fruits, its timber area, its minerel deposits, and various other topics, would be discussed in her letters to those young companions who had with her embarked in an undertaking which would have been considered futile by youths of the opposite sex. In one letter she wrote: "I like politics better than ever before. There is here a wide field and ample opportunities for developing a taste in that peculiar study. I long to see the time come when I may have something to say upon questions coming up for public consideration, and a work to do in this great and grand field."

Such sentiments were voluminously expressed in every letter she sent to Strawn. They not only encouraged the girls in their work, but principles and sentiments were imbued into their minds which would remain there during life.

But one of Mrs. Wise's callers impressed Ona at all favorably. From the first introduction, which was given after the season was over, Ona and Lillie Calhoun were devoted friends, although their political sentiments were as different as were the sections of country they represented. When they discussed these points of difference between them, it was in an argumentative, reasoning, unprejudiced manner, and much good was accomplished by both, as the mind of each was relieved of prejudices placed there through exaggerated statements regarding the peculiarities of either section.   Lillie prolonged her stay in Washington for no other motive than to enjoy the society of the fair young girl who had so effectually charmed her admiration and won her love and esteem.

CHAPTER XXIV.

THE DEATH BED SCENE.

A FEW years pass away and the acquaintance formed between Ona Leland and Lillie Calhoun grows into friendship and ripens into mutual love, one for the other.   Many weeks had been spent by Lillie basking in the pure mountain air which surrounds Cedar Hall, and summer after summer did these two friends spend together at the famed and famous resorts with which America abounds.

Now it was autumn; six years had passed since they first met.   At the end of their summering tour, Lillie thought it befitting to spend a few weeks at Cedar Hall before returning to her own balmy and flower laden home in the South.

She seemed languid, careworn and despondent. New Hampshire air did not bring the roses to her cheeks as it had in former times.   Finally, a week before the time fixed for her departure, she said:

"Ona, I must go home immediately!"

"Why, Lillie! you surprise me, I cannot entertain the thought of parting thus suddenly."

"I feel that I must go, there is a certain foreboding of evil seems to cling around me. I have a premonition that something terrible is about to occur, something entirely unlooked for. I cannot eradicate the thought from my mind and under its influence I cannot enjoy myself or add to your pleasure. I know my mind would assume a state of rest more readily at home than it does away. I shall then at least have the consciousness that I am not annoying others by my despondent expressions and dejected appearance."

"Be assured, Lillie, we shall suffer no annoyance by your indisposition. I can hardly realize that your feelings are caused otherwise than perhaps by our recent dissipation followed by hasty traveling, which was indeed wearisome and may have left its effects, as a prostration, partially of your nervous system, which depression you look upon as a mental affliction."

"Do not urge me to remain, I know myself sufficiently well, to know that I am not in error regarding my feelings, and I know further that you will, at my earnest solicitation, render me all possible assistance to start to-morrow. Will you not?"

"Although loth to part with you thus suddenly, I can only say 'yes' to your entreaty. I know how I should feel if, in earnest to go to my home, any barrier was interposed, even a kindly intercession to remain."

The next morning Lillie entered the stage to start for her home in the Sunny South, where the "magnolias bloom, and the orange grows." A smile played upon her countenance, as if she felt she had taken a step that would avert the calamity which had impended.

As she entered the stage, the postmaster of Strawn handed her a letter which had just arrived. She glanced merely at the postmark, and breaking the seal, said in her own mind: "It is from Hayden, yet it does not resemble his handwriting. But it surely is! It is mailed at London!" Tearing off the envelope, she threw it out of the stage-window, and perusing the contents of the letter, her very blood seemed to freeze in her veins. She sat pallid and cold as marble. Her young heart was crushed within her at the cruel, heartless words it contained.

All her bright day-dream was over. The idol of her heart was gone from her forever. The old creaking stage rattled on. She took notice of neither time nor objects. Sleep was banished from her eyes, and would not return at her bidding. The gnawings of hunger were suppressed, appetite had lost its relish. Desire was obliterated from her mind. The world appeared as a blank, except where in letters of fire appeared the words of that cruel epistle. Hearing was dead, except as all nature gathered its sounds and concentrated their forces upon the enunciation of those taunting words which rang as heaven's artillery upon her ear.

After many days' travel she reached home, almost unconscious of her surroundings. Repairing to her room, she carefully laid the fatal missive away and penned a line to Ona, saying: "I have come home to die."

Weeks passed, and she kept her bed. The physician gave no hopes of her recovery. At length she asked that Ona be sent for. A messenger was dispatched in haste, carrying the summons to her little friend in the North. Sad were the days and nights which passed in that Southern mansion as they awaited the arrival of the friend. At last Ona came. A happy expression of recognition spread over Lillie's countenance when she heard the sweet voice beside her. Opening her eyes for the first time in many days, she looked upon the face that bent over her and returned the affectionate kiss, but she soon relapsed into unconsiousness. She became delirious, and talked incessantly of the past; of Hayden, and of his marrying another. Then she besought him to come, that she might know from his own lips that he had broken his vow of constancy to her; that he had cast her adrift upon the ocean of inconstancy, without sail or rudder; that he had permitted her place in his heart to be usurped by another; that a siren voice had deadened his sensibility of right, of justice, o truth; that a fair face had charmed him, in imagination, and while it threw about him a vapor of delusion, led him on to self-immolation upon the altar of selfishness, greed and inconstancy.

There came a change seemingly for the better, she opened her eyes and recognized those around her. It was early one bright November morning, that delightful season, Indian summer cast its fragrant haze

upon the face of the earth. The early songsters
which had twilled their first notes in Northern clime
sought the balmy South to swell their first twitterings
into grateful songs of praise. These were abroad
upon this particular morning, making sweet music as
the golden sun, rising from its watery bed, glinted its
invigorating rays through the window full upon the
couch of the sufferer.

"What a beautiful morning," said she, "it reminds
me of the mornings at Cedar Hall. Oh! there I was
so happy."

"Are you not happy now?" asked Ona.

"Not as I was in worldly pleasures, but there seems
to be sweeter pleasures than earth can give, awaiting me on another shore. I imagine I hear the
sweetest music from the other side of this stream I
am about to cross. I see radient faces smiling at my
coming. I notice outstretched hands open to receive
me, and among that vast throng stands one, a smile
of welcome lights up his countenance, a halo of glory
surrounds his brow, and those around him smile
gladly as he addresses them as His children. Oh, I
know I shall be happy among that group. I so earnestly desire to have him place His hand upon my
head and say, 'my child.'"

She fell into a sweet sleep and her friends were
impressed with the idea that when she awoke she
would be better. After resting for nearly an hour,
she awoke suddenly, calling for Ona, she said, "get
my keys and open my letter-box, bring me the package of letters, you will find one in the top drawer of
my dressing-case, bring it also."

Ona brought the package and the crumpled note, and placed them in Lillie's hand. She placed the crumpled one among the others and returned them to Ona saying: "Take these, and when I am gone read them and answer the last one. Tell him that my heart was broken and I am sleeping the sleep that knows no waking. Tell him I forgave him, that my last thoughts and words were of him ; that I return to him all he gave me except the ring, that I will not have removed from my finger where he placed it. Keep the letters, Ona, until he returns to America, but be sure and answer the last one." Her voice grew weaker and the weeping friends bent over to catch the half-whispered and slowly uttered words.

As night drew near she closed her eyes as if she would sleep. Toward midnight she rallied, and casting a glance of recognition upon each of her friends, pleasantly smiled, and ceased to breathe.

The hand of Ona remained in the clasp of the one, that had often in life grasped it in friendship and still seemed to retain its grasp, though life had passed from it, and its power to act was dead. Ona was loth to withdraw from the bedside where she had long and faithfully watched.

Now that she could do no more to alleviate the suffering body or soothe the mind of the unconscious form before her, she gently unclasped the cold fingers and repaired to her own room where she threw herself upon the bed and wept until tired nature cast around her pillow the oblivion of sleep.

When she awoke, the sun was shining through the

open window of her apartment. As she raised her
head, she beheld to her great astonishment a dark
and vicious-looking man examining the contents of
her trunk—examinining, especially, letters and papers. She immediately thought of the letters Lillie
had given her and the silver case' which she had
brought with her. Finding them safe in her pocket,
she next thought how to rid herself of the presence
of the intruder.

She sprang from the bed, and reaching the door,
she threw it open before the man had time to gain
his feet. . Standing in the door, she demanded to
know the reason of the unwarranted intrusion. As
he cast his dark, scowling eye upon her, she, with
feelings of dread and fear, recognized the cruel visage; it was none other than the heartless wretch,
Guy Wren. He rushed past her without saying a
word.

She immediately instituted inquiries as to his presence in the neighborhood, and learned that he was
serving in the capacity of body servant and attendant of Mr. Calhoun.

"Does he have access to all parts of the house?"
asked Ona of the servant who had imparted the information.

"No, madam, I reckon not, but he always goes
where he pleases. Massa think a heap of him."

Ona felt that she should say nothing regarding his
presence in her room. Replacing the articles in her
trunk and arranging her hair, she went down to
breakfast, feeling a disgust for the laxity and want
of perception in people who would employ such a

man as Guy Wren for a servant companion when ordinary judgment would promptly condemn him by the rule of physiognomy. As she passed through the hall, she observed the human fiend standing at the farther end examining a revolver. He did not see her as she entered the sitting room.

Ona had loved the fair one now lying above them cold in death, and for Mrs. Calhoun her heart went out in kindly, affectionate sympathy, in this, the hour of her great affliction. They were no longer strangers to her. Her interest in the welfare of their lost one; her many kindly acts extended during her long sickness, had caused the tendrils of their hearts to go out and embrace the fair-faced girl of the North, and now their grief-stricken hearts looked to her as a comforter, while she, mildly and sweetly, called their attention to One who is able to comfort, willing to cheer and glad to receive.

As the family seated themselves at breakfast, a noise was heard in the room above where lay the corpse. The sound was that of heavy footsteps and scuffling.

"What can cause such a disturbance?" said Mrs. Calhoun, turning pale.

At that moment a servant entered, trembling and much agitated, who finally said: "Massa, de good Lor' ony know what is done! Dat dere ole Wren combed up-stairs a goin' to shoot Hanner and dis ole darkey jist cos we wouldn't let him take de ring off on Missus Lillie's hand, and he did tuk it off and weuns got it away from him an' is afeerd to put it back—we is—here it am."

Mr. Calhoun took the ring and asked Ona to re-place it.

"Where is the inhuman brute?" asked he.

"Massa, he go out ob de house by de back way. I seed him a crossin' de garden jist now. He went to Missus Ona's room dis berry mornin' and was a snoopen' in her trunk, when she seed him and drew him off."

"Is that a fact, Miss Leland?" asked Mr. Calhoun.

"Yes, sir," said she.

Mr. Calhoun immediately left the room in search of Wren, but he had left the premises. The deep grief at the loss of his daughter, alone prevented a thorough search being instituted by the old gentle-man. Contending emotions filled his mind as he returned to the room, where he and Mrs. Calhoun awaited Ona, who had gone to replace the ring upon Lillie's finger.

After breakfast, Ona returned to the silent cham-ber and watched by the dead body of her friend un-til night, when she occupied a couch in Mrs. Cal-houn's room, for fear of being intruded upon as she had been on the previous morning. Nothing, how-ever, happened to disturb the quiet of the mansion during the night. The early morning was devoted to making preparations for the funeral.

As the bell sounded its last doleful call and the hearse moved away, Ona observed from the family carriage a well-dressed, finely formed man who, with uncovered head, followed the carriage to the cem-etery. She could not see his face, but the form was familiar.

The procession stopped at the grave; the coffin was carried into the enclosure. There she met the young man face to face, and recognized Hayden Douglas. His eyes were filled with tears; the lineaments of his face bore positive marks of grief. Ona could not comprehend why such evidence of emotion should manifest itself in him, who had lost all interest he may have had in her whose body was about to be returned to its mother—earth—as her spirit was already with its creator—God.

Ona thought of the letters in her possession, especially the one last received from this man, who had informed Lillie in that letter of circumstances which, if true, branded him as a hypocrite in thus expressing emotion at the grave of her whom his perfidy had slain.

She thought of the obligation imposed upon her by Lillie to answer this last letter and return them all when opportunity offered. What should she do now that he was here?

After the funeral, Ona remained to transplant a little shrub at the foot of the grave and weep there alone by the grave of her departed friend. Soon one of those who had left the grave returned. It was Hayden, who, when he observed Ona, said:

"I hope I am not intruding, Miss ——.. Although I have met you previously under very different circumstances than now surround us, yet I have never learned your name, but that is a matter of no moment, as we both fill the same position here, I, too, being a mourner, having, in the death of Miss Calhoun, lost the dearest friend of my whole life."

"I think you are mistaken, sir," said Ona. "I am in possession of facts which conclusively contradict that statement, at least they should debar you of any right you may have previously had in acting the part of chief mourner at this service."

CHAPTER XXV.

ANOTHER DEATH-BED SCENE.

WHEN Guy Wren left the Calhoun mansion, he wended his way to New York, traveling most of the way on foot, carrying a budget of clothes with him, begging his food as he traveled through the country. It was toward night, one cold day, when he reached the metropolis. He immediately sought out an alley that, for filth and slime, was a disgrace to the city. Here, among the low hovels, he found one, more squalid than the neighboring ones, if such distinction could be drawn. He stopped at the door and gave a loud rap. In a short time it was opened by a woman clothed in the habiliments of poverty.

"You did come at last, Guy," said the woman in a creaking voice, as she closed the door after him.

"Yes, and I want something to eat, and that, too, in short order."

"Well, give me some money to buy something with, for I have nothing in the house, not a morsel to eat."

"You lie, you confounded old hag," roared he at the top of his voice. "Now get out of my house. I have kept you as long as I want to." While he was speaking, he had opened the door, and giving her a push, she fell in the deep snow outside. As she lay there, he muttered, "Go back to Strawn and hunt up your husband and children."

The woman sank down in the snow almost speechless. Not a wrapping of any kind shielded her half-naked body from the driving storm which had just renewed its fury. She seemed to realize her destitute circumstances, and in her despair she exclaimed, "Oh, what shall I do! No one to pity or care for me!"

Just at that moment, a fine carriage stopped and a young lad of noble appearance stepped out and lifted the freezing woman in, drove up to the Leland mansion and in a few moments she was comfortably wrapped in warm blankets and restoratives given. In a brief time the poor woman was sleeping soundly.

"Don't disturb her, Robert," said a sweet-faced old lady to the young man. "Sleep is the best medicine we can procure for her poor, suffering body, as well as for the mind."

"Well, you watch her, Aunt Nancy, and I will see if I can find any more who are exposed to this storm," and he was off without another word.

Kind reader, that youth was Robie Leland, and the kind old lady was his old nurse, Aunt Nancy. Mr. Leland had purchased a beautiful residence in the city and was sending his son to school. Ona had not returned from South Carolina, and Robie, on his return from school, had wended his way through the dark alleys, to assist those who were in extreme want. Not a day passed but what he contributed to the comfort of some one. As the cold weather continued, he found more to do than he could accomplish with the assistance of Aunt Nancy alone.

The poor woman above referred to, slept until bed time ere she awoke. Robie took up her thin, amaciated hand affectionately, when he started in surprise, exclaiming, "Why, Aunt Nancy! She has a high fever and we must send for medical aid."

Leaving the room, he dispatched a servant after their family physician, and with the assistance of the chamber-maid, he laid the poor woman on the bed. When the doctor came, he pronounced her case hopeless, her system being already to much reduced by starvation.

Asking a few questions of Robie regarding the manner and place of her discovery, he turned to leave, when his attention was called to a glittering ring, which was suspended from her neck by a dirty ribbon. Remarking to Robie, "This may be some clue to her identity, we will examine it." They cut it from her neck, and approached the light to examine it. Suddenly the Doctor stopped, turned deathly pale, exclaiming, "O, my God! it is the ring I gave my wife! Can it be she?" Going up to the bed, he took up her left hand and rubbed the fingers straight. "Yes, it is she!" sobbed he. "Poor woman! How sad, indeed, is your fate. Where have you been all these years?" Said he, as he bent over the only woman he had ever loved, and one unworthy to be known as the wife of such a man as Doctor Harris.

He had not heard from her since she left the village of Strawn. He had kept his little girls and sweet-faced boy, and had come to New York, and now resided there with his motherless family.

Addressing Aunt Nancy, he said, "You remember the sad occurrence of my wife leaving me some years ago, do you not?"

"Yes, Ona and I have spoken frequently regarding that dreadful time in Strawn, some years since, but I never thought of this poor creature being your wife."

"We know not what dire distress may overtake us in life. Indeed I have had my full share. I must summon others to assist in caring for her," said he.

Leaving the Leland home, he sought his own roof where he informed the children of what had transpired. "Here is the ring I gave her on our wedding day, and through which I recognized her."

With moistened eyes the children examined the ring.

"Can we go and see her papa?" asked one.

"Not now, children, you must wait until she becomes conscious."

He wrapped the ring in a piece of soft paper and placed it in his pocket-book, saying to the children:

"Wait until I come for you."

"He procured the best medical aid the city afforded, but days lengthened into weeks before the

9.

fever abated. During her delirium she had rehearsed
scenes and incidents in her life, from childhood up to
the present time. Much to the humiliation of the
Doctor, she spoke of her life of abandon in the city,
and how Guy Wren had abused her from time to
time. She would then call upon Wren to protect
her, and not forsake her, as she was alone in the
world.

Four weeks had passed, and late one afternoon,
just as the winter sun was emitting its last lingering
rays, which struggled through the half-opened shut-
ters, she opened her eyes for the first time and
glanced at each one who stood near the bed. Closing them again she shuddered and exclaimed, "Oh!
what a miserable dream I had."

Dr. Harris saw that there was little time to lose as
death was surely and rapidly approaching, he sent,
in haste, for the children who came promptly.

She smiled when they entered, but it was a smile
of delirium, not of recognition. Toward midnight
she breathed her last, among friends, though unconscious as to who had ministered to her wants.

Dr. Harris sent a messenger to Strawn with directions for her burial, and soon followed, accompanied
by his family and friends, bearing the remains of his
long lost and depraved wife. There in that quiet
village cemetery, beneath a tall, majestic cedar, they
laid her in her last resting place. When the last
shovel full of earth had been deposited the sexton
carefully replaced the mourning sheet of snow, thus
obliterating all traces of the newly made grave. But
a deeper chasm than the grave had grown in the

heart of him who had been her loving companion ; a chasm which could neither be filled nor obliterated.

Returning to New York, he endeavored to ascertain the whereabouts of Wren, assisted by the authorities, who desired to capture him on account of his escape from prison in New Hampshire, before his term had ended. He had killed a guard and had not been heard from until Ona saw him in South Carolina, and Mrs. Harris talked of him in her delirium. As before, he was successful in eluding his pursuers, and finally left for the far West, where he found congenial companions among the outlaws that infested Western Missouri. Thus adding another character of the darkest dye to that already criminally corrupt district, where outlaws made their home and horse-thieves reigned supreme.

Wren reached that neighborhood just in time to participate in the malicious murder of two young men from the Eastern states, their only crime being a disapproval of outlawry in any form. He had known them as innocent boys in the village of Strawn, and had often remarked the energy and manliness of Wayne Crowell and Gilbert Brooks, even in their childhood days. After the crime had been committed, he for a moment, when his thoughts reverted to them as happy boys, regretted the part he had taken in depriving them of life, but such thought was momentary. Another plot was developing in his perfidious brain.

CHAPTER XXVI.

THE FORGED LETTER.

WE left Ona and Hayden at Lillie's grave. Hayden had just returned from Europe and was on his way to call upon Lillie at her home when he learned of her death as he passed through the neighboring village. He returned to the sepulcher after the funeral services were over, that he might there pour out his grief upon her grave, the only spot of earth that seemed dear to him. But, alas! he was not granted that privilege, for there sat the blue-eyed lady he had seen upon three different occasions: once at Cedar Hall, as a child peeping over the stair-railing at him; again at the scene with the kidnappers in the Curry house, calling herself "Dickey Deane," and yet again in the throng in Washington, where she won the admiration of all present at the most fashionable fete given during the season.

Now her face was suffused with tears, and her heart, like his, was sad. When she became aware of his presence, her eye-lashes were glistening with tears, that caused them to seem darker than before, and when she said, "I think you are mistaken. I know some facts regarding you, Mr. Douglas," he was bewildered. Did she refer to his parentage? What could it be to her if he did not tell the world who he was? But in a moment he asked, "What do you know, 'Dickey Deane?'"

" My name is Ona Leland, and I know that your cruel letter killed my dearest friend, and one who loved you far more devotedly than you merit or appreciate."

" I am at a loss to divine your meaning, Miss Leland. My correspondence with Miss Calhoun was ever harmonious and treated of a subject dear to both of us, Love, as you perhaps know. My last letter to her was the most happy and joyful of all I had written in its tone, inasmuch as I had just arranged my business so that I could return to America and claim her as my bride. I told her that I should expect no answer, as the consummation of my business required that I should spend time in different places on the Continent, and I could not say where I should be. So from this statement, and the fact of my being here at her grave, when I expected to have been enjoying her society at home, you will certainly know that I am not deceiving you, her friend."

" Mr. Douglas, your statement, coupled with the emotion you have expressed to-day, is certainly entitled to credence. The fact that I referred to as being possessed of is contained in this letter which she received from you. Read it and you will know why Lillie Calhoun's body rests to-day under the cold sod."

He glanced hastily over it, and immediately said : " I never wrote it. It is not my hand-writing. I am not married, and never entertained such a thought, except in connection with Lillie Calhoun. This is the work of some evil-disposed person. My God !

was it thus my darling was murdered? Where did this letter come from? Where is the envelope? I will not rest until I have ferreted this wrong-doer out and have ground his unworthy body to atoms in the dust." Then calming himself, he said: "Miss Leland, excuse the show of extreme feeling I have just manifested. My heart is torn and bleeding at the loss I have sustained. My fiery nature has just cause to show itself when thinking of one who could be so base, so cruel, so unjust as to do so vile a deed."

"Mr. Douglas, I know your provocation is great. I am now thoroughly ready to rely implicitly on any statement you may make, regarding this affair which has terminated so unfortunately, and further, I am ready and willing to aid you in any way possible to enable you to arrive at the full knowledge as to who the guilty party is, and to commence, let me say, I have the envelope which contained this cruel letter, at my home in New Hampshire. Lillie received it after she was seated in the stage to return South, when she opened it, she threw the envelope out of the window and I picked it up, carried it home as a momento, and will send or give it to you, as the case may be, or the opportunity presents, as soon as I can reach home after leaving here."

"I am thankful, Miss Leland, for your kindly of-fer. The information, that you are possessed of the envelope gives me hope that its marks and stamps may lead to the detection of the guilty party. Let us not consider the matter further, but wait until time assuages our grief, when we can better apply reason to our acts. Let us devote the immediate present to doing the last sad office of dropping our tears upon the grave of her we loved. May each tear dropped be the germ that sprouts a flower to decorate the grave of the fairest of God's beings, and may each tear, as it leaves our eyes and wells from our hearts, be the reminder of some great good we have to accomplish in life, and plant in our minds germs that will bring forth good resolutions, which, growing and thriving, may cast a shade, in which may bask principles, developed and cherished by us through life, that will at last bring us in direct association with her among the redeemed saints in the celestial world."

"Mr. Douglas, I heartily endorse the sentiments you have expressed. It may be pleasing to you to know, that she whose mortal part now lies beneath our feet, expressed the abiding faith of the Christian ere she passed the stream of death. Smilingly she elated her bright, waking vision. She could calmly look across the dark river of death and behold the glorious scenes upon the other shore. She saw her Savior with the host of redeemed ones waiting to receive her. She expressed the desire to be near him, where He could place His hand upon her brow and say 'my child.'" She continued:

"As you have intimated, Mr. Douglas, there is a work for us all to do in this world, and I feel that here at the grave of my friend, is a proper place to re-consecrate myself to all that is for good in this life, that I may properly appreciate, while here, the joy and happiness that is in store beyond 'this vale

of tears,' for those who properly discharge their duty
toward their God and fellow mortals."

"I know nothing of the 'better life' you speak
of, Miss Leland, in practice. Oh, that I possessed
but one spark from the lamp of that life by which to
guide my wayward feet into the path that promises
perpetual enjoyment."

"Do you never pray, Mr. Douglas?"

"No. Yes. That is certainly contradictory. I
do pray in a certain way. I never kneel and unbur-
then my heart of its troubles, but when alone with
my own thoughts, there is a something that keeps
whispering in my ear, and I silently breathe a sigh
that my life may be pure, pure as Christ's was pure."

"You are on the right path, Mr. Douglas. Drive
not the still small voice from your heart. Encourage
it and abide by its decisions and heed its promptings, and your life may yet be pure."

"I will make an earnest effort to merit the approbation of Him who 'noteth the fall of the sparrow'
and remembers us in the time of our affliction, by
directing our thoughts toward good works and good
deeds, as has been the case to-day. I feel to-day,
Miss Leland, as if I could here consecrate myself to
greater efforts to lead a better life in the future than
I have in the past. I feel that the spirit of my departed friend will act the part of my guardian angel
through life, and with such an overshadowing presence I can do no wrong without being conscious of
it, and each good effort will meet the proper approbation of that angel."

"It costs an effort, Mr. Douglas, and only a strong,

earnest effort to be a Christian. That effort is nothing, at last. What is all the world to us when we
must die? We leave all behind."

"I know that I would willingly give of all this
world's goods at my command had I the faith and the
power to exercise it that you have, Miss Leland. It
is growing late, and I must bid you adieu. I need
rest for my journey. I am summoned to Concord,
and must be there this week. You are aware of the
business of our society as well, perhaps, as I am."

"Yes, Mr. Douglas, I leave here in the morning
for the same place."

"Ah! then, if agreeable, we will pursue our journey in the same coach."

"Before I leave this newly-made grave, I want to
plant an evergreen that Lillie brought from the
North with her. I grew it beneath our talismanic
tree at home, whose emblematical qualities you understand, being a member of our society. Lillie admired it on account of its resemblance to the parent
tree. I could not, of course, explain the nature of
its signs, but here, at her grave, in this beautiful
land, is a becoming place to plant such a tree."

"Allow me the pleasure, Miss Leland, of uniting
my effort with yours in thus planting in the Southern
clime our talismanic tree. In after years when I
think of her grave, I shall also not forget to blend
with it, in imagination, this tree, which I helped to
plant, and when its symbols have been accepted by
the world, I will be glad to point to one standing at
the grave of her I loved and of whom I was unjustly
robbed."

Thus saying, he took up the spade and dug a place at the foot of the grave, while Ona placed therein the little tree. He pressed the loam about its tender roots, and they left it to flourish and spread its green boughs over the grave of one dear alike to both, promising to return and moisten its roots with the tears of affection and love in after years.

Hayden walked with Ona to the Calhoun mansion. She introduced him to the parents of Lillie as a former friend of their daughter, whose memory he cherished. They knew of their daughter's engagement, but knew nothing of the forged letter and the presence of one whom their dear lost child had chosen for a companion through life, opened again the flood-gates of their grief. Thus the tears of friends from every clime almost mingled around the desolate hearth-stone.

Hayden remained with them but a few hours, when he returned to the village where he remained during the night. The next morning the two friends were on the way to Concord. Their departure left a warm place in the hearts of Lillie's parents for them both. For him a sympathy for his loss, for her a kindly remembrance of the sweet-faced Northern girl, who had been so dear to their lost one.

Ona felt no inclination to converse; while Hayden communed with his own thoughts, which carried him far back into the past, then to the forged letter which had wrought so much harm. Why should any one have committed so despicable an act? What a shadow it had cast upon that beautiful home! What a gloom it had thrown about many loving hearts!

Who could have been guilty of such a crime? Could it have been Ava Haynes? Hayden started at the thought, the recollection of her perfidious acts of the past came before his mind and forced themselves forward with such tenacity, that he felt a premonition that he had hit upon the proper clue.

After several days and nights' travel they reached Concord. Ona continued her journey to Strawn, offering to send the envelope to Hayden, but as he contemplated visiting that village soon, he suggested that he could then avail himself of the opportunity of examining it.

Hayden proceeded to the hall where the same society held its meeting, that he had so often in times past met with. A few of the old members were absent on business partaining to the society. Hundreds more were added to it. The business for this day was sending out committees, consisting of both men and women, to solicit emigrants for the West. Hayden was appointed to travel over the Atlantic States. He left the next day for Strawn where he had been on two previous occasions. He left his carriage before the gate at Cedar Hall and walked down the path. There stood the cedar tree, and there the cavity from which had been taken the smaller one which he had assisted in transplanting at Lillie's grave. He entered, and after the salutations of the day had passed, Ona produced the envelope, which she had accidentally saved, and handed it to Hayden.

CHAPTER XXVII.

THE BEGINNING OF TROUBLES IN THE WEST.

AS GUY WREN looked upon the lifeless bodies of those two young men, whose lives had been pure and upright, he was laying a plan to make their deaths known to their far away friends in the East. At last he conceived a plan which was submitted to his drunken companions. It consisted of publishing a false account of their many misdemeanors, and sending a copy of same to their friends in Strawn.

The skill of a swarthy Arkansas pedagogue was brought into play and soon the false statement was submitted for the approval of the dissolute rabble, who with applauding yells signified their approbation. In due course of time it was published in a pro-slavery sheet under the supervision of Esquire Barnes.

That night the lifeless bodies were thrown upon a building that was wood-shed and hen-house combined, while the murderers kept time to a squeaking fiddle in the miserable huts on the hillside.

The next day a hole was dug not far from the hamlet now known as West Point. There they were buried, having been stripped of everything except their underclothing. The earth was hastily thrown upon them. Thus without shroud or coffin were buried these young men, whose only ambition, and that unexpressed, had been to elevate the human race to the plane designed by the Great Architect.

In a few days the publication of the account of the hanging of those two young men appeared with the causes assigned. A copy was sent by mail to Strawn, where in course of time it arrived.

Some two weeks had elapsed when Guy Wren began to feel uneasy. What a fool he had been in allowing his name to appear in the paper which went where he was already too well known. But it was too late to repent now. He must look out. Would they send thousands of miles to look after those two boys? No, they certainly would not, and thus he reasoned with himself. But feeling unsafe, he went farther North and engaged to chop wood for a steam saw mill, until Spring should come. Having been closely hunted by Mr. Calhoun, he had tramped through to New York, and there ferreted out by Dr. Harris and others, he was compelled to go West, and after lying, house-breaking and many other crimes, he finally made his way to Bates county, Missouri. Fearing the people of Strawn, he had moved again.

If there be no rest for the wicked on earth, what can they expect in a world to come? If their minds are in a state of unrest here, can they possibly be happy in the great hereafter?

When Wren had been at the mill some two months, a Yankee pedler stopped one evening. He carried two large valises, filled with jewelry, which he was selling. He spent the night where Wren was boarding. The next morning he paid his bill and pursued his journey. Wren had left the house when the pedler started. When the proprietor, Mr. Jones, called where the men were working, Wren was not with them, and he ascertained he had not been there during the time they had been working. After waiting a brief time, Mr. Jones instructed some of the men to search for Wren and bring him back, dead or alive, the supposition being that he and the pedler were negro thieves. The search was continued until towards noon. A gun was heard, that being the signal agreed upon as denoting success. But when the scouts gathered they were surprised at beholding in the thicket the dead and mangled remains of the pedler. They discovered that his valises were gone, as well as his pocket-book and hat. The horror-stricken men carried the body back to Mr. Jones'. Scouts were sent out to scour the surrounding country in search of Wren. No trace could be found of the villain.

The dead man was cared for by the men at the mill as if he had been a friend. A good coffin and a nice suit of clothes were procured. He was buried in the village graveyard. A board bearing the inscription, "Here lies an Eastern man; name unknown; murdered by one Guy Wren," was placed at the head of his grave. An article was published in the St. Joseph Herald concerning the sad affair, and several copies were forwarded to Eastern papers, with the hope of attracting the attention of friends of the murdered man.

Thus, step by step, war began to rage on the Western border between the Anti- and Pro-Slavery factions. The outlaws and desperadoes who had congregated there, committed heinous crimes, pillaging and murdering promiscuously and charging the blame upon opposing parties, thus engendering a cruel strife, which marked the Missouri and Kansas borders as the second "dark and bloody ground." Respectable men of either party held aloof from such depredations, until public opinion was strongly expressed and excitement ran high, aggravated and inflamed by roughs from every State.

The settlers were generally respectable men from Kentucky and Tennessee, who owned a few slaves and thought it no disgrace to work along with them in the field. The slaves were well contented with their lot. They fared as did their masters, having plenty to eat and to wear.

CHAPTER XXVIII.

CAUGHT.

HAYDEN examined the envelope closely. He discovered that the post-mark was a false one, that the seal was not a foreign one, and addressing Ona, said:

"Miss Ona, I pronounce this as all false; will you permit me to retain this envelope? It may aid me, materially, in discovering the perpetrator of the crime."

"Most assuredly, Mr. Douglas. I promised to aid

you in whatever way I could, and although I value the envelope as a memento of Lillie, yet I cannot withhold it from you. Believe me, when I say, I hope your efforts may be successful."

"Thank you, kindly, for both the envelope and your earnest hope. Permit me to say adieu."

Hayden in a few days arrived in Washington. He learned that many of his former friends were spending the winter there, among whom was Ava Haynes, who acted as assistant to her brother who had charge of the distributing of foreign mails. He was at once convinced, in his own mind, as to the author of the crime, but what plan to adopt, to secure positive proof of the villiany, was a hard problem to solve. While pondering the matter over, he met his old friend and former companion, Arthur Holmes. He acquainted Arthur with all his troubles, as well as his suspicions regarding Ava's being concerned in the forgery of the letter.

The hot blood mounted to Arthur's face, and as quickly left. A deathly pallor overspread his countenance, a visible shudder shook his frame, but Hayden did not observe the evidences of emotion his accusations had brought about.

Hayden continued : "She has access to the Post-Office Department. She, on a previous occasion, created a false impression in the mind of Miss Calhoun regarding myself, and, considering all things, I believe she is the guilty party."

Every trace of emotion had passed from Arthur. His voice was calm and evinced strong determination as he said :

" Give me the envelope, write Miss Calhoun's name upon another, let me have that also, and if the party that you suspect is really guilty, I can soon arrive at the truth of the suspicion."

Hayden did as Arthur directed, after which they parted. Hayden left for Pennsylvania to solicit families to join the emigrants who were going West to settle the Platte country.

Arthur examined the envelopes closely and found them to be very dissimilar. He could hardly entertain the thought, that Ava Haynes could be so depraved as to intercept letters. But he had only known and seen the bright side of her life. He had felt his heart glow in love toward the bright Southern girl even before he went to Europe, and since his return they were fast growing in their friendship, hence his emotion when her name was associated with a deed that had been productive of so much evil. He said to himself, " I must lay aside all preconceived favorable opinions, and thoroughly investigate this matter for my friend Hayden."

He placed a sheet of blank paper in the envelope which Hayden had directed, and procuring the assistance of a wood engraver, had the name J. W. London cut in a circle, the unsuspecting workman supposing that to be the name of his customer. When in possession of the stamp, he erased the letters " J. W." and applied the stamp to the decoy letter he had prepared.

Proceeding to the wharf where the vessel lay, which had just arrived with the mails, he carelessly sauntered on board. He watched his opportunity and dropped his decoy letter in one of the apartments where the mail was being changed into "transfer sacks," which would soon be carried to the "distributing office."

He wended his way to that office, and presenting his card, was admitted to the hall. As he entered, he met Mark Haynes, Ava's brother, who was just leaving on urgent business, and could not remain to entertain his friend.

When he reached the apartment occupied by Ava, he fouud her busy arranging the outgoing mail. Seating himself where he could view her actions, unobserved, and yet not attract the attention of the assistants, he drew a paper from his pocket, and pretending to read, quietly awaited the arrival of the mail. Soon the heavily-laden trucks were wheeled through the hall, stopping at the various "department rooms," until Ava's room was reached, where two closely-filled sacks were placed upon her table.

After the men had withdrawn, she unlocked one of the sacks just as Arthur approached a shaded spot, where he could note her actions. As his eye glanced over the table, he saw his decoy letter lying by itself, not tied up with any of the packages, as if the official in charge at the boat had discovered it after the packages had been secured and threw it in the sack loose.

She glanced carelessly over the table until her gaze fell upon the decoy letter, which she hastily picked up and put in her pocket. Arthur trembled to such an extent that he felt his presence must become known in spite of every effort to the contrary. He thought: "What must I do? Hayden was certainly right. Shall I, this minute, tell her all, and possibly save her from a greater wrong in the future? or shall I inform the authorities? No, no! They will deal too harshly with her." And without further thought he walked into the apartment. She was not aware of his presence until she heard his salutation. She manifested a momentary surprise, but soon became calm.

He addressed her, saying: "I am authorized, Miss Haynes, to overlook the work of certain assistants in this department. There has been a gross dereliction of duty on the part of some of the clerks, and a careful watch has been established over their acts. You are aware that in the discharge of such duty as has been assigned to me, I must lay aside all considerations of former friendship with persons under my surveilance, and discharge my whole and entire duty without fear or favor."

"Do not say a word, please, until I am through," said he, coolly, as she attempted to speak, and he then continued, "With your permission, Miss Haynes, I would see the letter you, a moment since, placed in your pocket."

For an instant she trembled, then turning deathly pale, fell at his feet, at the same time throwing the letter upon the floor, she begged of him, "By all fond associations of the past, for the sake of her father's good name, for the sake of her brother's official station, for the sake of the spirit of her dead mother, for the sake of her own future, not to expose her acts to the authorities, and thus overwhelm her with shame, that would be as lasting as life itself."

"Calm yourself, Miss Haynes, let me ask, do you know the result of the act you perpetrated, last fall, in intercepting a certain letter and afterward forwarding one, expressing sentiments entirely foreign to those contained in the original? I will tell you. Miss Calhoun now sleeps the sleep that knows no waking. Her body rests in the quiet cemetery where the birds sing in tunefull melody and the flowers emit their fragrance. And why is that beautiful form thus situated? Miss Haynes, can I impress upon your mind the heinousness of your crime, when I say, the letter you wrote caused Miss Calhoun's death. Oh, let me advise you to have a greater degree of control over your selfish inclinations. Rather seek to give joy and happiness to others, than to selfishly intercept their joys. You can offer nothing in excuse for the wrong you have done, but what is based on selfishness. When your brother returns, tender your resignation of your position, and I will give you the assurance that none but interested parties shall ever know of your error, and they will be reticent upon the subject."

She could not await her brother's return, but closed the door, donned her cloak and hat with its heavy veil, and proceeded to her brother's house, where, on the plea of indisposition, she asked to be excused from further work in the office. She could not endure the mental strain she had been subjected to. She kept her bed for several days, and when sufficiently recovered, she sought her home in the South, a sadder and wiser girl. She put forth an earnest effort to redeem the past, by making her life more pure and unselfish, becoming interested in those around her, contributing to the wants of the needy, sharing of her bounty with the destitute, until, by a daily practice of unselfishness, her better qualities gained entire possession of her mind, and seeking the hallowed influence of a Savior's love, she became a kind and loving woman, whose presence brought sunshine and gladness wherever she appeared.

Years passed ere she again met those two men. They did not recognize her, but the expression of their countenances neither time nor place could remove from her mind.

Arthur wrote Hayden the result of his investigation and added, "I could not find it in my heart to subject her, who had occupied so exalted a position in society, to the shame and disgrace that would naturally follow the exposure of her wrong; besides, I must, in all candor, admit, that when discharging what I considered to be my duty toward you, my friend, and toward her, who sleeps among the orange groves, I had not entirely eradicated from my heart, the feeling of admiration and love engendered there for the person whose faults and misdoings I was endeavoring to substantiate. I hope, under the circumstances, when you calmly consider them, you will not censure me for my leniency toward her."

Hayden's reply contained these words: "I do not censure you, my friend, for being lenient toward the erring one. I was not aware that you entertained for her more than a kindly feeling, else I should not have had the temerity to have unbosomed myself to you. But inasmuch as you assumed the duty imposed upon you by me, you have established in my mind the fact of your entire unselfishness and your friendship for me. As regards Miss Haynes, I can truthfully assure you that for her I entertain only feelings of pity. I forgive her her wrong-doings, as I hope to be forgiven. While my heart is desolate at the loss of its idol; while I know who caused that loss, I can with truthfulness express the hope that her after life may abundantly atone for her past wrongs."

As Hayden finished this letter to Arthur, he received one summoning him to the village of Strawn. He hurriedly prepared to obey the summons. As he approached the village, evidences of sorrow and mourning attracted his attention from every side. From every door hung streamers of crape; the flag over the school-house floated at half-mast. "What can be the trouble," thought he, as he recognized many members of the Anti-Slavery party.

CHAPTER XXIX.

SADNESS.

ONA LELAND had returned from the South sad-hearted. Lillie's death had left its gloomy impress upon her brow and an aching void in her heart. Of all that were dear by the ties of friendship, Lillie Calhoun alone had been summoned by the relentless hand of death: one whom she loved from the great depth of her young and tender heart. Far away, under the glow of the Southern sky; beneath the rays of a Southern sun, she was calmly reposing, nestled in the bosom of mother earth. Hayden had just gone. Ona felt lonely.

No change of importance had occurred in the village during the past years. The members of the "Independent Band" were in different cities and towns, pursuing their respective avocations. Ida Crowell alone, with Ona, remained in the village. She had married Jasper Brooks, a prosperous young merchant of Concord. He had brought his household goods to Strawn, and left his little wife until he found a location in the far West.

Mrs. Brooks was spending one of the lonely days with Ona when the news of the death of Wayne Crowell and Gilbert reached Strawn. In a few minutes the church bell was tolling, indicative of sad news.

"What can be the trouble?" said Ida, rising to her feet. "Let us go to the village and learn."

They hastened to the village and found the people all wending their way to the place of worship. Vast multitudes gathered to learn the cause of the excitement. From the church door the announcement was made that "Wayne Crowell and Gilbert Brooks had been killed in Missouri." All was as if death stood at the door when the sad news was proclaimed.

Soon the attention of many was called to Ida, who was the picture of despair for a moment, then shrieked:

"Where is Jasper? He too must be dead, he went with them!"

She was informed that no mention had been made except regarding the two boys.

Public sentiment ran high. Many were loud in the expression of their fellings regarding the crime that had been committed. The fact of the bodies having been identified by Guy Wren, raised grave suspicions in the minds of those who knew his despicable character, that he was concerned, to a greater extent, than was indicated in the report.

Ona, with others, expressed herself forcibly regarding the character of Wren. She said, "How long shall the vile creature contaminate the earth with his presence? Surely the vengeance of a just God will overtake him. These innocent boys charged with stealing horses and hung, just to satisfy the cravings of the depraved mind of Guy Wren, who only sought an object on which to wreak his vengeance and bring sorrow to those who had been instrumental in frustrating one of his diabolical schemes."

She compiled a description of Wren and gave an account of his evil deeds, and had it published, sending many copies to the West, marking the article, to attract attention and cause a republication in local journals.

The next day a party was organized to proceed to the spot, exhume the bodies, and carry them to the village of Strawn.

Under the circumstances it was an arduous undertaking. To travel thousands of miles, on such an errand, under ordinary circumstances, would be no frivolous undertaking, and to penetrate a country infested with characters who were fugitives from justice in the older states; men with the brand of Cain upon their brows; men whose hands were uplifted against every one who was not of their own clan, or in harmony with them.

Six men volunteered to undertake the arduous duty. On their arrival in St. Louis, they procured two large wagons with teams. A strong wind was blowing, which to these Eastern men was not unpleasant, having left the rigors of winter in New Hampshire. As they pursued their journey, they thought the country a paradise. The grass was green upon the prairies and hillsides, the birds were singing among the budding trees as they reached the open country on their way to West Point. They were abundantly prepared in case they were compelled to contend with the ruffians. Said one, as they journeyed along : ·

" What beautiful weather for March. How balmy and salubrious the air seems! I do not blame industrious people for desiring to occupy this fair land."

" Yes," replied another, " it is pleasant to-day, but I remember having heard Western travelers say that often during March the most violent storms of the season prevailed, the change being so sudden as to give but little or no warning. Observe those clouds in the West. I take them to be an indication of a change ere long. I have been told that, at times, the sun would be shining gloriously, the air laden with the balm of spring, and within an hour the sky would become overcast with blackness and the temperature fall to a point many degrees below zero."

"I don't believe such stories," said one, "but we have an opportunity of testing its truth or falsity."

The next morning they were surprised to see a light snow, but the weather was pleasant and it had disappeared before noon, and they enjoyed riding in their open wagons. But toward sundown a change was visible; the wind blew from the Northwest; the temperature fell rapidly and could scarcely be endured by the travelers. It was yet a half-day's drive to the place of their destination. The snow filled the air and formed across the roads in drifts, which were soon scattered by the changeable, freezing wind and deposited in other places. Through the whirling, drifting snow they saw a habitation. It proved to be a farmer's home, where they found shelter for themselves and teams. They partook of the warm meal set before them, and were most cordially entertained by their host. He was a native of Virginia, and with the peculiarities of that people, was friendly with his neighbors, and ever ready to extend the hospitality of his home to travelers.

They told him the nature of their errand. He had heard of the execution of the young men, and stated further, that, in the opinion of the better class of citizens, the action was entirely unprovoked. During their conversation he informed them of the murder of the pedler, a few miles west of his place. He had purchased some silverware of him, and had viewed his body when it was brought to Mr. Jones' for inter-

ment. The description he gave of the man, plainly
indicated him to be Jasper Brooks, who had left
Strawn with the two boys.

"He was killed by one Guy Wren," continued the
farmer; "no doubt, for his money."   .   .

"He brought considerable money with him," said
one of the party. "It was his intention to select a
location for business, and he brought sufficient with
him to purchase a stock of goods after he had chosen
his location."

During the conversation which followed, they
learned from this gentleman many of the cruel atrocities of border life, as well as the peculiarities of those
who committed such deeds of violence.

When morning dawned, the storm still raged.
The air was filled with whirling frost, carried upward
and thitherward by the piercing wind. After dinner,
they started on their journey. The farmer had indicated the location of the grave to them, and had
cautioned them to make no inquiry in the immediate
neighborhood. He also furnished them with the
necessary implements for exhuming the bodies of
their friends, and instructed them to drive back to
his house as soon as their sad task was completed,
which, thanks to the prevailing storm, they accomplished without observation.

The following morning, they, accompanied by their
kind host, proceeded to the grave of the unfortunate
pedler.

When their errand was named to Mr. Jones, he
produced a number of coats among which they immediately recognized one which had belonged to

Jasper. Such evidence being conclusive, they repaired to the cemetery and exhumed the remains of their friend.

Overcome by the sad duty imposed upon them, they wept, wept when their thoughts reverted to the young widow who awaited their return. After thanking their friends for the many kindly offices rendered them in searching for the bodies of the dead, and the consideration extended toward the body of Jasper, they turned their faces Eastward. At St. Louis they sold their teams, and procured neat coffins, and proceeded on their journey.

Anxiety prevailed in Strawn. Some looking for the return of the six men who had assumed the arduous duty, some anxious lest they too should be cruelly murdered while in the discharge of their sad duty. At last they reached the village, bearing three instead of two bodies. When they imparted the intelligence of Jasper's death and named Guy Wren as the assassin, the quiet indignation and determination was plainly visible on many manly brows. " Shall they sleep in death unavenged? Shall Guy Wren go on his way rejoicing? No! Never! We will have revenge. The dead shall be avenged," said not a few. As they moved slowly from the graves, more than one brow wore an aspect of cool determination.

CHAPTER XXX.

ONA'S PLAN.

ONA had nothing to say after her return from the funeral, her mind was racked by contending emotions. She felt her entire inability to properly express her feelings, and she contented herself by communing with her thoughts. Mr. Leland was absent, and she had none with whom to consult. As she reviewed the past, she soliloquized:

"I am now twenty-four years old and have done comparatively nothing in the great work before me." Thus she mused, as she stood before the mirror. Other thoughts had presented themselves for her consideration, as she viewed her own fair countenance and elegant form, but she would not entertain them. She turned her mind upon channels that would develop thoughts leading to something useful.

Stepping to a drawer, she drew forth the silver case her father had given her. She read and re-read that secret pledge, until its teaching was indelibly impressed upon her mind.

"Why not begin work now? There will be no more appropriate time, and seating herself at her desk, she wrote some half-dozen letters to leading members of different Anti-Slavery organizations, communicating to them her plan, and soliciting their co-operation when she should demand their assistance.

The clock indicated the hour of twelve ere she retired, and the sun shone in upon her golden curls long before she awoke the next morning. She hasily attired herself and went down to breakfast. She appeared cheerful and happy. The gloom of yesterday had disappeared from her countenance. She looked out upon the valleys and mountains to-day with more zest and zeal than she had felt for many a long day. She had resolved to undertake a good, a grand work, and she felt already compensated in the exuberance of feeling which the resolution had brought to her mind.

"Mary, give this letter to papa when he returns. I shall be absent, perhaps, sometime," said she, and ordering her carriage, she drove to Mr. Crowell's place of business. Calling him aside, she said, "I go now to perform work in obedience to the instruction contained in my pledge, given years ago. Do not say, nay," and in a moment she was gone.

She was driven to the nearest station, and was soon on her way to St. Louis. Her trunk was packed with apparel designed more for use than ornament.

Ona Leland was one of the few who can properly assume to be privileged characters. Her native grace attracted attention; her self-discipline and self-control, inaugurated in early youth and zealously cultivated, imparted to her every act a nonchalance which, under other circumstances, could not have been commanded. Her perceptions were keen and active. She could tell at a glance the character that lurked behind a hypocritical smile, and divine its motive as readily as if it was emblazoned in letters of bronze upon the brow.

Every act of her life had a purpose. She meant·
well, and performed as she intended. Her object in
life seemed to be to magnify the beauty of anything
that was already beautiful; to elevate and ennoble
the low and debased. This she could accomplish
without being contaminated by the association sometimes required. Her well-balanced mind longed to
put forth greater efforts. She possessed the highest
accomplishment known to art; the art of living well.
In a well spent life she recognized the highest ambition of humanity. Such was Ona Leland, better
known hereafter as "Dickey Deane."

When she arrived in St. Louis, she hailed a cab
and gave her order for the "St. Charles." After
resting a day and procuring some necessaries, she
took passage on a boat bound for St. Joseph. Such
a mode of travel being new to her, she enjoyed it and
became deeply interested in the beautiful scenery
displayed on both banks of the river. She leaned over
the tafferel and watched the bubbling muddy waters
and different objects until they receded from view.
She occasionally walked forward on the boat and
admired the high bluffs, which were covered with
spring verdure. Such a sight was new to her, to
thus early in the season see the green grass and trees
in bloom. She thought: "Oh! how I long to roam
at will over those hills and valleys and the ·broad
expanse of prairie beyond the river bottoms."

"Miss Ona, allow me to restore the glove which
you dropped a moment since," said a voice near her.

She started in surprise and almost lost her self-
control, when she heard herself thus addressed. On

looking up, she beheld Hayden, who was holding her glove in his extended hand.

"Thank you, Mr. Douglas. Let me say, that for the time being, I have laid aside the name of Ona Leland, and, as a favor, ask that you will in the future address me as 'Dickey Deane.'"

He bowed assent to her request and said, "I presume any effort on my part to inform myself regarding your reason for the change of name, would prove futile. You have proved an enigma 'to me heretofore, and instead of beginning to comprehend you, I am constantly discerning new labyrinths."

"I was not aware that the gift of subtility had so penetrated my being, as to cause me to hide my personalities, or that those personalities were so peculiar, as to baffle one possessed of so great erudition as yourself."

"You flatter me by the expression of your opinion regarding my knowledge, and inasmuch as knowledge is gained by and through inquiry, may I exhibit my boldness, perhaps you will term it audacity, by asking why this disguise and assumed name?"

"I neither consider you bold or audacious, Mr. Douglas, yet I think you are endowed, to no small degree, with the peculiarity generally attributed to my sex, curiosity, and I must still further excite that curiosity in your mind, by keeping my own secret, another peculiarity your sex will not readily concede to ours. This, however, I will say, you will, probably, in due time become acquainted with my reasons."

"You surely are not alone in this country, Miss— Dickey Deane?"

"I have a protector whom you may not observe, in the person of the God above, who rules our destinies and on whom I implicitly rely."

Hayden soon became aware of her determination to keep him uninformed of her purposes. Her reserve would have at one time annoyed him. But he could not forget her whose form lay where flowers bloomed and balmy breezes blew.

As he stood conversing with her, she noted the mournful expression of his face; life and vivacity seemed to have departed from him. To the idler and passer-by they were, indeed, a handsome couple as they continued the conversation.

"What think you of the West, Miss Dickey?"

"I am entirely delighted with it. I had heard papa speak so favorably regarding it, that I was, in a measure, prepared to appreciate its beauties, but now that I am traveling through it, I cannot do justice to the subject by attempting an expression of my appreciation."

"We get but a limited view of its expansive beauty from the river. Beyond these bluffs it spreads out into broad prairies, whose extent can scarcely be imagined. There wild flowers bloom in profusion and fragrant odors are continually being generated."

"I can scarcely wait until the boat lands," said Ona. "I am so imbued with the desire to roam over these beautiful lands and inhale the fragrance emitted by those flowers. I can but think of the lack of wisdom displayed by many citizens of the East in living in laborious contentment when this glorious country invites their observation and skill. There

11

they are hampered, and often suffer for the conveniences of life, while here they would be free as the air itself, but little labor being required to prepare themselves for the thorough enjoyment of the pleasures of life."

"The beauties and opportunities of this country would afford an inexhaustible theme of conversation. I would indeed enjoy the prospect of watching the roses bloom upon the cheeks of many persons who are now in the East, could they be, as it were, transplanted in this rich and healthy country."

"To change the subject, Mr. Douglas, can you give me any information regarding that quiet, dignified, firm-featured gentleman standing near the bow? I have been observing him closely for some time, and, I must confess, I am already prepossessed in his favor."

"His name is John Brown. He is from Toronto. His mission and mine are identical, being the prevention of the establishing of slavery in the Platte country, to accomplish which we propose to colonize it with Eastern people, hoping thereby to control the country in the interest of freedom. Mr. Brown has a large family of boys, who will follow him as soon as the country is open for settlement."

"I am glad that you are engaged in so laudable an undertaking, Mr. Douglas. May prosperity crown your efforts! What a pretty town! What is its name, Mr. Douglas?"

"That is St. Joseph. It is, indeed, a beautiful place."

"I presume you are acquainted. Can you direct me to the best hotel?" asked Dickey.

"The 'Oyster House' is the leading hotel, or at least was when I was last here."

Bidding adieu to the young Englishman, Dickey was soon seated in a cab, en route for the "best hotel."

CHAPTER XXXI.

"DICKEY'S" NEW HOME.

THE cab stopped at a large two-story frame house. "Everything looks so cheerful and home-like," thought she, as she entered the large parlor. A sweet-faced, neatly-attired girl of fourteen years entered, and in a pleasant tone asked: "Miss, do you wish a room?"

"Yes, if you please," replied Dickey.

"Come this way, then."

Dickey followed the girl up nicely-carpeted stairs through the hall and into a large, well-furnished room.

The girl said, "Sister and I generally occupy this room, but as we are now entertaining many guests, she and I occupy a part of ma's room."

"Are you the proprietor's daughter?" asked Dickey.

"I am," she replied.

"And the name?"

"Oyster," said she. "My name is Kate Oyster. I will send your trunk up soon."

After Kate had gone, Dickey walked to the window. She saw upon the bosom of the muddy river a great many boats. Some were quiet, others were moving around slowly; one was going down the river, while the one she had left continued its course up the river.

"I wonder when I shall see Hayden again," thought she, as the two boys stopped at the door with her trunk. They placed it as she indicated, just as Kate entered with water and towels.

"Shall you remain long with us?" asked Kate.

"Until I obtain a situation."

"What employment do you desire?"

"I prefer teaching, if I can secure a suitable school."

"What, you a school-teacher? Excuse me, you appear so young, I was surprised."

"I am not as young as I appear," laughed Dickey.

"Where did you come from to this place?"

"My home has recently been in New York. I was raised in New Hampshire near the White mountains."

At that moment Kate was called and she hastened away. At supper Dickey saw Hayden and John Brown. At the head of the table sat an elderly gentleman. She occasionally glanced toward him and invariably found him gazing intently and earnestly at her.

From the position he occupied at the table, Dickey concluded it was Kate's father, Mr. Oyster, the proprietor.

Being weary, she retired early and morning found

her fresh as a school-girl. It was late when she went down to breakfast, and all were gone except the old gentleman. He occupied the same place and was reading the paper.

"Papa, this lady is a school-miss," said Kate, as Dickey took her seat. Kate, accompanied by her sister, brought her breakfast.

"Do you wish to secure a select school or a public school?" asked Mr. Oyster.

"I prefer a select school if I can secure such. I shall not then be confined to regular hours, as other business may, at times, require my attention."

"Are you a musician? Can you play?"

"Yes, sir."

"Do you teach music?"

"I have taught both vocal and instrumental music," replied Dickey.

"Why in the world are you then out in this heathenish land?" asked Mr. Oyster.

"Why do young men come West?" asked she in reply.

"Miss, there are many circumstances that bring them here. Some, by reason of misdemeanors, are compelled to leave their own state to avoid process of law and escape punishment. Others seek this fertile country to better their condition, in the way of homes. Some to fill their pockets with money and to have a jolly time, while others come to view the beauties of the country. Now, which class do you represent?" asked he mischievously.

"I do not know," said she laughing. "The money making class, I suppose."

"Well," said he, "you have come to a good place, teachers are scarce and money is plenty."

As she finished her breakfast, the old gentleman said, "We must now have some music, come into the parlor."

She seated herself at the piano, her soft, white hands swept over the keys. One selection after another was played. Mr. Oyster looked on in wonder, passers-by stopped to listen. Never had such wonderful skill in music been exhibited. All were in raptures. When asked to sing, she sang a favorite, "My heart is over the sea." It was rendered with such power and at the same time so pathetically, that Mr. Oyster exclaimed, "Well done, well done, my little school-marm! You must remain with us. What is your name?"

"My name is Dickey Deane."

"Deane, Deane, my wife's maiden name was Deane," said he. "She had no brothers, she had a sister who married a man in Boston, her name was Leona Deane. My wife's name was Ona."

Dickey could scarcely restrain her feelings. Beyond doubt, she was among friends. She had often heard her mother say that she was like her Aunt Ona, who married a man from Virginia and went West.

"Your name is Oyster?" inquired she.

"Yes," answered he, still looking steadily toward her.

She grew uneasy, fearing he would recognize her.

"You look like the Deane girls—like my wife,— but there were none of them near relatives, none

nearer than cousins. You are related, there is no
use disputing that, but it may be distant."

"I know but little about my relations," said
Dickey, but well she knew that she had found
friends. Yet she could not undeceive them. She
had too much work in view, and their knowledge of
a relationship existing between them, would be but
a hinderance.

After a short conversation, she agreed to teach
that family and to take in as many more pupils as
she could secure.

Thus pleasantly passed the day, Dickey and Kate
rapidly becoming friends. When she had gained
the seclusion of her room that night, she meditated
over the occurrences of the recent past. "I have
discovered," said she, "friends of whom we had lost
all trace, yet I dare not make myself known. Thus
far I realize the truth of the adage, 'All for the best.'
May I be as successful in the accomplishment of my
mission as I have been in finding friends! Papa will
surely be surprised when he reads my letter and
learns that I am domiciled with the family of my
Aunt Ona. There are unexpected pleasures opening continually before us in this world, and we can
discover such an abundance of work that we are
really happy in contemplating its results."

Early the next morning, she and Kate decided to
go "sight-seeing," as Kate termed it. When they
were ready to start, "Dickey" observed that Kate
was closely veiled, and asked:

"Kate, why do you wear your veil this morning?
I am sure the weather is sufficiently pleasant to dis-
pense with it."

"Why, bless your heart, if you don't wear a veil, the spring winds of this country will change your complexion, and you will soon be as yellow as saffron. Have you not noticed the peculiar complexion of everybody here? The men can hardly be distinguished from the Indians who are camped up the river. You must protect yourself if you desire to preserve your beauty."

They enjoyed their stroll around town. Kate was acquainted everywhere. They made some trifling purchases, and before returning, wandered above the settlement, some distance up the river, where they amused themselves kicking clods and chips into the stream, until a boat passed. Dickey saw Hayden on the boat and asked Kate if she knew him.

"No, I do not know him. He took supper at our house a few days ago. He and papa talked about his resemblance to some English lord, at which he laughed heartily."

They returned home for dinner. The exercise had imparted a rosy glow to their cheeks, and had given them a relish for their dinner.

While spending an hour at the piano, Mr. Oyster entered and listened appreciatively. He expressed his pleasure and proposed to take them for a drive out on the high prairie.

Mr. Oyster, like all enterprising men of the frontier, not only sought the comfort of his guests at home, but extended his entertainment to showing them the surrounding country, thus hoping to so interest strangers, that they would conclude to make it their permanent home.

After their return, while at supper, Mr. Oyster asked Dickey, "How she liked the prairie?" To which she replied:

"Oh, I should never tire of beholding it. The change from the dusty cities of the East is so remarkable. Everything is so refreshing, I should like to take a journey of two or three days' duration."

"You can do so whenever you wish, and Kate and myself will accompany you. How would you like to visit the Indian Mission up the river?

"I should be delighted to obtain a view of Indians and observe their mode of life. I have heard so much regarding the peculiarities of the Red Men, that I am really anxious and shall be glad of the opportunity of witnessing their maneuvers."

They accordingly started early the next morning and drove, leisurely, noting the many beauties which presented themselves for consideration. Toward night they saw a herd of ponies feeding on the young grass of the prairie.

"These ponies, Miss Dickey, represent a part of Indian life," said Mr. Oyster.

"How pretty they are! I wish I had one! Will they sell them?"

"I will arrange to secure one for each of you after we arrive at the Mission."

Soon after passing the ponies, they arrived at the Mission, which consisted of three large buildings that had been erected by the Catholic Church. Close at hand were the cabins of the Indians, who were under the care of and instructed by missionaries, representing the Church. The children of the Indians were taught to read and write, and the older members of the tribe were instructed in agricultural and mechanical pursuits.

Our friends had partaken of their lunch on the way under a clump of maple trees, which were putting forth green leaves, while the boughs were profusely hung with blossoming tassels. The air had proven so exhilarating, that the cravings of appetite were felt by the travelers, as they only can be felt on the Western prairies.

Mr. Oyster and Kate had previously visited the place and were acquainted with Isaac McCoy, the missionary, who met them within the enclosure and escorted them to his private dwelling.

To Dickey all was new, she looked upon the Indians with a mingled feeling of pity and awe. The sad and stoical countenances of the women attracted her attention. She thought, "Why do they wear such a gloomy look? Are they thinking of the loss of their country, or their frequent removals at the encroachments of the white men?"

She turned her attention to the men. They were tall and straight, and the majority were handsome, although, like the women, in the stoical expression of their countenances, yet they displayed a native dignity, not so generally beheld among their white brethren.

After supper, Dickey and Kate started out on a voyage of discovery among the huts. Dickey, for the first time, beheld Indians in a half-civilized condition. Some were sitting on the ground, which constituted the floors of their cabins, while they partook of their evening meal; a dozen or more dogs sat in an outer circle, waiting in anxious expectation for their share. The repast consisted of bread made from corn-meal, dried buffalo meat, pemmican and wild onions.

The squaws took great delight in displaying their ornaments of bead-work, which they had in store for the summer market. Dickey purchased a few articles and spoke kindly to them. So seldom had they heard a kind word or observed a sweet smile, that, as she continued to talk, their stoicism relaxed and smiles played upon their faces. One old woman clasped Dickey in her arms, and said: "You so good; heap good;—so good me eat you!"

Dickey patted her cheek and escaped from her kind embrace, at which they all smiled.

The next morning the ponies all came up and stood quietly before the huts, to be handled and petted by the men, women and children, as was their custom.

Dickey embraced this opportunity to examine the ponies closely, and when she had made a selection of a beautiful black one, she indicated her desire to purchase it to Mr. McCoy. He consulted with the Indian owner, who soon came, leading the pony by the lasso. The price demanded was twenty dollars, which she paid.

"I have one selected also, papa," said Kate. "It is a white one. Dickey's is as black as a raven, and mine is as white as snow. I shall call mine 'Swan.' What name have you for yours 'Dickey?'"

"You suggested the name when you spoke of his color. I shall call him 'Raven.'"

Kate asserted her intention of riding "Swan" home. Her father protested. She finally insisted on riding her pony, "just to break it," and without further ceremony, she vaulted upon its bare back, and was soon speeding like the wind on the prairie near the mission.

After Kate's return, the ponies were tied to the wagon, and they started on their return to St. Joseph. At noon, they stopped under the same clump of trees, to eat their lunch, as they had done the day previous. They had finished eating and were arranging their baskets, preparatory to replacing them in the the wagon, when Mr. Oyster said:

"Girls, yonder comes a pedler."

"Where, papa?"

"Yonder on the prairie south of us."

Dickey looked a moment in the direction named; her heart beat rapidly. Approaching Kate, she said: "Let us put on our veils; the sun shines so bright and the wind is rising, we shall become as tawny as the Indians."

Kate assented. They put on their hats and veils, and when drawing on their gloves, they watched the approaching man.

As he came near, Dickey drew herself up to her full height and grasped the pistol which she carried in a side-pocket. If her surmises regarding the man in sight proved correct, the mission on which she came West would soon be accomplished. The man surely was Guy Wren. She could not, at this late hour, attempt to explain to Mr. Oyster. Such a proceeding would require more time than could be commanded, as the man was already very near.

To avoid recognition, she withdrew to the shade of a large tree with her hand still on her pistol, unnoticed by Kate and her father, whose attention was drawn to the pedler.

The man carried a valise in each hand. He appeared too tall for Wren, yet he had the same swaggering movements peculiar to that individual. As he approached and addressed Mr. Oyster, Dickey said to herself, " It certainly is Guy Wren."

CHAPTER XXXII.

RODERICK LELAND.

" ONA gone!" exclaimed Mr. Leland, as he received the letter handed him by Mary on his arrival, one week after it had been entrusted to her care.

He had been riding all day. He was disappointed when he reached home and found none but servants to welcome him.

" When will she return?" asked he.

" I do not know, sir, she told me to do the best I could while she was gone."

Mr. Leland broke the seal and carefully perused the letter. After reading it, he exclaimed, " Just as I anticipated she would do, but she will come out all right. If any one can accomplish anything in that country, I feel assured she can."

He continued, " This is but a beginning. There is much to do, and when considering the vast amount of labor to be performed, the skill to be displayed, the expense to be incurred, and the sympathy to be enlisted, it seems disheartening. Yet, in spite of all opposition, the good work, already begun, must go on ; new fields are to explore, and renewed energy must be manifested."

Mr. Leland became absorbed in the supervision of his farm. He superintended the plowing and inspected the arrangements for planting. Thus two weeks passed, when he received another letter from Ona, containing statements regarding the Oyster family, her meeting with them, and her knowledge of the relationship existing between them and herself, dwelling to considerable length in her remarks about Kate, for whom she imbibed a great liking.

After reading Ona's letter, he mused, " What a strange world is this of ours. We are one moment surrounded by happy friends and joyous associations, the next we are drifting alone upon the ocean of time, surrounded by discontent and misery. Again our friends disappear from view, and we live over our season of lonliness, when those that have been lost, are suddenly and unexpectedly brought to view by the most unlooked-for circumstances."

In the interest of the " Emigrant Aid Society " he had traveled far and near. He had met Arthur Holmes, who had informed him of the success of Hayden and himself in Europe. He was known to all of the leading men of the North. Distinction was not his ambition. With Clay, " He had rather

be right than President." If affairs could become so
shaped, politically, that a true appreciation of right
would be entertained by the Government, he could
then feel that his labor had not been in vain. America
had been the birth-place of liberty, why should she
not become the birth-place of universal freedom."

The Anti-Slavery party was in a growing condition. Thousands of names were being added to its
roll daily. The great heart of the world was beating
in harmony with its principles. Thinking, active
men were flocking to its standard. Coffers were
thrown open to contribute wealth toward its advancement.

The Presidential election of 1848 occurred. The
candidates of the Whig party were elected by a de-
cisive majority. The Free-Soil party failed to receive
an electoral vote, but out of the popular vote, approx-
imating three million, nearly three hundred thousand
ballots were cast for its candidates, developing a most
remarkable gain during four years. Such men as
David Wilmot, of Pennsylvania, were laboring in its
interest. It was through the influence of the old
Anti-Slavery—now the Free-Soil—party that the
amendment known as the "Wilmot Proviso," passed,
which read: "Provided, That there shall be neither
slavery nor involuntary servitude in any Territory
which shall be acquired hereafter or annexed to the
United States."

There were extremes both North and South. Mr.
Leland took a determined stand. He advocated a
free country, free speech and free compensated labor.
His efforts were all turned upon such points. He

said: "Free the women. What! must we always be tyrants? Can we not give our girls the same privileges we extend to our boys? It costs no more to extend to them like opportunities with the boys. Try it, and be assured that our nation will then take precedence over every other nation in the development of Literature, Science, Art and Politics. In all we shall excel. Educate the mothers; extend to them like privileges with their husbands, and intelligence will beam upon the face of our offspring."

In his various addresses it was apparent that his mind was absorbed with the question of "Woman's Right." "I know, said he, "that a favorable consideration of this subject is opposed, bitterly opposed, by all religious denominations. Although claiming to be the followers of the meek and lowly Christ, who gave precedence to women, when he said, 'Remember my mother and my brethren;' yet, in opposition to every principle of right and justice and in violation of the proper consideration of the self-sacrificing devotion of women to the Immaculate Son, and with an utter disregard for her finer sensibilities and keener perceptions, she is entirely ignored in the temporal affairs of the Church, and unless she contribute liberally of her store, she is barred from participating in affairs spiritual. Is it justice? Is it right? I say, no. Open the doors of our colleges; throw wide the portals of our professions and invite her to participate. Elevate and ennoble her who has been heretofore oppressed, and a new star will appear in the constellation, and the intelligence of the world will flock to America, to bask in its lustrous brightness. We have an organization whose object is the freeing of the African, who is held in bondage. Can we be consistent while American women are in thraldom?"

In this strain he had been talking for weeks. Now he was thinking of Ona and her efforts to accomplish the right. She was now engaged in an undertaking which, if successfully accomplished, would proclaim her name over the whole country. While thus musing, a telegram was handed to him.

CHAPTER XXXIII.

CAPTURED.

THE pedler was the first to speak.

"How do you do, sir?" was his salutation, as he approached Mr. Oyster.

"Good morning, sir!" said Mr. Oyster.

"Would you like to purchase some fine jewelry, to-day?"

"No, sir. My girls are too young and I am to old to indulge in ornaments. Why do you not go to the mission?"

"I am on my way there now, how far is it?"

"I do not know, although we came from there this morning," said Mr. Oyster.

"I am very hungry, will you sell me some bread?" asked the pedler.

Mr. Oyster approached the wagon, and removing the basket, placed an excellent repast before the man. While he ate, the girls were taking particular notice and commenting upon his appearance. His hair was uncombed; the condition of his clothing indicated that he had slept without removing them, and his general expression was repulsive.

"This is a bad time for pedlers," said Mr. Oyster.

"Why so?" asked the pedler.

"Because it is not safe for a man to travel alone these days. There was a pedler killed in Cass county a few weeks ago."

"Is that a fact?" replied the man with comparatively little concern.

"It is, and the murderer has not yet been captured or even heard from."

"That's too bad. · Who was he? and who killed him?" asked the pedler.

"The man who was murdered was supposed to be an Eastern man, his name is unknown. The paper stated that the murderer's name was Wren."

"That is bad, indeed," said the man.

Dickey was standing by and had heard the conversation. The last word, "indeed," was spoken so indifferently, that she could restrain herself no longer. Throwing aside her hat and veil, she stood before him with pistol in hand, ready to fire, and said, "Guy Wren, you are my prisoner."

"Don't shoot me, Ona Leland, I am not armed."

"I will not take your word for it," said she. "Mr. Oyster, please search this villain."

Mr. Oyster and Kate had manifested the utmost

surprise at the proceeding of Dickey, but he proceeded to carry out her instructions, and found two revolvers on the person of Wren.

"Whose prisoner am I?" asked Wren.

"Mine, sir," said Dickey. "I have traveled thousands of miles to seek you out for murdering Jasper Brooks, besides being concerned in the death of those two innocent boys. By the most unexpected fortune I have found you and shall immediately convey you to St. Joseph. Were I gifted with your disposition, I would kill you here, without giving you an opportunity to be tried for your crimes." Calling to Mr. Oyster, she said, "Do me the favor to bind him."

That gentleman took one of the rope halters, and binding him securely, placed him in the wagon. He made no effort to escape, any such attempt would have proved futile. He quailed before the eye of that brave girl and her death-dealing weapon.

"I shall ride Swan home and you had better ride Raven," said Kate to Dickey.

"No, I shall ride in the wagon, and any demonstration on the part of this villain to escape, shall meet with summary punishment at my hands," said Dickey.

Mr. Oyster was puzzled at the scene in which he was taking a prominent part. He thought, "Who is this woman, or girl, rather, in whom I have placed so much confidence, and whose commands, I have, without questioning, obeyed? She has deceived me, her name is not Dickey Deane. The prisoner called her Ona Leland; It is a familiar name. Now, I remember, my wife's sister Leona married a man by the name of Leland. Can she be Lena's child?"

He turned and looked Dickey full in the face, she met his gaze, and said, "Uncle, I divine your thoughts, I will tell you all after we reach home."

Mr. Oyster was the more anxious to know who she was, but she would not undertake to satisfy his curiosity, for fear of having her attention drawn from the prisoner, whom she watched closely.

They reached town about sunset, and drove to the court house. Mr. Oyster called the attention of the Sheriff to the prisoner, giving a brief account of who he was, and the crime of which he was accused, adding, "You will detain him until the authorities of Cass county arrive and establish their claim. Here also, are the valuables that he took from the man whom he murdered; they must be taken care of."

"Mr. Sheriff," said Dickey, "This man has on his little finger a ring which belongs to Mrs. Brooks, the wife of the man whom he killed. It was given to her years ago. Will you be so kind as to take care of it for her?"

"What right have you, Miss, to give instructions in this matter," replied the ruffianly Sheriff.

"The right of a citizen of the United States. I have accomplished the arrest of this villain, and if you do not properly discharge your duty, I have the power to hold you accountable."

The Sheriff looked bewildered. "To whom am I talking?" thought he.

Dickey sprang from the wagon, and proceeding to the Clerk's office, she wrote some half-dozen dispatches, which she enclosed in an envelope, together with a check for payment of transmission, and hurrying to the post-office, she forwarded to the telegraph office in St. Louis.

When she returned, she found a large crowd assembled at the wagon who were loudly expressing their belief in the innocence of the accused. The facts being, he had killed a Yankee, and public sentiment being against that class of people, Wren's act was lauded rather than condemned.

Dickey hardly knew what course to pursue. She did not wish to leave her prisoner among men whose sympathy was favorable to him and who approved his crime. Finally, turning to Mr. Oyster, she said, "We will take him to the hotel, and I will guard him until he is cared for by the proper authorities."

Some of the bystanders interposed an objection to such a course.

She drew herself up to her full height and said, "A great and heinous crime has been committed, and now that the criminal has been secured, it seems strange that the proper authorities will cavil at committing him to jail. Although a Yankee may not be, in the estimation of this people, worthy of consideration, or the slayer of such deemed a criminal, yet common decency demands that the forms of legal proceedings, at least, should be carried out. This man is subject to trial in this country, and all I desire is, that he may be securely held for that trial. Proper means failing, I shall myself assume the responsibility of holding him." Saying which, she grasped the lines and drove to the hotel.

Wren was taken to a strong room up-stairs. Dickey asked Mr. Oyster to procure the ring she had spoken of. He entered the room and remained with the prisoner some time. When he came out, he had the ring, which he left in the possession of Dickey, saying:

"Wren says he found this ring. He further says he never murdered Mr. Brooks; that these valises are his own property: he found them in the timber, and the ring was tied to the handle of one of them, and that he never saw you before."

"Mr. Oyster, you heard him address me as Ona Leland. That is my name, "Dickey Deane" being an assumed name. I came here on purpose to search for this rascal. I have known him for ten years." She proceeded to relate facts which had come under her observation regarding Guy Wren as a criminal.

Mr. Oyster looked at her closely, and said: "I believe what you say, every word of it, but you cannot prove it, and I am afraid you cannot establish a case in court without positive proof, and further, if he has any friends, no matter how despicably mean and depraved they are, their evidence will be taken as well as that of the best citizens of the country. In fact, the rougher element predominates here, and officials are elected by that class, and like them, are corrupt. Now, I want to know regarding yourself, Miss Dickey."

Dickey related what she knew regarding her mother, and what she had heard that mother say regarding her sister Ona; how she had married and gone West, and their soon losing trace of her; how she herself was well aware that he was properly her uncle, and Kate her cousin.

"Yes, there is no doubt in my mind," said Oyster, "regarding you being Leona Deane's child. You resemble your Aunt Ona very much. I was at first struck with the likeness. We must establish our claim and keep you with us."

"No, no, I must return home. My only object in coming was to search for Wren. I had intended to stay until I found him. Now that I have discovered my own relatives, I do not propose to ignore them, but shall keep up a correspondence with you through Kate, and in time visit you. Papa will be here before many days, and then I may gain his consent to remain a short time, but my present impressions are that I shall be needed at home."

"Pshaw! pshaw! all these things make no difference to me. You must stay until fall, at least, and probably you'll find some one else to arrest. You are, indeed, a grand-looking officer, especially when you are displaying your revolver, which brought Guy Wren to terms. Why, I verily believe a regiment of ruffians would not frighten you in the least."

"You must not laugh at me, uncle. I am fully determined to do what I deem to be right, if it costs me my life. When I recognized Wren, I at the same-time realized that I could not reach the city and have the proper officers follow with the assurance of his capture, therefore I concluded—with your help, for which I thank you—to undertake it myself."

"You are right, my dear girl, I am proud of you, you are both good and brave." As Kate entered, he continued, "Kate, here is a new cousin for you," at which the kind-hearted girl tenderly clasped

Dickey in her arms, saying, "As a cousin, I do love you, but I was just a little afraid of you, when you arrested that scoundrel with your revolver."

While they were talking, a loud noise was heard on the street in front of the house. Kate looked out of a window and hurriedly returned to her father, saying, "A mob, papa! A mob is coming to release Dickey's prisoner."

CHAPTER XXXIV.

THE TRIAL.

MR. LELAND was surprised when he read: "Come to St. Joseph, I have caught Guy Wren," signed, "Ona, alias Dickey Deane." Ordering his carriage, he was in a brief time on his way to the railroad station. Others in Strawn had received telegrams, and were as promptly on their way. Officials in Cass county had been notified. Thus, from many points people came to St. Joseph. The town was in a state of excitement.

A mob had collected on the first evening of Wren's arrest, some of whom succeeded in entering the house, ere Mr. Oyster became aware of their purpose. Dickey drew her revolver, and standing on the stairway leading to Wren's room, said, "No man passes here alive!" They fully realized that the woman before them would do as her words and looks

indicated she would. Through her boldness they
were the more readily induced to listen to the mild
persuasion of Mr. Oyster. They withdrew one at a
time, feeling mortified, yet giving the Yankee girl
credit for her display of pluck.

" I was afraid," said Kate, after they had gone,
" that papa could not control them, and I verily believe they only pretended to listen to his persuasion,
as a subterfuge to cover the fear of Dickey's
weapon."

Three days passed, before the officials of Cass
county arrived. After consultation, they concluded
to remain until those from a distance arrived. During the time intervening, the Sheriff of Cass county
held frequent interviews with Wren, the nature of
which was unknown, but an after conversation between the same official and Mr. Oyster, was, no
doubt, based upon suggestions from Wren. The
Sheriff said, " Mr. Oyster, I fear there has been a
mistake made here, an innocent man is made to suffer."

To which Mr. Oyster replied, "I know that my
niece cannot be mistaken in the man's identity, she
has known Wren for ten years and recognized him
from a distance."

" I don't dispute his identity, no doubt he is Guy
Wren, yet he may not have killed the pedler," said
the Sheriff."

" She is in possession of a ring taken from Wren,
which she recognizes as having been owned by the
wife of the murdered man, and worn by him when
he left home."

"I don't apprehend that such a statement will be considered proof, as he may have lost or disposed of it, and it accidentally came into Wren's possession. Merely a coincidence."

"I have nothing more to say. I am not the attorney for the State," said Mr. Oyster.

In a short time they were on their way to Harrisonville to attend the trial. Mr. Leland had just arrived, and taking a carriage, accompanied by Kate and Dickey, followed. At her father's suggestion, Dickey had her friends separate, for fear of arousing the animosity of the ruffianly crowd, who zealously watched them. They reached Harrisonville before the Sheriff and Wren did.

The next day, being the one set for the preliminary trial, or examination, was bright and clear. At eight o'clock, an hour before the time set for trial, the court-room was crowded. Among those near the witness stand were Dickey and Kate. Near them sat Mr. Leland and Mr. Brooks, of Strawn. Among others present were Mrs. Crowell, Mrs. Strawn and Dr. Harris.

The Sheriff appeared with the prisoner. The first witness called was Mr. Jones. He testified that the murdered man had stopped with him the night previous to his murder; to Wren's having boarded with him for some time previous; to his leaving the house on that morning before the other men with whom he worked; to his non-appearance on the ground where the men were chopping; to the search instituted for him on the suspicion of his being connected, in some way, with the pedler in tempting negroes to leave

Missouri; of the result of the search in finding the
dead and mangled body of the pedler, and at the
same time finding Wren's hat. He recognized Wren,
also identified the valise as having been in the possession of the pedler when he left his house.

The next witness was the tall, long-necked school
teacher from West Point. He testified that Wren
was at West Point on the morning that the murder
had been committed, and had been there for several
days. He had associated with Mr. Wren a great
deal; had not been separated from him a whole day
during a year, until within the past ten or twelve
days. Wren had always been an honorable, straight-
forward man, and other statements, such as was necessary to establish an alibi.

Dr. Harris was called. He disproved the schoolmaster's evidence by asserting that Wren was in New
York City during the past winter.

Dickey was called and refuted the same point in
the schoolmaster's evidence by repeating her experience with Wren at the Calhoun mansion in South
Carolina during the previous autumn.

Others swore in substance the same as the Arkansas schoolmaster. The examination ended. As the
judge arose, quiet for the first time pervaded the
room. He folded his arms, and in a slow and deliberate tone said: " I have listened with much interest
to the evidence adduced. The statements for and
against have been of the most positive nature. If all
parties concerned were equally well known to the
court, it would, indeed, be difficult to decide, but in
weighing the testimony in this case, certain allow-

ance has to be made for sectional prejudice. Personal considerations also, if permitted, work gross injustice to any party accused. I must say that the evidence tendered, favorable to the defense, is of a character that is beyond question, and the evidence, stripped of prejudicial motives, seems to preponderate in favor of the accused, and permitting all prejudices to remain unnoticed, as I before remarked, it would be difficult to determine in point of preponderance. It is always best, if we err, to err on the side of mercy. Therefore I declare Brother Wren 'not guilty.' "

Never, perhaps, was there such a farce in the way of a trial. Justice did not reign in Western Missouri at that time. The trial of Wren was but a fair sample of trials in that country, in those days. Thanks to progressive civilization, Western Missouri stands to-day the peer of any country in dealing out justice.

During the trial Wren manifested no excitement, not even sufficient to develop an interest. He, no doubt, had reason to judge how the trial would terminate. When dismissed he smiled defiantly at Dickey, who said to herself, " Never mind, Wren, I shall yet bring you to justice."

CHAPTER XXXV.

TWO YEARS OF REST.

MR. LELAND and Mr. Oyster had met but momentarily at St. Joseph, before proceeding to Harrisonville, and had, of course, conversed but little. Now, that the excitement attending the trial was over, and they were on their return to St. Joseph, they occupied the same carriage, leaving Dickey and Kate to follow in a buggy. The first subject of conversation, naturally, was the trial and its result. They agreed upon the weakness of the law, and the injustice of its administration, as had been abundantly exemplified in the recent trial. Thus they continued to talk upon various subjects, seeming at all times jovial and happy; never once touching upon their relationship. Although entertaining for each other the greatest respect, there was an innate dignity existing in each, that held him aloof from manifesting familiarity toward the other.

The old Virginian tracing his genealogy back to the " blue blood " of the English nobility, made no concession to him of the equally as pure blood of Scotland's chieftains, although he was possessed of greater talent and ability than could be boasted of by him, whose ancestry alone was his pride.

A happier couple were pursuing the same road, in the persons of Dickey and Kate, who by nature was an excellent girl. Her few faults had been eradicated in early life through the watchful care of her father. She was of a kind and loving disposition, and having become greatly attached to Dickey, was using her greatest effort to induce her to remain with them during the summer.

She said, "Why not remain with us? We will have a grand time riding our ponies over the praries."

"I can not determine as to the course I shall pursue. I can more properly, arrive at a conclusion after we reach home and consult with papa."

"Cousin, must I always call you Dickey?"

"For the present, you must, I have a great work before me, its nature I cannot even impart to you, in fact, I have not, as yet, fully developed my plans, neither have I fully comprehended its magnitude, but whatever I accomplish toward that work, I desire to do under the name of Dickey Deane, though my proper name is Ona Leland."

"Why did you assume that name, cousin?"

"I presume the idea of an assumed name was, at first, merely a whim, and in selecting one I chose Deane, on account of its being my mother's family name and having heard papa laugh so much about his family nick-naming him 'Dickey' when he was a child. I concluded to blend the two. Hence the sobriquet 'Dickey Deane.'"

"Won't you tell me what you *expect* to accomplish, Dickey?"

"No, I cannot. It is to be developed in the future, and our Heavenly Father alone knows whether or not it will be successful. It may prove to be all in vain. I am under no restraint in the matter. I am free in all things to do as I please. I can either continue to progress in the work, or withdraw from it at my pleasure. I choose the former."

"I don't want to be free. I would rather remain at home, petting the chickens and calves, than doing for myself," said Kate.

Dickey had observed the peculiar fondness of Kate for fowls and animals, and on their arrival home, half an hour before sundown, Kate's first thought and attention was given to her dumb, yet appreciative pets.

After Dickey had laid aside her traveling wraps, Kate asked her if she would go and see Swan and Raven. They were soon at the stable door. Kate ran in, and patting Swan on the neck, jumped on and cantered out of the stable. Returning in a few minutes, she asked Dickey:

"Now, don't you want to mount Raven and have a ride?"

"No," said Dickey, "I will not undertake to ride him without a saddle."

"May I ride him?" asked Kate.

"Why, of course. Whenever you wish to, you may."

Soon Kate had mounted Raven and put him through the same maneuver, to the great delight of Dickey, who exclaimed:

"Cousin Kate, you would be a good circus-rider."

"No, indeed, I don't like that name, nor their way of doing. They are too cruel to their horses and ponies. Won't you get a saddle to-morrow and go with me for a ride?"

"I will determine by to-morrow what I shall do. If I go home with papa, I shall not need a saddle until I return."

Kate fed the ponies some oats, and turning to Dickey, said:

"This is the way you must pet these Indian ponies, if you want them to be gentle. They know their friends," and she proceeded to fondle their heads, comb their manes with her fingers and pat them, all the while talking kindly to them. "Now you come in and approach one of them and see what it will do."

Dickey approached Swan, and it laid back its ears, snapped its teeth, stamped its foot on the ground and looked angrily at her.

"Now, Cousin Dickey, you see what I told you is true. They don't like strangers."

"Why, Kate, are you not a stranger?" asked Dickey, in surprise.

"No," said Kate, laughing. "Before we went away, I was here so often—every morning before you were up,—and I fed them and I shall continue to feed them, and, of course, they recognize me as a friend."

Dickey had been a teacher and had instructed children, but she had learned several lessons from Kate Oyster of a different nature. She had always been kind in her consideration and treatment of brutes, but she had never succeeded in teaching them to love her, as these did Kate. Here every calf, pig and chicken about the premises would permit her to fondle and play with it.

As they walked to the house, Dickey resolved to rise early in the morning and cultivate the acquaintance of Kate's pets and observe her manner toward them.

Although she was out early the next morning, Kate was out before she was, and was deeply interested feeding her chickens, which clustered around her, while the pigeons were perched upon her shoulders, cooing for their share. When she observed Dickey, she said, " Good morning, cousin, I am glad you have come, we will now go and feed the ponies. You see I am feeding them corn, they are not accustomed to it. The Indians feed them only hay, but after they begin to relish grain, they thrive better and become more beautiful."

Hastening to the house, they ensconced themselves in the parlor where they talked of their pets until Dickey's attention was called to an oil painting, a portrait which she had not heretofore noticed. Kate, observing her, said:

" That is mamma's picture. I have frequently thought you resemble her so much. You will observe it was taken when she was young. O! come to think, I really believe I saw your picture once, I almost know I did. I was looking at mamma's picture one day, when a young man who was stopping with us, exclaimed, ' I have a picture just like that,' and taking a daguerreotype from his pocket, we compared them, and sure enough, they, in expression of countenance, were alike."

" Do you remember the young man's name?" asked Dickey, experiencing a throbbing sensation at

13

the heart. Strange that such feeling should permeate the heart of one who had never acknowledged that "love" had occupied her inmost thoughts.

"His name is Strawn, Walter Strawn, I saw him at H——— when we attended Wren's trial. You should become acquainted with him."

Without deigning a reply, Dickey approached the piano where she stood a moment, fingering the keys. Turning quickly, she said, "Kate, favor me with your morning song before breakfast to-day, will you?"

Kate seated herself at the piano, saying, "I will sing my dear old song," and tears gathered in her eyes as she bent over the instrument and sang:

> "I've no mother now, I'm weeping,
> She has left me here alone,
> She beneath the sod is sleeping
> And all joy from home has flown."

Never did the rendering of a song touch the heart of Dickey as did this one. She had heard it many times, but it had never seemed as touching as now.

At breakfast Mr. Leland and Mr. Crowell expressed their intention of returning home immediately. Mr. Leland, at the earnest solicitation of Kate, consented that Dickey could remain with them until autumn.

She passed the summer pleasantly in instructing Kate and practicing horse-back riding. She became much attached to Raven, and every morning she spent considerable time in the stable petting him.

She made, with Kate, several visits to the Indian Mission, and became thoroughly acquainted with the Indians and their ways. Late in the autumn she went home, accompanied by Mr. Oyster and Kate.

The former to remain a month or two at Cedar Hall, while Kate would not leave there before spring. Mr. Oyster returned West at the appointed time, and the following May, Kate and Dickey parted, after a most enjoyable winter.

CHAPTER XXXVI.

KANSAS TERRITORY ORGANIZED.

ON Mr. Leland's return from Missouri, he publicly expressed his disgust with the manner in which the people of that state executed their laws, and to members of the " Free-Soil " party he spoke forcibly, regarding the sectional prejudice which prevailed in the West.

Two years passed. The Democratic party had gained the ascendency, and under Mr. Pierce's administration the bill had passed organizing the territories of Kansas and Nebraska.

Previous to the final organization, the Government had purchased such parts as were held by the Indians, and provided them with a temporary reservation, pending the organization of the Indian Territory, farther south, where they finally removed.

This action on the part of the Government, at once threw Kansas and Nebraska open to settlement by the whites. Mr. Leland and his brethren were not asleep. Day after day they sought out families who were willing to emigrate to the West. Kansas became the great attraction, it was more fertile, its climate so delightful. But before action could be taken by Free-Soil men, the people living on the border passed from Missouri into Kansas, and selecting the best locations, put their marks upon them, hoping in this manner to establish their rights to such lands under the "pre-emption laws," the real object being to organize and hold the Territory in the interest of Slavery. But few of them removed to Kansas, or had a desire or intention of so doing.

When the news reached them of what was being accomplished by the Free-Soil party in the New England states, the Pro-Slavery party in Western Missouri determined to prevent, by fair or foul means, the Eastern people from making settlements in the Territory, and seeing that the lands were not being promptly taken by their own friends, they, in July 1854, called a meeting at Weston, Missouri, where it was resolved, "That all persons taking part in this meeting, shall and will, whenever called upon by the citizens of Kansas Territory, promptly respond, and ever hold themselves in readiness to remove all persons now in that Territory under the auspices of the Northern Emigrant Societies, and to resist the entrance of others, under the same auspices."

John Brown and Hayden Douglas were traveling in Missouri at the time, and attended the meeting, listened to the inflammatory speeches and heard the above resolution. In a few days letters were on their way to the leaders of the Free-Soil party, apprising them of what they had to contend with.

The first party sent out by the New England Aid Society, arrived at a point on the Kaw river, near the middle of July and located, and began erecting buildings for a town which they named Lawrence, in honor of Amos A. Lawrence, of Boston. Near the last of the same month, they were joined by another party of emigrants, numbering about seventy, and the work of founding their town was pushed forward with renewed energy. They were all honest, hard-working, God-fearing men and women, and were determined in the efforts to succeed in their undertaking.

They were in legal and peaceable possession of their land and had molested no one.

Among these settlers were some of our former acquaintances, Mr. Brooks and his family. He had been engaged in the dry goods business, and had brought a stock of goods with him. Visitors were arriving daily. To accommodate them, a large sod house was built by the settlers, afterward known as the "Pioneer House." Among the boarders were Sir Richard Burns and Pat Devlin, Arthur Holmes, Hayden Douglas and his companion, "The Mysterious Englishman." The only name by which they were known in the West was, "Hayden and his companion." No time was ever lost in ascertaining particulars. If a man was—to use a phrase peculiar to the times—"right on the goose," he was "all right." It made no difference whether he had a name or not.

All went well until one day Pat rode hurriedly into town, announcing that a crowd of drunken men were approaching.

"Are they armed, Pat?" asked some one.

"Yes, they have weapons all around them."

The settlers had been abundantly supplied with arms and ammunition before leaving the East, and as soon as the alarm was given a tap on a large bass drum called the men to arms. They formed in rank behind the tents and houses to drill. The sentinel observed in the distance three men approaching, riding slowly. As they drew near, he discovered that they were heavily armed, and he raised his gun as if to fire.

CHAPTER XXXVII.

AT OSAWATOMIE.

MR. LELAND left New York City for the West in company of a dozen or more families, his own among the number. They did not stop at Lawrence, but proceeded further south down the border, their object being to establish a town, so as to prevent the Missourians from taking possession of the "Border-tier Lands." They crossed a beautiful stream, called by the French "River of Swans." It to-day bears the same name, expressed in the French tongue, *"Marias des Cygnes."*

On the south bank of this beautiful stream they pitched their tents and began building a town, which they named Osawatomie. The Marias des Cygnes river being frequently called the "Osage," and one of its branches the "Potawatomie," the town name was compiled from these two names.

The settlers had brought provisions and building material from the then hamlet of Kansas City, in Missouri, on the Missouri river, forty miles distant. These were hauled through by teams of oxen, or horses, as the case might be. Most of these settlers were wealthy men. They and their families were intelligent and highly educated persons, who were endeavoring to overcome oppression, and for the accomplishment of their object they were willing to sacrifice comfort and comfortable surroundings.

Mr. Leland and his family occupied a tent, as did the balance of the families. His purpose was not to make it his permanent home, but merely by his presence to encourage others and assist personally in building up and protecting the town. Robie hauled lumber from the river landing at Kansas City. Ona, still known as Dickey, acted as baker and baked the bread for most of the families. Every evening she rode her pet pony Raven after the cows that grazed on the prairie.

Early in the spring of 1855, four men and their families came from Illinois, where they had spent the winter, having started from Ohio the previous autumn. On account of their being Free-States men, they were frequently insulted openly as they passed through Missouri. They took claims about eight miles west of Osawatomie, and immediately began work, as peaceable citizens should, in building their cabins and improving their land. They had horses and cattle in abundance, and never did a more quiet people settle down on the fertile prairies of Kansas than were those brothers, sons of a man whose name is inscribed high upon the Temple of Fame.

Dickey often rode out and spent the day with those freedom-loving people. One day she received a letter from Mr. Leland, who had gone East to solicit aid. He had met John Brown at a meeting. The old man had asked for money and arms to supply emigrants. It had been granted. Some time afterward he reached Osawatomie and built his cabin near his sons. Mr. Leland soon followed, bringing funds for the erection of public buildings for the use of the Free-States men.

One bright night, as Dickey was sitting just inside of the open door, two men passed near. She heard one of them say, " Come to that large post-oak tomorrow evening about this time and I will be there, and I know Guy will."

She held her breath, lest they should discover her presence. Not until their footsteps had died away, did she move. The next day she prepared a suit of men's clothes, and as night approached, she donned them, and slipping out of the back door, she sought the shelter of the bushes near the house and stealthily moved toward the large post-oak tree.

Strangers had been in the settlement for several days. She had overheard some of them making remarks derogatory to the Free-States men, and had suggested that they be watched, and when she learned of the meeting at the post-oak, she was fully confirmed in her suspicions, and determined, if pos-

sible, to learn the nature of that secret meeting. So
she crept to the spot indicated, more than half a mile
from her home. She nestled down in the grass under
the bushes near the tree to await the coming of the
men.

· From this little circumstance she took the name of
"The Spy of Osawatomie," which appellation she
held until Slavery was extinct. She had just settled
down quietly, when a horseman came riding up from
the west and stopped near where she was secreted.
He dismounted and tied his horse. Owing to the
darkness, she could not discern his features.

After the lapse of an half-hour another person approached on foot, soon he greeted the first one with
"All right? Field clear?" to which he answered,
"Yes," and coming nearer, they shook hands and
talked on general subjects for an hour, when the third
one arrived. The moon had risen, Dickey could
plainly see them.

CHAPTER XXXVIII.

AT LAWRENCE.

THE sentinel who watched the approach of the
Missourians, was Hayden Douglas. He held
his Sharpe's rifle in readiness to fire. They
had almost stopped, when they beheld Hayden's defiant look and attitude.

" Halt ! " said he.   " What do you want ? "

One of them advanced and said, " We, the rightful citizens of this Territory, are sent by a company
of a few hundred of our fellow-citizens, to inform
you Yankees, that you must leave this place and return East, in one day, or you will be assisted in so
doing, by us, the rightful citizens."

Hayden recognized one of the trio.   It was Guy
Wren.   He looked steadily at Hayden, but said not
a word.   During the conversation which followed,
he was not idle.   His eyes were noting the plan of
the new town, and he saw, west of the town, men
with their Sharpe's rifles and bayonets drilling.

" Yes, I understand what you say," answered Hayden.   " When you establish the fact that we are tres-
passing upon your lawful or rightful possessions, then
we will remove to some other part, but not until
then."

They turned and rode off toward their camp,
where they were received with applause.   When
they reported the result of their observations and
that there were men in that settlement who had been
in trouble with Guy Wren in the East, and that there
were thousands of men, in marching array, in the
town, they quietly " pulled up stakes," and returned
to Missouri.

Some of the boldest leaders went South to enlist
recruits for the border war, and by the last of
autumn, 1855, thousands of criminals had been taken
from the prisons and penitentiaries and enrolled in
the ranks of that " Army of the Border."

Guy Wren commanded a company of some two

or three hundred, who, for over a year, made the
western border of Missouri their homes. Every little village and town had a portion of them to main-
tain, while they lent a protecting hand to the Pro-
Slavery settlers in Kansas, who arrived slowly, as
compared with the Free-States men. Guy Wren was
stationed at H——, C—— county, Missouri, and it
was his duty, assisted by his drunken men, to examine every family that passed near that point on their
way to Kansas. If any weapons were found, they
were confiscated, and the emigrants commanded to
return East, under penalty of death.

For such reasons, thousands of emigrants came to
Kansas through Iowa and Nebraska, in order to avoid
the ruffians stationed on the Missouri border.
Among those who came by that route was John
Brown, with provisions and arms, which had been
contributed by prominent Free-States men, and collected at meetings during the summer of 1855.

One year had passed since the settlement of Lawrence, and it had grown to be a beautiful, thriving
town. Hayden and his companion were still among
the visitors. The old gentleman had nothing, apparently, to do, except to spend time, but Hayden
had been, and still was, ever on the alert, watching
the movements of the border ruffians by scouting
in the eastern part of the Territory.

While on one of his excursions south, toward Osawatomie, riding slowly, admiring the beauties of nature, which had been bestowed with a lavish hand,
his attention was directed to an object in the distance, which, by the aid of his glass, he made out to

be a horseman ; whether friend or foe, white man or Indian, he could not determine.

Seeing none but the solitary horseman, he pushed on to meet him, feeling able to cope, successfully, with any person, one-handed. After some time had elapsed, as he was riding up a slope, leading to the crest of a "divide," he beheld the head-gear of the opposing horseman approaching the same crest from the other side. While but a few paces apart, he drew his revolver, exclaiming in the usual salutation of the border, "Free-State or Pro-Slavery ?" when a low, sweet and melodious voice answered, " I am lost, please tell me the way to Lawrence ?"

" This is the trail leading to Lawrence," answered Hayden, as he approached, when the stranger uttered a joyful cry of recognition.

CHAPTER XXXIX.

THE PLOT.

"HALLO ! old fellow," cried number three, as he approached the oak tree, followed by, "By jing, Wren, are you here ?"

" Yes, I came down from Dutch Henry's crossing, to-night."

" What's the voice up there to-day ?"

" They say for us to come and take Brown's horses and cattle, some night this week."

" What will we do with them ?" asked the other.

" Why, send them to Missouri, to feed and equip our soldiers with, of course."

" Can it be done this week ?"

" Yes, it can."

" I don't think we have men enough for that, until we can send to. Missouri."

" Yes, we have, Wren, them Dutchmen up at the crossing, will help us, and there are two or three here in town, that are only waiting for a chance to pop over old Leland or any of these low-down Yankee trash."

" Well," said Wren, " we must, then, begin now to make our plans, so as to be ready to strike here, at the same time Pate does, at Lawrence."

" Ain't you going to help take Lawrence, Wren ?"

" No, I've been there and saw some I once knew in New Hampshire, and I won't risk myself there. My company are made up of criminals from South Carolina, and they are ready for any kind of work. That's why I came over here, to see if there was any one to be put out of the way. And when we do come, we want to take all the stock, for it is too hard for the citizens along the line in Missouri to feed our men so long, if it is nothing but corn-bread and bacon. We must take all we can get."

" You are right, Wren. What day must we look for you ? "

" Friday night, if we have no bad luck. Martin White said he would guide us in from Miami Mission on that night, and Capt. Pate is going to Lawrence when we strike here, so as to weaken both places at the sametime.   I will have to let him know when I am ready.   This is Monday.   I will have to go to Westport and see him, and then to West Point to see Capt. Hall, and then go back to Harrisonville.   They say these Brown boys have plenty of arms and a store of ammunition, which the old man sent them. It will pay to take them in.   By the way, did you hear of the Kickapoo's raid?"

"No, what did they do?"

"They went in for the arms at St. Joe, and took all they wanted one night."

"Did they arrest any of them?   What did they do with them?"

"Old Oyster got on his ear and said they were the ones who stole them, and that they had been put up to it.   He said he believed in slavery, but there was no use carrying anything so far.   They knew it was all right with the officers, so they let old Oyster howl it out, and a week ago last night they took Kate's pony. Kate is his youngest girl—about sixteen years old. The pony was snow-white.   You bet he is pouting about it, but that's the way to keep them under."

"By the by, Wren, have you any good doctor down with you?"

"I don't know as there is.   Why, Bill?"

"We must have one here in the place of Strawn. He is a good enough doctor, but he is an abolitionist, and when we scoop 'em in he'll have to go with the rest.   Listen! I hear some one coming on horseback.   I think we had better hide. Come this way."

They whispered a moment, and soon they were crouching on the ground near Dickey.   She could hear their quick breathing. The midnight rider came hurrying on. Wren's horse was hitched in the bushes; it neighed loudly as the horseman approached.

"Now, if that devil takes my horse?" growled Wren, the same growl that Dickey had heard before.

But the lone rider passed on, taking no notice of the horse in the bushes.

"That was Dr. Strawn, going to see my oldest boy," said one. "He is quite sick, and the doctor could not come to-day, but sent word he would come to-night. He is a kind-hearted man, always ready to do good."

"That makes no difference," said one of the others. "He goes when the others go. The right way is to topple some of them over in the ditch, and that will frighten the rest."

"Wren, who do you intend killing?" asked one of the others.

"Those Browns and some half-dozen others, whose names I don't remember. Most too sultry in here. Let's get out, so we can get our breath"

They crept out under the bushes. One came near tramping on Dickey. She trembled, for fear they would find her. They soon separated after they reached the road, promising to meet Wren Friday night at the VanHorn ford.

Waiting until all was silent, Dickey crept out, to find the coast clear, and going toward home, she soon reached the house. She seated herself upon the steps, waiting for Dr. Strawn to return. Presently she heard him coming from the west. As he

approached, he stopped, saying in an undertone,
" Who is there ?"

" Dickey Deane," said she, in the same suppressed
tone, and continued, by asking, " Where have you
been, Doctor?"

"Why do you ask me that?" said he, rather
loudly.

·'Speak lower," said she,- coming nearer, and in a
low tone told him all.

" I will go," said he, "and stir the men up, so as to
be ready.   Some one must go to Franklin, and some
one to Lawrence.   We must be very quiet, not a
child must know of this.   I will see you at sunrise."

"Come just at day-break, for I shall ride, yet to-
night, to see the Brown's," said she.

Dickey strapped a blanket on Raven and donned
a heavy coat of her father's, and a hat of Robie's,
and was soon riding on her way to the Potawatomie
settlement.

Alone in the bright moonlight that young girl rode,
thinking of what she had heard.   Her heart bounded within her, and her pulse beat faster, as her mind
dwelt upon the scenes about to be enacted.   Bloody,
cruel war and rapine was about to desecrate and
make desolate the happy homes of honest settlers.
Many who had forsaken homes of comfort to establish this fair, young State upon a basis of freedom,
were to be mercilessly butchered in their beds, or
cut down upon the streets.   Criminals and demons
had been let loose by legal authority, upon condition
that they would still further darken their hands with
blood, and blacken their hearts with crime.   As she

thought of the injustice following such a course, she lifted her eyes to heaven, and in agony of soul calmly prayed, " O, God ! Thou who rulest immensity ; Thou, who noteth the fall of the sparrow ; Thou, who art omnific, omniscient, omnipresent and omnipotent ; in trouble, as well as in comfort, in sorrow as in joy, we come to Thee, asking, pleading and entreating, that Thou will grant us strength, to endure the affliction which now bears so heavily upon us. If it be Thy will, remove this cup of bitterness we now imbibe. Thou knowest our devotion to Thy cause. Teach us to rely implicitly upon Thy promises. Give us strength to endure the suffering imposed upon us, knowing that Thou chasteneth whom Thou lovest. May this, Thy own fair land, be possessed by honorable, God-fearing people. May the crime of Slavery never sully the fair fame of this beautiful land."

Ere she was aware, she found herself near the home of Jason Brown ; riding up she called in an undertone. She heard no response. She called again in a louder tone. Mrs. Brown came to the door. Dickey said:

" I desire to see Mr. Brown. Tell him I am a friend."

Jason Brown came to the door, revolver in hand. He had heard the first summons, and not knowing whether the person was friend or foe, he prepared himself for any emergency that might arise. When he approached, Dickey made herself and her errand known. When they separated, it was with the understanding, that Jason should carry the information

14

to Fay, Jones and others living in that neighborhood.

Just at daybreak, Dickey arrived home. Removing the blankets which had served for a saddle, she led Raven to the stable and fed him. Entering the house, she procured a suit of Robie's clothes, of a dark color, which she substituted for those she had worn, which were damp.

Just as the faint rays of approaching day glimmered through the timber, a horseman approached from the south part of the village. As he drew near, she said in an undertone, " I am ready."

" So I observe," said Dr. Strawn.

She brought Raven from the stable and sprang lightly upon his back.

" I went to Middle Creek last night. They will be ready," said he.

" I went to Potawatomie and gave them warning. They are on the alert," said she, and turning, rode west, until they reached the ford, where they crossed the Marias des Cygnes river.

CHAPTER XL.

HAYDEN'S SURPRISE.

NEVER was any one so surprised as was Hayden when the stranger burst out in the joyous laugh.

" Dickey Deane," exclaimed he, " what are you doing here?"

"You were the last person I expected to meet," said Dickey, for it was she.

Briefly she told him of what she had heard and what had been already done in the way of warning the settlers, and advised him to hasten to Franklin, thence to Lawrence.

"It would seem ungallant to permit you to return without an escort. Had I not better return with you?" asked Hayden.

"No, no, under the circumstances formalities must be laid aside, in order to deal promptly with things that require immediate attention. Although, Mr. Douglas, I must not accept your kind offer, yet I thank you sincerely for your consideration."

Each sent by the other kindly messages to friends in either settlement, and bidding each other adieu, they retraced their steps.

After Dr. Strawn left her, she pursued her way through the brush, from which she was about to emerge, when she heard a horse approaching rapidly. She drew Raven into the thicket, which was dense on either side of the path. As the horse passed, she noticed that he carried none other than the cruel and notorious Guy Wren. He turned not his head as his horse shied, when he passed the thicket where Dickey was concealed, gently patting Raven to keep him quiet.

After she parted with Hayden, she remembered that she had made no provision to supply the demands of appetite. Feeling hungry, she left the trail to procure a meal at a log-house not far away. She ascertained that the proprietor was away with the "boys," as his loquacious spouse denominated the Pro-Slavery men. Dickey being clad in boy's habiliments, personated a Missouri school teacher. Her hostess had many words of censure for "Free-Soilers," and commendatory ones for Pro-Slavery men, in which Dickey acquiesced. She had just returned from the river landing at Kansas City, and had learned that "We'uns are jist about all set to wipe out Lawrence and the hull raft of settlements whar' the darned Yankees have squatted, and I'm afeared we'uns 'ill have it kinder nip and tuck at Lawrence, 'kase ther's a hull God's-pacel on 'em thar'."

At this juncture she announced dinner by saying, "Wal, stranger, yer dinner's ready, square yer cheer 'round to the table now. We haint got nothin' much for nobody to eat, nohow, but I recken you kin stand it fur onst, if we'uns make out to live on't."

Dickey seated herself at the table which had no cloth spread on it. The food was good and very well cooked, and the coffee was splendid.

"John Andrew, run to them air oxen, at onst, an' see what on airth is ailen on em, hurry up, or I'll bust yer crust fur you, this very minit. Move, d'ye hear me," screamed the woman.

Dickey ate her dinner in silence, and when she was through, paid the sum demanded. Strapping the blankets on Raven, she was soon hastening toward Osawatomie, thinking of the peculiarities of nature improperly trained, as was exemplified in the case of the woman she had just left. A rough, rude woman, who made a practice of driving three yoke of oxen, and who could swear before her children, even cursing them for little inattentions peculiar to children.

Having reached the Marias des Cygne, she waited until darkness threw her mantle of blackness over the earth, hoping thus to avoid observation in her unusual apparel, she quietly rode to her home.

CHAPTER XLI.

DICKEY AT WORK.

WHEN Hayden left Dickey, he hastened to Franklin and notified the citizens of that settlement. They soon secreted their goods and hastened to Lawrence. A preacher, by the name of Martin White, had been conducting a meeting in the settlement. When he heard Hayden's announcement, he expressed his determination to hasten to his home near Osawatomie, but instead of so doing, he hurried to Westport, where he found Capt. Pate, and informed him that the whole plot had been discovered.

When the news reached Wren and his men, they became terribly enraged, fearing that they had a traitor among them. No one had been in Kansas lately except Wren, and he was known to be true to the cause he had espoused. They knew nothing of the little New Hampshire girl who had declared vengeance upon Wren, years ago, when a mere child, listening to Aunt Nancy's story of her wrongs and suffering.

Now destiny had made them workers in the same field, but with opposite purposes. He to tear down and destroy, to lead criminals and felons to greater crimes for the perpetuation of a curse that long had been a blight to American civilization. She working earnestly and zealously to establish the beginning of the extinction of that curse from our fair land. To him immediate excitement was necessary. He had neither principle nor property at stake individually, but there was a promise of an opportunity to wrong his fellow beings, to indulge in his unholy desire for crime; voracity existed in his corrupt mind, and he could not withhold the insatiate greed that ever governed his actions.

She made sacrifice of comfort, left the society of friends, devoted her energies and lavished her wealth for a principle—a principle involved in the glorious declaration which freed the Colonies from the oppression of a mother country; a principle which had established the American people upon a basis broad and expansive as the earth itself; a principle which, for height, reached high as heaven and brought smiles to the faces of angels as they rejoiced in the advancement of mankind—the principle that all men are created "free and equal."

When Dickey reached home, she called Robert, who cared for Raven while she entered the house and sought the repose that tired nature demanded. She remained quiet until Friday afternoon, when she

donned her peculiar costume, and walking through
the bushes, reached the VanHorn ford, where she
removed her shoes and crossed the stream. Scarcely
had she reached the opposite bank, when she heard
the sound of approaching horses as she sat in a
densely tangled thicket. They came near. She
discovered one to be the villainous Wren. The
other was a stranger. After crossing the river, they
took the road leading to Dutch Henry's crossing, on
the Potawatomie.

Being satisfied in her own mind, she returned to
the town and told what she had seen, and volunteered an opinion that no attack would be made, else
Wren would not come without his men, but for fear
others would come after night set in, a strong guard
was placed at the ford, to watch during the night.

Valuables, clothing and bedding belonging to citizens, were secreted in the dense thickets which surrounded the town. None slept during the night.
Morning dawned bright and clear. The watch was
kept up at the ford. Wren and his companions re-
crossed on their return. No attack was made. The
ruffians did not consider their number sufficiently
great to cope with the settlers, of whom there were
scarcely one hundred, while the Pro-Slavery band
was known to be over fifteen hundred.

During the summer, emigrants had poured into
Kansas, principally by the Nebraska route, and Osawatomie had received·many accessions to its numbers. Dickey spent considerable time in Missouri,
visiting Kate Oyster and noting the movements of
the Border Ruffians. She ascertained that it was

their intention to utterly annihilate the entire number of Free-Soil settlements in Kansas during the coming autumn.

When she had gained all the information she could, she returned to Osawatomie, where she made known to the principal men what she had learned. Each town, acting under instruction of its acknowledged leader, appointed guards to watch day and night for any demonstration the Border Ruffians might make. Dickey volunteered to act as spy. Leaving Osawatomie, she reached Missouri, where, clad in man's apparel, she passed as a school teacher hailing from South Carolina, having been sent West by Mr. Calhoun, showing Lillie's daguerrotype, with her name and residence engraved upon the case.

She had dyed her hair black and assumed the name of Dick Richards. Soon, by her easy manner, fluent address and her many accomplishments, she had charge of a school, made up of children of the first families of Westport. Although, ostensibly, a teacher, yet she closely observed all that was transpiring around her, keeping a record of sayings and occurrences during the day, she sent, nightly, a letter to a friend in Osawatomie, through the mail to Harrisonville, where it would be taken by some neighbor who was there trading.

Everything went on pleasantly, until, one day, on which Dickey had dismissed school on account of a feeling of indisposition, which she had experienced for several days, a horseman galloped through town, calling out to the citizens to prepare for a raid into Kansas. Now realizing that her sickness was "all for the best," she announced her intention of going to Harrisonville to procure medicine. She accordingly took the stage and reached town about ten o'clock at night. Going to a stable for a horse, she observed Kate's white pony that had been stolen in St. Joseph. She asked to hire it to ride out to the "old man's," as she expressed it.

Procuring the pony, she was soon hastening toward Kansas. Before daybreak she crossed the State line, having had no trouble in crossing the streams, the weather having been very dry and the water low. Reaching Osawatomie while the citizens were at dinner, she alighted from her pony, and rang the large bell, which had been provided and was to be rung only as a warning of danger, at which all the men were to assemble.

Leaving the men to evolve their own plans, based upon the information she had brought, she took Raven and hastened to the Potawatomie settlement, where she found old John Brown, lion-hearted, and his equally brave boys, at dinner. Soon after she had imparted her information, they were on their way to Lawrence. They had already suffered the loss of much stock at the hands of the Border Ruffians, and, like all honest men, they were ever ready to lend a helping hand to prevent further depredations.

Although Dickey's inclinations and desires were to accompany the settlers to Lawrence, and aid them in their efforts, yet she fully realized, that in order to continue her espoinage over the Pro-Slavery factions, she must immediately return to Missouri. To be

away from there at such a time, would attract attention, and suspicion against her would naturally follow. She was soon ready to start. Taking Raven
and sufficient money to pay for Swan, she rode brisk-
ly away.

The men of Osawatomie, under the leadership of
Arthur Holmes, had determined to assist in the defense of Lawrence, and soon departed for that place.
Thus in a brief time nearly five hundred citizens from
all parts of the Territory, had assembled at Lawrence,
that being the objective point of attack. A special
animosity existed in the minds of the leaders of the
Border Ruffians against this place, and every effort
was made, on their part, to overcome the settlers and
utterly destroy the town.

About ten o'clock great excitement and rejoicing
prevailed among those assembled at Lawrence, which
was caused by the appearance of "Old John Brown"
and four of his boys. As they stopped in front of
the hotel, a deafening shout rent the air from the
crowd assembled around the wagon, many of whom
had followed the wagon down the street, attracted
by the unusual display of fire-arms it contained, each
man being abundantly supplied with rifles, revolvers
and sabers, besides there being many poles, on which
were fastened bayonets.

At that time John Brown was not generally known
to the settlers, yet as he sprang from the wagon, a
voice in the crowd shouted, "Here is our Captain,
whoever he may be." Acting upon the suggestion
the remark conveyed, a company was promptly organized, of which Brown was placed in command.

Captain Brown immediately proposed that an attack should be made upon the enemy that night and surprise them in their camp near Franklin. He, with a dozen men, even went so far as to make a start in that direction—"to draw a little blood in the cause of 'Universal Freedom,'" as he expressed it, but at the earnest solicitation of General Lane, he returned to the town, chafing under the restraint.

Gen. Lane sent for him to participate in a council of war. The old hero replied, " *Tell the General that when he wants me to fight, to say so; that is the only order I will obey.*"

John Brown, ever afterward, regretted that he complied with Jim Lane's request at that time. He said: "Many a man's life I would have saved to after time, had I pounced upon them at Franklin." But the opportunity had passed, and he must bide his time.

Peace was at last established by Gov. Shannon —peace upon the principle which declared "Equal rights to all," which the Pro-Slavery element soon perverted to " *Southern* rights to all."

Brown and his men returned to their homes, disgusted with the terms upon which "Peace" had been declared.

Among those who, in like disgust at the proceedings of the "Peacemakers" left Lawrence, were Hayden Douglas and his old "companion." They united their fortunes with Brown and his determined band. A feeling of respect, of admiration and almost adoration existed in the minds of all who were associated with or had ever studied the character of the brave, freedom-loving old man.   Thus often in times of adversity, attachments and friendships are formed and cemented, which death alone can sever. So it had been with Hayden and his companion in espousing the cause of Freedom and forming the acquaintance of the champions of that cause.

These two companions of "Osawatomie Brown" survived him sufficiently long to see the principle for which he died promulgated throughout the land.   It was accomplished ere they laid aside the spy-glass and rifle which the old hero had placed in their hands.

Although peace had been declared, yet, when the invaders withdrew, it was with the determination existing in the minds of their leaders, that ere spring Kansas should be purged of the Free-Soil element that existed within its borders, and for the furtherance of such plan, frequent raids were made upon the settlers, carrying off horses, cattle and provisions, and killing two men, who refused to open their doors to them.   Many families were thus left to suffer from hunger and exposure, all their effects having been carried away by the " Legal settlers from Georgia," as they termed themselves.   The care of persons thus conditioned by "Southern rights to all," was assumed by friends in the Free-Soil party.

Hayden and his companion made themselves useful in their new home, the cabin of Brown, intending to return to Lawrence in the spring.   One day, as Hayden and two of Brown's sons were hauling wood, they were surprised by a dozen men who demanded their arms, to which demand they were forced to sub-

JOHN BROWN'S CABIN.

mit. They bound their hands together, the end of the rope being held by the captors, as they trotted toward Missouri by the side of the horses. They were not permitted to walk, and if they lagged, they were forced, at the point of a bayonet, to resume their pace. Thus were they hurried until they reached Harrisonville, where they were paraded through the streets, to the great pleasure of the hundreds of ruffians in arms and the hostile citizens. The exertion was more than Hayden could endure, and from fatigue and excitement he swooned. Having resuscitated him, he, with the others, was conveyed to the jail, where two or three hundred men guarded them during the night. The next morning they started for Boonville in a conveyance, which had been kindly tendered by some unknown party. Many days passed, long days to those men who were chafing in confinement, not knowing what was the design of their captors toward them. Many visited them out of curiosity, but not a friendly smile did they see, or a friendly word hear, from the many who came. One day, as Hayden was looking from the window through the grating, his heart bounded within him, as he recognized a familiar face, which was turned, in seeming curiosity, toward him for a moment, and then disappeared.

CHAPTER XLII.

THE PRISONER'S ESCAPE.

DICKEY was worn and weary as she traveled toward Harrisonville from Osawatomie. When night approached, she stopped at the most convenient house, where she remained until morning, when she resumed her journey. She was anxious to return before the proprietor of the stable should become uneasy about his pony and institute a search for it. The morning being cold and frosty, she gave Raven free rein, and was not long in reaching the town.

The proprietor of the stable jokingly expressed surprise at the transformation which had taken place in his pony. Said he, "I hired you a pure white pony and you have returned with one which resembles it in every feature, except color, which is coal black."

Dickey answered by saying, "Your pony was taken from the stable while I was away, and I was compelled to procure this one. I am prepared to recompense you, in full, for the loss of your pony. I have taken a great fancy to this pony and wish to keep it, or I would give it in place of the one I lost."

"Well, you can suit yourself about that, if you want to pay me for the white one, you can do so by paying ten dollars, all I hope is, that the pony won't fall into the hands of the Kansas 'Jayhawkers.'"

Dickey paid the amount, and after dinner mounted Raven and continued her journey toward Westport, where her pupils were anxiously awaiting her. On her arrival, she learned from the landlord, who took charge of Raven, that all the men servants had been forced to accompany the Border Ruffians on their raid into Kansas; what had taken place, and the purpose of the movement. She expressed herself as well pleased with the prospect of Pro-Slavery success, and regretted that she had not been present to accompany them.

Although assuming pleasure, yet down deep in her heart were feelings of anxiety to know what was transpiring in Kansas. She was anxious, yet dreaded to hear the news, fearing that some deed of horror had been committed by the drunken rabble, who constituted the so-called army, that was endeavoring to establish " Rights for All " in Kansas, provided, such rights were not inimical to " Southern " principles; an army that was composed of men thirsting for the blood of Yankees.

The citizens of Westport were decidedly Pro-Slavery in sentiment, yet the absence of the rabble inaugurated a feeling of peace and security, which, for some time past, had not been experienced.

One day, when the landlord was estimating his losses at their hand, he said to Dickey, " I am keeping account of the damage done by our own men, so that when we capture the Yankee's goods, I can get my pay out of them."

At last the rabble came back, boasting of their deeds. They had burned the hotel, destroyed the

printing presses, torn down bridges, and killed one
man by the name of McCoy, who refused to accompany them to Lawrence, and even, after killing him,
abused his helpless family.   Such was chivalry.
Brave men, indeed, to kill a helpless and defenseless
man.

Aunt Nancy and Robert had returned to New
York.   Mr. Leland was traveling in the East, endeavoring to secure property and money in behalf
of Kansas. Vast amounts reached Lawrence through
his efforts.

One day, a letter addressed to her as Dick Richards, desired her assistance in liberating the two
Browns and Hayden, who were held somewhere in
Missouri.   None could be found among their friends
who could, with safety to themselves, search for
them.

Fortunately, in two days, she was to have a vacation.   During the day she read an account, in one of
the county papers, of the incarceration of three
horse-thieves from Kansas.   They were held in
Boonville jail to await their trial.   Well did Dickey
know what "holding for trial" meant in Missouri.
It was only awaiting the arrival of a sufficiently
large mob to make an "execution" a gala-day.

As soon as she closed her school, she started to
visit friends in St. Joseph, but soon turned toward
Boonville, where she sought to make up a class in
music.   She visited the homes of many of the leading families.   Having been a teacher in Westport,
and a friend of the Calhoun's, no suspicion was
aroused, and she was very successful.

The prisoners had been there nearly a week, and yet the whole town was in a state of excitement. Fear predominated in the minds of the citizens, lest they should get away. Hundreds, out of curiosity to see a live Yankee, flocked to the town, and they, too, felt fearful for their own safety. Thus three men, chained and incarcerated, frightened thousands.

In her perambulations about town, she frequently passed the jail, endeavoring to obtain a view of the prisoners. Finally she was successful, having seen Hayden, a glance from whom convinced her that she was recognized.

On the arrival of gentlemen from the South, they were taken to see the prisoners. She resolved to accompany one of these parties, who were just ready to start as she arrived at the hotel. Manifesting the utmost unconcern, she was admitted as a member of the party. The prisoners were very reticent, only speaking in answer to questions. Dickey seated herself in one corner of the room and pretended to read a paper which had been furnished for the use of the prisoners. After the visitors had left, she drew a note from her pocket and threw it along the floor to Hayden, who read the note, nodded his head understandingly and returned it to her in the same manner.

She withdrew in the same careless manner in which she had entered.

Two days had passed, when a crowd came from St. Louis. Accompanying some of these, she again entered the cell. Watching her opportunity, she dropped something on the old quilts which composed

15

the prisoners' bed, at the same time kicking some of the old rags over it.

Hayden's eyes were on every movement. As night approached, he lay down carelessly on the bed and found a file and two packages, which he knew to be designed for their use. One package contained a narcotic, the other a preparation for coloring the hair. Hayden instructed the Brown boys as to their manner of proceeding. The guard slept in the same cell with them. As soon as he evinced a desire to sleep, a portion of the quieting potion was to be administered.

The inside guard assumed his position on his mattress about nine o'clock and was soon fast asleep, being somewhat under the influence of liquor. When he entered, the prisoners had been, seemingly, asleep for two hours.

After all was quiet on the outside, save the pattering of the rain upon the roof, under ordinary circumstances a doleful, dismal sound, but now a joyful one, as it drove pedestrians from the street, and lessened the chances of the prisoners being observed in their efforts to escape.

The time had arrived for action. The prisoners crept cautiously from their pallet. One of the Brown boys held the narcotic near the nostrils of the sleeping guard, while the others proceeded to remove their chains with the file. Their worn and bruised limbs felt light and fresh when the heavy burden was removed.

Approaching the grated windows cautiously, they listened attentively for a few minutes, and hearing no one, they began work upon the bars, which alone stood betwixt them and liberty. Rapidly did their hands move for a brief time, then they listened. Nothing could they hear but the soughing wind and pelting rain, the former of which increased in force and violence each moment, while the latter fell in torrents, seeming to be striving for the mastery over its companion thé wind.

After the window had been freed from its iron bars, Hayden listened for some sound, but none being heard, he said :

" Extinguish the light ! "

" Why not leave it burn ?" said one.

" No, put it out," said Hayden. " Besides that was to be the signal that we-were ready."

After the light had been extinguished, they dropped, one at a time, to the ground, the distance not being great. They listened for the signal; in an instant, almost, they heard it. It came from an-alley, a few feet beyond them. Silently did they move toward the low, patting sound, where they found two persons in male attire, who held three horses. " Two mount the large horse, and one the small one near him," said one of the persons, in a whisper, "and follow me." They were gone, leaving one standing in the dark alley, while the storm raged with increased fury.

CHAPTER XLIII.

AVA HAYNES.

FAR away to the Southern States had the news flown of the arrest of John Brown's sons and Hayden Douglas. The papers contained voluminous accounts of the deeds of valor the champions of the cause of "Southern Rights" were accomplishing. They had entered the Free-Soil settlements and carried away three of their most active men as prisoners. Great rejoicing existed throughout the whole country. The news reached a palatial residence in South Carolina, where dwelt Ava Haynes, now Mrs. Blair, the wife of General Blair, and the controlling spirit of the splendid mansion.

She read the account of the capture of the men. When she read the name of Hayden Douglas, her heart sank within her. Her thoughts flew back to years gone by. She remembered the handsome face, the elegant form, and above all, she remembered her heart's devotion toward him, whose love to gain, she had stooped to commit a crime. She thought of her, whose spirit was driven to the sheltering bosom of its Maker before its allotted time through her wrong. She thought, that to seek in the excitement of the border, forgetfulness of the past, Hayden had gone. She thought the result of her crime had driven him from society, and that, thus,

he had become associated with that—to her mind—
rabble, denominated " Free-States" men, whom she
believed to be guilty of all crimes and misdemeanors
attributed to them through the Southern press.

She soliloquized, " I have now an opportunity to
atone for the wrong I committed against Hayden.
No doubt, I am, indirectly, the cause of his being in
his present unpleasant situation. Mr. Blair has been
anxious to go West to command our army. I have
never consented that he should go. Now I shall
urge him to go, and I shall accompany him. Once
there, I shall have him use his influence in securing
the liberation of Hayden. Then I shall feel that I
have, at least, in part, atoned for the wrong I committed against him."

The next morning, at breakfast, Mr. Blair said,
" My dear, it does not, really, seem proper, that I
should remain here in idleness, while our friends in
the. West are battling for the protection of our
rights and the perpetuation of our institutions. I
have been frequently solicited, earnestly solicited, to
assume command of all our forces on the border of
Missouri, and all that has restrained me from taking
an active part is your consent. May I hope to gain
it this morning?"

Mrs. Blair had been cogitating in her own mind as
to the manner in which she should broach the subject to the General, but now he himself had given
that opportunity, and she blandly replied: "I have
not heretofore withheld my consent because I had
fear for your personal safety. I have sufficient
knowledge of military affairs to know that your posi-

tion as commander would not necessarily be an exposed one; neither do I lack interest in the cause you would represent; my only fear has been that you would require me to remain at home, which thought I could not for a moment consider with any degree of happiness."

"Then am I to understand that I am to have your permission in this matter, provided I allow you to accompany me?"

"Yes, Mr. Blair, upon such condition I give my consent."

"I regret that you had not named it sooner. In my considerations of this subject, I had ever calculated that you should accompany me. If you can so arrange, we will start immediately."

The carriage was ordered, and they were soon on board the train—he, to fight for the perpetuity of an error, a wrong, a crime; she, to atone for the past, in order that her future should be brighter and happier. How strange is life! The present is faulty. The past is filled with regrets. The future alone affords brightness, joyousness and happiness, and that only in anticipation. Is it not a cheering thought that "The future never comes?"

In a few hours the train whirled past the Calhoun home, where was the grave of Lillie. O, the anguish of that moment to Ava Blair! That fair form seemed to stand before the vision of her mind and accuse her of duplicity and perfidy. She, whose body was sleeping in the valley, seemed to rise up before her and demand a herculean effort on her part to rescue him whose incarceration was due to her crime.

On, on sped the train, leaving the plantations of rice, cotton and tobacco behind, stopping at each station to take on passengers, most of whom were going West to assist in establishing "Southern rights for all" upon the soil of Kansas. Proclamations had gone forth over the South calling for men. Jails and penitentiaries were depopulated to procure the class of men desired for the work in hand; hardened, wicked, wretched, inhuman beings were gathered up and sent without cost to battle—more appropriately, rob and murder—on the Kansas borders.

At St. Louis passage was taken on the boat for Boonville. Suddenly the weather changed, as if the face of Nature was o'erhung with a mantle of sorrow. Boreas turned loose in all his power, and the very flood-gates of heaven seemed to open as the boat landed at Boonville after midnight. General and Mrs. Blair proceeded in a carriage to the "Bigelow House," the same hotel where Dick Richards, the music teacher, was stopping. As they hurried up the steps to the entrance of the hall, a traveler, whose clothes were saturated with rain, entered with them.

The next morning Ava arose early, and from her window, looked out upon the surrounding country and the beautiful town. The rain still continued to deluge the buildings and streets, while the wind whistled a mournful dirge, as it bounded with an unresistable force from its secret den in the northwest. Not a person was visible upon the streets. Animated nature sought refuge from the power of the elements.

Eight o'clock, and breakfast was announced. Ava

addressed her husband saying, "Mr. Blair, let us attend the early breakfast, I desire to observe the
guests, with the hope that I may recognize some
companion or friend of former days."

He signified his consent by a polite bow and gracious smile, as he offered her his arm to attend her
to the table. Opposite to Mrs. Blair, at the table,
sat a handsome youth, with bright blue eyes and
curly hair. That person was Dick Richards, the music teacher—our Dickey.

Dickey recognized the person before her, at the
same time she remembered the forged letter and the
cold and dark grave on the slope beneath the austral
sun. Something about Dickey seemed to attract
Ava, she glanced at her several times during the
meal. Little did she think that the boy before her
was none other than Ona Leland, for whom she had
been searching for years.

Conversation flowed freely at the table upon the
all-absorbing topic, "The Yankee prisoners." Dickey
watched the expression of Ava's countenance. She
noticed the shadows come and go as the name of
Hayden Douglas was mentioned.

Breakfast was nearly finished, when a great noise
was heard upon the street. The doors were thrown
open and the cry, "Help! Help! The prisoners have
escaped," was echoed and repeated through the halls.
Crowds of men, boys and negroes went hurrying toward the jail, until a vast multitude surrounded the
building. The Sheriff addressed the crowd, telling
them all to immediately join in the search. Search
every house and barn thoroughly; leave no place

unsearched, bring them back dead or alive. Many
hastened to begin the search. Dickey ordered the
blanket strapped on Raven, and was soon galloping
away southwest. The rain still poured upon the pursued and the pursuers. At noon no trace of the
Yankees had been found.

The outside guard had waited until eight o'clock
for the door-keeper to come out to breakfast, and
feeling uneasy, he rapped loudly on the door, but receiving no answer, he went outside, and looking up,
saw the iron bars were gone from the window, then
he realized the truth, and in order to secure help
promptly, screamed " murder!" in a loud voice,
which attracted the attention of the populace, who
hastened to the jail, and burst open the door, where
they beheld the guard, not yet recovered from the
effects of the narcotic. The chains of the prisoners
lay on the floor, but no sign of the instrument used
in their removal.

The stupefied man was resuscitated. He could
throw no light upon the subject. Hopes were entertained of their capture, but with the approach of
night, the majority of those who had been sent in
pursuit returned, reporting that no trace of them
could be found. They then concluded that they
must yet be somewhere in the town. The following
morning a renewed search was instituted, all points
having been guarded during the night.

Dickey continued in her work until she had organized and taught the music class; while Mrs. Blair
scanned every paper closely, hoping for the success
of him whom she would have assisted. Not a word

could she find, until on the wings of rumor came the word that the three were safe on Kansas soil.

For a time great excitement prevailed as to who had aided the prisoners, but nothing could be learned. Suspicion pointed to no one, yet they must have been assisted by parties on the outside. The irons bore evidence of having been filed off. Where did they procure the file? No such thing had been sold by any of the merchants; mechanics missed none from their work-benches.

As soon as Dickey reached Boonville and noted the surroundings, she sent word to Dr. Strawn and submitted her plan to him. By rapidly riding during the night, he reached the vicinity of Boonville the day previous, and mingling with the many strangers already there, he gave the file and packages into her possession, with accompanying instructions, and returned to the place where he had left the extra horses. It was he who stood in the alley with Dickey, holding the horses; it was he who accompanied the men and guided them safely into Kansas.

Dickey returned to the hotel, and entering with those who had just arrived on the boat, she was not observed.

Dickey, as "Dick Richards," returned in two weeks to Westport and resumed her school. General and Mrs. Blair soon followed her, he having been assigned to the command of the Pro-Slavery troops, who were being drilled near that town. Although Ava was Mrs. Gen. Blair, yet she was unhappy; a gloom had settled upon her fair brow. She sat at her window gazing far to the West. The only thrill of happiness and joy she had experienced was when she learned of the safe arrival in Kansas of the three escaped prisoners. Dickey taught from day to day, with as much interest, seemingly, as though she had no other object in view.

One day she learned that the armed bands were to invade Kansas at a time not far distant. She felt a desire to know and understand more thoroughly their plans. The chief officer's room was in the second story of the hotel at which she boarded. She knew by the assembling of subordinate officers, who immediately on their arrival repaired to General Blair's room, that something of moment would occur in that room. She resolved at all hazards to ascertain. Removing her shoes, she crept noiselessly up the stairs and took her station close to the door of the room occupied by the officers.

CHAPTER XLIV.

JOHN BROWN'S HOME.

UNDER instructions from Dr. Strawn, the prisoners took different courses at day-break of the morning following their escape. Before separating, they stopped at a farm-house for breakfast. They informed the farmer that they had been down to Boonville to see the Yankee prisoners, and that one of their horses was missing, and in search-

ing for it, they became lost themselves. Before they
left the Doctor purchased another horse, so that all
now were well mounted. At noon each one stopped
for dinner, stating that he expected to join some
friends who were going into Kansas, with the hope
of meeting with some more of the Yankees, and if
they could capture them, they would take them to
Boonville, where there were already three. Thus,
they not only secured their dinners, but were invited
to return with their prisoners, as the men wanted to
see a live Yankee.

During the following night they each reached Osawatomie and went to the Western House, and when,
in the light of the bright morning, they stood upon
the porch, they were the recipients of such a greeting as never before had been expressed in Osawatomie.

Among those assembled to extend congratulations
to the boys on their escape from the hands of the
Border Ruffians was an old man. He was sedate
and calm, seemingly unmoved by the demonstrations.
When the cheers resounded upon the morning air,
his hat was not lifted, neither did his voice join in
the shouts. His small blue eyes flash a fire never
before observed. As the vociferations died away,
he stepped forward from the crowd, and mounting
the steps to the porch, in a calm and deliberate voice
said :

"It has been said that I am a member of the Republican party. It is false. I despise the Republicans, I am an Abolitionist; not only opposed to the
extension of Slavery, but in favor of its *extirpation.*

What does the Republican party teach? It teaches
that we must content ourselves with resisting the extension of Slavery. The Republican party cries
halt! I say, 'Forward to the Rescue.' I am an
Abolitionist of the Bunker Hill school. I am following neither Garrison, Seward, Gerritt Smith, nor
Wendell Phillips, but I am following the teachings
of the Golden Rule ánd the Declaration of Independence. The Republican leaders of to-day will
be the Democratic leaders of 1860. Now, we, the
Abolitionists must fight. I say fight, if we be free
men. You all know what we have endured already.
Our crops have been destroyed, our horses and cattle stolen, our friends carried away into the heart of
their state and confined in felons' cells. Must we endure it further? I emphatically say, no. You, who
will fight follow me, step to the front and bring your
guns, if you have none, I will furnish you with all
the weapons you need."

Among the first to step forward was a man, older
than Brown, whom all knew as "the companion of
Hayden Douglas," whom we had met years ago, an
English nobleman. Next came Hayden and soon
all but two of the assembled multitude, stood by the
side of Old John Brown, that noble champion of
freedom. Two alone stood aloof. They were the
midnight companions of Guy Wren at the post-oak
tree.

"Come with me," said Captain Brown as he led
the way to his home on the Potawatomie. It was
not a gorgeous structure; it was not a palatial residence. The home of the predestined leader of the

second and holier American Revolution was but a
low log-cabin, containing a door and two windows;
its roof of boards rived from trees fallen by his own
hand. It was from here those evergreen trees had
been taken that now ornamented so many New England homes, and the man who now stood here as the
Captain of a resolute band of freedom-loving men
was the same who carried those trees to the East
and gave with them the secret pledge whose import
we shall, in years to come, ascertain. Near his cabin
was the spot from whence they were taken.

You ask, Why did he choose this secluded spot?
Go view its surroundings and you will learn. · Once
there, without a guide, you cannot return to the path
by which you came. The soil is not as fertile as that
of the surrounding country, but what enemy dare
venture upon that home when its inmates were there!

As they approached the cabins, they observed the
departure of a band of Pro-Slavery men from the
houses of the old man's sons. During the absence
of the men, these ruffians had shamefully abused
their families, and in leaving, had told them that if
they and their husbands did not leave by the next
day, they would return and kill the last one of them.

The old man turned to his aged follower after he
had listened to the story of the women, and said:

"Now war must begin. I wish I could see·Dickey
Deane. I want her with me, but you come; perhaps we can make arrangements for to-day."

They left the camp. Soon a light wagon, equipped
with a surveyor's outfit, stood near the cabin. The
old man came out, dressed in a different costume.

A surveyor's compass hung by his side, and he carried a spy-glass in his hand.

"I want two more men," said he, calling them from the camp.   When they came they mounted into the wagon and drove in a southerly direction.   After driving some distance, they left the wagon.   As they walked along, the two old men talked of former days, when they had first met in England, where Brown was engaged as a wool-dealer.   They talked of the time when this Englishman had given Brown money to assist in procuring homes for the Africans who had already thrown off the galling yoke of slavery and sought protection in the Northern States and in Canada.

"There they are," whispered Brown, and they began their work of surveying.   In a short time they were "running their line" right through the camp of the invaders.

CHAPTER XLV.

"DICK RICHARDS" SUSPICIONED.

DICKEY stood at the officer's door a moment, all was still.   Placing her ear to the key-hole, she could hear the words of their whispered consultation.

"You are right, Wren, there is a spy among us, who it is, I can not tell, neither have I any suspi-

cions." These were the first words Dickey heard.
They were followed by others from Wren, who said :

"I have been watching this school-teacher, Dick
Richards, for some time. He was gone from here
when those Yankees escaped from Boonville, and I
think he needs watching."

"Yes, we must be on the look-out, for they are up
to every trick," said another voice.

"Wilkerson and Sherman were here yesterday,
urging us to come and knock that Brown out-fit
over, or they would soon have the lead," growled
Wren.

Dickey turned and crept away to her own room,
down stairs, where she packed her few articles of apparel, and securing Raven, she galloped away over
the prairie, following the trail made by the Pro-Slavery men in making their raids into Kansas.

The following morning, at the instigation of Wren,
a warrant was issued for the arrest of Dick Richards,
but when the Sheriff came to serve the warrant,
Dick could not be found. Earnest search was made
of every house in town, but without avail. The
honest, fair-minded citizens believed their teacher
had been killed, having fallen under the suspicion of
such unscrupulous men as Guy Wren, and, that his
pony had been secreted, to convey the idea, that he
had escaped. This belief was confirmed beyond
doubt, when, during the day, a suit of clothes were
found, which were identified as having belonged to
Dick.

Orders were issued to "fall in," and "form ranks
for Kansas." Banners were thrown to the breeze,

on which were inscribed various mottoes, the following being the most prominent:

"Yankees tremble and Abolitionists fall !
Our motto is 'Southern rights for all !'"

A bountiful supply of spirituous liquors was carried along, as an antidote for snake bites and the ague.

Grandly, bravely, superbly did that host march forth with drums beating and colors flying; each heart beating high with expectation. Patriotism, as a sentiment, if it existed at all, existed to a very small degree, in the hearts of those composing that band, therefore their expectations were high, and their anticipations bright. They expected, as individuals, to return laden with valuable plunder, and with the proceeds derived from its sale, continue the bacchanalian orgies which had characterized their conduct since they had joined the army of the Border Ruffians. They anticipated, by force of numbers, that the Yankees would flee upon their approach, and thus their victory would be easy.

On reaching the State line, they divided into three divisions, the first going to Lecompton, from whence it would sweep down upon Lawrence. The second proceeded to a point six miles south of Osawatomie, while the third entered Kansas on the Santa Fe road. It was the second company that the pseudo-surveyors espied, and "ran their line" and "drove their stakes" through the heart of the camp, the occupants of which not doubting but what the party were really government surveyors, asked no questions concerning their political sentiments.

16

The surveyors left their instruments and sat down to dinner with them. While eating, they talked freely of the object that had brought them into that neighborhood. They said, "There was an old man by the name of Brown, who had several sons. They had come especially to put him out of the way, besides they had the names of other men in this vicinity, whom they proposed looking after as soon as they had disposed of Brown and his sons."

They continued, "Since our arrival here we have learned that a young woman, from Osawatomie, is now in Missouri acting as a spy upon our movements. We shall do our best to find her, and when we do, we will hang her to the first tree we come to."

While the conversation between Brown, for he it was that was personating a surveyor, and the invaders was going on, a young man, small of stature, clad in the military uniform of the United States, walked leisurely into camp and joined in the conversation.

The old man's eyes sparkled as he beheld the young soldier, who gave a certain sign as he approached. Brown now knew that one of his bravest and most energetic workers was here. A smile played upon the features of those two, as they listened to the boasting, bragging remarks of the invaders.

When the "surveyors" resumed their work, they "back-sighted," as is the custom of such men, and pretending to find an error in the placing of their stakes, retraced the whole line to ascertain where the deviation began. The soldier, pretending to wish to observe how such errors were corrected, accompanied them, and they were soon free from observation from the camp, when they hastened to the cabin of John Brown, where his friends were awaiting his return, as he had instructed them to do.

To them he conveyed the information he had obtained. A merry laugh followed, and three cheers were given for Captain Brown and his Gunter's chain. They watched closely the movements of the young soldier. There was but one, Hayden, who recognized him. No disguise could hide from him the brightness that flashed from those blue eyes—which belonged to none other than Dickey Deane, the spy.

Hayden cast upon her a look of indifference. Dickey saw that look and understood its origin. She knew that he lacked stability. Anything might call forth his energies, as long as it yielded a measure of excitement, but as soon as that ebbed, his interest was gone. His efforts were well intended, and his plans properly conceived, yet he lacked the will-power and energy to properly execute these plans. Besides, jealousy was another characteristic of his nature, and the peculiarly indifferent look he gave Dickey, as he recognized her in the soldier's uniform, showed that he was jealous of her, on account of the confidence extended to her by Captain Brown. She feared that the day would come, when he would prove the Judas, and consign them into the hands of their bitter enemies.

Thus thought Ona Leland, as she stood in the character of "Dickey Deane, the spy," and person-

ating a United States soldier—of one, who had been
of great service to the Free-States men. Her pre-
sentiments had ever been of assistance to her, and
she had learned to heed them, no matter how para-
doxical they appeared.

The name of Dickey Deane was now being proclaimed over the land. Her friends, though unknown
to many of them, thought of her with pride when
considering her services to the Free-State cause.
The same name was spoken in derision among the
leaders of the Pro-Slavery faction. They traced all
their misfortune to Dickey Deane, "The Spy of
Osawatomie." An account of her doing had been
published in the Southern papers, and a reward of a
thousand dollars offered for her capture. But she
was not the least disconcerted. She was as calm as
when entertaining friends in Mrs. Wise's drawing-
room in Washington. She had, it is true, discovered
their various plans, and in some manner conveyed
her knowledge to her friends, thus enabling them to
be prepared to receive those who came to slay and
rob. Such a state of affairs was, indeed, aggravating
to the Pro-Slavery men, and in their wrath and ill-
feeling toward her, had in their newspapers described
her as "horrid and hideous," thus enabling her to
continue her work without fear of detection, as her
beauty attracted universal attention.

Old John Brown and the young "soldier," accompanied by two ladies, left the cabin and drove to
Osawatomie, where the "soldier" left the wagon,
and proceeding to a stump near the residence of Mr.
Leland, drew forth a key and entered the house by

the back door. Proceeding to a room up-stairs, he selected from the wardrobe a becoming dress of black with dark cuffs, and collar trimmed with gold. Going to a trunk, he produced curls, gold-headed hair pins and jewelry, and in a few moments the "soldier" was transformed into Ona Leland. She herself could hardly believe that the transformation could be so complete as was revealed by the reflected image from the mirror.

In a brief time, some half-dozen of her nearest neighbors had gathered at her home, where they pressed her with questions as to where she had been during the recent troubles.

Even as Ona Leland, she had to, in a measure, continue in disguise. Brown, Hayden, and her immediate family friends, were all who knew that Dickey Deane and Ona Leland were one and the same person.

She told her neighbors that she had kept herself informed of what had occurred in Osawatomie, and regretted that she had not been here to rejoice with them at their success in receiving information of the intended raids of the invaders and of the safe return of those who had been captured and carried into Missouri.

Thus they conversed on various subjects pertaining to their trials and sufferings, until Ona expressed her intention of taking a ride. Proceeding to Mr. Robers', she found Swan where he had been sent when Aunt Nancy and Robert went East. Then to Mr. Gedins', where she had left Raven the night previous, on her arrival from Westport. Having strapped a blanket on Raven, she donned a heavy black riding habit, and was soon on her way north of Osawatomie, leading Swan, much to the surprise of her neighbors, who exclaimed, "Where can she be going?"

She crossed the river and was soon traveling rapidly on the well-beaten trail leading to the landing on the Missouri river at Kansas City. She was attracted by and pleased with the beauty of the surrounding country. Wild flowers of every hue and odor gave forth their fragrance on the balmy air. She had never before traveled on this road in springtime, and it seemed a new country to her.

After traveling about five miles, she came near to a high mound or knob, upon its apex she discovered something, which her glass revealed to be merely a loose pile of stones. She rode to where the ascent was too steep for safety, and dismounting, clambered up to the pile of rocks. "What a beautiful view!" exclaimed she, and taking out her glass, she looked far away to the east. There she beheld the glittering spires of Harrisonville. To the southeast were the large orchards and dark-green corn fields. To the south she could see across the Marias des Cygne, and on the bluffs she discovered the camp of the Missourians, where she had been, disguised as a soldier, the day previous. More to the southwest, she saw upon a high mound near the Marias des Cygne, the outlines of two men, who seemed to be watching her movements. They belonged to Brown's band of surveyors. They were standing on Grand View, a mound southwest of Osawatomie, a favorite "lookout" of the old hero. Although she had often seen from a distance this mound, yet she had never learned its name, and she concluded she would name it, which she accordingly did, calling it " Pilot Knob," which name it yet bears.

As the tourist glides along on the cars, after leaving the city of Paolo, bound for the fertile fields and blooming prairies of Kansas, that knob attracts his watchful eye, as the train rushes with the speed of the wind at its base. As his vision is greeted by that monument of rough stones will his thoughts revert to that little New Hampshire girl who gave it its name, as she stood in the fresh green grass of the fragrant spring and gazed far away over the vast expanse of prairie?

As she turned to retrace her steps, she heard a faint moan. She, ever on the alert, stopped to listen. Again the sound was repeated. Grasping her revolver, she looked cautiously about her. She glanced among the rocks composing the rude monument; again she heard the noise, this time it seemed to be farther north. Advancing a few steps in that direction, along the crest of the mound, she beheld lying in the long grass, with no protection save the blue canopy of heaven, a helpless child. She lifted it in her arms, wondering how it had ever reached that place. Upon examination, she found it was alive. Descending the mound to where she had left the ponies, all the while exclaiming, " What shall I do with it."

CHAPTER XLVI.

THE STORM.

WHEN John Brown left Osawatomie, he proceeded directly to Grand View, where Ona
had observed him from Pilot Knob. The
old hero also saw his spy as she stood upon the
mound north of him, but he lingered not on his
watch-tower. He hastened on to other duties. He
was sounding the tocsin of war, and gathering the
clan in martial array, to inaugurate the strife which
continued to be waged for years, between the Free-
State and Pro-Slavery factions.

The following morning dawned bright and beautiful. All nature was clad in loveliness. The air was
laden with the perfume of the flower-bedecked prairies. A quiet reigned over the face of nature and
men should have been at peace. But it was otherwise. The Border Ruffians again visited the quiet
settlement on the Potawatomie, and grossly insulted
the helpless families of the settlers, who had remained at home. They reiterated their threats of
extermination and for the time withdrew.

At noon there came a change. Although the sun
continued to pour his burning rays upon the earth,
yet a strong breeze had arisen, which, instead of
bearing refreshment upon its wings, caused the hot
air to appear only the more oppressive. Many remarked, "Such a state of affairs indicated a storm."

During the middle of the afternoon a sultry haze overpread the face of the country. An hour later a deep, dark, portentious cloud appeared in the west. The zig-zag lightning flashed across its face; night had suddenly appeared. The cloud passed on toward the east; the wind ceased; the stillness of death reigned over all. How desolate were those women and children in their cabins on the Potawatomie! Fathers, husbands, brothers and neighbors all gone; not a man remained in the settlement, they were hiding for protection in the bush.

The wind changed, coming from the direction of the cloud which had so recently passed. With the wind came the cloud, the same lurid flashes illuminating its face, while thunder loud and deep pealed and reverberated up and down the valley. In a moment the storm burst in all its fury upon that settlement, which seemed predestined to be destroyed. The wind whistled through every crevice between the rough logs of the cabins; windows were burst open and doors torn from their hinges.

In vain did the inmates strive to keep their goods together. The wind whirled them from their grasp. Huddled together under the beds were the mother and children in each cabin, awaiting the result of the terrific force of the storm. The day grew darker; the rain fell in torrents and ran in sluices down the walls and over the floors. Peal after peal, crash after crash, the thunder rolls above the din of the muttering storm. Will their cabins withstand the united forces of the elements?

Fences are blown down and carried away, yet the

cabins stand against the fury of the storm. Suddenly and unexpectedly the wind ceaseth; rain falls no longer; calmness again settles upon the face of nature; bright stars twinkle out their gladness; the atmosphere is balmy and fresh, yet quiet does not come to the hearts of those women. A deep gloom, an anxious, expectant look rests upon their countenances. Their thoughts were not of the "wreck of matter" around them, but out in the gloom toward loved ones who for protection had sought the shelter of the wild wood. How had they fared during the storm? Had they been torn asunder by the "bolts of heaven, or had the Great Ruler miraculously preserved their lives?

During the night their friends return. From them they learn that they had found shelter from the wind in a neighboring ravine. That is all they learn, and now that they have returned, it is all they desire to know.

Let us follow them during their absence. While the elements were at strife; the disrupted heavens pouring out wind and rain; the booming thunder echoing from hill to valley; the forked lightening glinting from cloud to cloud, concentrating its powers to hurl upon earth and demonstrate to man his weakness and insignificance; the minds of men were busy, thoughtless of the surrounding strife, maturing plans already conceived, to wreak vengeance upon their kind.

After the storm had abated, the homes of men whose sympathies were with the Pro-Slavery faction, were visited by masked men and five of their num-

ber carried away. Their bodies were found the following day perforated with bullets. None, except
God and the participants. knew who had been guilty
of the crime. " Patience had ceased to be a virtue " .
with the Free-State settlers. War had begun in
earnest. Blighting, desolating guerilla war claimed
its victims on every hand. Massacre and murder ran
riot throughout the land. Men scarcely knew whom
to trust. A line was drawn, there was no neutral
ground. Free-States men grouped their families for
protection. Men could not be seen during the day.
Occasionally, as the gloom of night lowered its mantle upon the earth, they would creep, stealthily, to
their cabins and softly commune with their loved
ones.

Nearly a week after the storm, a band of Border
Ruffians, commanded by Capt. Pate, came to the
settlement, searching for old man Brown and his
boys. They succeeded in capturing John Brown,
Jr., and Jason Brown. They were afterwards joined
by Capt. Woods' company of dragoons, and together
they burned the store of Wines, on the Potawatomie.
Brown himself was away at Lawrence. They carried their prisoners away, and as they were camped
one night at the head of a creek or ravine, called Black
Jack, a woman entered the camp, carrying a bundle
of clothes in one hand and a field glass in the other.
She said : " I am lost."

CHAPTER XLVII.

THE BABE OF THE PRAIRIES.

ONA took the sweet-faced child in her arms and caressed it, smoothing back the long, golden curls, which reminded her of her own silken tresses when she was a child in her mother's arms.

She continued to caress it until a smile played upon its features, in answer to her own. She in a sweet pleasant tone asked :

" What is your name? little pet."

" Me name is Ota," answered the child.

" Ota, can you tell me where your mamma is?"

" Mamma gone."

Ona saw it was useless to question the little one further, and replacing the little pink sun-bonnet upon its shapely head and securing it, she led Raven to a low place and with the child in her arms, she sprang upon his back, leaving Swan to follow. Arranging the child comfortably upon her lap, she pursued her journey.

She stopped at the Indian Mission on the east side of Moody Creek, to make inquiries concerning the child. She learned that a woman had passed the morning previous, carrying a child and had returned at sunset without it. She was thought to be insane. She was very sick, lying in one of the Indian huts unconscious of her surroundings. Ona thought best to retain the child, and procuring some food from the

Indian woman, she fed it. Indications of an approaching storm induced her to remain, but on further consideration, she concluded to press on, which she did, reaching the Shawnee Mission in time to secure shelter just as the storm burst over the place.

After supper she rocked the little one to sleep, all the while softly humming a sweet lullaby song. As she thus sat, she heard the name of Dickey Deane mentioned by some one of a party who were holding an animated conversation in the adjoining room. The child by this time being asleep, she laid it gently upon the bed, and with her head resting against the partition between the rooms, endeavoring thus to obtain a knowledge of what those persons in the other room were conversing about, in order to be prepared for any emergency, should she be identified.

The subject of conversation had changed; she heard a low, sweet voice mention the name of Lillie Calhoun. At the mention of that name she forgot her purpose, as her mind wandered to scenes of earlier days when she and Lillie were boon companions. Those joyous days of mirth and merry-making; those halcyon days of love, when each thought the other more deserving. Then she wandered in imagination to the last parting at Strawn, when Lillie carelessly threw the envelope from the stage as she bade her friend adieu; she thought of herself as she picked it up with the determination of cherishing it as a simple memento of the past; she thought of her summons to the bedside of her dying friend, of the cruel letter which caused that death, of the flower-laden grave in the far-away Southern clime.

Such thoughts occupied her mind until tired nature demanded attention. She lay down by the side of the sleeping child, with her revolver under her pillow. When she awoke, day was dawning in the east. Ordering an early breakfast, much to the surprise of her hostess, she was soon on her way, having thus avoided answering innumerable questions.

She pressed on, carrying the child until noon, when she stopped under a tree on the bank of a ravine, where bubbled a fresh spring of water, to partake of the refreshments she had brought for the child and herself.

When she had rested sufficiently, she resumed her journey. Not desiring to enter St. Joseph at an early hour, she rode slowly. When she reached the immediate neighborhood of the city, she secured a heavy veil over her head and face. As the last lingering rays of a setting sun elongated her shadow and marked its outline upon the distant plain, and gilded the spires with a golden sheen, she entered the suburbs of the city.

As she passed a party of boys who were playing on a corner near the hotel, she heard one exclaim: "Look, there goes Kate Oyster's white pony!"

She alighted in front of the hotel. The family and boarders being at supper, her arrival was unnoticed. She ascended the steps, passed through the hall and entered the parlor where Mr. Oyster and Kate were sitting.

As Kate arose to receive her, she removed her veil, when Kate exclaimed:

"Oh, Cousin Ona," and hastened forward to embrace her.

When she beheld Ota, she started in surprise and ejaculated:

"What a pretty child! Where in the world did you get her? Whose is she, Ona?"

"Before answering all your questions," said Ona, "I want to call your attention to the pretty ponies I have. They are in front of the house."

Kate bounded from the room in great haste to see the beautiful ponies. Soon her exclamations of surprise and delight reached the ears of her papa and Ona.

"Oh, papa, do come and see Swan! He is here."

Mr. Oyster hastened to rejoice with Kate over the return of her long-lost pony. During their absence, Ona removed her riding habit and the bonnet and impromptu wraps from Ota. Kate forgot entirely the presence of her cousin and her curiosity regarding the child, and not until Raven and Swan were properly cared for did she enter the house to assail her cousin with innumerable questions.

Ona related to Mr. Oyster and Kate her past experiences, especially regarding the manner in which she became possessed of Kate's pony, and how and where she found the child, adding:

"When I discovered the child, my first thoughts were as to the manner in which I should dispose of it. I was about to return to Osawatomie with it, when I concluded I would bring it here, with the hope that I could induce you to care for it, until I had time to arrange for its future. At one of the Indian Missions, I saw the woman, who, no doubt, is its mother, but some great calamity has pressed so heavily upon her that she lost her mind, besides suffering from exhaustion and disease. I felt that she could not long bear up under her afflictions, and must soon pass from earth away."

"You did right, Ona," said Mr. Oyster; "we will care for the child, and I shall leave it entirely to the care of Kate, and now she can have a pet to fondle night and day."

"Oh, cousin, I'm so glad you found this child, and glad that you brought it here. I will take the best possible care of the little one, but I do not like the idea of your 'arranging for its future' elsewhere than here with us. You can, during your stay, instruct me how to care for it."

"I should be glad to remain and instruct you in the matter of caring for her, to the best of my ability, even if I am deficient in such knowledge myself, but I am now on business that must be promptly looked after. I would like my breakfast as early as possible. I would like to leave the city by sunrise. I do not desire any one, besides yourselves, to know that I am here, or, after I am gone, that I have been here."

The next morning early, she was on her way to Lawrence, leaving Ota with Kate, who was well pleased, and before Ona left remarked:

"What shall we call her besides Ota?"

"I have thought of no name to bestow upon the little foundling," said Ona; "besides, I have no choice. I shall leave that to you entirely, Kate."

"May I call her Ota Chance?"

" Yes, that will answer the purpose as well as any, until we ascertain her proper name," replied Ona.

While Kate was planning and arranging to supply Ota with suitable apparel—so she could take her to Sabbath school, the next Sunday—Ona was closely observing the prominent features of the country she was passing over on her way to Lawrence. She also moved cautiously, as she had observed freshly-made tracks of horses, which unmistakably indicated that a troop had passed that way recently.

On approaching the Kaw river, she observed a body of men on horseback approaching, to avoid which she turned into the timber to the right of the road, and awaited their disappearance in the distance before she resumed her journey again on the highway.

CHAPTER XLVIII.

A SCENE IN THE BORDER RUFFIAN CAMP.

"YOU lost!" exclaimed an uncouth-appearing individual, as he approached the woman who had entered the camp at Black Jack. She was almost exhausted from walking so long. The uncouth salutation of the ruffian frightened her, besides her attention being called just at that moment to the prisoners, who sat near loaded with chains. She at length rallied sufficiently to ejaculate: 17

"Yes, I am lost. I am anxious to find General Blair's camp."

"You bet you want to find General Blair's camp. Come, boys!" shouted one, "here is that old hag, Dickey Deane. We have her safe now," and before she could utter another word a half-dozen of the " Chivalry " seized her, while others held their weapons in readiness, pointed toward the helpless woman, the leader standing by, laughing at her distress.

Her pockets were rifled of their contents and her field-glass broken to pieces. Her hands were securely bound behind her back, and she was gagged so she could not speak.

Two women from Westport were in the camp, acting as cooks. Although they expressed feelings of sympathy for the men who were prisoners, they had no word of comfort for the unfortunate woman in bonds.

For three days was she kept in that unpleasant and annoying posture, her bonds removed only at such times as she was permitted to eat of the miserably-prepared food, yet during her sufferings she found time to feel for and sympathize with the unfortunate prisoner, whose suffering had caused reason to depart from his mind, and he was now a raving maniac. Such was the scene the camp presented at Black Jack.

They had left Westport a few weeks previous, fully determined to capture "Old John Brown." They had succeeded, they thought, in capturing some of his men, of the truth they were not quite certain. They felt assured that they had, for a certainty, captured the notorious spy, "Dickey Deane."

They had sent for Guy Wren to identify her and also the other prisoners. Late one afternoon as they were waiting Wren's arrival, scouts brought in the word "that Old John Brown and his company were approaching and were now in the next ridge, with the intention of killing every Southerner."

"Put these prisoners out of the way," shouted the Captain. "Let them die first," and seizing the weak woman they supposed to be Dickey Deane, they dragged her to a neighboring tree, where one of them had already thrown a rope over a limb. Removing the gag from her mouth, they placed the rope about her neck, when she made a demonstration to speak, at which one more cruel than the others suggested that they tie her tongue, which suggestion meeting with favor from the majority, they procured a string, and seizing her face with their rough hands, they fastened her tongue securely and amused themselves by pulling on the string to cause her as much suffering as possible and almost depriving her of consciousness.

As they paused a moment to more thoroughly arrange the rope, they heard the tramping of horses approaching. In a moment they beheld some of their friends who belonged to General Blair's command.

"Hallo! what are you doing here?" shouted one of the foremost of the new arrivals.

"We've got that old spy 'Dickey Deane,' and we are going to swing her up. Come, give us a lift."

By this time, General Blair had approached to note the appearance of the world-renowned spy. A sudden pallor spread over his countenance, and he shouted:

"My God! Untie this woman, you villains, or I'll shoot you down like dogs!" at the same time springing from his saddle, he hastened toward the now unconscious woman, and clasping her tenderly in his arms, exclaimed:

"Oh, Ava! my wife! are you dead?" Then turning to the ruffians who were hastily removing her bonds, said:

"Vile wretches, how dare you thus treat any one wearing the sacred habiliments of a woman? Have you, in your thirst for blood, lost all respect and decency? Do you propose to wage war upon helpless women? Is it your purpose to destroy every woman you meet, thus hoping to be sure and destroy one, who, by her former acts, has proven herself too shrewd to ever be captured by such a set of desperadoes as your acts clearly demonstrate you to be? Away, vile dogs! I never want to look upon your murderous and villainous faces again."

One by one, they quailed before his wrathful expressions and crept away, feeling far different than they had a moment previous.

Their captain rushed forward to learn the cause of the excitement, and was much surprised on learning that the prisoner, for whose execution he had recently given orders, was the wife of his commanding General. He assisted the General in restoring her to consciousness, and gave orders to let the other prisoners remain as they were.

While attention was being given to the resuscitation of Mrs. Blair, a new-comer appeared upon the scene in the person of a young and active man clad in the jaunty costume of a midshipman in the navy. Approaching the General and Captain, he produced a pass from the authorities at Washington, giving him permission to enter all the towns, hamlets and military camps in the territory. He produced a sketch-book as soon as the officers had returned his pass, and walking into the camp looked about for a favorable position, seemingly from which to make a sketch of the camp.

To some of the men near, he expressed the greatest surprise that they should be compelled to punish their men for insubordination as those were being punished, at the same time pointing to the prisoners. When informed they were prisoners, he intimated that they might possibly deserve the treatment they were receiving.

The prisoners had recognized in the person of the young sailor a friend, and realized from the happy expression that illumed his face that assistance was near.

Seating himself near the prisoners, he began sketching the camp and its surroundings. The Border Ruffians gave no attention to his presence. They were on the lookout for Old John Brown, of whose approach their scouts had warned them, besides the mistake they had made in treating the General's wife in the manner they had, led them to think they were acting too hastily.

As the sailor glanced toward the prisoners, he saw

the blank expression of countenance of one who seemed utterly unconscious of events transpiring around him, a quick glance of inquiry toward the other, who pointed toward his mate, and tapped his own head with his finger tips, at same time shaking his head slowly. The sailor understood the pantomime, and an expression of sorrow crept over his face.

The sketch-book contained only the lay of the camp and its surroundings. When General and Mrs. Blair left for Westport the sailor accompanied them. On the journey he learned of the treatment Mrs. Blair had received. She being unable to talk, wrote down every particular and handed it to her husband for perusal, who in turn passed it to the young sailor.

While at Westport, Mrs. Blair had expressed the opinion that the people of the North and East were as a class more generous and kind than were the Southerners. The expression had been reported on the streets, and it raised the ire of some of the " Chivalry " who had assembled after the departure of the army. They threatened to tar and feather her and send her to the Missouri River.

Fearing that she should suffer ere the return of her husband, she resolved to seek his camp and there gain protection. She started one night and stopped at Shawnee Mission the same time that Dickey Deane sought shelter from the storm for herself and the little waif which she had found.

It was Mrs. Blair whom she had overheard speaking of Lillie Calhoun. She was telling the missionary of her death, he having been acquainted with Lillie in Washington.

When the General had read what his wife had written, he said calmly:

"To-day severs my connection with this unholy warfare. There are two sides to every question, and for once I acknowledge I am in error in making my selection. I am an honorable man, and as such admire and love a properly-conducted war, but such a warfare as this I condemn. When innocent women cease to find protection even from the enemy, I cannot endorse it; where greed, lust, murder and every felony takes precedence over honorable strife, I must obey the dictates of conscience and withdraw."

To which the sailor replied: "General, I for one cannot find it in my heart to censure you for the resolution to withdraw from the army, you have just expressed. The injury your wife has sustained under a misapprehension, which before being hastily acted upon should have been thoroughly investigated before action was taken thereon, is sufficient to produce feelings antagonistic to friends even who are guilty of such gross negligence. Permit me to thank you, General, for the kindness extended to me in permitting me to make a sketch of the camp, as well as for the privilege of riding thus far with you, I will now bid you and your estimable lady, whom I hope will soon recover her accustomed health, a kindly adieu," saying which the sailor sprang lightly from the wagon.

While General Blair and his wife continued on their way to Harrisonville—where he had chosen to go instead of to Westport, where his wife had been treated with such disrespect—the young sailor took a northwesterly direction and disappeared in the thickets in the ravine.

The camp of the ruffians was in such confusion that they had not noticed the departure of the sailor for half an hour after he had gone, when, fearing he might be an emissary of Old John Brown, they started in hot pursuit. They saw the wagon far in advance, and putting spurs to their steeds they overtook the wagon and found it belonged to their own company, and was carrying General Blair and his wife into Missouri. They learned that the young sailor had started toward Lawrence, and they hastened on in pursuit. As they reached the top of a divide they saw him enter the thicket on the ravine.

CHAPTER XLIX.

"DICKEY" IN JOHN BROWN'S CAMP.

THE advancing horsemen did not observe "Dickey" as she rode in among the bushes on her way to Lawrence from St. Joseph. She sat quietly on her pony, gently patting his neck as they passed by. She could see that they were the scouts from the camp of the Southern invaders. They disappeared in the distance, and she emerged from her hiding-place and hastened toward Lawrence.

When she arrived at that place she found all in

confusion on account of the steps taken by the
invaders to avenge the murder of their friends on
the Potawatomie. A company of dragoons had
been sent to compel all Free-State settlers to leave
the Territory, and to bring Old John Brown to
Lecompton for trial.

" Has any one been sent to Brown's camp to
apprise him of the danger?" inquired Dickey as
she dismounted before the hotel.

" No one has gone yet," answered one.

She turned to Mrs. Baker, the landlady, and asked,
" Are there any of those sailor suits in the house
that those visitors had who were here a few weeks
ago?"

" Yes, they left a number of them. I will procure
them for you as soon as you have eaten some dinner, which will soon be ready."

After dinner, she secured the suits, and selecting
the newest, she proceeded to make some slight alter-
ations, to suit her taste, and putting it on, she appeared upon the street as a sailor. In the jacket
pocket she found a card bearing the name " Harry
Owen." Replacing the card in her pocket, she said :
" That will be my name on this trip."

Stopping at the book-store, she purchased a
sketch-book, in which she wrote the name " Harry
Owen, U. S. N."

She rode along up the Potawatomie trail for some
miles, when she turned in the direction of Black Jack.
Stopping at the house of a Free-Soil man, she made
inquiries for the camp of John Brown, and also for
the camp of the dragoons. He could impart no information on either point.

She entered the ravine and followed a path made by cattle on their way to and from the water. She slowly wended her way over the fallen trunks of trees and through the bushes, until just ahead she noticed two branches broken from trees on either side and lopped across the path, such being the sign that the camp was near.

"Halt!" commanded a voice near. Looking ahead, she saw a man well-armed standing directly in front of her. He had glided from behind a large tree, and carried a revolver in his hand.

She looked at him steadily as she grasped the reins tighter in her hand, and said in a low tone:

"Hayden Douglas, I am Dickey Deane."

"Dickey Deane! I thought you were in Missouri," exclaimed he in surprise.

"I have been there. Where is the Captain's camp? I must see him."

Hayden turned and led the way to the camp.

She dismounted and gave her pony in charge of Hayden and followed the path leading to the camp. She was frequently stopped by men who unexpectedly darted from behind trees and halted her, until she could give the pass-word of the company.

Dinner was being prepared. There stood the brave old John Brown, with his sleeves rolled up and a large piece of pork before him, from which he was cutting bountiful slices, preparatory to cooking it. She stood for some minutes unnoticed. She was admiring that old man as he stood near the blazing fire, preparing supper for the company, assisted by Pat Devilin.

The old man was poorly clad. He wore a suit of coarse cloth, and his toes protruded from his much-worn shoes. But his eye reflected the fire and his countenance bespoke the noble, determined man he was.

"Never can I forget the scene at that camp," wrote she to Ida Brooks, "as I came upon it in that secluded place. Several horses were tied near, with saddles on them, to be in readiness, if needed. A dozen rifles and sabers were stacked near a tree, while four men well armed lay on some blankets near, conversing in a low tone, while on the opposite side stood two handsome young men, leaning on their guns. One was the noble Hungarian who came to America with Louis Kossuth at the close of the insurrection in Hungary. We call him 'Brave Lavanda.' While in the center, preparing food for the coming meal, was the brave, noble old man, John Brown."

The above extract from "Dickey's" letter gives a true picture of the camp as she found it. Each man having his duty to perform; each moral, kind and polite. Profane or vulgar language was not permitted. The men of that camp were honorable, law-abiding men, who would gladly live peacefully and quietly with their neighbors—men who regretted that stern necessity forced them to fight, but since they were so compelled they would fight to the bitter end.

As she stood contemplating the weird scene which that camp presented, one of them noticed her presence and exclaimed:

"Come on, Miss Dickey, the hospitalities of our camp are ever open to you."

In a moment all had assembled about the place where she stood, and listened patiently while she hurriedly related the latest news, advising them of the impending danger.

Early the next morning the camp was astir, and she took leave of the company—Hayden and "B ave Lavanda" escorting her beyond the picket lines.

She rode up the ravine to a point beyond the path by which she had entered, as she had been instructed to do. She was riding leisurely, in deep meditation, thinking of the hardships and exposure calmly endured by those brave men, whom she had left, in defense of a principle.

Her pony suddenly stopped and snorted, and had she not used a restraining influence on the rein it would have turned. Just ahead in the path flashed the fire from two green eyes. On closer inspection she observed an old coyote with her young by her side.

Pat Devilin had once said: "That a coyote was the only animal that was meaner than an Indian." The remark came to her mind as she watched the brute for a moment. She drew her revolver, but the thought occurred that she must not shoot the infuriated animal, as the act would betray her presence to the enemy, should any happen to be near; besides it would cause her friends in the camp she had just left much annoyance.

She looked the wolf boldly in the eye for a moment, when its gaze relaxed, and giving a low whine as a signal to its young, they bounded away in different directions. The old one stood a moment, until seemingly satisfied that her young were safe, when she too bounded up the path.

Dickey pursued her journey over deep washes and gulleys and high ridges until she reached the open prairie, and turning toward another ravine, which was known as Black Jack, she soon found herself in the vicinity of the camp of the ruffians. Leaving her pony secreted in the dense underbrush she continued her journey on foot, entering the camp as an artist, and leaving during the excitement caused by mistaking the wife of one of their leaders for "Dickey Deane, the spy."

She noted the approach of the men who followed her after she left the wagon, and hastening to her pony, she led him some distance above the only path which led through the ravine, and stopped under a projecting rock, which cast a deep shadow, where she felt safe from observation.

CHAPTER L.

THE STRANGER.

ROBERT and Aunt Nancy returned to New York at the close of the winter, leaving their little home in Osawatomie in the care of Dr. Strawn and Ona.

On their arrival East they became earnestly engaged in soliciting aid for the Free-State settlers of Kansas, while Ona kept them informed regarding the events which transpired there.

Late in May Mr. Leland sent on a quantity of supplies, which he placed in charge of Robert, who accompanied them. On his way to Kansas, Robert was joined by a number of young men, whose only aspiration was to meet and become acquainted with John Brown and fight under his standard.

Upon their arrival at Lawrence, by the way of Iowa and Nebraska, the young men who had accompanied Robert remained there, while he continued his journey to Osawatomie in search of his sister, although a friend had said:

"You may possibly find her there, but it is far easier to catch a flea than to find Dickey Deane."

Robert moved on slowly with his large canvas-covered wagon toward Osawatomie. On his arrival he learned that all the men had gone to Lawrence, except a few who were unable on account of sickness to go.

Being unable to find the key to his house, he proceeded to the hotel kept by Mrs. Benning. There he found one of the sick men, whose ailment had assumed a serious nature. Dr. Strawn had left a quantity of medicine with him on his departure for Lawrence, but now typhoid fever had set in and raged with all its virulent malignity.

Robert realized at once that he must render the stricken one all the aid and attention it was possible for him to do. Although he was an entire stranger, yet sympathy and a sense of justice and right were predominating characteristics in Robert's mind.

He hastened to the Doctor's office, and forcibly entering, procured such medicines as were suited to the old gentleman's case, and instituting himself as nurse, saw that they were properly administered.

Only once had the stranger showed signs of consciousness, and then only for a brief time. He opened his eyes and gazed for a moment into the boyish face above him and said:

"You are Roderick Leland's son."

"Yes," answered Robert.

"I have often seen you, but could not find you when I wished to speak with you," continued the sufferer.

He closed his eyes and continued to talk of a far-off land, calling for his mother and sister to come to him; then he talked of Roderick Leland, asking where he had gone and why had he not come to his own home in Scotland.

He, in his delirium, continued to talk of Scotland and Roderick Leland until Robert began to think that something had transpired, in times past, compelling his father to leave Scotland; otherwise he would return to his old home among the highlands.

For two weeks Robert watched by his bedside, until at last the fever subsided, leaving the old man pale and weak as a child. He opened his eyes and looked inquiringly about, but his young nurse had gone.

Orders had been sent for Robert to report immediately at Lawrence, and he had hastened away.

When the sick man looked around the room for a moment, he said:

"What a strange dream I have had! When I was a young man, living in my old home in England, I had many friends. Among them was a young—"

Just at this moment a woman rushed into the room, exclaiming:

"The Missourians are coming!"

All who were able to leave the house, hastened for protection to the neighboring thickets, except Mrs. Benning and her little daughter. They remained in the sick man's room to defend him, if need be.

"Who are they, Etolia?" asked the sick man, addressing the little girl, as he heard the tramp of horses' feet coming up the street.

The child looked from the open window and saw the approaching cavalry, and replied:

"I don't know, but they have a banner on which is printed in large letters: '*Guy Wren and his brave three hundred.*'"

"Yes, they are, indeed, brave men," said the sick man scornfully. "Etolia, hand me that revolver."

She handed him the weapon, when he said:

"Now watch and see that they do not fire this house."

From the window she watched the plundering band, who had begun their pillaging by emptying all the liquor they could find into their canteens.

"They are coming in, mamma," said Etolia, running to her mother.

"I have no fears, daughter, only for the sick man," and turning to him, said: "Let me hide you."

"Do as you think best," said he.

She hastily concealed him where he lay by covering him with a feather bed, to which she added quilts and pillows, thus giving to the bed the appearance of having no occupant.

Ten or a dozen of the gang entered the house. They searched each room; forcibly opened trunks and satchels, taking possession of everything of value, such as clothing, money and jewelry. They entered the sick man's room, removing the pillows from the bed in search of valuables.

As they lingered, the liquor began to produce its effect, and each moment they became more abusive, threatening the helpless women and children with every manner of punishment if they did not reveal the hiding places of their treasures.

They had just entered the dry-goods store, proposing to transfer all the goods to wagons which they had brought for the purpose. When some one of their number called out:

"Look! yonder comes the Yankees."

"Yonder comes the Yankees," was shouted throughout the town. The ruffians mounted in hot haste and galloped off toward the southeast as fast as their horses could carry them, still retaining such plunder as they could secure about their persons. Their scare had been produced by the return to town of three or four boys who had been fishing. They carried the poles on their shoulders, and the drunken rabble had mistaken them for armed men.

As the ruffians retreated, they met a well-known Pro-Slavery man, who asked:

18

" Where have you been, boys ? "

"We have been fighting Old John Brown, and sacked the town back here and left it burning," answered Wren.

Such was the manner of boasting adopted by the invaders upon all occasions. They had succeeded in burning two or three houses, the women being unable to procure water in time to arrest the flames. By the watchful care of Etolia, the hotel was saved, she having extinguished a number of fires which the demons had started.

The excitement strengthened the old gentleman. Sooner than he anticipated, he was able to be about the house. As he sat by the table one day at dinner, he asked Mrs. Benning :

"Madam, who was my nurse during my sickness?"

To which she replied :

"I do not know his name. He was a youth somewhere in his 'teens,' is all I can tell you."

"I sometimes think I saw him, yet it must have been only a dream," he said as he withdrew from the table.

It was not a dream, the transpirings of the brief past had left their impression upon his semi-unconscious mind, and he now recalled them indistinctly.

He wrote a letter to England, which was addressed to the young lady whom we saw at the bedside of Theodocia. He wrote : "Pet, control your anxiety until Hayden and I return. I feel that my efforts will soon be successful in attaining the object for which I so long have sought. This being the case, I shall, upon my arrival in England, inform you regarding that which you so much desire to know as to who were your parents. With this you must be content until I come." The letter revealed the fact that she was anxious to know regarding her parentage. But Sir Charles was hoping for a brighter day to dawn ere he satisfied the longing desire of the anxious girl.

CHAPTER LI.

A WESTERN HOME.

WHILE murder, plundering and rapine were desecrating the fair fame of the new Territory of Kansas during 1856, many of those who participated in the earlier troubles had returned to the East and there spending happy days.

Among such were Arthur Holmes and Sallie Strawn, who, in their early childhood days, had played together, but the removal of Mr. Strawn had separated them, and until a year previous they had not met; their meeting at that time being accidental.

Sallie, during the absence of the editor-in-chief of a religious journal with which she was associated as assistant editor, was occupying the editorial chair, when Arthur, who was a contributor, entered on a matter of business.

The recognition of each by the other was mutual. The friendship of their childhood days was renewed, and as time grew on apace they learned that each was necessary to the other's happiness. Love superceded the claims of friendship, and on a bright and cheerful morning in May, the ceremony was performed that united their hands as their hearts had long been united.

Leaving the church, they hastened home, where Sallie laid aside the orange blossoms and satin dress and donning a plain traveling attire preparatory to starting to Kansas.

Arthur had already forwarded his goods and a new printing press to Lawrence, and soon he and Sallie were on their way to their future home.

At St. Louis they learned that they must continue their journey by the way of Iowa. When they reached the Kaw or Kansas river, they were compelled to await the falling of the waters ere they could cross to Lawrence.

In search of shelter, they drove some ten miles down the river toward Missouri, until they reached a small log house, where they procured food and the desired shelter.

It was a true type of the Pro-Slavery settler's home, who came to the Territory for the purpose of "jumping the claims" of others, and thus holding all the land in the interest of his political faction. Sallie stood a moment hesitating at the door step before she could muster sufficient courage to enter.

The house was small—twelve or fourteen feet square—containing but one room, which was warmed by the fire of logs which blazed upon a rude fireplace. The same fire served the purpose of cooking,

there being a large spider or oven sitting on the
coals which contained corn-meal dough, prepared
with water and seasoned with salt alone to make it
palatable, while suspended on a hook above the fire
was a pot containing some kind of meat.

Near the fire sat a lean, lank man of about forty
years.   He was clad in coarse brown home-spun
clothing. His head was covered with a broad slouch
hat that had once been white, while his unkempt
beard and uncombed hair, with their accumulation
of dirt, gave to him a horridly repulsive appearance.

His legs were crossed; his jaws were constantly
moving, masticating a huge quid of tobacco, while
his occupation seemed only to be whittling on a stick
with a huge jack-knife.

He merely looked up as Sallie stood at the door
making known her wants.   When she had finished,
he resumed his whittling, leaving his wife to attend
to those wants.

The wife, a large red-faced woman, was bending
over the pot, holding the lid in one hand and a large
black iron spoon in the other.

On hearing the voice of the stranger at the door,
she replaced the lid, and using the skirt of her dress
to protect her hands from being burned, she drew
the oven off the coals, and approaching Sallie, who
had seated herself on a rickity chair near the door,
exclaimed :

"Thar' is a plenty to eat sich as 'tis. If yer want
to stop over with we'uns awhile you can do so."

"Thank you," said Sallie, as she went to inform
Arthur, who returned to the house with her.

As they entered the house they looked around, to discover, if possible, anything that indicated a home-like comfort. In one corner hung two or three sides of bacon, against the wall of logs, near by, was suspended a piece of flannel that had once been red, but was now smoked to such an extent, that its original color could not be recognized, on this flannel were stitched small pieces of cloth, making little pockets, in rows, its entire length. This was all in the way of ornaments that the room contained. Rough boards formed the roof. There was an opening for a window, which had not been supplied with glass. The floor was composed of rough, thick boards, whose weight kept them in place. The door swung on wooden hinges, all convincing evidence that a higher or more appreciative evidence of civilization did not exist within the rude structure.

"Whar be you'uns gwine?" asked the woman, as she seized a rag, the color of which would indicate that it had been used as a pot-rag for half a century, and wiped the dust from a pan, into which she dipped some flour from an open barrel.

"We are on our way to Lawrence, but were unable to cross the river," answered Sallie.

"La sakes! The Yankees will kill you sartin as you go thar, they are dreadful. My Bill, thar," said she, pointing toward the man in the corner, " he's jist come back from that Yankee hole, an he sez its the meanest place he ever seed. Why, the poor trash up thar put on as much airs as the rich amongst we uns, an they ar a follerin all the tricks you ever heerd on to make a livin. You Bounce, you black pup,

you jist keep your nose outen that oven, git outen
the house, I tell you." Thus she screamed at the
large dog, while she worked the dough with greater
vigor. She continued, "I want the niggers to have
this yere work to do, an they will, sho, if this is a slave
state. Mr. Capt. Guy Wren says he'll give my Bill
two niggers, if he'll jist stay here till nex spring."

By this time Arthur concluded to feed his team
and Sallie went with him to consult upon the propriety of stopping at this place. They concluded
they could humor the political views of the woman,
by seeming to agree with her in her condemnation
of the Yankees.

When the meal was announced, Arthur and Sallie,
with the man and woman, seated themselves at the
table, which was, like the surrounding furniture, made
of the roughest material, without paint or even a
cloth, to hide the finger-marks made by the children
and the accumulation of milk and grease-spots which
adorned its surface.

Plates of the roughest ware, and large earthen
bowls contained the food prepared for the visitors,
while tin-cups served as drinking vessels. Knives
and forks that had never known the virtues of brick-
dust or sand, while the latter occasionally could boast
of one tine, yet generally they were minus the han-
dles.

On a tin pie-pan lay corn bread—called corn'
dodger—on top of which lay the buscuits—called by
the children "flat-outs." A large dish of bacon and
beans occupied the middle of the table, containing
the same large iron spoon or ladle that was used in

stirring the vessel over the fire. On one end of the table sat a plate of butter, which seemed to have been bleached—the only really white article the cabin contained. The coffee, made of parched and pounded rye, was poured from an earthen vessel that was smoked by the coals and streaked by the ebulitions of years.

"Bill," the man of the house, bent over his plate without looking up; his uncombed hair and whiskers contained numerous feathers and many straws. His hands were of the same somber hue as the bare feet of the children who clustered near the table, looking toward it whistfully until the eldest mustered sufficient courage to ask his mother for "one of 'em yere flat-outs."

Poor child! One effort to obtain a "flat-out" was sufficient. His hope was crushed and his aspiration killed, when his mother yelled at the top of her voice:

"You, John William, you jist shut yer mouth or I'll bust it wide open. Git yout o' this ere house right away or I'll mash yer snoot."

At this time Arthur addressed the man:

"Mister, are you a hunter?" asked Arthur as he glanced toward a rifle and guns of every variety suspended from hooks upon the wall.

"Not much of a one," drawled he so slowly that Arthur gave up the effort of inducing him to speak.

They continued the meal in silence, save when the old lady thought proper to abuse one of the group of children who still persisted in demanding "one of 'em air flat-outs."

After they had finished their repast, they concluded to take a view of the surroundings. As Sallie
took up her hat, she observed that the trimmings
were sadly out of place and one of the bows missing.
She glanced toward the children and observed that
one of the little girls had the bow pinned to her
dress and seemed to be lost in admiration of the
beautiful ornament.

The mother at the same time noticed the ribbon
in the child's possession and in an instant began
abusing the little one, who, in the unconsciousness of
youth and innocence, had appropriated the gew-gaw
to her own use.

The child seemed to feel hurt; tears flowed freely
from her eyes as her mother ranted about, more like
a beast than a human being, until Sallie thoughtfully
suggested that the child be permitted to retain the
ribbon, and thus secured quiet to the household and
saved the innocent one from a severe punishment.

As Arthur and Sallie walked from the house, he
said: "It takes all manner of people to make a
world, and here is a phase of Western life that is new
to you. What do you think about it?"

"Well, Arthur, to be candid, my surprise has been
so great, that I have had scarcely sufficient time to
collect my thoughts, to say nothing about expressing them. But it does, really, seem strange to me
how such a man can sit, listlessly, in one corner of a
house on such a beautiful day as this has been and,
seemingly, make no effort to work. His appearance
indicates that he does nothing, or certainly he would
not present so slovenly an appearance. His wife

seems to be energetic, and I cannot comprehend how she can submit to be tied to such a good-for-nothing man."

" I do not, entirely, agree with you, Sallie," said Arthur. "I think the woman has, in this case, usurped the management of affairs generally, until the man has become disheartened."

" Disheartened, indeed! A pretty state of affairs, when men become disheartened and quietly sit, waiting for a woman to keep their spirits up. It is, merely pure laziness, if that man had one iota of energy he would either go to work or leave home. I have observed the ways of the world to some extent, and I always find that these come-easy, go-easy people never amount to much."

" They don't eh?" said he, patting her on the chin.

" No, indeed, they don't, and I will assure you, that ' My Bill,' as she calls him, was one of these good, easy, young fellows who spent his time loafing around bar-rooms, playing cards, or leaning against the fence, listlessly watching a horse-race, and finally married that woman because she was industrious. I feel sorry for those children and that woman."

" Do you not feel sorry for poor Bill, too?" laughingly asked Arthur.

" Indeed, I do not. The world is ever ready to sympathize with just such men as Bill, and never speak one good word for the woman. I'll admit that this woman displays too much temper, but it may be that she is disheartened. Temper in women is an excellent thing. I do not admire it when it be-

comes demonstrative, as in this case, but I do love to
see it flash in the eye and glint across the cheek.
Where there is a properly controlled temper, there is
industry, skill and energy. Come-easy, go-easy ap-
plies to women as well as men."

"On my previous visit to this country, I observed
the same peculiarity in very many women, as we see
demonstrated here to-day, their tendency is to be
loud and boisterous."

"Yes, I will admit all that, and I will venture the
assertion, that had you been a close observer, you
would have noticed that in just such places the men
were lazy and shiftless, good-for-nothing sort of beings. The women have some energy and pride
about them, and, in all probability, have begged and
coaxed, and pleaded with the men to stir about and
accomplish something toward the support of the
family, until their patience has become exhausted,
and finally resorted to scolding and the use of harsh-
er language, until it has become almost second nature, and they cannot refrain."

"You are quite a champion of the rights and privileges of women. But you have forgotten, that
while many of the men of the West make no great
display of energy, they are only following in the
footsteps of the women of the East. Where will
you find greater indolence than among the women of
the cities?"

"I'll admit that there are too many there who submit to be the slaves of fashion and think it ignoble
to be industrious, yet they have no hesitancy in accepting the hard earnings of father or brother who,

by labor or business tact, may have secured a competency. I can not see that this woman is lazy. Her hair is nicely combed and neatly braided; her hands and face are clean, while 'Bill' is evidently too lazy to either wash his face or comb his hair."

"But what a dirty house she keeps!"

"It is just as I said before. No allowance is made for women. Is it her duty to provide things to do with? If 'Bill' would display the least energy whatever, I feel assured that his wife would appreciate his efforts and use to advantage anything he could secure tending toward beautifying their home. But who are those men approaching yonder? Perhaps, Arthur, you had better find shelter from observation. They may be some of the invaders."

"I shall not leave you," said Arthur, as he stood by her side, "although I believe you are right in your surmises. They are at least thoroughly armed."

CHAPTER LII.

THE BATTLE OF BLACK JACK.

THE approaching horsemen caused Dickey to seek the shelter of a cluster of grape-vines, where she secreted herself, grasping her revolver, prepared for any emergency.

They hurried on in pursuit. When they had passed her place of concealment, she proceeded in another direction, until she found her pony, which she had hidden, ere she entered the invaders' camp as a sailor.

She led the pony cautiously up the ravine, pausing frequently to listen to the sound of the receding footsteps of the horses as they hurried on, their riders imagining themselves to be close upon the audacious sailor.

After moving thus quietly for about two miles, she emerged upon the high prairie. Proceeding to a house which she saw in the distance, she was surprised on beholding Dr. Strawn's pony, with saddle and bridle on, grazing near the door. Her near approach was heralded by the barking of dogs, of which each settler had an abundant supply. The demonstration on the part of the dogs brought the inmates to the door, among whom Dickey, in glad surprise, recognized her brother, Robert Leland.

After a moment's greeting and anxious inquiry, Dickey hastened on toward the camp of John Brown, to whom she had promised to convey all possible information at the earliest practicable hour regarding the disposition of the invaders between his camp and Hickory point, a prominent position near the ravine where he was encamped.

After she had imparted the information, but few minutes elapsed ere the men were in the saddle, to form a junction with Captain Beach's company and move on the enemy early the following morning.

Dickey watched them as they passed from camp up the ravine by twos, Brown himself leading, closely followed by "Brave Lavanda" and Hayden Douglas, riding side by side.

The following day being Sunday, a few men gathered at Dr. Foster's to hold religious services, each man carrying his rifle or weapon of some description. The doctor himself was a prisoner in the camp at Black Jack. Rev. Mr. Jones preached from the text, "The wicked flee when no man pursueth." The congregation were singing the last hymn, preparatory to being dismissed, when a watcher cried out, "The Missourians are coming." The benediction was omitted, as each man seized his gun.

The ruffians, six in number, had galloped near, not expecting to find any besides the family at home. As the congregation rushed out, they succeeded in surrounding four of the gang. The two hindmost, although many bullets were sent after them, succeeded in effecting their escape.

Two days previous, this same gang had brutally shot and left for dead, a young man on the Kaw river, and were now on a mission of blood toward Prairie City, but were, fortunately, intercepted by the worshipers.

The prisoners were disarmed and secured. They were left in charge of two men, while the balance went in search of Brown and Beach's commands.

The companies were soon united and taking up the line of march, they reached the vicinity of the enemies camp late at night.

They left their horses in the ravine and proceeded cautiously toward the camp. Each Captain had selected from among his own men, those who were skillful as marksmen.

Early on Monday, as the ruffians were preparing

their breakfast, their outer pickets were driven in by the three advancing men of Brown's company.

" The Abolitionists are coming," shouted the fleeing pickets, as they rushed into camp.

Brown in the ravine below, and Beach above, poured volley after volley into the camp of the frightened invaders until they hoisted a white flag, although half of their number had disappeared over the ridge toward Missouri.

The result of the surprise was the release of the friends of the Free-State men and the driving of the band from the Territory.

The next morning Brown had a consultation with Dickey, after which she hastened to the house where she had left Robert, when they both proceeded to Lawrence, where Dickey exchanged her gaudy sailor suit for a plainer one, and taking a pedler's case, set out for Missouri. Robert accompanied her as far as Shawnee Mission, where he purchased a roan pony for her, Raven being too well known on the border.

The second night she stopped at a house near which was a camp of nearly two thousand Georgians. After supper she, accompanied by the gentleman of the house, proceeded to the camp, carrying her pedler's case.

CHAPTER LIII.

ARTHUR HOLMES SHOT.

SALLIE clung closely to Arthur as the horsemen approached. As they came near, one in a low gruff voice asked :

" Who are you ?"

" My name is Arthur Holmes," said he.

" Are you the Holmes from New York who sent that printing press to Lawrence?"

" I sent a printing press to Lawrence this spring," replied Arthur.

" You had better turn and run for your life or be shot where you stand, just as you choose," and before he could make a show of resistance or offer one word in defense, they drew their guns and fired upon him. He fell to the ground, and they galloped away in the direction from which they came.

The firing brought the man and women from the cabin. They saw the horsemen riding away and heard the heart-rending cries of the young wife. The woman hastened to where Sallie was standing and beheld the prostrate form of Arthur, covered with blood, while Bill came poking leisurely along. When he arrived, his wife exclaimed :

" Bill, see what the bloody hounds have done. Help me carry him to the house. He is awfully shot up, but ain't dead, and maybe we can do something for him."

They carried him to the cabin and laid him carefully upon the only bed it contained. The woman drew a box from under the bed which contained many and various sized bottles. She soon removed Arthur's coat and began her examination. In a brief time she exclaimed:

"No bones broke; two holes in the arm and one in the shoulder. Guess we'll fetch him through all right. Don't yer be oneasy, Miss. I reckon he'll be around soon as he gits over the loss of blood. My sakes, Bill, what yer doin'? Ain't yer got them air bandiges yit?"

All the while Sallie, almost unconscious, sat near the pillow. The rough, though kindly attentions and words of the woman, gave her great encouragement, and by a great effort she calmed herself.

The woman watched over the wounded man carefully, applying liniments and lotions and arranging the bandages as needed, until at the end of three days he was able to walk out, as the woman had predicted.

As he and Sallie sat near the house under the wide-spreading branches of a tree, he said:

"Sallie, I must agree with you in your opinion of the readiness of resource of a woman in a case of emergency as compared with men. Had I been surrounded with men, I have no doubt I should have bled to death ere proper assistance could have been rendered."

During the afternoon they bade their friends adieu and drove toward Lawrence, Sallie assuming the management of the team.

19

Upon their arrival, Arthur learned of the destruction of his press by the invaders, and everybody was excited over the battle of Black Jack. The report was also current that Dickey Deane had been captured and carried away by the Missourians.

Sallie met Robert Leland in Lawrence, but he could give no information regarding the missing spy. Arthur could find no employment, so as soon as he was able, he hastened to join Brown's men. Going toward Franklin, he learned that a body of men were encamped near there, and following a path down the ravine, he soon found himself in the midst of a company of dragoons from Georgia. The leader addressed him by saying:

" Hallo, young man, which way ?"

" I am hunting a pony that strayed away the other day," replied Arthur.

" It's more probable you are trying to steal one of ours. Here men," said he, calling to a couple of men who stood near, " look after this horse-thief."

He was released the next morning and started on his way without his breakfast. He had gone but a short distance, when he was overtaken by two men who accused him of stealing two horses that were missing. He denied the charge and returned to the camp, where the Captain ordered him tied and held for trial. Arthur knew it was only an excuse to hold him until opportunity offered to send him to Missouri.

CHAPTER LIV.

THE COMPANIONS.

AFTER writing the letter, Sir Charles seated himself upon the porch of the hotel, enjoying the beautiful scenery. As he sat there, he noted the approach of a young gentleman on horseback, who reined up in front of the hotel and politely inquired, if Mrs. Benning was at home.

The lady, in passing the door, heard the inquiry and stepped out to learn the wants of the inquirer, when the young man, producing a letter, said, " Mrs. Benning, will you favor me by handing this letter to Dickey Deane, should she return to this place ere I see her?"

Mrs. Benning consented to act as requested, whereat the young man, bidding her adieu, returned by the same way he entered the village.

After his departure, Sir Charles, in some excitement, addressed the landlady, asking :

" Mrs. Benning, who is that young gentleman who just rode away?"

She replied by saying, " I think he is Dickey Deane's brother."

" Dickey Deane, the spy?" inquired he.

" Yes, sir," answered Mrs. Benning.

Each resident in that community had learned to be cautious, and Mrs. Benning was not an exception to the rule. Although Sir Charles had been an inmate of her house during his sicknes and had developed the proper spirit in resisting the invaders, yet Mrs. Benning did not feel at liberty to converse with him freely upon political affairs, therefore she did not tell him that the youth was a member of John Brown's company, or that the same youth had been his nurse during his illness.

Sir Charles, in a few days, determined to return to the company, from which he had been absent nearly two months, so procuring a small, rickety old spring wagon, he set out for Lawrence. At Prairie City he learned that the "boys" were encamped at Hickory Point, whither he proceeded on horseback.

Approaching the camp, he dismounted and proceded slowly, being frequently halted by the outer guards, to whom he gave the countersign. As he drew near the encampment, he hesitated, taking note of the arrangement of the camp and of those on duty.

To the left stood Hayden and "Brave Lavanda," engaged in cleaning their weapons. Others were similarly engaged in other parts of the camp, while John Brown was arranging a number of letters, preparatory to entrusting them to a messenger to carry to the nearest post-office.

Hayden glanced in the direction of his position and momentarily started. A second look seemed to convince him of the correctness of his first impression, and he eagerly sprang forward to meet his "old companion."

He grasped him earnestly and lovingly by the hand, and made anxious inquiry regarding his health, being alarmed at his failing appearance, as

denoted by his blanched cheek and weakened step.
Hayden had not learned of his recent illness, and his
emaciated appearance caused him much anxiety,
Sir Charles being the only friend he possessed in
America.

As they were seated, conversing upon topics of
interest to themselves, they were observed by Brown,
who was still writing. As he recognized them, he
wrote to North Elba, his home :

"Noblemen and scholars of other lands have
joined me in this strife for freedom here on the broad
prairies of the West. Then why should I cease to
hope?"

Sir Charles intimated his intention of returning to
England during the coming autumn, and urged Hayden to accompany him, to which Hayden replied:

"Sir Charles, as you are well aware, my greatest
pleasure is to be near, and, in fact, constantly with
you. Your location during the past few months being unknown to me, has caused me much anxiety,
and although I should be pleased in accompanying
you to England, yet I, at the same time, feel that
duty compels me to remain here while this strife con-
tinues and put forth my greatest efforts in the establishment of freedom on the soil of this Territory, besides in England there are none to care for me, except yourself, and I prefer to remain in these woods
rather than return to the crowded salons and thronged
thoroughfares a stranger, where none love or care for
me, though surrounded by thousands."

"Well, well, my boy, are you not judging too
harshly?"

"I think not, Sir Charles. There are some in England, who are my friends, but only by reason of your patronage, you being a leading man of the nation, friendship must be extended to your *protege.*"

"Is not such the case the world over?" asked Sir Charles.

"Not invariably," replied Hayden. "Here in America friendships are formed by associations, which time can not sever. Privations are endured here which eternally cement the friendship of the participants. I feel to-day a feeling of friendship, nearer and dearer toward the companions in this camp who have struggled for the everlasting principle of freedom, than I do for any of my friends of former days in England. Wealth nor social standing causes neither difference nor distinction here. Caste is discarded, and men are judged as men, so long as they act the part of men, and are industrious and energetic. No, Sir Charles, I cannot forsake duty and true friends to accompany you to England."

"I shall not endeavor further to induce you to forsake, even for a brief time, the noble cause in which you are engaged. Be true to the cause you have espoused. It is a noble and grand one; adhere firmly to the principle you have avowed. But as for myself, I must not remain here longer than the middle of September."

Hayden pulled his hat down over his eyes and whipped the long grass with the ramrod which he held in his hand.

He had formed ties of friendship in the New World and he was loth to sever them. His early life had been one of seclusion. When a mere child, he had been domiciled in a gloomy castle on the Thames, where his education was supervised by a stern and strict old German professor. He had wearied of the restraints and formalities of the Old World, while in the New World there was ample scope for his freedom-loving mind. His native romance led him to appreciate the camp and give it precedence over the parlor. The common cause of freedom developed friendships which could not be acquired where formality reigned.

"There comes 'Dickey Deane, the spy of Osawatomie,'" said Hayden to Sir Charles, as they still sat upon the log.

"Who is she?" asked Sir Charles.

"Sir Charles, it is rumored that she is descended from the Scotch family of Macdonalds, of which one of the later members won great distinction with Bonaparte. Her bearing certainly indicates noble blood."

"What do you mean, Hayden?"

"Just what I say, Sir Charles, although I cannot vouch for the truth of the report," and he stepped forward to meet his little friend.

Sir Charles soliloquized, "Who of noted and noble descent is not engaged in this struggle for freedom?" and he continued to gaze upon the noble looking little woman, who had won the applause of the world by her brave acts as "The spy of Osawatomie."

CHAPTER LV.

THE MISSING SPY.

DICKEY felt a certain degree of timidity, as the contents of her pedler's case were inspected by the ruffians in the camp, but she betrayed no outward emotion, being conscious that the contents of the case would not betray her.

She remained in the vicinity of the camp, visiting it frequently for nearly two weeks, never losing an opportunity to be present during any meeting of the officers, thus gathering up many items of interest regarding their future intentions and movements.

At the close of two weeks she ascertained that they contemplated an early move into the territory of Kansas.

On her departure, she intimated her intentions of going to St. Louis for a new and larger supply, and would revisit the camp on their return from Kansas, but she was soon hastening toward Brown's camp in the Territory.

She had crossed the State line and was urging the pony to its greatest speed, when, upon attempting to cross a small stream, the pony suddenly stopped, and she could neither persuade nor compel it to go further. Such procedure on the part of the pony was to her unexplicable, and she endeavored to ascertain, if possible, the cause. Her attention was called to a movement in the bushes which fringed the stream, and in a moment, a human form stood before her and a voice exclaimed:

" Bress de Lord, Massa Dick, whar is you come from?"

In a moment Dickey recognized the negro woman who had charge of the cooking at the hotel in Westport, and asked:

" Aunt Mary, what are you doing here?"

"Don't talk loud, Massa Dick, an I tell you all bout it. Dem air men in Wespo who owned slaves, tuk a big scare lest Ole John Brown should drop down on em, some night, an carry off all de darkies, so dey sole us niggas fur to go Souf an work on de plantation, so as to be suah of not losen on us, an when de buyers come, dey put us all in a camp and chained de boys and put a guard ober us all. De night was berry dark, an wen all de oders was asleep and de guards busy playin' keerds, I jist slipped away in de woods an kep on agoin Souf till I runned inter dis road a runnin west, an I follered it till broad day, then I shinned up a tree and staid till dark."

" Why, Aunt Mary, have you had anything to eat?"

" Yes, Massa Dick, I just helped myself to de green corn. I heerd you a comin and hid in de bush. When I seed you, I was mighty glad, cos I knowed you was my fren. I was a huntin' Ole Massa John Brown's camp. Dey say he helps de niggas a heap."

" Where is your baby?"

Aunt Mary burst into tears at the mention of her child, and sobbed, " I luf it home. Ole Missus sed as how she would keep it an I could cum back an see it, some time, but, bress de Lord, Massa Dick, I can sooner go widout eaten, dan be widout dat are little honey. O, Massa Dick, I wish to de good Lord, dis poor lone nigga could die."

"Aunt Mary, why did you come to me? Are you not afraid I will tell the buyers where you are?"

"Ise aint a bit afeerd, Massa Dick, cos I heerd Massa John say hissef, as how you was one of Massa Brown's company, an you had spided out all dar plans. I dis wish I could get some of Massa Brown's men to dun fetch me dat ar, little baby," saying which, she gave way to her feelings and wept bitterly.

"Dickey felt keenly for the poor woman in her distress, and she felt it her duty to put forth an effort to assist her. She at last asked, "Do you think, Aunt Mary, that I can get your baby if I go to the hotel?"

"I don know, Massa Dick. Spec you could if you try. Wish to de good Lord you would."

"I will make the attempt. You stay near this place and take care of my case until I return."

"Bress de Lord, Massa Dick, is you a goin? I dis do anything what you says. I foun dis yer ole quilt dis mornin an I can lib on de berries and de corn till you cum back."

Handing her case to Mary, Dickey rode away toward Shawnee Mission. Night had settled her gloom over the earth, ere she entered the place. She met a young Indian of whom she purchased a hat and jacket which she secreted, and sought entertainment for the night. The following day she repaired to the timber where she donned her Indian costume and staining her hands and face, she proceeded leisurely toward Westport, arriving there about sunset. As she passed down the street leading to the hotel, she noticed many familiar faces, but none recognized in the Indian boy, the notorious Abolition spy, Dickey Deane.

Riding up in front of the hotel, she dismounted, and seating herself upon the curbstone, held her pony by the bridle. She sat thus for some time, manifesting no interest in events transpiring about her, until the landlord, noticing the somewhat jaded pony, inquired of the Indian boy his wants, to which the reply was made:

"Sewansee want feed for pony and place to spread blankets."

This sentence was uttered slowly, with the peculiar brevity of the Indian race.

The landlord, knowing the peculiarities of the Indians, without further inquiry, took the bridle and led the pony to the stable, the Indian boy following, and carefully noting where the saddle and bridle were placed, and followed the landlord to the house, carrying a large blanket.

Supper being over, the Indian boy rambled about the yard, carefully noting the location of gates and paths leading to the stable.

While eating supper, Dickey noticed the child playing upon the floor of the dining-room.

When bed-time came, and the landlord was wondering what disposition he should make of the dirty young Indian, Dickey quietly picked up the blanket, and pointing to the floor, looked at him inquiringly, as much as to say, "Can I sleep there?" The landlord gave immediate and willing assent, glad indeed of any excuse to keep the Indian out of his neat beds.

Before Dickey spread the blanket, she saw where little Jim, the colored baby, was put to bed, in an old crib in the kitchen, near the dining-room door.

Rolling herself in the blanket, after the manner of the Indians, she lay down, awaiting sleep and quiet to visit the household.

Near midnight she quietly arose, and going to the stable, saddled the pony and led it out to the gate in the rear of the kitchen.

The passing clouds obscured the moon, which cast out a somber light over the earth. Hastily, yet quietly, she entered the house, picked up her blanket, and lifted the child gently from its bed, wrapped it comfortably in the blanket and hastened to mount the pony and rode away.

She left a twenty-dollar gold piece upon the table in payment for the child, having thus, Indian-like, fixed its price without consulting the owner.

At day-break the next morning, when the cook came down to prepare breakfast, she discovered that the Indian boy was not on the floor. No suspicion arose in her mind until, on entering the kitchen, she discovered that little Jim was missing from his crib. She immediately called the proprietor, informing him of the facts. He immediately suspicioned the Indian as being connected with Jim's disappearance, and on

going to the stable, he found the pony had been removed.   Search was made everywhere upon the
premises, but no further trace could be found.   At
the table, the matter was discussed and the conclusion reached that the Indian had been employed by
some one to steal the child, possibly some of the
men who had bought the older slaves.

Some were sent to the camp of the slave dealers,
while others went to Shawnee to make inquiry.
They had scarcely left town when two men appeared
from the negro camp, stating that Aunt Mary had
escaped.· Then many supposed that she had returned to the house and stolen therefrom her own
child.

CHAPTER LVI.

THE WICKED FLEE.

ARTHUR HOLMES found himself a prisoner
in the camp of the dragoons.   He was sufficiently conversant with the manner of conducting such trials as he was doomed to undergo to
know what the verdict would be.   He recognized in
the commander one with whom, in former times, he
had had a disagreement over some trivial matter.
His proud spirit would not permit him to look with
complaisance upon one who would thus take advantage of his official position, to seek vengeance when

his personal ability had been unequal to the task of protecting him in the argument which had taken place.

He became sullen and refused to answer the questions propounded, and when an order came, requiring the troops to move to Osawatomie, he likewise, refused to go, saying, "I am a free American citizen and if I am longer detained, I shall seek redress by notifying the Governor of my own state. My friends know of my being here, and should anything occur to prevent my return, the proper authorities will be promptly notified."

A consultation was held and it was decided to release him, which was accordingly done, some of the men, however, retained his revolver. After he was released, he went on toward Prairie City, where he met some half-dozen of Brown's men who were on their way to Potawatomie. He procured a horse and accompanied them.

After traveling some eight miles toward Osawatomie, which place they would have to pass to reach their destination, they espied a moving object in the distance, which, upon inspection by the aid of field-glasses, they discovered to be a body of troops numbering about one hundred. They hastened on to get a nearer view, to note the character of the troops. When they had approached sufficiently near, they ascertained that they were a body of Border Ruffians, who had stopped upon discovering the approach of the few men.

"What shall we do?" asked one. "If we turn away they, being better mounted, will overtake us."

" Let us play a 'Yankee trick' on them," said Arthur. " Here, give me a couple of handkerchiefs."

The handkerchiefs were tied together, and ordering the men to stand between himself and the main body, he began a series of signalings, as if communicating with some one in the ravine, from whence they had just come.

The Ruffians had noticed the men dismount, and being supplied with glasses, had observed the signals, as if calling for reinforcements, or giving directions for intercepting them as they proceeded.

Being unable to divine the object of the signals, the Ruffians started slowly toward Missouri. The signaling was carried on more energetically, until the Missourians concluded that some rapid movement tending to their interception was being executed, when they hastened and at last, panic-stricken, they were riding at the top of their speed toward the State line.

The few men started in hot pursuit, not giving up the chase until the Missourians were across the border.

The idea of safety being bounded by State lines, did not enter the minds of the pursued, who continued their flight until they reached Harrisonville. Some days after, they learned from a Pro-Slavery settler the true state of affairs.

" It was no laughing matter," said Wren, who was the commander. "We could not tell how many there were, and we had to run or take the chances of being caught, as we were at Black Jack."

Many of the Border Ruffians by this time began

to entertain a holy horror at the mention of the name of John Brown. They supposed him to be a supernatural being, having power to protect his men with bright steel armor. His long dirk knives and Sharpe's rifles were a terror in their eyes. Distance seemed no obstacle to the destructive properties of his guns.

A few days after they had been so humbugged, they concluded to return to the Territory, in fact, circumstances compelled them to make a show of activity. The residents in Missouri, wearied of their being quartered on them continually, besides the so-called troops were of that character, personally, that the citizens could no longer endure their depredations and debaucheries. Petty stealing was carried on continually; the good housewives found it next to impossible to realize anything from their henerys or gardens, while the vicinity of the camps bore abundant evidence as to where the poultry had gone, feathers being found everywhere.

They reasoned that if the action of these troops had in any instance been productive to benefit in establishing their views regarding slavery in the Territory, then small inconveniences and discomforts could be borne by the citizens, but in no single instance, with all their boasting and display, had they accomplished their undertaking. The Yankees had not only defeated them in their depredations, but the Free-States men were multiplying to such an extent that the Pro-Slavery force was inadequate in numbers to compete with them, or at least soon would be.

This state of affairs, both at home and across the line, induced them to so soon undertake another invasion. Orders were accordingly given to prepare to move. The citizens well knew what such an order meant. It meant for them to furnish abundantly of everything they, by hard labor, had laid by for their individual use. Without consulting the citizen or farmer, a levy was made upon him for goods, provisions, cattle, horses and sometimes money, all to be used in establishing the institution of human slavery upon the fertile soil of Kansas.

The outfitting of this heterogenious army required one article not generally used, even in larger bodies. Breadstuff and bacon, generally considered necessaries, could, with this army, be laid aside, but whiskey must be freely furnished. Each wagon carried an abundant supply of the vile stuff. The leaders, though with few exceptions, used it freely, for they deemed it necessary to encourage the men, otherwise they would not fight when called upon, being as they were of that character who had no vital interest in the principle for which they were contending, and nothing to lose, should they be defeated.

Even the citizens of Missouri were happy when the Ruffians were in the Territory ; happy not in anticipation of any great victory they would gain, but that they were gone and quiet and security reigned, as it had done before their advent. Besides, while the troops were in Kansas, a hope prevailed among the citizens of Missouri, that they would secure sufficient by foraging, on which to subsist for a brief time, at least, and thus relieve them of their support.

When all was ready the company moved away in good spirits, yet they were not as hilarious as they had been on former occasions. They made their first camp in Kansas, near Middle Creek, south of Osawatomie. From this camp a number of men were sent to join Bill Stout, who was in camp on one of the branches of Moody Creek, awaiting reinforcements and an opportunity to burn Osawatomie.

CHAPTER LVII.

AVA AND KATE.

AS soon as Mrs. Blair had sufficiently recovered to travel, the General accompanied her to St. Joseph, where he left her at the hotel kept by Mr. Oyster.

A strong and lasting feeling of friendship sprang up between Mrs. Blair and the beautiful and lovely Kate. Mrs. Blair's whole nature had undergone a change since Lillie's death. In her life, since that time, she had endeavored to atone for the past, and in cultivating a lovely and lovable disposition, she soon found greater pleasure in harmonizing her views to the consideration of the comfort and happiness of those by whom she was surrounded and with whom she was called upon to associate, than she had experienced in her younger days, when her only object and desire was to win the admiration of such as others of her sex loved.

Kate, especially, attracted her attention from their first meeting, so gentle, so kind, so considerate of the wants of others, not only of her own kind, but her kind disposition manifested itself in the care of the brute creation, which recognized her voice and step, as she visited the yard to attend to their wants.

In conversation with Kate, Mrs. Blair was surprised to find her so well-informed on various subjects, and as their association continued, they each talked freely of their experiences in life. Mrs. Blair related the story of her early days in the South, of her winter visits to Washington and her associations there, of her marriage to General Blair, of the interest she took in the cause of establishing slavery in the new Territory, of her disgust at the manner of conducting the strife, through incompetent squad commanders, and finally, of the change of feeling that had been brought about in her mind through witnessing and experiencing the atrocities committed by their own men, and the corresponding sympathy for the Free-State settlers.

Kate, in turn, related scenes and incidents connected with her early associations in the West, of the number and proximity of the Indians, of her visits to their camps, of their beautiful ponies and their filthy manner of living, and comparing the Indian as he exists in reality with Cooper's description, which she had read with interest. She then would dwell, at length, upon the exploits of Dickey Deane, her cousin, especially dwelling upon the accidental finding of little Ota, of whose history they knew nothing further than her mother had died unknown at the Indian Mission.

Ava took a deeper interest in little Ota, her circumstances calling forth the whole and entire sympathy of the now really kind and considerate Southern lady, and when the news reached St. Joseph of the supposed capture of Dickey Deane, Ava felt as much interest and consideration for her safety as did Kate, and promptly wrote to her husband, asking him to use his influence in having her properly cared for, with the view of her final release.

Strange to say, Kate had concealed the identity of "Dickey Deane" and Ona Leland.

Other efforts were put forth in the interest of Dickey. Mr. Oyster visited the various influential Pro-Slavery citizens of St. Joseph and wrote to Roderick Leland, under the impression that she might possibly have taken a journey home. Mr. Leland's reply informed them that she had not been home and directed them to again advise him, and if the continued search had proved unsuccessful, he would himself try to find her.

A day or two after, while Ava and Kate were discussing the propriety of informing Mr. Leland regarding Dickey's continued disappearance, a young man rode up and hastily dismounted.

"O, see!" exclaimed Kate, "there is Cousin Robert. We shall hear some news of Dickey now."

Mrs. Blair watched the young man attentively as he secured his horse and walked hurriedly to meet his Cousin Kate, who welcomed him kindly and affectionately.

As she noted his movements, she thought of the young sailor who had visited the camp where she was held a prisoner and where she received treatment that would have disgraced the wildest hordes that inhabited and fought upon the steppes of Russia. She subsequently had learned that the sailor was Dickey Deane. She thought of the resemblance that existed between the spy and the new-comer, who was introduced as Kate's Cousin Robert. Might they not be one and the same? Might not the titled of woman be applied to this boy as a blind, or might not this youth before her be in reality a woman? The same deep blue eyes; the same calm and happy expression; the same golden hair; the same peculiarly high forehead; all this Mrs. Blair saw in one brief moment.

CHAPTER LVIII.

THE KILT AND KIRTLE.

AS Dickey reached the suburbs of the city, she urged her pony to greater speed, carrying the "involuntary refugee," as she in after years designated the little colored boy. So gently did she carry it and so easy was the long swinging gallop of the pony, that he slept on, entirely unconscious of his rapid transit, but when the little fellow did awake he uttered a long and loud protest against his strange surroundings. Dickey became anxious, lest his cries should arouse the inhabitants, and to secure quiet she was compelled to pin the the blanket closely over his mouth.

At day-light, she had reached a point near where she had left Aunt Mary. Cautiously descending into the valley, she entered the bushes, but before she had moved far through the dense and tangled thicket, Aunt Mary met her, and with outstretched hands asked for the child. Dickey handed her the bundle and watched her as she removed the blanket, which she dropped to the ground, clinging convulsively and lovingly to the child, alternately addressing it by endearing names and calling upon "de Good Massa to bress young Massa Dick."

In all her efforts to do good, never before had the glow of perfect happiness so entirely pervaded her mind, as it did when she witnessed the happiness she had been the means of conveying to this poor, lone and destitute woman, in the restoration of her child, whose absence she had mourned.

In her happiness Aunt Mary forgot her poverty, her destitution, her loneliness, and even forgot the danger of being apprehended by those who were searching for her, until Dickey said :

"Come, Aunt Mary, we must leave here as rapidly as possible, we are not yet free from danger."·

"Bress de Lord, Massa Dick, Ise ready to go anywhere now. You jist lead an dis po chile foller an pack de pickaninny."

"No, Aunt Mary, you have had nothing substantial to eat, and I must insist upon your riding while I, who am strong, can walk."

Without further ceremony Aunt Mary mounted

the pony and took the child. Dickey led the way
on foot toward Brown's camp, which they reached in
safety.

Arriving at the camp, Dickey left the fugitives
outside, while she went in search of the Captain, to
inform him of what she had done. As she entered
the camp, Hayden was the first to recognize and
hasten forward to greet the long lost spy.

She soon met Capt. Brown and informed him of
her adventure and its successful termination. The
old man kindly and gladly approved her action, and
soon Aunt Mary and her boy were comfortably fixed
in camp, to the great surprise and joy of all.

Sir Charles' whole attention was given to Dickey,
as she moved about the camp superintending the arrangements for Aunt Mary's comfort. There was a
charm about the expression of her face which he
loved to dwell upon. She entered the ladies' tent
and laid aside the costume she had worn, and donning one which she always wore in camp, which consisted of the plaid stockings, short dress and neat
jacket, in fact the " kilt and kirtle " of the Scottish
lassie, she again appeared, and entered into an earnest and vivacious conversation with Capt. Brown,
giving him in detail the information she had obtained
while pedling in Missouri.

At sight of her in the familiar costume of the Old
World, with her golden ringlets waving in the wind
and displaying a brow, the beauty of which was as
famous as were her deeds, his thoughts carried him
away to scenes of childhood, when he " roved, a
young Highlander o'er the dark heath." He ap-

proached nearer, and as he traced the lineaments of her face, he said, "Can she be the daughter of Roderick? She certainly bears a family resemblance, and the story of her being connected with the Macdonald clan, gives favor to my apprehensions."

After she and Brown had talked for some time, the old man said:

"Miss Dickey, we have missed your cheering songs. May I inform the boys that you will sing them a favorite?"

She smiled assent, and the old man called the men together and Dickey sang the song known as "The Old Granite State," and each time as her strong, yet sweet voice warbled the refrain,

"O, thy mountains and hills are still dearer to me
Than the broad, sweeping plains of the West."

the eyes of Sir Charles would glisten with the gathering tears as his thoughts carried him back to "Bonnie Scotland," roaming over her hills and dales, listening to the songs of the loved and loving "lassie" who accompanied him. His thoughts wafted away to the days when a brave girl sang to the hills and vales of the land where freedom found friends and liberty was a birthright.

Hayden witnessed the emotion of his friend and companion, and imagined that the song had revived memories of the past in the mind of the old gentleman, as it had done in his.

She had just finished the song, when a messenger arrived from Lawrence, bearing letters for members of the company. Among the number was one bearing the post-mark of Osawatomie, addressed to her.

Breaking the seal, she read the contents of the missive, which merely said : " Thursday evening, at Van Horn crossing." Signed " Friend."

She handed it to Capt. Brown, remarking :

" There is certainly some foul play connected with this affair. I have no familiar acquaintances at Van Horn crossing. Robert is not in Osawatomie, and Dr. Strawn did not write this letter. To-day is Tuesday. I shall rest to-morrow and meet the appointment the next day. I may be enabled to learn something to our advantage."

" Do as you think best, Dickey, but be very cautious."

On Thursday morning she mounted Raven, and accompanied by Hayden, " Brave Lavanda," Pat Devilin and Bill Stout, Dickey and Hayden took the lead and rode rapidly toward the appointed place of meeting, the others following. Each man carried, besides his rifle, two large revolvers, while Dickey carried her trusty weapon in the pocket of her kirtle. Scarcely a word was spoken. Each person was busy with his own thoughts, as they hurried along, generally by twos and often in single file, after the Indian mode of traveling.

The word "evening" in the letter was understood, after the manner of the country, to mean at "sundown."

As they neared the place designated, the last glimmering rays of the sun gilded the tops of the mounds. The party had arrived at the river, some distance west of the appointed place, and followed its course under the protection of the trees, so as to avoid an ambush, if such was the design of the party sending the letter.

They halted in a thicket of post-oaks, about one half mile from the crossing. As the gloaming grew deeper, they rode nearer to the ford, when Dickey dismounted and in her moccasins crept to a dense thicket near the ford. She could neither see or hear any one. In the distance she finally heard the sound of horses feet, which approached rapidly. When they came near the river, the riders dismounted, one of whom approached the crossing cautiously, and finding no one in view, he gave a low whistle, which was promptly answered, and he was soon joined by two other men.

As they drew near, the former said in a low, gruff voice, which Dickey recognized as Guy Wren's:

"I did not think your plan would work. You see she is not here."

To which the other replied, "Wait awhile, she may come."

"You might wait here until doomsday, she is too sharp to be caught by such chaff," said Wren.

"Bill Stout said he would let us know if she would not come, and I think she will be here. If she don't come, it will be because Bill has put her out of the way himself. He is true to his word."

"Would Bill Stout kill a woman?" asked Wren scornfully.

"I know of his killing an old Indian woman once, just for the fun of it, for I was with him when he did it. He has grit enough to do anything he says he'll do. · He said that if she came he would manage, some way or other to come with her."

Dickey now felt that her first impression when she read the letter was correct, that they meant to do her some harm individually. But what pained her most, was the fact, that there was a traitor in their camp in the person of Bill Stout, for whom she had never entertained a favorable impression. She had heard all she desired to know, and creeping out of the bushes, she returned to where the party anxiously awaited her. "Brave Lavanda" stood near to Bill Stout, before whom she appeared with her revolver drawn and said:

"Villainous traitor! You have conceived this plot to have me captured, remove your weapons. Lavanda, take possession of them. He has promised some of Wren's friends that he would betray me into their hands, and had I refused to come here to-day, he would have stabbed me in the back. I have heard it all." Then, addressing Stout, she said, "Miserable miscreant! If you were treated as you deserve, you would be hanging to one of the limbs above you."

Stout quailed before the words of the brave girl and handed his weapons to Lavanda, as she had directed.

"Have they, indeed, come?" asked Hayden.

"Yes, there are three of them now at the crossing waiting for me."

"Let us charge them," said he, as they mounted their horses.

Lavanda lifted the little spy to her saddle, and ordering Bill to ride before them, they galloped down the road to the place where the three were awaiting the arrival of their victim.

As they drew near, the ruffians knew that there were more than Bill Stout and the spy. So they hastily hurried to the brush, leaving their horses where they had tied them. The advancing party sent a number of bullets after them. As they dismounted to untie the horses, Stout slipped from his horse, and plunging into the dense thicket, made his escape. They took possession of the horses and carried them to Osawatomie, where Dickey proposed to remain a few days.

When Hayden returned to Black Jack, those in camp were much surprised to learn of the treachery of Bill Stout and the result of the meeting at Van Horn's crossing.

Dickey knew of the invaders being camped on Middle Creek in considerable force, and feeling a desire to know something of their intentions, she disguised herself to represent a washer-woman who lived in town and was of the strongest Pro-Slavery type. Having completed her disguise, she rode out toward the camp in question. She had not proceeded far when she met three men, who came from the invaders' camp. She drew the old greasy sunbonnet of blue gingham close about her face, and stopping her horse, gazed steadily toward some cattle that were grazing in the distance.

When the three rode up, one of them asked:

"Mrs. Laird, which way are you going?"

"O, I am just out looking for my cow. She has been gone—let me see—yes, three days, and I'm afraid her milk will be of no force unless I find her soon."

" Have you heard anything from Brown's men lately ?" asked the man.

" Yes, they say Brown is a coming down in two or three weeks. All his men are with him at Black Jack."

" You tell our friends in town to be on the look-out, as we will be in town in a few days."

" I will, and I do believe that is my cow away off yonder by herself."

She turned to go after the cow, and the men rode off toward Moody Creek, in search of Bill Stout and Guy Wren, to make arrangements for the attack upon Osawatomie.

CHAPTER LIX.

THE BATTLE OF OSAWATOMIE.

THE summer had drawn nearly to a close, and nothing of importance had been accomplished by either party. It is true, the number of Free-States settlers had been greatly augmented through the earnest and never-tiring efforts of the " Aid Societies " of the East.

Robert spent two weeks in St. Joseph, in anxiety concerning Dickey. Being discouraged in searching, or rather impatiently waiting, in that quarter, he hastened to Osawatomie to there continue his inquiry. Imagine his surprise, as on dismounting near the hotel, he was addressed by Dickey's familiar voice, on turning, he saw only a person attired as Mrs. Laird, the well-known washer-woman. In a moment he became convinced that the personage was, in reality, Dickey, for whose safety he had almost ceased to hope.

She, too, was rejoiced at meeting Robert, but brief time was allowed for conversation, on account of the impending danger to the settlement. She told Robert of what she had recently learned regarding the contemplated attack of the invaders, and instructed him what road to take in order to most thoroughly arouse the settlers, while she rode as promptly in another direction.

The settlers promptly rallied at the call of danger, though there were but few who were not already with some one of the different commands guarding important points. During two days messengers brought the news that the invaders were approaching the settlement from the north. The crossings at the river were constantly guarded and swift messengers hovered near, to quickly convey the news of the coming of the foe.

Brown and his company had not yet arrived. It had been expected they would be promptly on the ground, consequently great disappointment and anxiety prevailed among the few who were there. They feared that some unknown and well conceived plan of attack had been devised by the foe, to engage Brown where he was, and thus prevent him from joining in the defense of Osawatomie.

The near approach of autumn caused dense fogs

to hang over the river far into the morning of each day, and those who did duty in watching during the night, were prostrated by the malaria which filled the atmosphere and were, by reason of the ague and fevers thus induced, incapacitated for duty.

In a few days Captain Brown arrived with a part of his company, who watched faithfully until it was thought that the enemy had given up the idea of attacking the town, and most of the men returned to watch at more seriously threatened points.

As an assurance of safety prevailed, Dickey, Robert, Fred. Brown and others, went out one evening to visit a friend, who resided west of town. The house was built of logs, and consisted of two large rooms, as were the then better houses of the neighborhood.

The invaders were in camp on Moody Creek, where it afterward appeared, they had been waiting for a clear night in which to make the long contemplated attack.

While the young folks slept, the foe began their movement. Their attacks had been so often frustrated by the settlers, that they had learned caution, and through the advice of Bill Stout, who was familiar with every path in the country, they resorted to the stragetic movement of marching up the river, far above the guarded crossings, where they effected a crossing in a shallow place, and approached the town from the west.

As they were discovered and identified along the line of march, the settlers gathered their valuables together, and with their children sought the protection of the bushes, cornfields and ravines, and the men hastened by circuitous paths to join Brown at Osawatomie.

Day, bright and beautiful, had just dawned when the head of the column reached the house where the young folks were stopping.

The young men had arisen and were standing in the door as the troops filed past. Thinking they were some of Captain Beach's or Hope's command, and not expecting the enemy from that direction, young Leland and Fred. Brown started toward the road, a few rods distant, to speak to them.

At that instant Guy Wren passed, and recognizing the boys, exclaimed, " There are two of the young Yankees, somebody look after them."

In another instant a volley was fired from a dozen guns and the youths fell to the ground.

Those in the house had been aroused by the rattling of guns and bayonets, and were looking from the windows as the boys fell. Dickey, from her window, saw her only brother fall to the ground before the murderous fire of the invading horde, she did not weep, but patiently awaited the disappearance of the men, and then hastened to care for the murdered boys.

She found Robert still alive but fearfully mangled, while young Brown was stiff and cold in death. Dickey went in search of Mrs. Davis, the lady of the house, who had sought protection in the brush.

While they were carrying Robert to the house, the boom of the cannon east of them saluted their ears, quickly followed by the sharp, keen and reveberating crack of the Sharpe's rifles told those, not engaged, that old John Brown was there.

The two women, sorrowing for the dead and caring for the wounded, heard the roar of the musketry, the boom of the cannon, and the shouts of the invaders, as they repeatedly charged the block-house which Brown and his men held, the sharp detonating and rapidly repeated crack of the rifles of the defenders, told them how bravely their friends were fighting.

The few settlers who came too late to enter the block-house took positions, singly, in the bushes and on the mounds, and as coolly sent forth their messengers of death, as did our forefathers, from behind fences and trees from Lexington to Concord.

The sun had turned to the west, the clock on the mantel indicated the hour of one, when the tramp of horses feet and the rattle of wagons was heard as the invaders percipitately retreated.

"Here they come," said Dickey, as they appeared in sight, and she hastened to Robert, who had regained consciousness. As she embraced him lovingly, he said:

"Don't be alarmed, Ona, they can only kill us at most."

The retreating horde had, in their hasty retreat, no time to devote to pillage and murder. They were giving attention to their own dead and wounded and their own safety from the hurtling messengers of death that the defenders still hurled after them.

Some of Brown's men were killed while crossing the river, but the enemy lost far more from the long-

21

range rifles of the settlers. The cannon which they had brought to demolish the block-house proved ineffective.

The last volley of the settlers, aimed at a tall officer who was directing the retreat, brought him off his horse, and created more than an usual degree of excitement in their ranks.

Among the missing of Brown's men were Fred. Brown and Robert Leland. Not until night did they find the innocent boy who was murdered in cold blood.

His body was gently carried to the house, where tender hands removed the gore that matted his hair and clouded his fair face.

The old man, when he learned his loss, repaired to the scene, and, lion-hearted, knelt by the dead body of his dead boy. His impassioned voice breathed forth the anguish of a broken heart.

As the friends stood weeping in sympathy with the sorrowing old man, a carriage drew up at the door, and a voice inquired if Ona Leland was there.

"Yes, that is my name," answered Dickey, as she, in her kilt and kittle, stepped to the door to meet her visitors.

CHAPTER LX.

GENERAL BLAIR.

"WHAT can woman do in the way of making her own liven', I'd like to know,"
said one rough and dirty-looking man
to another in Mr. Oyster's bar-room, where General
Blair was enjoying the fragrance of a cigar.

"'They can't do nothin', John Ubanks, an' you
know my opinion on that score, so what the use of
askin' me?" answered the other.

"I agree with you thar', but did you never notice
they are allers a medlin' with somebody's affairs.
You bet, I believe in them a stayin' home and at-
tendin' to their work."

The General cast a furtive glance at the two individuals, who, to evolve new ideas, were gulping
down liberal doses of "invigorator" in the shape of
whisky.

As he gazed, he thought, "Where on earth can
the woman be found who, judging from external appearances, is not better qualified to judge of what
will be conducive to her benefit than such degraded
beings as you, with your uncomely and unkempt
appearance, your uncombed hair and beards, your
torn and tattered clothing. Is it possible that you
belong to an age of civilization and intelligence?
Are you not some relic of the barbaric age, when
education and enlightenment were unknown? Are

you not, by an eternal edict, just temporarily dropped upon this mundane sphere, that we may take a retrospective view of the condition of the human race in antedeluvian ages, and by comparison continue to eliminate the dross, and introduce a greater degree of intelligence ?"

In disgust the General withdrew to the porch, where he was joined by his wife and Kate.

He forgot that the basis upon which ignorance grew and continued to thrive, was human slavery. It does seem that African slavery, as it existed, destroyed the finer perceptions and keener sensibilities of those who were contaminated by its influences, and, assuredly, association introduced contamination. These individuals who were thus ably discussing the rights, privileges and duties of women, in Mr. Oyster's bar-room, were, individually, not the owners of a single " nigga," yet, following the precedent established by their more able neighbors, the larger landholders, they must talk of slavery, and had talked it until they, considering themselves superior beings, must reduce something by which they were surrounded, to a level comparing favorably with the slaves of their neighbors, and thinking too much of their dogs as companions, had had recourse to their wives and daughters.

Their further conversation on the subject was, whether or not woman should be educated. The conclusion arrived at was, that further than " readin' and spellin' " was unnecessary and would work to her disadvantage. Especially did they deplore the idea of woman exercising the privilege of the ballot or attending literary societies or lyceums.

Could we have visited the home of this dictatorial individual on election day, we would have found his wife gathering corn in the field with the hired negro.

General Blair intimated his intentions of visiting Kansas to consult with the Free-States men, especially with John Brown. Mr. Oyster had known, for some time, of the change in the mind of General Blair toward the Free-States settlers, and he encouraged him to proceed at once, hoping that some definite plan, leading to harmony and peace, might result from his visit.

The battle at Osawatomie had been fought, and the General, on his way, met many of the invaders on their return. They were far from happy at the defeat they had met with. Their enthusiasm was visibly cooling.

When Gen. Blair arrived at the town he was informed that Capt. Brown was at his home, west of the village, whither he proceeded, finding the young Hungarian, Lavanda, on guard, who saluted him in true military style as he halted him and politely asked him his business.

The General returned the salute and said, " Do me the favor to present my card to Capt. Brown and say, with his permission, I desire to speak with him," at the sametime handing him his card.

Lavanda withdrew to the house and in a moment returned, bidding the General enter.

As he entered the rude log cabin, a feeling of awe and reverence pervaded his mind. Each side of the door was guarded by a strong, hearty and intelligent looking young man, whose hand rested upon a heavy

Sharpe's rifle. Others occupied the room engaged in reading, while on a low couch in one corner of the room, lay the old man whom the General desired to see. As the General drew near, Brown said :

"General, I know you by reputation, and am glad to have the honor of entertaining one, who; though recently in arms against us, has ever deported himself as becomes a gentleman. Pray, be seated," at the sametime motioning him to a seat.

The General replied by saying :

"Captain Brown, the approbation of a man occupying the position you do in this Territory, regarding the part I have borne personally in the existing strife, gives me great pleasure. I need not tell you that I deplore the ungenerous manner in which this strife has been conducted, and regret that certain elements of society, unworthy the name of men, have taken so prominent a part in it."

"I believe myself," said Brown, "that the better element of Pro-Slavery society has been averse to the manner of conducting this warfare. I feel assured that all bloodshed could have been avoided had not this mercenary element established itself as the dictator in the matter. Individually, I have suffered much. I have been robbed of almost every earthly possession. My family has been abused and my child murdered in cold blood."

"Is it your intention to leave the Territory, Captain?" asked the General.

The old man started, and quickly assuming a sitting posture in bed, frowned for a moment, and said :

"General, excuse my apparent excitement, but

your question being of a nature far remote from my idlest thought, for a moment roused my feelings. No, sir, I shall never forsake my undertaking, and should this strife continue to be pressed upon us, I assure you I shall be abundantly avenged for the wrongs I have suffered."

"Allow me, Captain Brown, to ask, Are you a representative of either of the Eastern Aid Societies?"

"No, General, I came to this Territory entirely upon my own responsibility, and have continued to act under the same. It is true I have been East and solicited aid in the way of arms, ammunition and money since these troubles began, and I am glad to say that I have personal friends now there upon whom I can call for assistance at any time, with the assurance that it will be promptly forthcoming."

General Blair gazed in silence upon the care-worn face and emaciated frame of the old man and regretted that he had lifted a hand against him, thoroughly convinced that his every act was prompted by the purest and noblest motive, knowing full well that such a face as John Brown's could never be crossed by a shadow of shame arising from an ignoble act.

The General spent the night with the old hero, and the next morning, accompanied by Hayden, went to visit Robert, whose acquaintance he had formed in St. Joseph.

He had not learned that Dickey Deane was Ona Leland, a sister of Robert's, and was much surprised when Hayden informed him of the fact. After a moment, he laughingly said:

"Well, I must ackowledge women can keep se-
crets, for Mrs. Blair and Kate certainly knew of this,
and, although we have often talked freely of Dickey
Deane, yet neither of them ever intimated to me her
true name or character."

As they passed over the battle-ground, traces of
the conflict were yet visible. Here the grass was
matted where some poor fellow had lain and, perhaps, died, there the boughs were lopped off the
trees where the cannon balls had plunged through.

Said Hayden, pointing out two trees close together
wonderfully scarified by bullets, "That is the tree
behind which Capt. Brown fought, and this one I had
the honor of holding."

The General watched the dignified movements of
the young man, listened to his firm, well-modulated
voice, noticed his handsome appearance, and noted
his unassuming yet noble manner. The longer he
was with him, the more he became interested in him
and finally said :

" Excuse me, sir, but I infer you are an Englishman.   Am I not correct?"

" Yes, sir, my home is in England."

" May I be sufficiently bold to inquire your name ?"
continued the General.

" My name, at present, is Hayden Douglas."

" Then you are one of the men of Brown's command known as "The Mysterious Companions."

" I have the honor to be frequently spoken of as
such," replied Hayden.

" Think me not impertinent," continued the General, " but who is the other companion ?"

" Sir Charles," answered Hayden in a low tone, and continued, " further than that, General, I am not permitted to speak on this subject, by reason of a compact entered into between the last named gentleman, Capt. Brown and myself. Our own men know nothing further. I sincerely hope the time may come, when we can discuss such matters without reserve."

The General seemed perplexed. He desired to know more regarding Hayden, but delicacy forbid further questioning.

As they approached the house where Robert lay wounded, they noticed a fine carriage standing near. It was an unusual sight, in those days, to see even a common spring-wagon in Kansas, and they wondered as to whom the fortunate person could be, who possessed so fine a carriage so near the recent battle-ground.

CHAPTER LXI.

THE SURPRISE PARTY.

DICKEY drew near the carriage with some degree of hesitation, until she recognized the familiar faces of Arthur Holmes and his wife. Dickey had heard of their marriage, but was not aware of their presence in Kansas.

A hearty welcome was extended to them as they alighted from the carriage, when Dickey said :

"The sight of a carriage and rustling silks are unfamiliar sights in this country, Sallie."

To which Sallie replied, "I am myself ashamed of my dress, since I noticed the beauty of your Scottish costume."

Dr. Strawn, Sallie's brother, sat by Robert's bed, watching the youth, and did not notice the vehicle, nor was he aware of the arrival of his sister, until she stood before him and addressed him by the familiar name of "brother," when, with outstretched arms he received her tenderly, then Arthur came in for his greeting from his new brother, while Sallie tenderly clasped the hand and addressed kindly and sympathizing words to the wounded boy.

Two days had passed, and Arthur and Sallie were contemplating an early return to Lawrence, when two gentlemen drew near, who, as they reached the door, were recognized as General Blair and Hayden Douglas. The meeting between the latter and Arthur, although each was surprised, was most kindly.

As the General was introduced, Dr. Strawn looked up in surprise. As they exchanged glances, a mutual recognition took place, having, in times past, when attending the Medical College in St. Louis, been warm friends and jolly companions on many boating and hunting excursions.

Dr. Strawn ejaculated, "Why, Blair, how in the name of goodness does it happen that you are in this country?"

To which he replied, saying:

"To be candid, Doctor, I left my home in the South to take command of the Pro-Slavery forces

operating on this border, and did so associate myself, for a time, with them, but in considering the social element constituting those forces, and calmly
investigating the principle actuating the strife, I have
withdrawn from the conflict, and shall personally use
my influence in a prompt discontinuance of these
invasions."

Conversation turned upon familiar topics, and the
bright September was nearing its close. All had
enjoyed themselves, even Robert had been wonderfully invigorated by the reminiscences related in his
presence.

While at supper, Arthur remarked:

" This has, indeed, been a 'surprise party.' "

" Yes," said Dr. Strawn, " I know of none that
can yet appear to contribute to our enjoyment."

The words were scarcely uttered, when a spring-
wagon drove up to the door, containing two men,
One, a tall, noble-looking man, alighted and walked
toward the house.

As Dickey noted his approach, she unceremoni-
ously sprang from the table, exclaiming:

" O, Robert! here is papa," who tenderly embraced
the dear child whom he, until recently, had supposed
lost.

. Mr. Leland had not learned of the injuries sustained by Robert until he entered the house. He
was much agitated, until Dr. Strawn assured him
that the symptoms indicated an early recovery.

At this moment Dickey received a message from
Brown, stating that he had that morning started for
Lawrence, which was seriously threatened by a large
force under Guy Wren.

Dickey motioned to Dr. Strawn and Hayden, to whom she communicated the intelligence and resolved to hasten to Lawrence.

Returning to the house, they seized their guns, saying to Mr. Leland:

" We are off now, and shall leave yourself and the General, with Sallie to look after Robert."

Raven was brought out and hurriedly mounted, while Hayden, Arthur and Dr. Strawn occupied the wagon with the driver who had brought Mr. Leland from St. Joseph.

They traveled all night and at dawn of the next day passed the sentinels in the suburbs of the town. Considerable uneasiness prevailed in the minds of the few men in Lawrence. The enemy numbered over two thousand, while the defenders, all told, numbered but thirty-nine, to such an alarming extent did sickness prevail among them, brought about by almost constant exposure and excitement.

On the Saturday following the arrival of our friends at Lawrence, the smoke of the invaders' camp fires were seen at Franklin. Dickey rode out toward their camp until she could distinctly see the many forms clustered and passing about the campfires, and hear the outer pickets discussing the probable strength of the Yankee forces at Lawrence.

On her return, she found men of determined visage calmly preparing for the conflict of to-morrow.

CHAPTER LXII.

MORE PLOTTING.

SUNDAY morning dawned bright and clear, not a cloud darkened the face of the azure heavens.

The settlers at Lawrence were on the alert, anticipating an attack from any quarter and at any time.

In a short time the voice of Pat Devilin was heard exclaiming, "Here they come, riding like Jehu." About fifty mounted men were hurrying toward Lawrence. On reaching the Wakarusa river, they plunged through the water in self-important style, which caused Pat to remark : "Look at them, Douglas, the Young Guard of Napoleon's army never put on more airs than those devils."

Arthur who heard the remark, said : "The 'Guard' you speak of Pat, were brave fellows, while these are arrant cowards and will run at the sight of their own shadow by moonlight."

They still advanced until within about a mile, when they halted. As they were closely grouped, Pat, without saying a word, raised his rifle and fired. In a few seconds one of the foremost fell from his horse. His comrades dismounted and placing him across the saddle, moved back toward their camp.

Late that afternoon the invaders started in a body for Lawrence, with banners flying and fifes whistling they drew near the apparently doomed town.

" Wait until they come nearer," said Brown to his men who lay behind hastily constructed earthworks.

At the proper time the order came, " Now, boys, give them hot shot in rapid doses. Be sure of your aim and don't waste your ammunition." As he spoke the last word his finger pressed the trigger of his rifle and its detonating report rang out sharp and clear upon the evening air.

In an instant the whole line was ablaze. The whiz of the bullets were distinctly heard, as well as the dull thud as they found a resting place in the body of horse or man.

Shot guns and squirrel rifles, which constituted the arms of the horde, were not effective against such weapons as the settlers used. After a few well-directed shots from the earthworks, the invaders manifested uneasiness, and in a few moments fell back in confusion. The approach of night was accompanied by dark, lowering clouds, which indicated an approaching storm.

Around the town stood sentinels all through the night, weary and worn, contemplating the past, meditating upon the present and endeavoring to anticipate the future, but thought would not go beyond the morrow, and who of the noble thirty-nine had need of it beyond that time? Did ever thirty-nine men, however brave, successfully contend with two thousand?

The next morning found every man of Brown's command on duty and ready for further duty. They could have, during the night, escaped and saved their lives individually, but they were men who fought for a principle and were not governed by mercenary motives.

When day dawned, the enemy were nowhere to be seen. They had been satisfied with the taste of the settlers' mettle, and fearing a more determined resistance, had withdrawn to safety in Missouri, carrying their dead and wounded with them.

The next morning a colored woman appeared, making inquiry for Capt. Brown. When she had found him and conversed with him for a few minutes, he sent for Dickey.

As the trio talked for some time, Pat Devilin remarked to Hayden:

"Another plot is brewing. We'll hear of it when it is over."

Early the next day, Dickey set out on her journey to West Point, the very center of Pro-Slavery sympathy, where she arrived, habited in a suit of brown jeans, making inquiry for work of each person she met, such persons directing her to some other one, until, having left her horse at the village, she approached a house where three men were sitting on the porch.

As she drew near, she asked, adopting the customary inquiry of the neighborhood:

"You'ens don't know nobody what wants to hire nobody, do you?"

One of the men straightened himself, and yawning, said:

"Wal, I reckon as how your outen a job, I mought gin yer suthin· to do in a few days, fur we'er about gwine to send our niggas South some day fore long. If yer want to stay an jine in the drive, go inter that thar room thar and git yer dinner."

Dickey entered the low log shanty. Near a smoky fire-place sat an old negro woman, endeavoring to quiet the cries of a small child, while a younger woman was busy washing the clothes.

"Yer dun want yer dinner, sir, I reckon, cos I heerd Massa a tellin on yer to go inter dat room an git it," said the old woman.

"Yes," said Dickey in a pleasant tone, "I shall stay here a few days."

After partaking of a light dinner, she lay down upon a bed, and pulling the old straw hat which she wore over her face, pretended to be asleep. As she thus lay, she listened attentively to the conversation of the women as they gloomily talked of the suffering and misery they expected to endure on the Southern plantations.

Toward evening she arose and wandered to the south side of the place, where she observed a solitary log cabin, just as Hannah, the woman who came to Lawrence, had described. She examined it closely, and returned to the house to find supper ready.

After the family and company were through, Dickey and the colored persons belonging to the place partook of their supper.

"Who are those men?" inquired Dickey of a negro boy who sat near her at the table.

"Nigger buyers from way down Souf," answered the youth.

"Are you going South with them?" asked she in a different manner.

"No, sah, I'se not gwine," said he.

"Yes you is a gwine, Tim," said the younger woman, shaking her head in a significant way at the
boy, who dropped his head and remained silent, occasionally casting an inquiring and suspicious glance
at Dickey.

When the family retired, the man of the house instructed the old woman to show the "new-comer"
where to sleep, but instead of occupying the place assigned, she lay down on a pile of shavings under a
tree in front of the house, where she remained until
the lights were extinguished, when she arose from
her chosen bed and carefully wended her way to the
cabin she had visited during the afternoon.

She seated herself upon a log near the deserted
cabin, watching the lowering clouds as they gradu-
ally obscured the twinkling stars, and listening to the
distant voices of the negroes as they sang familiar
hymns and songs while attending to the chores.

Two hours passed, and in the distance she dis-
cerned the twinkling of light, which continually grew
brighter as it drew near the cabin. The light came
from a small lantern, so shaded as to light only the
path which its bearer and his companions had traveled. They drew near the cabin, and removing
the fastening from the door, cautiously entered.
Presently another group from a different direction
came, and after knocking at the door, were admitted.

Dickey knew that all had arrived, and cautiously
approaching the cabin, gently rapped upon the door.
The hum of voices ceased within. The dim light
which had shown through the chinking was entirely

22

obscured. She rapped again, and in a low voice said: "I am Hannah's friend."

As by magic, the door opened; the light was restored, and a house full of colored persons was revealed to Dickey.

The old woman who had prepared Dickey's dinner, looked a moment in surprise, and exclaimed:

"Wal, I du clar, Massa, I nebber would ha tooken you to be our fren. I fought suah, yous one ob em fellas as was a gwine to help em ya buyers fur to tote us niggas off Souf."

"Yes, I am your friend. Capt. Brown sent me here to find out when you would be ready to leave with him, provided, you wanted to go," answered Dickey.

"Dats wat wes heah fur dis blessed night, fur to hold a consultin on dat berry pint, an I specs dese darkies are all on em a wantin to go wid Massa Brown, an I kin jis say wes got to be dun gone some night dis berry week, cos nex Monday em ar nigga drivers is a gwine to set off Souf wid all on us."

All present seemed to endorse the opinion of the old woman, and an understanding, regarding the night Brown was to send for them, was soon arrived at, and they separated.

Dickey persuaded Tim to accompany her to the village where she had left the pony.

It was not yet light when she aroused the landlord and requested her pony.

"Why so early, young man?" asked he.

"O, I have engaged to do some work for Mr. Bond and want to be there in time," answered she.

"Yes, yes, I'll agree that you're a right smart hand," said he, as he brought out the pony and received the pay for keeping it.

As she and Tim were about to part, Dickey remembered that she had left her bundle at the cabin, and for a moment considered whether or not she had better return for it, but finally she said: "Tim, you get the bundle I left at your house and burn it as soon as you get home."

Tim hastened home to obey the command, while Dickey was riding rapidly toward Osawatomie, which place she reached near noon, where she found Brown awaiting her return.

The next morning two large emigrant wagons started toward Missouri in charge of Brown, accompanied by six men. Arriving near the State line, they camped in the timber until the inhabitants along the route had retired, when they resumed and hastily pursued their journey.

At Bond's house they were met by Tim, who guided them to the cabin where the negroes, eleven in number, had congregated. They hurriedly climbed into the wagons and were soon on their way to Kansas.

When near Bond's house, Brown directed two of his men to procure two of the best horses as they passed the barn, saying, "These black men have, long since, each earned a horse, and they shall have it."

As the men led the horses from the barn, a man appeared from the house. A revolver was pointed toward him, and he was ordered to mount one of the horses and accompany them, which he did without a murmur.

CHAPTER LXIII.

GENERAL BLAIR'S DEPARTURE.

GENERAL BLAIR remained some days at the Leland home, until he was well assured of Robert's final recovery. He felt it a duty incumbent upon him to assist Mr. Leland in watching by the bed-side of the youth, as there were none others who were present to render such assistance.

Immediately after the battle of Osawatomie, the settlers, both Free-State and Pro-Slavery, loaded their valuables and sought protection in Missouri. Many left their cattle and extra horses to graze upon the range. There were, in fact, but three families who remained on all the scope of country lying between Prairie City and the Marias des Cygnes river, so general was the stampede.

Those who sought protection in Missouri found little comfort on their arrival in that State. They were intercepted by the troops; their horses and wagons taken; their furniture destroyed; their trunks broken open and their money taken, until the citizens compelled the ruffians to desist.

When Dickey arrived at the house where her father and brother were, she found them just bidding the kind-hearted and gentlemanly General Blair adieu, who, as he took her hand, said:

"Allow me the pleasure of assuring you, Miss Leland, that all indications point to your brother's early recovery. I hope to hear regularly from you all until we again meet. May more auspicious circumstances surround us in the early future. I do sincerely desire that strife and contention may soon cease to exist in this otherwise highly-favored country," saying which, he mounted his horse and rode away.

As he passed along, busy with his thoughts, his horse followed the trail toward Harrisonville, instead of St. Joseph, and had proceeded a number of miles before the General discovered it.

After a moment's thought, he turned north and continued his journey across the country, following no trail. Some miles south of Shawnee Mission he discoverd a lone log cabin in the ravine below, from the chimney of which smoke was curling. In a moment he, unconsciously, turned his horse toward that cabin. When he neared the door, he called to arouse the inmates. An old man, apparently very feeble, appeared, leaning upon a stout cane, who, in answer to the General's pleasant greeting, replied:

"Good afternoon, sir. Please alight."

As the General dismounted, the old man continued:

"You are the first person I have seen for weeks."

Taking a chair, the General began questioning the old recluse as to why he remained in this secluded place alone.

"I will tell you," said the old man.

"My son and myself came here in the spring of '54. We built this cabin and began work improving our land. The next fall my son returnud to Ohio and brought his young wife out. Time glided by, and they worked on, well pleased with the country and its prospects. Our live stock increased and Charley Chance—that was my son's name—was known far over in Missouri, as a well-to-do farmer. One day a crowd came for him to go with them somewhere to vote. He told them that they had no right to enter this Territory for the purpose of voting, for which expression they abused him unmercifully, and told him they would call again soon an make him change his mind."

"We were not troubled again until the spring ' '56, when ten or twelve men rode up where we wei working, near the house, and began abusing u Charley told them that he had not been concerned i politics and wanted no trouble with either part They then said that they intended to kill him, an before he could make a show of defense, they cr elly fired at him, and he fell to the ground as th rode rapidly away. His wife came out and we ca ried him into the house and laid him on the flo where you see that blood-stain. He soon began i choke and strangle, and in a few minutes died. rode many miles ere I could find help to bury hin I finally met five men, who proved to be old Joh Brown and his men. They all came with me. Son staid, while others went to procure a coffin. The placed the coffin, containing his body, in one wagon while his wife and child, and myself were taken i another. In the grave-yard at Lawrence, sir, lie my only son."

As the old man's utterances carried him back t

the sad scéne, he could speak no more, and giving
way to his grief, the tears coursed down his wrinkled
cheeks.

The General's lips trembled and tears bedimmed
is eyes, as his whole heart went out in sympathy to-
vard the old man.

After the old man had regained his composure, the
General sat for sometime contemplating the woman's
apparel which hung upon the wall, knowing, from
the dust and cob-webs that prevailed everywhere,
that the tidy hand of woman was no longer known
in that cabin, and he wondered what became of the
young widow and child.

CHAPTER LXIV.

THE "JAYHAWKING" BOY.

AMONG the members of Brown's company were
men as brave as the world knew, such were
not confined to native Americans, men of almost every nation and clime had seen the star of
freedom dawning in the West, and sought to bask in
its resplendent light. Men of noble antecedents
fought under the banner of "Universal Liberty"
with as much ardor as did those who created the
idea.

Englishmen who boasted of the blood of the Stu-
arts, wielded the sword and endured the hardships.

Hungarians, inspired by the example of Kossuth, sought the field on which to die for freedom. Polanders, while they wept for the serfdom imposed upon their people, by a power it were futile to resist, lent a helping hand where their services were welcomed and appreciated. Scotchmen, whóse ancestors fought with the noble Wallace, and in whose veins coursed the blood of the most renowned clans of the Highlands; and Ireland too, furnished her representatives, in whose breasts the smoldering fires of freedom lay, awaiting the slightest zephyr of liberty to fan them into flame.

The fairest representative of the Celtic race existed in the person of Pat Devilin, whose happy disposition, under adverse circumstances, more than once cheered the hearts of those who, without his presence, would have desponded. His ready wit would turn the chagrin of a present defeat into a prospective hope of the future. While sickness and despondency overcame the many, Pat grew hale, hearty and hilarious. The more arduous the duties imposed upon him, the more carefully and surely he fulfilled them. To his mind idleness and inactivity were the bane of life. As soon as one foraging expedition was ended, and he saw smiles of gladness flitting over the faces of those among whom he distributed willingly what he had hazardously won, he was impatient to be off securing more booty. A single horse could not endure the repeated loads he would compel it to carry. Oftimes he would take two horses and from six to eight large sacks, which he would invariably fill. While many returned sad and dejected, by reason of their failure, Pat's cheerful voice could be heard singing snatches of song, long ere he reached the settlement.

On the advent of the colored people from Missouri, an extra supply of provisions must be secured. Each forager, as he departed, was instructed to, if possible, return bountifully loaded, but when Pat appeared, Brown said :

" Pat, there is no necessity of instructing you, I contemplate appointing you 'Instructor General of Forager,' should this state of affairs continue."

To which Pat replied in the rich brogue he would occasionally use, " Niver do ye mind, Captain Brown, Pat Devilin's the boy to stay wid yes as long as the feadther grows upon the back of a chicken, or a bristle sprouts from the skin of a pig, and the Marias des Cygnes afford a drink of wadther," saying which he sprang upon his horse and with a wild whoop dashed away.

As each day passed some member of the foraging party returned, laden with provisions. Three days had passed and none had heard ought of Pat. Uneasiness regarding him prevailed in the town, but on the morning of the fourth day, as the early risers strode forth to resume the duties of the day, the happy and cheerful voice of Pat came floating through the still atmosphere, and ere long, he appeared.

What a sight greeted the settlers. Pat, mounted upon his horse, carried a long pole with which he frequently "persuaded" a yoke of cattle to increase their speed as they weariedly dragged a heavily

loaded wagon.   As the settlers examined the contents of the huge wagon-bed, they exclaimed, " How
in the world did you get all this forage, Pat ?"

" Be aisy now an I'll tell yez," said Pat, and he
proceeded to relate.   " Indade, an the forage was
gittin scarce where I had made so many raids, an sez
I to meself, I'll take another route an go furdther.

"So the furst night I called at a large stone house,
an', indade, it was a foine place.   An' whin I would
ask could I rest meself awhile, there was nary soul
there to answer me.   So I just unsaddled me pony
an' helped meself an' horse to a liberal supply of
the best I could find.   An' I tell yez whin I was en-
joyin' meself to me utmost, I thought of yez poor
divils at home, an' sez I to meself, Bedad, an' I'll
take a foine supply back wid me, an' as I began to
fill me sacks wid chise bacon, the thought come to
me mind that I would hide the heft of it an' come
back wid a crowd an' take it home.   Whin I went
into the woods wid me furst load I found the oxen,
an' I had seen the ould wagon.   Thin I hunted up
the yoke, put the cattle ferninst the wagon, and yez
all see me here."

An immense quantity of bacon was in the forward
end of the wagon.   Chickens and pigs filled the center, while flour and meal in sacks occupied the rear.

Some one remarked :

" Why, Pat, this is stealing."

" Indad, an' yez can call it by any name yez wish.
I call it 'jayhawken.'   There is a burd in the
ould country that watches the fish-hawks and other
burds an' stales from them; that burd is called a

jayhawk. Now I truly belave, upon me soul, that that ould fellow where I jayhawked these things stoul them himself. Whin the ould coot comes home he'll find naither chicken, nur pig, nur flour, nur meal, nur bacon; and won't he be in a pickle?"

The abundance of the supplies which Pat had brought in induced Brown to start North with the colored persons he had confiscated. The next morning he was on his way to Tabor, Iowa, with the negroes, accompanied by a few trusty and tried companions. They tarried a few days in Lawrence, and pushed on through Nebraska. At Plymouth, Brown became very sick, where Arthur Holmes found him. He afforded the old man all the assistance possible for him to render in the way of medicine and attention ere he resumed his journey toward Lawrence. He had proceeded but a few miles, when he met Dr. Strawn, coming to notify Brown that the Dragoons were pursuing him. Arthur returned with the Doctor. As they approached the hut where the old man lay, they were met by a young man, who expressed a desire to see Brown. Thoughtlessly they indicated the place where the old man lay, when, to their surprise, the youth rode rapidly south. On reaching the cabin, they apprised Brown of their suspicions, and urged him, if possible, to cross the Nebraska line. The old man, in much misery, resumed his journey and entered Nebraska just as the Dragoons came in sight a few miles south. Arthur and the Doctor met them and informed them that Brown was now more than two miles over the line in Nebraska.

The warrant issued by the Pro-Slavery government of Kansas, would give them no right to pursue into Nebraska, and they felt mortified and chagrined at their ill luck. Arthur and Dr. Strawn passed on, leaving the disappointed troops consulting as to the best course to pursue. Arthur stopped at Lawrence, while Dr. Strawn continued on to Osawatomie, accompanied by Hayden Douglas, who joined him at Lawrence.

They arrived in Osawatomie just as Mr. Leland, Robert and Dickey were starting for St. Joseph.

The face of Mr. Leland was immediately recognized by Hayden, this being their first meeting in the West. After they had gone Hayden felt wretchedly lonesome. The sun appeared as a ball of fire suspended in the heavens. A thick smoke hung over the face of the earth. He wended his way to Fair View, but not a living being greeted him on his way. His friends and companions were all gone, among them all he missed Dickey more than the others. He had contemplated asking her to correspond with him, but his heart failed him, and now that she was gone, he felt desolate and disconsolate.

CHAPTER LXV.

HAYDEN'S SURPRISES.

WHILE Hayden stood upon Fair View the smoky atmosphere brightened, the day became bright and beautiful, but his sad heart enjoyed not its brightness and lustre. His thoughts were far away, reviewing the past. As he seated himself upon the soft grass, he noticed in the distance an approaching horseman, who, on his near approach, proved to be Sir Charles. Hayden went forward to meet him.

"A pleasant day for viewing the country," said Sir Charles, as he dismounted.

"Yes," said Hayden, indifferently.

Sir Charles looked upon Hayden in astonishment and exclaimed: "What wave of trouble has marred the beauty of your sea of happiness, my young friend?"

"No particular wave has caused me undue annoyance, but accumulating grievances and vexations have culminated in this day, which I recognize as the loneliest of my life," answered Hayden.

"I do not doubt your latter statement, for I met a party this morning among whom was your 'little spy,' over whose acts you became so enthusiastic at our last meeting," answered Sir Charles, as he noted ' the flush which spread over the young man's face, as he toyed with the long grass.

Receiving no reply to his last remark, Sir Charles continued by asking: "Who was the old gentleman for whom she seemed to be acting the part of guide and escort?"

"Her father," answered Hayden.

"You seem, young sir, to be in deep meditation, I hope I shall not intrude upon your reverie, but, in times past, you excited my interest in the young lady and I desire to inquire further regarding her. Is she a native American?"

To which Hayden replied : " Excuse me, kind friend, if I have seemed inattentive. I have, for sometime, been absorbed in topics pertaining to myself, especially as to my individual identity. The home of the young lady in question is in the state of New Hampshire."

" If I remember," said Sir Charles, you told me her name was Dickey Deane ?"

" Yes, sir, I so informed you, but such name is an assumed one, her proper name being Leland, Ona Leland."

" Leland !" ejaculated Sir Charles. " Do you know her father's name ? tell me quickly."

Hayden was surprised at the interest manifested by Sir Charles and also noticed the excitement the name of Leland had produced, as exemplified by the manner of his last question, and quietly replied :

" Yes, sir, it is Leland, Roderick Leland."

The old gentleman started in greater surprise and exclaimed : " My Heavens ! Is it possible I met Roderick Leland this morning and did not recognize him !"

Hayden now became interested and said : " Sir Charles, I am at a loss to account for the unusual degree of interest manifested by you for the members of this family."

" Your interest, however, does not attract my attention as much as does your apparent excitement."

Sir Charles replied : " Why, boy, have you forgotten that Theodocia's family name was Leland and that she had a brother, Roderick ? "

" Yes, Sir Charles, I now distinctly remember the

oft-repeated name of Roderick, which I so frequently heard in my boyhood days. Yet I am impressed with the idea that he was killed or at least lost in the mountains of Scotland. I have heard that his companion was found desperately wounded, but could give no rational account of the accident."

"Now that I think further," continued Hayden, "I remember certain incidents of the past, especially my first meeting with Mr. Leland, in whose face I detected a familiar look, a family resemblance, but certain circumstances occurred which rendered it necessary for me to devote personal attention to his bodily ailments, he having fainted, and after his recovery we were so absorbed with the business in hand that I thought no more regarding the resemblance."

"Hayden, boy, I have, through all these long years, been untiring in my efforts to find this man. He is an old friend, a friend of my youthful days. I have ever had a presentiment that he was yet alive; but hope of finding him had almost died out of my breast."

At the hotel Sir Charles wrote a long letter to his charge in England, giving in detail the facts concerning his discovery.

Two days passed ere Hayden could procure a horse; Sir Charles being restless during the time on account of his anxiety to follow the Leland family.

When they reached Lawrence they learned that Mr. Leland and his family had gone East. Taking a stage coach they started for St. Louis. The ride was dreary, on account of the condition of the roads, which, by reason of recent rains, were mis rable.

At St. Louis they were joined by Pat Devilin, on his way to New York. The trio journeyed together until the great city was reached, where Pat bade them adieu, and they continued on to Boston.

On arriving at Cedar Hall, they learned that Mr. Leland, by last advices, was in St. Joseph, awaiting the more complete recovery of Robert. The two Englishmen determined to remain at Cedar Hall until the owner returned home.

On one of Hayden's trips to Boston he obtained a letter addressed to Sir Charles, which, upon being opened by that gentleman, proved to be an importunate request that he and Hayden—if he could find him—should immediately repair to London, as a person had there appeared who claimed to be rightful heir to the Douglas estate.

To the great surprise of the people of Strawn, the strangers, who seemed so wonderfully anxious to meet Mr. Leland, disappeared as suddenly as they had come.

At an early day they set sail for Liverpool, where they took the train for the suburbs of London, where they entered the—to Hayden—gloomy halls Sir Charles called home.

Hayden's mind had been filled with foreboding thought. Gloom and despondency had long claimed his thoughts. Doubts as to his antecedents pervaded his mind, and now that a claimant for the estates he looked upon as his by inheritance had appeared, his mind was so wrought upon that it affected him physically. He retired at an early hour, but bodily ail-

ments and mental trouble kept him in a state of unrest, and when morning dawned he was haggard and
worn.

CHAPTER LXVI.

A WESTERN WOMAN.

GENERAL BLAIR remained silent for some
time, contemplating the many articles of dress
suspended from pegs on the wall. After the
old man had become calm, the General asked:

"Where are his wife and child?"

"I cannot say. Lola, his wife, went to Lawrence,
where we buried Charley. She carried the child
with her, but when the services were over I could
find neither Lola nor the child. I have waited for
her but she does not come, neither has she written
me."

"Of course you have continued to inquire regarding her?" asked the General, much interested.

"Yes, I have; but I am of the opinion that the
same villains have killed her and soon will kill me."

After a moment's hesitation, the General said:

"Suppose you go with me to St. Joseph, and I will
institute an organized search and assist you in any
possible manner."

The old gentleman acceded to the proposition, and
after extinguishing the fire and securing the cabin,

23

they proceeded leisurely to Shawnee, whey they remained during the night.

The next morning, the General procured a horse for the old gentleman and continued their journey. They soon overtook a heavily-loaded wagon drawn by three yoke of cattle, which were managed and driven by a perfect Amazon of a woman. As they passed, they lifted ther hats and the General said:

"Good morning, madam."

To which she roughly replied:

"Mornin', sur."

Such a sight being an unusual one, the General concluded to institute such inquiries as would lead to his learning the circumstances which forced a woman to adopt su ch means to obtain a livelihood, therefore he 'said:

"Excuse me, madam. Let me ask if you are accustomed to driving oxen?"

"In course I is, or I wouldn't be a doin' on it."

"Allow me to inquire your name."

"Jane Ann Morgan, Bill Morgan's woman," answered she.

"Is your husband dead?"

"No, mout as well be. ' He ain't fit for nothin', but I dew make him stay to home and take care of the brats."

General Blair was surprised, but concluded to ask further, and continued:

"Is your husband sick?"

"Sick? Not a bit of it! Sometimes he sez as how he is about gone up, but I keep a tellin' on him that he needn't go to 'peggin out' now an' leavin me so many darn'd brats to look arter."

During her remarks, the oxen had not followed the trail properly, seeing which, she whirled her huge whip, at same time calling out in a coarse voice:

"Whoa, gee, buck. Git up, Dick, you black divil."

At that moment they drew near a small stream, where sat a man who asked to be taken across, as the water was too deep to wade, to which she replied:

"Yes, I'll take you across for two bits, pay in advance," and turning to the General, exclaimed:

"I'm old bizness, I'm darned if I ain't."

The man clambered into the wagon, while Jane Ann took her position on the tongue of the wagon, and by roughly-spoken commands and well-directed blows from her huge whip, she piloted the team safely across.

As they pulled up out of the stream, she stopped, and addressing those on horseback, said:

"Men, look ahere. Here's this cuss that I toted across the creek for two bits has dead oodles of money. Sposin' we'd upset and he'd got drownded, he had plenty of money to pay his way into heaven or hell, and I'll bet he'd agone to hell, cos he's too lazy lookin' to get away from the devil."

The General, although he felt mortified at her uncouth expressions, felt inclined to indorse her ideas.

The General and old Mr. Chance left her driving her team toward the river landing to procure goods for her family. She was the same woman with whom Dickey had dined when on her return journey to Osawatomie after having met Hayden.

"One of those rough, energetic Western women,"

said Blair, and continued, "who, unfortunately, ignore education and are submissive only in one thing, that being an indulgence in laziness, extended to the husband. Not having associates and neighbors, they soon learn to depend upon their own energetic labor, and in so doing become rough and uncouth. Keeping, as they do, in advance of civilization, their children assume the same role, therefore no improvement can take place.

Late at night, the travelers reached St. Joseph. At Mr. Oyster's hotel the family were still in the parlor, listening to Ona's sweet music, as her voice accorded so harmoniously with the music of the piano. There was a glad surprise for two of the group.

CHAPTER LXVII.

KATE'S TROUBLE.

SOON after the arrival of the Leland family at the hotel, Ona discovered that Kate's mind was in a state of unrest; something seemed to be weighing it down; her accustomed hilarity and joyousness had departed, and one evening after they had withdrawn to their private room, Ona said:

"Kate, you seem to have grown prematurely old. What is the cause of your changed appearance?"

Kate burst into tears, and Ona feeling deeply

her responsibiliy in thus increasing her sadness, sought to comfort her. For sometime she refused to be comforted. Finally mastering her emotions, she tenderly embraced Ona, and said with choking sobs:

"O, Ona! I am in so great distress. I am engaged to marry Sylvanus Vance, and I have recently learned that he uses ardent spirits and spends much of his time playing billiards; and intemperance and idleness are distasteful to me." ,

Ona answered by saying calmly:

"Cousin, I was not aware that an attachment of heart existed between yourself and any gentleman, but if such is the fact and circumstances have developed other facts regarding the character of your affianced, and such facts are repugnant to your finer feelings, my advice is that you immediately break such engagement. I say immediately because such action, in such cases, can not be taken too soon, and by so doing you may preserve yourelf from a life of misery, shame and, perhaps, contempt. Do not allow your mind to be worried and harassed by such trifles. Before we retire, write and inform him of the changed state of your mind toward him, and at the same time do not omit to state the reason."

Kate produced writing materials and attempted to write the letter, but her hand trembled and her heart failed, and looking imploringly toward Ona, said:

"I cannot. I cannot write such a letter."

"May I write it for you?" asked Ona.

"Yes, write it, but I cannot send it."

"Cannot send it!" said Ona in surprise and asked, "Why?"

"O, I fear him! I dread him!"

With much dignity Ona said:

"Am I to understand, cousin, that you entered into an engagement affecting your life's interest with a man whom you fear and dread?"

"Yes, Ona. But I love him," said Kate.

"Indeed, you cannot love and at the same time fear a person. If you love a man truly, you certainly cannot fear him. Love does not excite such feeling. It is possible that you may fear and dread him and at the same time become submissive, but submission is not love."

"I cannot think otherwise than that I love him, yet at the same time I have dreadful forebodings for the future in an association with him," said Kate.

"Tell me further regarding him. Who is he? What are his prospects in life, and all you know regarding his antecedents." demanded Ona.

"Why, you ask an impossibility. I know but little pertaining to him. I met him for the first time at the house of a friend, where he was for a brief time tarrying. He proved to be splendid company; highly entertaining; had been connected with some business, in the discharge of which he had traveled considerably; had nicely furnished rooms when at home in Cincinnati, but had stored his furniture, which was very valuable, while he journeyed to the West. It is true, at our first meeting he talked much of love and marriage. Although he is not young, he had never met a lady in whom he felt the interest that he did in myself, and told me that he knew that I loved him, and if I did not, the time would soon come when I would, and that if from any cause we should soon become separated and I in the meantime should marry, that I would then see my error and gladly leave my husband and flee to him."

"His conversation was indeed entertaining," replied Ona haughtily. "You do not realize, Kate, that you have fallen into the fascinating society of a professional 'love-maker,' a real 'masher,' whose crimes may out-number his love affairs. You are young and somewhat inexperienced in the ways of men, while I am older and more experienced. Therefore let me assume the office of advisor to you. There are men in this world who seem to be endowed with that same subtle power which reptiles possess over lesser animals. They cast a halo of fascination around and about that which they would destroy. The lesser or weaker animal becomes first fascinated and attracted by the peculiarly graceful movements of the reptile; its bright, dazzling eye calls forth the admiration of the now infatuated one, and requiring a nearer view, it approaches the cause of its infatuation until sufficiently near, when, with one fell swoop, the wily serpent envelops the deluded being in its coils, crushes out its life and devours it. If I am to judge regarding yourself and Mr. Vance, you occupy the place of the infatuated and deluded animal, while he occupies that of the destroyer. To break this spell, this hallucination by which you are surrounded, may and will, dear cousin, cause you pain. It is a fact in natural history that animals which, by an interven-

tion of a stronger power, have been rescued from this peculiar attraction, have given evidence of the greatest pain just at the moment the spell was broken. You stand in this affair upon dangerous ground. Let me urge you to bring all your will-power into force and cast aside the tempter."

"O, I wish I could be brave and firm as you are, Ona," replied Kate.

"You have the power so to do within yourself. Take a secondary position to no one. Be not subservient to any man or his wishes. Think and act of and for yourself. Deposit the letter in the office in the morning. Force yourself to appear happy, even gay. Ignore Vance and all who are equal and below him. Aspire to a higher position. If you do not immediately gain it, do not be discouraged, you will eventually gain any position your aspirations denominate."

"I fear, Ona, you are too severe in your judgment of Mr. Vance," said Kate.

"I am not severe, Kate; I am only just. Every occasion demands to be justly considered; some require a greater degree of severity than others. You must, in dealing out justice, neither be sympathetic nor philantropic. You know the character of the man with whom you are dealing. Marry such a man and become submissive. Permit him, when under the influence of whisky, to repeatedly beat you, and as submissively excuse him for the whisky's sake," said Ona.

"I would not, after being once beaten, permit a repetition. I would leave him immediately," replied Kate.

"So women, from time immemorial, have said, and what have they accomplished? They have invariably done as you seem to desire to do in this case, cling to the serpent and end their days in the alms or mad-house, or even worse, and then talk about Fate or Fortune being unpropitious. I tell you we mark our own path through life, and gods nor goddesses have aught to do with it."

"Is there not some hope for the reformation of such men after being happily married?" said Kate, her mind still dwelling on Vance and his failings.

Ona, somewhat impatiently, exclaimed:

"Now, there it is again. We women *must*, it seems, be continually extending our pity to some abomination in the shape of a man, because he chooses to lay aside principle, pervert his acquirements and become worse than a beast. We, even in the hope of effecting his reformation, marry him. Did you ever know of a man marrying a degraded woman with the hope and for the purpose of reforming her? No, indeed, you never have. No matter how much man degrades himself, he still looks for perfection in his wife, and when a woman unites her eternal destinies with such a man she generally subsists on corn-bread and water, after having herself raised the corn and carried the water. Yet, with all the experience of the past, people cry that 'it is the duty of women to reform these drunkards.'"

"I know that your expressions are true, Ona. But I would not marry such a man," said Kate.

"How long, cousin, shall you entertain that opinion? Until your mind again reverts to Vance and your fear of him and dread of giving him offense?"

At this moment the step of a child was heard in the hall, followed by a gentle tap on their door, while a sweet voice exclaimed:

"O, Katy, tum see who tum. Somebody tum to see Ota."

CHAPTER LXVIII.

THE MISSING CHILD.

WHEN the Border Ruffians realized that John Brown had again eluded them, they disbanded and returned to Missouri. While the older settlers were leaving the Territory, new emigrants were constantly arriving, whose doings the dragoons from Georgia remained to watch.

A part of the disbanded ruffians reached Missouri at St. Joseph, the leaders putting up at the hotels. At Mr. Oyster's could be seen Guy Wren and some of his leading men.

He was there when Mr. Leland and his family arrived, but did not recognize in the fashionably-attired young lady Dickey Deane, the spy. These men were sitting on the porch, near the parlor, regretting that Ona and Kate had just left when Gen. Blair and old Mr. Chance arrived. The General entered and was on the point of introducing Mr. Chance to the occupants of the parlor, when little Ota, with a joyful cry of recognition, sprang forward and exclaimed:

"O, grandpa, I'se so glad you tum."

Every eye was turned toward the old man and the child. Wren recognized the old gentleman, having been at his house frequently, besides being one of the number who murdered his son.

He had often admired the innocent little child as she played about the house, all unconscious that he was the cause of her being there, but now when he witnessed the evidences of affection of one for the other, a frown played upon his hardened features. It did seem that he was so constituted that he could not behold evidences of love and affection, as it existed between others, with favor.

The old gentleman's eyes were bedimmed with tears of joy as he pressed the pretty child to his gladdened heart.

Mr. Oyster informed him regarding the finding of the child by his niece. Wren, with others, heard the particulars and formed the vile scheme to again cast sorrow and gloom upon and over the mind of the old man. He was not aware that Mr. Chance was a protege of General Blair's, or his cowardly heart would have failed to co-operate with his depraved mind, in carrying out its vile conception.

Suddenly the child exclaimed:

"I must do and tell Aunt Katy that dranpa has tum for Ota," and clambering down from her grandpa's knee, she hastened to the door, which General Blair smilingly opened, at same time saying:

"It is too dark, little one; wait until I can procure a light."

But Ota darted through the opened door, and the

patter of her little feet were heard as she tripped down the hall in search of Aunt Katy's room.

Her summons was answered by Kate, who said:

"Go back, Ota, and we will join you in the parlor as soon as we replace our shoes," which they had removed, preparatory to retiring.

As the young ladies made hasty preparations to return to the parlor, they each conjectured as to who the new arrival could be. In a moment, heavy and hurried footsteps were heard passing through the hall and out into the darkness.

When the young ladies reached the parlor, they met General Blair and Mr. Chance, who, in tenderest words, thanked Ona for preserving and Kate for kindly treating his little pet.

Kate entirely forgot her love-sorrow in her interest in Ota, and said:

"What a strange coincidence! We named Ota 'Chance' on account of her accidental discovery and rescue, and her name proves, in reality, to be such. I hope, Mr. Chance, you will consent to leave her with us; we are all much interested in her welfare."

Before Mr. Chance could reply, Kate had looked around, and failing to note Ota's presence, exclaimed:

"Where is the child?"

Mr. Oyster replied:

"She went in search of you," and rising hastily . from the sofa, ejaculated:

"Did she not return with you?" .

"No," said Kate, "I told her we would meet her

in the parlor in a moment, and I thought she returned."

An anxious look dwelt upon the countenances of all as the child was repeatedly called and no answering voice was heard. Prompt and energetic search was instituted in and around the house, but no tidings of her whereabouts could be obtained.

At last Ona said :

"We heard a heavy step passing through the hall toward the outer door, and I apprehend that step is connected with Ota's disappearance."

The boarders were questioned, but they knew nothing concerning the child.

Ona approached Mr. Oyster and quietly asked :

"Uncle, where is Wren ?"

"I don't know. Has he gone ?" asked he in surprise.

Immediate search was made for Wren, but he could nowhere be found. When the suspicion flashed upon the mind of Kate, she could scarcely control her grief; she knew too well the nature of the demon, Wren.

General Blair and Mr. Leland enlisted the whole police force to aid in the search, but it was unavailing, although continued during the next day.

The friends continued to inquire for two weeks, when, losing hope, gave up the search.

General and Mrs. Blair bade adieu to the few friends at the hotel, and in due time reached their home in the "Sunny South," while Mr. Leland and family, accompanied by Kate, traveled eastward, leaving old Mr. Chance with Mr. Oyster, who was to look after the needs of the old man, while renewed search and inquiry was established for Wren and Ota.

Some weeks had passed, when Mr. Oyster received a letter from Gen. Blair, stating that Wren was in Atlanta, drilling troops for a renewal of the campaign in Kansas during the next spring, and suggested that an officer be sent to arrest him.

Without informing Mr. Chance, Mr. Oyster applied to the sheriff, who replied:

"I can't go. Possibly the Governor can assist you."

"Can't go? What are you here for?" ejaculated Mr. Oyster.

The sheriff replied:

"To do what I can. In many things I am hampered. This man Wren is free to go where he pleases and when he pleases, until the troubles in the Territory are over; then, if he is guilty of any misdemeanor, we can look after him."

Mr. Oyster was visibly excited, and as he left the officer, he exclaimed:

"I'll not wait until the troubles are over. I'll look after this case myself, and begin looking soon."

Mr. Oyster was not quarrelsome, neither was he cowardly, but he was determined that right should prevail, and securing a brace of pistols, he left for the South, instructing Mr. Chance to assume control during his absence.

CHAPTER LXIX.

MR. LELAND GOES TO EUROPE.

THE beautiful scenery along the river route to St. Louis and the confusion of the transfer to the cars, kept the mind of Kate busy, and Vance and his fascinations were obliterated from her mind. The roses returned to her cheeks and the smiles to her face.

As they stopped one day to change cars, she said:

"There is but one thing, Ona, that would or could add to my enjoyment."

Ona, with much apprehension, fearing that her cousin's mind was dwelling with the same absorbing interest upon her unfortunate infatuation, asked:

"Cousin, is it in my power to supply the one thing needful; if so, do not hesitate to ask it."

To which Kate replied:

"I fear it is not in your power, Ona. I so much miss the pleasantry that little Ota would afford us in watching her pleasurable emotions and listening to her childish prattling."

Thus the conversation turned upon Ota, with the usual regretful feelings at her loss.

Days passed, and they arrived at home. To Ona Cedar Hall held all the attractions of her life. As she noticed the beautiful tree, she soliloquized:

"I have seen the place where you grew. I have stood upon the ground where flourish your mates, and upon that ground I have put forth my greatest effort to consecrate that beautiful land to freedom. I have, in part, redeemed the vow I made beneath thy shade. How I should love to behold thy tender off-shoot, which I planted by the grave of my girl-hood friend, in the clime where the austral breeze is laden with the fragrance of the orange bloom. When eternal and everlasting freedom is established, thy rough boughs shall quiver with delight at the loud acclaim of joy reverberating from these rugged hills."

As these unuttered words passed through her mind, the door opened and Aunt Nancy, who had been apprised of their coming, appeared to welcome them.

Mr. Leland learned that two gentlemen had for sometime awaited his arrival. Concerning them, he could learn nothing further than that one of them was in Strawn when the attempt was made to kidnap the Curry family.

From the tenor of letters recived from Walter Strawn and Arthur Holmes, Mr. Leland concluded that the incoming settlers in Kansas would be sufficiently strong to successfully contend against any force the Pro-Slavery party could send during the winter, and he was cogitating as to how he should dispose of the time.

Visions of childhood days flitted constantly before his mind, and a longing desire to again behold the land of his birth, fixed itself firmly upon his mind, and thither he determined to go.

To think was to act, and in two days he was en route to Boston to sail for the home of his childhood and youth.

Slowly the vessel weighed anchor on the bright November morning, to cross the turbulent Atlantic, freighted with many anxious souls, among whom was Roderick Leland, who, in youth, had sought the Western Continent, feeling that to be alone in the world would solace his wretched thoughts; wretched, because of an imagined crime he had committed.

When he arrived in Edinburgh, the day seemed the same, and the sights as familiar as when he left, long years ago. Miles beyond the city, he left the cumbersome stage coach and slowly climbed the hills and winding paths around the cliffs, until he reached the Kirk of Glennarcan, from which he beheld the roof of the house in which he was born and which had sheltered him through succeeding days of childhood and youth.

He drew near. The gates stood ajar, as if waiting his return. Nervously his feet pressed the graveled walk as he approached the door-where "Welcome" had been so often uttered on his return from school. He raised his hand to grasp the old brass knocker and paused. He thought: "Am I a stranger here? Why should I knock? Can I not decorously enter where I in youth dashed through without restraint? Where are the familiar faces I once knew? Where are father, mother, brothers, and most of all, where is the much-loved sister, Theodocia? Will she know me? Will she expect me to-day?"

Thus did the thoughts course through his brain as he hesitated to rap at the door of the house he had so long known as home.

Presently his hand reached the knocker, whose

24

detonating sound reverberated through the massive
building, and to him sounded hollow and mournful.
The door swung back upon its rusty hinges, and before him stood a girl. "It cannot be Theo.," thought
he.   "The face is familiar, but it is child-like. Theo.
should be grown.   Thirty years I have been away.
This child is but little more than half that age."

CHAPTER LXX.

KATE IN THE EAST

THE approach of winter found Kate and Ona at
Cedar Hall. _ During the late autumn, they
had wandered through the woods, gathering
nuts; rambling in the meadows, selecting wild flowers and curious grasses; clambered over hills, to view
the wild and picturesque scenery; coursed along the
streams, picking up variously-colored shells and peb-
bles, and passed the evenings at home, answering
letters, reading aloud or singing choice selections and
discoursing sweatest music from the piano.   Neither
had a desire to mingle with fashionable society, but
each preferred the unrestrained life and liberty of
home.

On pleasant days they would ride far out into the
rough hills, where but an occasional family dwelt;
at other times they would drive through the more
thickly populated valleys.

Kate could not harmonize her views of an agricultural district with the small farms of the East. She also noticed that the utmost economy was practiced by the majority of the people, in order to eke out a miserable existence, and on their return from such a drive one day, said to Ona:

"Ona, do the rich or better class of settlers in this country emigrate to the West? Are such selected by the Aid Societies?"

"Not generally," replied Ona. "Such people receive aid from the different societies as are not able to pay the expenses of the trip across the country, but why do you ask such questions?" replied Ona.

"For the simple reason that in our journeyings I notice but few who are blessed with the evidences of prosperity, to say nothing of a competency. I refer particularly to those outside of the small towns, such as dwell in the farming districts. In St. Joseph I have noticed almost invariably that the Eastern people who arrive there make a great ado about the poverty and peculiar appearances of the Western people, and have much to say regarding their condition before they left the East, speaking especially regarding the social surroundings of their 'wife's people,' and I cannot see but the Western people are enjoying far better surroundings to-day than are the majority of the residents of this older country."

To which Ona replied:

"I admit, Kate, that the middle and lower classes in the West have advantages superior to the same classes here. That is, they have better opportunities to seek a higher position. There is more land to cultivate, and land that in itself is productive without the aid of fertilizers, which must ever be employed here. Having more land, they have greater scope for their energies, and after certain pressing seasons, they have opportunities of frequently meeting, which develops more sources of amusement and consequent happiness. Here the farms are small, and each member of the family must occupy every moment of his or her time in some employment that will augment the scanty supply on hand. The peculiarity of the emigrants' conversation which you noted is brought about, no doubt, by his future prospects, it being a peculiarity exclusively Yankee, when elated over a bright prospect, to boast of the past, however dark it may have been. You must admit, cousin, that our people when they settle in the West are industrious and soon acquire the competency for which, in laboring here, they became discouraged."

"I have not a word to say against them as citizens, but I was led to believe, through their peculiarity, as you term it, that people in the East generally were rich. As regards the surface indications of the country, I much prefer the West, where plenty and an abundance abounds."

Thus discussing the merits of their respective sections, the girls passed the greater part of the winter. They made a ten days' visit to Washington, and business concerning the Aid Societies called Ona to Boston, whither Kate, of course, accompanied her.

A letter from Mr. Oyster informed them that Guy Wren had returned to Missouri, and surrounded as he was by cut-throats and outlaws, it was impossible to bring him to justice.

On the approach of summer, Ona was assigned by the Anti-Slavery party, soliciting funds wherewith to purchase the freedom of slaves and colonize them in Liberia. For her field of operation she sought the fashionable resorts at the seaside. The plan was soon found to be not feasible, and was abandoned. Yet Ona and Kate remained at the seaside, enjoying the refreshing breezes and mingling with the fashionable society there congregated.

One day as the two wandered along the beach watching the light boats mounting the fleecy waves, they were startled by a childish voice, which sounded familiar, exclaiming:

"There is Aunt Katy! There is Aunt Katy!"

They both turned in the direction of the sound, and then beheld little Ota, who ran to Kate and was soon clasped in her arms. A well-dress lady followed, who seemed surprised at the happy meeting between her little charge and the two young ladies. On being questioned by Ona, she told how she became possessed of the stolen child.

She was stopping at a fashinable Southern resort, where Wren appeared with the child, saying that he had found her begging in St. Louis. She became attached to the little orphan and begged Wren to allow her to have the child. After some consideration, he fixed a price which the lady paid, and thus brought the child to the Northern States.

Ona and Kate related the sad history of the child and told of the anxious waiting of her grandpa at St. Joseph, to learn of her whereabouts. The lady would not give the child into their possession, although the little one clung convulsively to Kate and refused to go with the lady.

Ona hailed a carriage and all returned to the hotel, where it was agreed that the grandfather should be sent for. Ona accordingly sent a message to Mr. Oyster and Mr. Chance. On their arrival they identified the little one, who, once in its grandpa's possession, could not have been purchased with the wealth of the Indias.

The happy group returned to Cedar Hall, carrying the child with them.

After a brief rest, Kate accompanied her father, Mr. Chance, and Ota to their Western home, where she assumed the duties and cares devolving upon her. Her association with Ona; her introduction to society, although limited, gave her a better insight into life, its hopes and its expectations. She had acquired Ona's firmness and easy style and manner. She had not forgotten Vance, but her admiration and feeling for him had undergone a radical change. Instead of loving, she despised him. To such as he she extended her sympathy, but the idea of descending to their common level, or elevating them to hers at the risk of sacrificing self never once entered her mind.

During her brief stay in Washington, she had become acquainted with a young French gentleman, Francis Orlando, who was sent by his government to convey certain instructions to the French representative at the Capital. He had expressed more than usual interest in her and had manifested great solicitude in things pertaining to her comfort and pleasure. She had received his attentions merely with courtesy, but now images of him personally passed before the vision of her mind, and thoughts of his kindly attentions ever presented themselves for consideration.. When she left Washington, he, wearied of the cares and vexations of business, sought recreation at the fashionable resorts of the United States.

The many cares and duties pertaining to hotel life were supervised by Kate, besides directing proper care and instruction for Ota, whom Mr. Chance had left exclusively to her care when he returned to Ohio, where he lived among other relatives.

Autumn and winter passed, and Mr. Leland yet lingered in Scotland, while Ona, deeply interested in affairs at Washington, could not find time to visit Kate, who had repeatedly written for her. In the following spring she, in obedience to earnest solicitation and her own desires, journeyed West. Spending two weeks with Kate, who had many duties to perform ere she could leave the house in care of the servants, they together visited Lawrence.

Ona was surprised at the manifest change which had taken place. Where once stood only sod houses now arose stately buildings of brick, stone and lumber. Emigration had poured into the Territory from the Eastern States, and money for improvements had been bountifully supplied.

She became, with Kate, the guest of Arthur and Sallie Holmes, who had rooms in the Free-State Hotel. Arthur conducted a newspaper, which was in itself a powerful aid in properly representing the affairs of the Territory.

As they sat at table one day in the public dining room, an old man of stately, noble mien entered and took a seat with them. Ona viewed him a moment and excitedly arose from the table, at same time extending her hand to him.

CHAPTER LXXI.

AT HARPER'S FERRY.

AS Ona approached the old man at the table, he looked up in evident surprise for an instant, when a smile played upon his noble, intelligent face as he hastily rose and eagerly clasped her extended hand, saying:

"I am, indeed, glad to see you, 'Dickey Deane.'"

To which greeting Ona replied:

"Your pleasure, Captain Brown, cannot be greater than mine in having met you."

Every eye in the room was turned toward the two persons who had, in former times, been so well known throughout the Territory. A number of men were seated at that table who had been members of Capt. Brown's company, yet they had not, until his name was spoken by Ona, recognized him. Now all arose from the table, to pay respect to the brave old man and determined leader.

He appeared younger, by many years, than when he left the Territory. His small blue eyes gleamed with pleasure and a smile of delight overspread his countenance as he finished his meal in silence.

Strangers who had heard of the world-renowned "Dickey Deane," gazed in wonder and amazement upon the handsome and elegantly-attired lady. They could not, seemingly, in their mind associate "The Spy of Osawatomie" with the beautiful and refined lady before them, who had been so prominent an actor in the Border warfare.

Captain Brown, too, received his share of attention. Many of his old comrades now in Lawrence, on learning of his arrival, hastened to the hotel, where their cheers "made the welkin ring," so great enthusiasm did his presence create.

By-standers said: "It is no wonder Missourians fled from him. Determination, such as his countenance expresses, will cause an enemy to flee as readily as do swift-flying bullets."

He remained in town a few days, during which time he was the recipient of one continued ovation. He went to Osawatomie, where a like reception awaited him. On his return to Lawrence, he was heard to say to Brave Lavanda:

"Be ready, I shall need you. Do not forget your promise!"

He stopped a short time in Tabor, and returned to the East.

To the outside world his movements were unknown. Only his chosen few knew where he was. In such a noiseless manner were those few assembled, night after night to drill, that none heard of it.

Ona had returned to her home in the East, sum-

moned thither by her father, who intimated his speedy
return to the United States, and hoping she would
be at Cedar Hall to receive him and the news he had
for her.

Time passed, and yet Mr. Leland came not. Ona's
mind was in a state of anxious unrest, fearing some
accident had happened to the vessel. Her mind was
thus absorbed in thoughts of her father as she stood
watching the falling snow-flakes on that memorable
17th of October, when she was suddenly startled by
the hasty clang of the village bells, as they dolefully
tolled.

Calling Robert, they hastened to the village and
learned that the Anti-Slavery Society demanded
volunteers. Men, in groups upon the corners, talked
seriously. A solemnity prevailed everywhere. She
learned that John Brown was a prisoner at Harper's
Ferry, and friends were trying to effect his release if
possible.

Ona hurried home, where she hastily arranged for
an indefinite absence, and departing, took the train
for Baltimore, thence to the scene of battle.

But what could she do there alone? A messenger
called her to Lawrence. Before she left, she visited
the old man in the jail at Charlestown, where he had
been removed for safe-keeping. The old man was
lying upon a worn and dilapidated bed. His countenance wore the pallor of death, but the same stern,
calm and serene expression lingered there, as it had
in by-gone days. He opened his eyes and faintly
smiled as she extended her hand.

For the first time in her life she gave way to fear-

MARBLE BUST OF JOHN BROWN.

(Made by Brackett, at Charleston, Va., by order of Mrs. Mary E.
Stearns, of Medford, Mass., during Brown's imprisonment and previous to his execution.)

The Publisher is indebted to Hon. F. G. ADAMS, Secretary Kansas
Historical Society, Topeka, Kansas, for the use of this cut.

" Mr. Stearns, I consider the Golden Rule and the
Declaration of Independence one and inseparable."

JOHN BROWN.

MEDFORD (near Boston), *January*, 1857.

ful apprehensions. She saw no hope of rescue for the lion-hearted old man, and hiding her face, she wept tears of sorrow. The old man placed his hand upon her head and said:

"We have accomplished, we think, a great work in the last few years, but it is only the beginning. Great ends cannot be attained without sacrifice. If it be my lot to be given as a sacrificial offering toward the cause of freedom, I am resigned to my fate. Let me repeat: This is but the beginning. The seed we have sown in the West is being scattered by the breeze of public opinion, and will soon germinate and diffuse its influence over the whole world. Human slavery must be obliterated from our beautiful land."

He, after a pause, said:

"All I can ask of you is to remember my family, who, no doubt, have suffered from my interest in this cause. And furthermore, Dickey, watch closely the Judas of our band. You know him. He has betrayed me, his best friend."

Ona dried her tears, and kissing the old man, passed the guards who paced before the cell, unconscious that Dickey Deane, the Spy, had been in consultation with old John Brown, the Liberator.

CHAPTER LXXII.

TOO LATE.

WHEN Ona had left the cell, she conceived a plan by which to serve the interests of the prisoner. She hastened to Kansas, accompanied by some of Brown's best friends. Excitement ran high in Kansas. A company had been formed for the purpose of releasing the old man. Money had been contributed to properly arm all who would defend their homes in the North.

Confusion prevailed in the South. Men were afraid of Old John Brown, though fearfully wounded and in prison. To the extreme limits of the South drums beat, calling for volunteers to guard the lone prisoner at Charlestown.

That miserable miscreant, Guy Wren, traveled from State to State, making speeches and collecting money to pay the expenses of guarding Old Osawatomie Brown and urging each State to send a rope with which to hang the old man. South Carolina, Missouri and Kentucky each sent a rope.

Friends of the old man hovered near, but they were powerless. Ona, accompanied by the braves of Kansas, reached Baltimore the day preceding that set for the execution. Realizing the futility of any effort that they could put forth at that late day, they could only weep as they listened to the tolling bells and minute guns fired in honor of him who was soon to be at rest.

It was over!. The rope from Kentucky had done its work. The hero of Osawatomie was no more. His lifeless body was placed in the walnut coffin and sent to his friends. Mournfully and silently they followed it to its last quiet resting place in the cemetery at North Elba, where the last respects of the few were paid to him whom the many have since called great and good.

At the head of the grave stood the family of the departed. The people gazed with amazement upon the little company who, headed by a young woman, bearing in her hand the rifle of the deceased, while the other supported a banner bearing the inscription, "The heroes of Osawatomie. In God we trust."

Yes, every survivor of that band was there, his arm draped in mourning for the man who had given his life for a great cause, that of the welfare of a fellow being.

On the faces of that chosen band was an expression of grief and determination. The careless observer did not see the silver locket that each member grasped in the right hand and placed upon the heart, with left hand uplifted, as the coffin was lowered into the grave. They saw the banner lower and the hand press upon the breast, but they did not know of the high resolves and nobly replighted vows which were made as that casket of lifeless clay was lowered to its last resting-place. Nor could they realize the heart-felt emotions which this band felt as the eulogistic words were uttered by the most eloquent of men over the grave of "The Martyr of Freedom in America."

How differently was this scene viewed! In the North business was suspended; bells were tolled; eulogistic sermons were delivered and sympathy for the cause of freedom received an impetus which never lagged or diminished, until the cause of slavery was no more.

In the South it was a day of rejoicing. Cannons were fired; bells pealed forth glad notes; balls were given, and all were merry and happy in triumphing over the death of one whose name is high emblazoned upon the temple of Fame.

The boom of the cannon; the glad peal of the bells; the happy sound of merry voices, were all gathered up by the spirit of "Old John Brown," to be, in after years, handed down to the African slave, that he, too, might rejoice and be glad when the object for which the hero died had been attained.

As they journeyed home, Dickey thought of the words of Brown pertaining to his betrayal. She knew, in her own mind, who the person was. She had detected him as easily as she had discovered the treachery of Bill Stout. She felt at a loss as to how she should inform the "Band" of the treachery of one of their number formerly. She desired first to confront him personally with the accusation. But she knew not when an opportunity would be presented.

She, on her way home, stopped, in company with Mrs. Wise, to attend an Anti-Slavery meeting in Boston. As they were seated, a handsome gentleman approached and extended his hand to Dickey, who rose from her seat, and with a finger pointing to

the west, said, as the hot blood suffused her cheeks:
"Away, traitor! and mourn at the grave of thy
best friend."

CHAPTER LXXIII.

QUANTRELL IN KANSAS.

WITH the prospect of the establishment of
peace along the border of Missouri and
Kansas, emigration was renewed. The
fame of the new Territory as an agricultural district
had spread far and wide. Every Northern State
contributed its proportion to swell the tide. Honest,
industrious men, hoping to better their individual
condition and increase the prospects of their children, hastened to this fertile Territory.

In 1857 some half-dozen families from the little
village in Ohio where Bill Quantrell was born, and
had since lived, determined to emigrate to Kansas.

As they were about ready to start, Bill appeared
among them and informed them that he would like
to accompany them. It was with reluctance that
they consented to accede to his wishes, and thus it
was that he left his native village for a clime, the
associations and surroundings of which, in after times,
proved to be more congenial to his nature.

On the arrival of the company, they selected lands
some eight miles north of Osawatomie. Here Bill

spent the first year in the Territory, after which he went to Lawrence, where he was when Dickey Deane met and recognized Captain Brown, he being a guest at the same hotel, and at the time was seated at the same table.

He had become acquainted with many who had participated in the early troubles, among them Arthur Holmes, from whom he had learned of the fame and renown of Dickey Deane, the spy. When he saw the beautiful young lady he importuned her many friends, especially Arthur, for an introduction. Arthur refrained from complying with his request until circumstances were such that he could no longer avoid it. He noticed the cool indifference with which Dickey received the introduction to the would-be school teacher, that being the object of Quantrell's visit to Lawrence.

"What do you think of Mr. Quantrell?" asked Arthur of Dickey, as she entered their apartments.

"I must be candid and say I am not favorably impressed with the gentleman," replied Dickey.

"Indeed!" exclaimed Arthur. "He, although a new-comer, has identified himself with our interest; in fact, is one of our most active and efficient pickets."

"That does not change my individual opinion regarding him. Furthermore, Mr. Holmes, I have my reasons for prejudging him. His cast of countenance, especially the expression of his colorless eyes, is enough to identify him with meanness, treachery and deceit. He so strongly resembles Guy Wren that he should be his son. I can at least aver that they are related. Note carefully his facial expression and the construction of his head and neck, and if you do not determine that he is nearer allied to the brute than the human creation, I will lay no further claims to physiognomy."

Dickey threw more energy than usual in her remarks concerning Quantrell, to which Arthur calmly replied:

"I think differently. I think Mr. Quantrell is a well-meaning young man. We will allow after events to establish the correctness of our judgment of character."

The conversation turned in a different channel, and Bill Quantrell was forgotten by both, but in an adjoining room, with his ear pressed against the thin partition, sat Quantrell, catching every word. His heart sank within him as he heard the outspoken and candid opinion of himself as entertained by the renowned woman for whose favorable consideration he would have given life itself. But as all men of like nature, instead of making an effort to establish himself properly before the community and thus winning favor, he permitted the baser propensities of his nature to predominate and govern his actions.

He soliloquized: "I am mean and despicable by nature. Am I? I look and act like Guy Wren. Do I?" His passion controlled him, and with glaring eyes and clinched hands, he paced the room, muttering: "Dickey Deane shall, in the future, consider Guy Wren an angel, when compared with me. Every element of my nature calls loudly for revenge, and I swear to so indulge that nature that in after

25

years the name of Quantrell shall be a synonim for
'Devil.'"

The next morning when he appeared at breakfast,
the scowl had not left his face. Dickey did not,
apparently, notice his presence. Arthur's mind, at
sight of him, reverted to Dickey's opinion, as expressed the night before, and he thought: "She is
right," and the favorable opinion he himself had conceived was suddenly dispelled.

Dickey's sojourn in Kansas, on account of the
press of business, soon terminated, and she returned
to Cedar Hall.

Quantrell had not forgotten her expressions. Her
words burned into his brain as a hot iron. The more
he thought of them, the stronger grew his determination to be revenged. He even contemplated taking
her life, but a cowardly fear of apprehension alone
prevented the act. Something must be done to satisfy the cravings of his agitated and depraved mind.
He opened a correspondence with Wren, making
known his wishes, and afterward visited him in Missouri, where they held an earnest and private consultation.

His acquaintances at Lawrence were not suspicious of him, even when, in after time, he was frequently absent. Being a member of the "Secret
Force" of the Territory, he was privileged to go and
come as he desired, and was not suspected, even
when he left Lawrence and stationed himself nearer
the State line, to more effectually carry out his base
designs.

A year had passed since the attack on Harper's

Ferry, and Guy Wren had returned to Missouri. The Missouri farmers were suffering much annoyance and inconvenience from the depredations that were constantly made upon their stock of cattle, and more especially horses, and no clue could be obtained as to where they were taken, while some of the Pro-Slavery settlers in Kansas seemed to prosper in the accumulation of such stock.

A prominent man in Missouri, who owned many fine horses and had a number of slaves, kept constant guard over his stables, and had threatened to kill any one found prowling about his premises at night.

Quantrell visited Lawrence frequently. On one of his visits he called a select number of the Free-State men together and told them that a number of negroes were anxious to leave their master and would do so if they could obtain assistance and guidance from men in Kansas. Arrangements were made to assist them. Quantrell immediately visited the Missouri gentleman who kept watch over his stock.

Hitching his horse, he approached the door and rang the bell. He waited patiently and was about to ring the second time, when the door was opened by a young lady whose attire was neatly arranged, except that her hands were incased in kid gloves and her face enveloped in a woolen shawl, which was closely held by one hand.

" Is Mr. Baily at home?" inquired Quantrell.

"He is somewhere upon the premises. Walk in, sir, and I will send for him," replied the lady in a whining voice.

They entered the finely-furnished parlor, when the lady rang the bell and a servant soon appeared at an opposite door, of whom she asked:

"Where is papa, Dinah?"

To which the servant replied, "I dunno, Missus!"

"Go and find him. Tell him that a gentleman awaits him in the parlor. Close the door," and turning to Quantrell, she continued:

"We have to exercise great precaution in protecting ourselves from the pertinacious influences of the South winds, which predominate here, else our complexions would be utterly ruined, sir."

Quantrell merely nodded acquiescence, and now understood the delay in answering his call. As she removed the shawl and slowly removed her gloves, he thought, "What a consummate fool!"

CHAPTER LXXIV.

MR. LELAND AT HIS EARLY HOME.

MR. LELAND followed the young lady who had answered his summons, and was soon ushered into the family room. There, in the same old arm-chair his grandmother had occupied when he was a child, sat an aged woman. "Can this be my mother?" thought he. Near her sat a middle-aged man, who had, apparently, been reading aloud, but now arose to welcome the stranger.

Mr. Leland, with forced composure, said:

"I am an American gentleman, traveling for recreation, and wish to rest a brief time."

The gentleman politely handed him a chair. He laid aside his great-coat and hat and entered into conversation with his host. The young lady entered and seated herself near him.

After some moments' conversation in a cursory manner regarding America, Mr. Leland asked:

"Who is the proprietor of this estate at this time?"

"I am, sir. My name is Leland—Robert Leland."

"I was here once when I was a boy," continued Mr. Leland, still putting forth great efforts to retain his composure.

The old lady glanced over her glasses and said:

"I don't remember of receiving a call from any one from America, but I am so forgetful. Do you remember such, Robie?"

"No, mother, I do not remember," answered Robert.

"I spent two days here, but the family was larger than now. There was a pretty blue-eyed lassie, three boys and an old gentleman, the father," said Roderick.

The old lady began to weep, and Robert answered:

"Father is dead. Roderick was lost—we suppose he was killed. Scott went to India, since which time we have not heard from him. Theodocia, our pet and idol, married an English nobleman. They removed to Paris, and we lost all trace of her. So you see, sir, that we have been most unfortunate in losing all trace of many members of our family."

"Permit me to ask the name of the gentleman whom the young lady married," said Roderick.

"Gordon, sir.   Cyril Gordon."

"Cyril Gordon!" ejaculated Roderick as he started in surprise, but promptly controlling his excitement, calmly said, "I think that was the name of the young man who was said to have been killed while I was here or near here."

"He was not killed," answered Robert.   "He was seriously wounded, but ultimately recovered.   It was then that brother Roderick was missing."

"And you have not since heard from him?" continued Roderick.

"No, not one word."

"I knew a man by the name of Roderick Leland in America," said Roderick.   .

The old lady rose hastily from her chair. Robert drew nearer, and excitedly asked:

"Do you think it possible that it is my long-lost brother?"

The old lady had closely scanned the face of the stranger, and ere he could reply to Robert's question, the old lady hastened toward him, exclaiming:

"You are my long-lost bairn.   I know every line of your face."

She threw herself into Roderick's arms, where she was lovingly embraced while Roderick said:

"Yes, mother, I am indeed your boy.   I am Roderick Leland."

He bore the happy old lady to her seat and extended his hand to his brother Robert, who eagerly grasped it.

The young lady stood amazed, until Robert said:

"Brother, this is my Theodocia.   She was named for our sister."

The young lady joyously received the extended
hand of her kinsman, who said:

"She so much resembles in appearance our sister
that, except for the disparity of their ages, I should
have addressed her as 'sister' when I entered the
hall."

As he talked, his mother stood near, parting his
hair. Presently she exclaimed:

"You are, indeed, my son Roderick. Here is the
same lock of black hair—unsilvered, like the rest, by
time—that you wore when a lad."

Roderick now meditatively recalled the past and
thought: "Would he not have been happier to have
remained in Scotland, since Cyril had not been
killed?" Then his thoughts wandered to America,
where he had taken so prominent a part in the endeavor to establish "universal freedom." Amidst
conflicting thoughts, he realized that, despite all his
efforts toward the freedom of others, he now, for the
first time in thirty years, felt himself untrammeled
and unrestrained.

The bullet aimed at the innocent hare had glinted
from a stone and wounded Cyril in the breast as he
sat, with sketch-book in hand, limning the surrounding scenery.

Roderick related incidents and circumstances of
his life since he left Scotland; told them of his wife
and children; showed them a picture of his wife,
Leona, and the little ones which the aged lady admired. Conversation turned upon the political troubles in the West, and when he related the experiences of Ona, the old mother's frame quivered with

an exciting thrill and the eyes of the younger Theodocia glowed with the fire of enthusiasm, while Robert declared her to be "a worthy scion of a noble
house."

After strolling for some days among the familiar
scenes of Glenarcan, Roderick proposed to Robert
that they should visit Paris and institute a search for
Theodocia and Cyril. Robert acquiesced, and they
accordingly made arrangements to start in a few
weeks.

On their arrival, they began a diligent and sys-
tematic search. Finally, at the "Census Bureau,"
they found a record of the family, consisting of
"Cyril Gordon, wife and two children, No. 96 ——."
They afterward could only learn that such a family
had lived at the designated place, but had removed
to another, unknown, quarter.

In conversing upon the subject uppermost in their
minds, the oft-repeated saying of their mother was
quoted: "That Theodocia was predestined to care,
trouble and anxiety, as a shadow ever darkened her
path."

The brothers started for London to continue the
search.

CHAPTER LXXV.

THE DOUGLAS ESTATE.

AFTER Sir Charles and Hayden had spent a few days in recuperation, they repaired to the hotel of the "Aspirant to the Douglas Estate."

On announcing their business, they were ushered into the presence of a young gentleman, who received them kindly, at same time handing each a card, bearing the name of Francis Orlando Douglas, in exchange for theirs.

Hayden manifested much agitation. He could plainly discern that the young gentleman, whether legally entitled to the estates or not, was, without doubt, a scion of the house of Douglas.

The young gentleman, having excused himself, returned, bringing with him innumerable papers, saying:

"These are the evidence I have to offer in substantiation of my claim to the 'Douglas Estate,'" and at same time offering one for the inspection of Sir Charles and Hayden. It proved to be a certificate of a marriage contract performed in England, the contracting parties being Cyril Gordon Douglas and Vivian Orlando, Countess of Lorrea.

Hayden could not control his emotion; his eyes were fixed; his face was pallid, and he sat uprightly and motionless as a stone. The new claimant looked· at him a moment and asked:

"Are you, sir, an heir to these estates?"

To which Hayden replied:

"Yes, I am a son of Cyril Gordon Douglas and Theodocia Leland, of Glanarcan, Scotland."

Francis gazed in astonishment at the statement, and in a hesitating voice asked:

"Was Cyril Gordon Douglas twice married?"

To which Sir Charles replied:

"Yes, if your papers are correct. He divorced this young man's mother, whom we had supposed was his first wife, and married a wealthy demi-monde, who yet resides in this city."

The sympathy of Francis was touched, and turning to Hayden, asked:

"Is your mother in the city?"

"She is dead," answered Sir Charles.

"Were you an only child?" continued Francis.

"No, I have a sister, who is now at school in the city."

After a moment's hesitation, Francis said:

"It is not in my nature to destroy the prospects or blight the expectation of any one. My identity can be easily and thoroughly established. I shall submit my proofs to you, outside of what I have already shown you. My desire is, since I have met you, to arrange this business in such a way that the gentleman present, his sister and myself shall be and constitute one family. I submit this as a proposition for your consideration, after you have become thoroughly satisfied regarding my identity."

"Truly thou art a Douglas," said Sir Charles, who continued by saying: "Permit me to inquire regarding your mother. Is she living?"

" No, sir," answered Francis. "She died in India when I was but four years old, since which time I have not met my father or any of my relatives, until the unexpected pleasure you have this day afforded me."

"Have you remained in India since the death of your mother?"

"No, sir, I was sent to Paris, where I spent my school days. I have been some years on the continent, and have had no correspondence with England except through my counsellor, who notified me to appear in London to establish my claim as the lawful heir to the Douglas and Gordon estates. I have learned, since my arrival here, that there are two heirs to the latter besides myself. I shall make no efforts in that direction."

"Your information is correct. I have the honor to be the first, and my brother Geoffrey is the second."

"Is your name Charles?" asked Francis.

"Yes, I am Sir Charles Gordon, a brother of Cyril Gordon Douglas."

"How did Cyril, the third son, receive the name of Douglas?" asked Francis.

"His mother was not my mother. She was Lady Douglas, the second wife of my father, Sir Geoffrey Gordon, and by her request he attained the name of Douglas, in order to inherit the estates belonging to her."

"That is correct. Should you ever need proof to establish that fact, I shall be pleased to furnish it. Please examine these papers, which contain the facts you have just stated," said Francis, at the same time handing a bundle of worn papers to Sir Charles, who carefully examined them, while the young men conversed upon general subjects.

When Sir Charles had perused the papers to his satisfaction, he returned them to Francis with thanks, after which he and Hayden took leave, for the present, of their kinsman.

Arriving at the home of Sir Charles, they dispatched a carriage for Addie. The three consulted for some time regarding their arrangements for the future. Hayden was almost penniless, and Addie entirely so, she having depended upon the liberality of Sir Charles for many years. He had ever been her friend. Her deserted mother and herself had dwelt for years in the small cottage furnished through his kindness. Even in the shadow of the mansion home they once enjoyed, they became the recipients of bounty, while she who had usurped their place in the heart of husband and father, deprived them of the privileges and pleasures of home; wronged them personally; derided them publicly; cast contumely and shame upon them; gloried in their distress, sat comfortably at home in the palatial residence, enjoying the pleasures she participated in at so great cost to others.

When the cold hand of Death was laid upon that deserted wife and mother, it was a welcome touch, and she gladly sought refuge from further care in the clammy arms of the so-called Destroyer. Yet even as her lifeless body was borne to its last resting place, the shadow of that house fell athwart its path, while the usurper's face smiled from the lofty window upon

the ruin she had wrought and the wreck she alone
had made.

Hayden felt that he was, indeed, alone. He had
not been as a brother, neither had he been as a son
to his mother. He had spent the greater part of the
alimony bestowed by his father when he procured
the divorce from his mother. He could have claimed
and become established in the home and estates of
his father, had he not been idle and indifferent. But
the natural propensity inherited from his father, led
him to prefer roaming in the wilds of the United
States to becoming a titled noble of the English
realm.

He could not now enjoy the revenue of the Douglas estate, except by the charity of Francis, which he
would not accept. And when Sir Charles handed
him a draft for several hundred pounds, he refused
it, saying:

"Sir Charles, I have been already too long a subject of your bounty. If it has not been bestowed
upon me directly, it has been extended to my mother
during her misfortunes, and continued to my sister
since that mother's death. I realize, when too late,
that I am an ingrate in thus permitting you to supply wants it was my duty to anticipate. This will be
beneficial to Addie. Give it to her. But as for me,
inasmuch as the Divine Creator has ordered that I
should have an older brother, and the law counts me
a nonentity, I bow submissively to the Divine edict,
but spurn the land that inaugurates such injustice."

Through the aid of the law and its officers, Francis succeeded in ejecting from his premises the last

wife of his father, and surrendering to her the sum named as alimony, he became established in and possessed of the ancestral halls of the Douglas estate, while Hayden, as much a Douglas-as Francis, became an outcast and wanderer.

Hayden was indignant at first, but "Time changes all things" and cools the hot blood of youth. So as time rolled on and Francis solicited Hayden to repair with Addie to his mansion and assume its management, while he spent the season in Canada and the United States, whither he was commissioned from the French Government, no objection was raised in the mind of Hayden, and he accordingly assumed the management requested.

Time hung idly upon his hands. Trained servants performed the allotted duties from day to day. He visited clubs and places of amusement and strolled over the lands of the estate. One day, as he was returning from a stroll, he met two gentlemen, one of whom was attired in American costume. In a moment he recognized Roderick Leland, and politely raised his hat.

Mr. Leland paused, and said to his brother as Hayden drew near :

"That is Hayden Douglas."

Robert extended his hand, saying :

"I have not forgotten you, Hayden, although you were but a child when I last saw you. I am Robert Leland, your mother's brother, and this is Roderick Leland, a brother also, who recognized you without having known you, at least so I presume."

"You are wrong, sir," replied Hayden. "I have

had the pleasure and honor of meeting Mr. Leland frequently in America, and I censure myself for not recognizing him as a kinsman at once, from his most striking resemblance to my mother."

"I, too, am deserving of censure for not placing you where your lineaments so plainly indicate you belong, among the Gordens, who were the fast friends of my youth," returned Roderick.

Hayden invited them to return and partake of the hospitality of his home. On the way the brothers learned, for the first time, of the fate of Theodocia. On their arrival they met Addie, who, in family resemblance, favored the Douglases more than either the Lelands or Gordons.

Hayden could now recognize the noble-looking man as his uncle. But the thought that the little blue-eyed "spy" must therefore be his cousin, was not pleasant to contemplate. Had she not been the subject of his thoughts by day and his dreams by night? Had she not been the only inmate of the palatial halls he thought to occupy? Even since his dependence had become known to him, had he not, in imagination, wended his way to the shores of America, where the accident of birth is not a bar to privileges, and there again, in imagination, basked in the sunshine of her smiles. Now these day-thoughts must become hideous blanks upon the tablet of the past; those beautiful night-dreams be turned into huge goblins, to annoy, instead of to solace his rest; and imagined smiles, which cheered his heart, will now become frowns, to disrupt it; and cherished sweets, although only anticipated, are even now turning to gall and bitterness within his bosom.

When they reached the mansion, a messenger was dispatched, asking Sir Charles to visit Douglas Hall. The old gentleman started promptly, all the while wondering what pressing need demanded his attention at the Hall.

Hayden met him at the door, and said:

"Sir Charles, be prepared for any surprise. We have a great one in store for you here. Verily, the dead has been restored to life."

They entered the room. Sir Charles paused to view the strangers.

Roderick returned the glance, and rising, said:

"Is it possible that I stand in the presence of Charles Gordon?"

"Yes, and I behold my long-lost friend," exclaimed Sir Charles; as he eagerly stepped forward to meet and lovingly embrace Roderick, who as tenderly returned the greeting.

Robert cordially returned the grasp of the now happy Sir Charles, although in times past a coolness had arisen between them in some manner connected with the settlement of affairs after the death of Robert and Theodocia's father.

Roderick and Sir Charles had at Oxford experienced a feeling of regard and love for each other seldom witnessed among men, but at the time of vacation Sir Charles had become piqued over some trivial affair and would not accompany Roderick home, as had been agreed upon. Cyril, his brother, took his place; then came the accident and the disappearance of Roderick, for which Sir Charles censured himself alone. To, if possible, atone for the wrong he had done, he had for thirty years sought the friend of his youth.

.In all his travels; amidst all his recreations, and among all his associations, he had never experienced the pleasure that this meeting brought to him.

Their after conversation developed many surprises, but none greater than Roderick felt when he learned that Sir Charles had been one of "The Mysterious Companions" of Old John Brown.

They spent weeks together, until the Lelands were called to Scotland on business. Hayden and Addie accompanied them. Information of their coming, and facts concerning Theodocia and the children, had been conveyed to their mother. When they arrived, the grandmother welcomed the children of Theodocia. Hayden, impressed with her resemblance to his mother, tenderly embraced the old lady. Addie, too, offered many expressions of love for her grandmother, which favorably impressed her.

Roderick had, in his letters home, made no mention of his discoveries, hoping to find time to return, but the partially reunited family would not permit of his doing so. They traveled on the continent until nearly three years had passed, when a letter from Boston summoned him home to assist at Harper's Ferry. Accompanied by Sir Charles and Hayden, he set sail for the United States.

26

CHAPTER LXXVI.

"DICKEY DEANE" IN EUROPE.

WHEN Hayden heard the slowly but firmly uttered words which denounced him as a traitor and saw the eyes of the speaker flash with the fire of indignation, his head dropped upon his breast and he, blushing with shame, withdrew to the opposite side of the hall, where he had time to collect his thoughts.

When the meeting adjourned, he had regained composure, and meeting Ona in the vestibule, smilingly advanced and addressed her, saying:

"I have arrived at the conclusion, Miss Leland, that when you addressed me in the Hall, you must have mistaken me for some other person."

To which she promptly replied:

"The conclusion at which you have, with great effort, arrived, I beg to inform you, sir, is incorrect. I was then, as I am now, fully conscious that I addressed Mr. Douglas."

With evident confusion Hayden said:

"I beg leave, Miss Leland, to inform you that your remark then made does not apply to me, for I—"

Ona interrupted him by raising her hand and saying:

"Mr. Douglas, do not add the sin of falsehood to the wrong you have already done. You must not deny that you were instrumental in exposing to our enemies the plans of Captain Brown. I have in my possession evidence which indelibly stamps you as a traitor. You were kept informed of the movements of Brown by himself, he all the while relying upon you to assist when the time should come. You, sir, basely betrayed those plans. Further, you wrote a letter to inform him that you had died while on your way here; although you endeavored to disguise the writing, I assure you, sir, it is yours. Please examine this," handing him a letter. She continued: "Yes, for the insignificant, paltry sum of two thousand dollars you betrayed your best friend."

"Where did you get this? How did it fall into your possession?" stammered he, pointing to the letter.

"I dare not tell you, sir. You were never, sir, fully initiated into the mysteries of our band, else you would know how such business falls under my consideration. You have the money, and let me assure you that you are more earnestly despised by the men who paid you than are we, who are their open enemies."

"Miss Leland, I have not their money, nor will I ever receive it. I acknowledge I wrote the letter containing the proposition you have named. But, Miss Leland, I have much to offer in extenuation of the act. At the time I committed the wrong I was not properly myself. I had just been deprived of estates which I had long looked upon as indisputably mine, by the appearance of an older brother. To be sure, I could have become a dependent upon his bounty, but a subsistence gained through crime is more honorably acquired than through charity. You can act at your pleasure regarding that missive. You have my permission to publish it, that the world may know my dastardly act. I feel that I justly merit the severest punishment that can be meted out by an indignant people."

Ona looked upon the handsome face, fired, as it was, by the spirit of a good resolution. She knew his kindly disposition, and her heart softened toward him. At length she said :

"Mr. Douglas, the knowledge which I have of your perfidy shall never be made known, provided you never repeat the wrong and as soon as possible withdraw as a member from our political society. Let me ask further, Mr. Douglas, that your after life be governed by principles of Right and Justice, so fixed and founded that an irresistible power, which annihilates alone, can prevail against your morality."

Hayden, overcome by shame, conscious and repenting the wrong he had done, and with the resolute and advisory words ringing in his ears, bowed assent and turned away.

In a moment he returned, bearing in his hand a letter, and addressed Ona, saying :

"Miss. Leland, in the confusion and surprise which followed my effort to address you in the hall, I had, until a moment since, forgotten the object for which I sought you out. I have the honor to be the bearer of a letter from your father to yourself, which permit me the pleasure of delivering," at same time passing the letter to her.

Ona thanked him kindly, and wondering where

he had met her father, opened the letter, which was voluminous. Her father had written this when on the eve of starting for the continent with his friends. In this letter he conveyed the intelligence he had withheld in others regarding the family affairs, giving particulars pertaining to each individual.

When Ona had finished reading, she approached Hayden, saying :

"This letter is a complete genealogical record of members of our family; from it I learn that you, whom I have so long known, are my cousin. Please accept a cousin's welcome to her home, where I propose going in a few days."

Hayden accepted the proffered hand, glad to be now recognized as a friend to her whom he had ever loved.

Ona was pleased herself to know that a relationship existed between them, for it would afford a better opportunity for her to administer kindly advice to him and reforming his weaknesses, thus leading him in the path of higher motives and holier ambitions.

He had often felt that he could meet and combat more successfully the temptations of the world had he but the influence of her presence, endowed as she was with will and self-possession.

On their arrival at Cedar Hall, Ona wrote to Kate, repeating much she had learned from her father's letter, especially that part pertaining to Francis Orlando, stating further that when they returned to America she should inform her, and expected to be favored with her presence.

We pass over the time of Hayden's travels to the West, his return to England, the many newsy and interesting letters passed between Ona and each member of the party traveling in Europe. She took an especial interest in her cousin Addie, and looked anxiously for the time to arrive when she should greet her in her own American home.

That time arrived; Kate was duly notified, and, accompanied by Ota, arrived from the West on the same day as did those from the East.

Long years had passed since Cedar Hall had witnessed so much of joy, pleasure and happiness. Each person vied with others in making everything pleasant and home-like. All restraint was removed; all formality laid aside, and as one family, united through the influences of love and good-wishes, they passed the time.

Hayden communicated with Francis, telling him of their joyous surroundings and naming the Western lady as one of the guests. With the early spring came Francis, to swell the number and add to the interest of the scenes enacted at Cedar Hall. He was ushered in by Hayden and presented to Ona, who received him with her becoming dignity and suavity of manner, which impressed him favorably, but when he was presented to Kate a mutual recognition took place, while the blush which adorned the cheek of each told the tale their minds would conceal.

Francis, in after days, sought the company of Kate and boldly, yet kindly, told of the feelings of love and affection which permeated his whole being, that,

without wavering, had withstood the crucible test of
absence and time amidst the blandishments of England's fair lassies. He told her how that feeling of
love which she alone had called into existence had,
since its inception, continued to grow and gain
strength amidst the responsibilities and cares of life
which he asked her to share with him.

Kate could but acknowledge that since their previous meeting she had entertained for him the kind-
liest feeling, and the knowledge that she had been
thought worthy of his consideration, gave her, indeed, much pleasure.

Thus, by frequent interchange of thought which
followed the removal of the restraint under which
they had labored when they first met, they fully
comprehended the motives one of the other. As
time passed, the engagement was made known.
None were surprise. Each seemed so entirely calculated for the other, that it seemed to be a natural
conclusion, at which all had arrived ere it was made
known.

Kate did not desire to return to the West, so Mr.
Oyster was notified of the engagement and of the
time set for the nuptials. Late in May the ceremony
which united Francis Orlando Douglas and Kate
Oyster was performed at Cedar Hall. The happy
couple soon after sailed for England, accompanied
by the Leland family, Sir Charles, Addie and Ota,
while Hayden accompanied Mr. Oyster to the West.
The trip across the Atlantic was pleasant and much
enjoyed by all, especially Ona, to whom it was a
novelty. It is true her thoughts were not all of a

pleasant nature. Her mind would ever revert to the old hero whose body lay entombed at North Elba. She could, in imagination, behold him in the various phases of life in which she had seen him—the well-dressed traveler on the boat; the active and earnest, hard-working settler near the Potawatomie; the eloquent speaker appealing for manhood's boon—freedom—from the porch in Osawatomie; the brave and defiant leader of free-born and freedom-loving citizens against the ruffiantly hordes sent to establish slavery upon the soil of Kansas. She could see him as he encouraged the men in the camp at Black Jack; she saw him hurrying through Nebraska and Iowa, piloting by day and guarding by night fugitives from slavery; she saw him at Harper's Ferry, wounded, yet defiant, offering his life for the principle he had advocated; she saw him in the poorly ventilated and uncleanly furnished cell at Charlestown, and in imagination she saw him surrounded with bristling bayonets, his worn and wounded body suffering with pain and a smile beaming upon his countenance as he was led out to become the sacrificial offering which the curse of slavery demanded. These were all sad thoughts. Thus in life, surrounded, as we are, by happy scenes and joyous associations, our minds will, in spite of our every effort, dwell upon such scenes.

When the vessel landed, the party repaired to the church, where, in conformation to the English law, the marriage service was re-performed, after which they repaired to "Douglas Hall," the home of Francis, where the festal occasion of the other side of the

Atlantic, like the marriage ceremony, was renewed.

Early the following week, the Leland family started for the family home in Scotland, where as warm a welcome was extended by the aged grandmother to the children of Roderick as she had extended to those of Theodocia.

Grandmother Leland became much interested in Ona, whom she thought resembled her own dear child. Often she would sit for hours listening to the rehearsals of Western life as depicted by Ona.

When they had been in Scotland some weeks, they concluded to protract their stay longer than they had at first contemplated. Ona became anxious regarding Aunt Nancy, who had remained with the servants at Cedar Hall. She feared that Wren would become apprised of her unprotected position and do her some injury. She accordingly sent a letter, urging Aunt Nancy to join them in London.

Roderick roamed over the cliffs, ferreting out the favorite haunts of his boyhood with no less ardor than was displayed when he knew every nook and cranny of the neighboring mountains. Ona and Addie often, accompanied by little Ota and Theo., made choice collection of wild plants for future consideration during their review of their botanical lessons upon which they had determined.

On the approach of winter, Addie returned to London, accompanied by the children, who were assigned to the care of a governess. Ona remained with her grandmother and Nancy, who had arrived, and proved an agreeable and interesting companion for Grandmother Leland.

Ona wrote frequently to Hayden. Her letters were, for the most part, advisory and encouraging. Occasionally, after reading some passage of his condemning English laws, she would endeavor to arouse his energies by writing: "You have both acquired and natural ability. Cultivate them, so that when the time comes that you háve confidence in yourself, endeavor to arouse the people upon the subject; portray its injustice; demand the repeal of the law which works so much misery and has become so obnoxious."

Hayden had not the energy of his American cousin, and although her expressions would arouse his enthusiasm for the tme, he had not fixedness of purpose sufficiently strong to adhere closely to anything that did not produce a continuous degree of excitement.

Each letter that found its way to Hayden or Robert, her brother, who was at the military academy at West Point, contained a draft for some hundreds of dollars.

Two years had passed when the signal gun was fired which ushered in the Rebellion in the United States. Its echo reverberated from hill to hill and bounded over the waves, striking upon the lofty crags of Scotland and arousing from inactivity those who sought rest and recreation there.

Hayden wrote: "The great army for which we formed the skirmish line is massed. The forces have rallied upon the line we held so long alone. The great battle has begun; the rattle of musketry, the clash of saber, the boom of the cannon is heard from

East to West, and 'Old J⟩hn Brown's soul goes marching on.' "

Mr. Leland and Ona could not be disinterested spectators to the scenes being enacted upon American soil, and fired with patriotic zeal and adhering strongly to their old principles of "universal freedom," they hastened to lend a helping hand to the cause they so long since had espoused.

CHAPTER LXXVII.

QUANTRELL THE MURDERER.

QUANTRELL repeated mentally the expression of condemnation as he watched the young lady remove her gloves, which were evidently used only to protect her white hand from the summer air.

In her own estimation Rose Baily was handsome and intelligent. But a casual observer would readily notice that too much attention was given to the adornment of her person to leave more than a limited scope for mental improvement. She seated herself before a large mirror, and while listlessly conversing upon the deleterious effects of the Western air upon the complexion, complacently viewed the reflection of her slender body upon the glass.

Quantrell, who had one redeeming trait, that of detesting affection, mentally quoted :

> "While thousands fall by clashing swords,
> Ten thousands fall by corset boards."

Mr. Baily appeared, which relieved Quantrell to a

great extent of the embarrassment thrown around him by the affected lady.

He informed Mr. Baily that he had some business with him of an exclusively private nature, and the two withdrew to the lawn, where Bill Quantrell began his career as a "Border man."

He remained with Mr. Baily during the night. The nature of his business was made known to Rose by her father. She thanked him for so kindly warning them of impending danger. Quantrell had informed Mr. Baily that a number of men from Kansas were intending to attack his house the following night.

Quantrell left early the next morning. At sundown the family were sent to a neighboring plantation. Mr. Baily remained. with the trusty watchers he had summoned to assist him. Just as the last stroke of twelve sounded upon the bell of the clock, five men came through the gate and passed to the back part of the house. Mr. Baily said:

"Keep still. The gentleman said he would send them back to the front."

Soon a sixth person appeared, who carried a lantern. In a brief time the five returned, two of whom stooped upon the porch as if feeling for something. One said in a low voice:

"This is where Bill said we would find the key."

In an instant a volley of buckshot and bullets was poured upon them. One of their number fell dead, the other four hastened through the gate, closely followed by those from the house. The pursuers lost sight of them in the dark, and the pursued sought the protection of the timber, to await the dawn of day.

Quantrell, who was the sixth person to appear, returned to the house with the baffled pursuers. Mr. Baily took five hundred dollars from his safe and presented it to Quantrell, saying:

"Your prompt action saved me the loss of my slaves and other property. This shall be your reward."

Quantrell returned to his quarters in an unceremonious manner. Some of the men were found wounded and promptly killed by Wren and his men, who were summoned to search for them.

To a comrade Quantrell said as they walked down the bank of the Marias des Cygnes river:

"I have begun to take my revenge upon 'Dickey Deane.' I received some money, and found a relative besides."

"What relative do you refer to?" asked his friend.

"I found an own cousin, in the person of Guy Wren. He is my father's sister's child."

At this moment a number of horsemen approached, who demanded Quantrell to surrender. Seeing no hope of escape, he gave up his weapons and was carried to the block house at Stanton, to await his trial. But nothing could be proven against him, and he was permitted to go, while the friends determined to watch his further development in villainy.

He returned to Lawrence, where he fared sumptuously upon his ill-gotten gold, until the drum beat called the armies of the opposing forces to face each

other. He hastened to Missouri, where he was welcomed by Mr. Baily and his daughter Rose, who forgot her gloves, and ran anxiously to meet him as he
appeared at the gate. He ever acknowledged that
Ona Leland was the only woman who had called
forth his admiration and love. To her he could have
bowed in submissive homage. But fate had decreed
it otherwise, and in time he and Rose agreed that
"after the Yankees were whipped," they would marry.

The border war waxed warm, and Quantrell's
name became a terror to Union men. At last he
gathered his forces for a raid upon Lawrence. His
outlaws rode madly through the streets, killing promiscuously, not sparing women or children.

On their return to Missouri, part of the band joined,
Wren, and they departed for richer fields of booty.

Late in the last year of the war, a federal bullet
laid Quantrell low upon the blue grass of Old Kentucky, "The Dark and Bloody Ground" of the Indians. Such are the characters whom War makes
famous, while Peace confines in the prison cell or
turns over to the hangman.

Wren saw the desperado fall. As he realized that
Death's messenger had overtaken him, he drew a
picture from his pocket and threw it aside, muttering: "Thoughts of you made me wretched for life,
and miserable in death."

Wren picked up the picture. It was that of Ona
Leland. He had stolen it from Arthur Holmes in
Lawrence, and carried it near his heart during all
these long years. Who knows but his dare-devil
nature could have been moulded into a powerful

element for good by the woman who rejected his kindly advances and spoke severely, perhaps unjustly of him?

CHAPTER LXXVIII.

THE DEDICATION OF JOHN BROWN'S MONUMENT.

WHEN Mr. Leland and Ona arrived in the United States, everything was in a state of excitement. Soldiers were hurrying from all directions toward Washington as a common center. War was the topic upon every corner and within every house. Anxious mothers, with pallid faces, bid adieu to loved sons who rushed to the fray. Loving wives and tender sisters clung lovingly to husbands or brother who went to mingle in the strife. Brave and stern old fathers, with trembling voice and grasp, gave parting words of encouragement to those on whom they had relied as being the staff of their declining years.

We pass over the sad scenes, and would willingly force back the soul-harrowing thoughts when considering the darkened shadows which fell upon many peaceful homes during the years of blood, when loved ones were known to be no more.

Mr. Leland rendered efficient service in one of the departments at Washington. Robert went South with the "boys in blue," while Ona was forced to a life of inactivity, on account of the failing health of Grandmother Leland, at whose request she returned to Scotland and cheerfully nursed the old lady through her declining years.

The years rolled by, and the war was over. The blow struck at Harper's Ferry echoed and re-echoed through the North until the few of then had become the hundred thousands of now, and the name of "Liberty" in America had taken one grand stride in becoming nearer a synonym for "Freedom."

Time passed pleasantly with our friends. Robert, Mr. Leland's brother, Sir Charles and Francis having been, during the war, anxious spectators of the scenes, returned to their homes across the Atlantic.

War raged upon the continent of Europe. Powerful potentates no longer being able to dictate terms to each other, attempted forcing such terms. Prussia and France were contending for the mastery, with no principle involved.

While the enthusiastic majority of France rallied to the support of their popular Emperor, there were many thinking minds cogitating upon the principles which Lafayette had taught and for which he had suffered.

These men, though deeply concerned regarding their home affairs, had previously arranged to send to the widow of John Brown a gold medal, commemorative of his efforts and the efforts of his followers in inaugurating the strife which gave freedom to the slaves in the United States, thus showing that they held his name in holy memory and appreciated and endorsed his motives.

Ota, now in the blush and bloom of womanhood, had been selected as the representative of France in conveying the token to its destination. She, accompanied by Kate, repaired to Paris, in accordance with the terms of her invitation.

The war closed. The Emperor was deposed. France stepped forward and upward and took her place among the few bright stars denoting the field "Republic."

Ota sat in one of the elegant parlors of the French President, where she was to receive from the former nobles of France, but now the foremost Republicans, the token commemorative of the "Freedom" they had learned to adore.

The position, when the committee was announced, was an embarrassing one to the beautiful American, but with commendable tact she overcame all hinderances, and in the display of dignity she won the praise and admiration of those by whom she was surrounded.

Besides the committee, distinguished personages had been admitted, each of whom had a word of praise and encouragement for the beautiful American lady. Besides the medal, a letter to the Governor of Kansas was read by Prince Lionel, and for delivery intrusted, with the medal, to Ota.

Ota, somewhat weary, returned with Kate to London, and in a few days, with Francis, started for America. Arriving in Boston, they repaired to Cedar Hall, where they found Mr. Leland and his family, Sir Charles, Addie and Hayden Douglas, all awaiting the time to arrive when they should start for

27

Osawatomie to participate in the unvailing of the monument erected to the memory of Brown and others who had struggled for freedom on the soil of Kansas.

The morning of the thirtieth of August dawned bright and clear. Long before noon vehicles of every description began to arrive at Osawatomie. The sun poured its scorching rays upon the unsheltered people, thousands of whom gathered around the graves of those who offered their lives upon the altar of Freedom twenty years before.

As the speakers were taking their places upon the stand, a murmur of applause ran through the immense audience. A beautiful French landau, drawn by four black horses, followed by some dozen open carriages, approached the stand. The people gave way on either side, until they stopped in front of the stand.

On the front seat of the landau sat two beautiful women, one attired in Scottish, the other in French costume. The beautiful Scotch woman, in her "kilt and kirtle," held in her right hand a brightly polished Sharpe's rifle, while the left contained a silver locket. The assembled multitude gazed in wonder, until the name of "Dickey Deane" was repeated. At the mention of that name cheer after cheer rent the air, and again "The Spy of Osawatomie" looked upon familiar surroundings.

The other lady carried in her right hand a golden salver, upon which, wrapped in silvered paper, lay the letter addressed by the French committee to the Governor of Kansas, while from her left hand depended the gold medal.

THE BROWN MONUMENT.

Upon the other seat sat two gentlemen in English costume; the older, a nobleman by title and noble by nature; the younger, a man of the most remarkably handsome features, whose symmetry and beauty were admired by all. These men were "The Mysterious Companions of Old John Brown."

The "Stars and Stripes" floated with the English "Jack" and French "Tri-color" above the carriage. On another staff floated a torn and tattered battle-flag, which had been carried through the war of the Rebellion and had been perforated by many bullets.

The other carriage contained those who had fought with the old "Martyr," among whom were Arthur Holmes and his wife, Dr. Strawn and the estimable and beautiful lady who had become his wife.

The occupants of the various carriages dismounted and walked in couples around the shaft of marble and stopped in front. Sir Charles made an appropriate speech in behalf of the English delegation, which he represented. Ota stepped forward, and in neat and appropriate sentences presented the letter, and medal, in the name of "Liberty and France." With the expression of her last words she bowed at the foot of the monument and placed upon the pedestal a *fac simile* of the medal, one side of which was adorned with the raised profile of John Brown, with brow contracted in profound thought, the whole face being indelibly stamped with energy. Around the brow the inscription: "John Brown; born in Torrington, May 9th, 1800."

The reverse was inscribed with: "December 2d, 1859," being the time the presentation was consid-

cred by the French committee, and "To the Memory of John Brown, his Sons and Companions, the
Victims to the Cause of the Liberty of the Blacks."

She stepped aside, and Ona appeared. Resting the rifle against the marble, she placed the silver
medal near the one Ota had deposited. The silver
locket which we saw in the beginning was upon her
arm. It was still locked. A small card hung from
the chain, on which were the words: "We let not
our left hand know what our right hath done." That
silver case still keeps its secret. None but the pos-
sessor knows its contents. Part of its prophetic mission has been performed, and when women become,
under the laws of the land, equally endowed in privileges with men, the silver case will be unlocked,
and one as fair and energetic as Ona will read aloud
to the world the messages it contains. Till then we
can only conjecture its contents.

While the bands discoursed sweet music, and
eloquent men pronounced eulogistic words, Ona and
Ota wended their way to the north, where stood
"Pilot Knob." They climbed its steep side and
stood beside the pile of stones known as the "Look-
out," which may ornament the grave of some Indian
chief. As Ota surveyed the scene, she exclaimed:

"This, then, is the spot upon which you found me,
a poor, lost and friendless child."

"Yes, Ota, I found you here. You were not long
friendless. To-day I am proud of you. I am glad
to be known as your friend. I care no longer for
the plaudits of the multitude. My mission is not
accomplished, and I feel that I can depend upon you
as an earnest assistant."

She bent over and kissed the young lady as she had years before kissed the lost and orphaned child. Each became occupied with her own thoughts as they, seated upon a large rock, watched the rockets in Osawatomie and saw the glinting of the lights in the city of Paola.

Descending the hill, they entered the carriage waiting to carry them to the hotel preparatory to taking part in the reception tendered them as the guests of the State by General S——, of Paola.

The residence of General S. was ablaze with splendor. Flowers were suspended in the halls, until they seemed built of roses. The evening zephyrs were laden with their fragrance. Pyramids and arbor, constructed of flowers, decorated the dining rooms. The elite of the city, representatives of literature, genius and wealth, had assembled.

A buzz of admiration pervaded the room as Mr. Leland and Sir Charles, with Ota and Ona leaning upon their arms, passed through the rooms, to be presented to the assembled guests by General and Mrs. S.

Ota, surrounded by friends; the adopted child of wealthy parents; the representative chosen and approved by the French government, was not happy. She thought of the cruelty which had deprived her of a father and caused reason to forsake the mind of her mother. She thought of that mother, lying near, yet in an unknown grave. How gladly would she have forsaken the scenes of splendor, to have shed a tear and place a wreath upon that grave!

Ona was merry. She was, in imagination, living

over the earlier scenes of her life. There were many familiar faces around her, whom she delighted by her hilarity and happiness. She wished for Raven, that she might again course with freedom along the neighboring highways, which had taken the place of the grand old prairie trails.

The reception was over. The carriage was sent East by the train, and the visitors bade adieu, for the time, to Kansas. They tarried for a few days in St. Joseph, and went down the majestic river on one of the palace boats to St. Louis, where they were joined by Kate, who had remained there to visit her sister.

Let us look up our friends to-day. Ona is in Washington, looking after the interest of women; Ota is in England, soon to be married to a young French officer; Addie has given her attention to literature, and is to marry Lord L——; Aunt Nancy dwells with the Lelands in Scotland; Hayden Douglas married an actress during the Rebellion, the union was an unhappy one. Parting, he left Osawatomie and went to California, where he died wretched in mind and broken in heart, made wretched by the injustice of English law. While Hayden's body lies upon a beautiful slope of the Santa Clara valley, where a plain slab, containing the words, " I was one of the Mysterious Companions of Old John Brown," Francis, no more the son, nor less the brother, dwells in splendor.

Sir Charles and Roderick Leland are visiting places of interest together, more firmly cementing the friendship of their youth.

Pat Devilin, noble, generous Pat, perished on the plains of Colorado, rather than desert a fatally wounded companion. Rose Baily still lives and mourns for her dead Quantrell. Guy Wren roams, at the head of a band of outlaws, through Texas and Mexico.

Arthur Holmes is conducting a paper, assisted by his wife, who was Sallie Strawn, a poor New Hampshire girl.

While I write I hear the tolling of the bells in Osawatomie, echoing to the world the fact that another hero has gone. Walter Strawn is being carried to his grave in a land where he struggled for the maintenance of the principles of Liberty and Freedom. A newly made grave in the cold earth, now covered with the deepest snow ever known in Kansas, awaits its occupant, whom nations will venerate and mourn, though "he wore neither the Blue nor the Grey."

One by one that historic band is passing away. Shall they be forgotten? Who will in after years gather flowers to bedeck their graves? We as a nation forget not "The Blue and the Grey." Then let us remember those who wore neither "The Blue nor the Grey."

The wild jasmine and rose then go gather for those
Who in Death's long repose sleep unconscious of foes.
Yes, in morning's light hours bring the brightest of flowers
From Nature's own bowers for those true heroes of ours.
They, the friends of the slave, are now Kansas' own brave.

THE END.

www.ingramcontent.com/pod-product-compliance
Lightning Source LLC
Chambersburg PA
CBHW030938110726
47900CB00004B/1039